PRAISE FOR
HEIR OF LIGHT

"A riveting, emotional ride with unforgettable characters and relentless pacing that leaves you breathless. Pure magic."

—C.J. REDWINE,
NEW YORK TIMES BESTSELLING AUTHOR
OF *THE SHADOW QUEEN*

"*Heir of Light* captivates from the first page. Jill Williamson has found a true treasure with Niki Florica. The evocative prose we've come to expect from Jill's novels does not disappoint. Blended with Niki's fresh voice and raw talent, readers will be transported into a world of intrigue and magic. The tension between Rigil and Sethe will keep slow-burn romance fans swooning and reading into all hours of the night, while also reminding them what true love and beauty look like. Don't miss this fantasy novel full of heart, grit, and second chances!"

—SARA ELLA,
AWARD-WINNING AUTHOR OF *THE WONDERLAND TRIALS*,
UNBLEMISHED, AND *GLASS ACROSS THE SEA*

"*Heir of Light* is a pulse-pounding and wholly enthralling fantasy that kept me hooked from the first page. With striking character arcs for the dashing Sir Rigil as he confronts the failures in his past and for the fierce survivor Sethe as she fights to find freedom, this story sings with powerful themes and a compelling second-chance romance. Add to that a touch of swashbuckling adventure and the quirky and utterly endearing Mezaedo, and I loved every moment of this tale."

—GILLIAN BRONTE ADAMS,
AWARD-WINNING AUTHOR OF *THE FIREBORN EPIC*

"Spies, thieves, smugglers, and reunited would-be lovers in need of a second chance? What's not to love? Niki Florica's entrée into the world of Er'Rets brings intrigue, new powers, and a complicated relationship readers can't help but root for! It's a great reminder of what true freedom is and where it comes from."

—JOHN W. OTTE,
AWARD-WINNING AUTHOR OF THE LEGACY OF INK TRILOGY

HEIR OF LIGHT

HEIR OF LIGHT

←BLOOD OF KINGS: LEGENDS→

NIKI FLORICA

JILL WILLIAMSON

sunrise
PUBLISHING

Heir of Light
Blood of Kings: Legends Book 4

Copyright © 2025 Sunrise Media Group, LLC
Published by Sunrise Media Group, LLC

Print ISBN: 978-1-963372-64-9

This book is a work of fiction. Names, characters, places, and incidents are either products of the author's imagination or used fictitiously. Any similarity to actual people, organizations, and/or events is purely coincidental.

All Scripture quotations, unless otherwise indicated, are taken from the King James Version.

For more information about the authors please access their websites at www.jillwilliamson.com and nikiflorica.com

Published in the United States of America.
Cover Design: Emilie Haney, eahcreative.com

Blood of Kings: Legends

Squire of Truth
Lord of Winter
Lady of Shadows
Heir of Light

Blood of Kings

By Darkness Hid
To Darkness Fled
From Darkness Won

To Jesus, my Author and Finisher,
whose mercy is more.

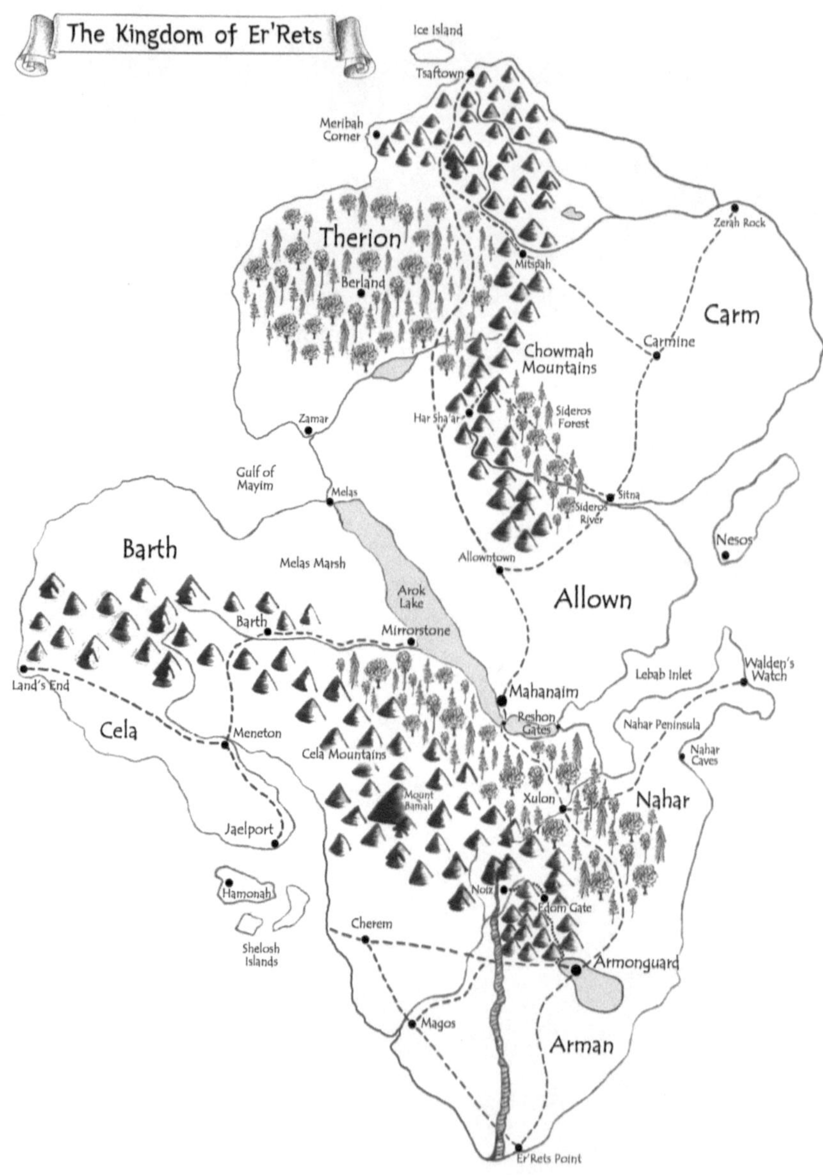

The Kingdom of Er'Rets
Ice Island
Tsaftown
Meribah Corner
Therion
Zerah Rock
Berland
Mitspah
Carm
Chowmah Mountains
Carmine
Zamar
Sideros Forest
Har Sha'ar
Gulf of Mayim
Melas
Sitna
Sideros River
Nesos
Melas Marsh
Allowntown
Barth
Arok Lake
Allown
Barth
Mirrorstone
Walden's Watch
Land's End
Mahanaim
Lebab Inlet
Cela
Reshon Gates
Nahar Peninsula
Meneton
Cela Mountains
Nahar Caves
Mount Bamah
Xulon
Nahar
Jaelport
Hamonah
Notz
Cherem
Edom Gate
Shelosh Islands
Armonguard
Magos
Arman
Er'Rets Point

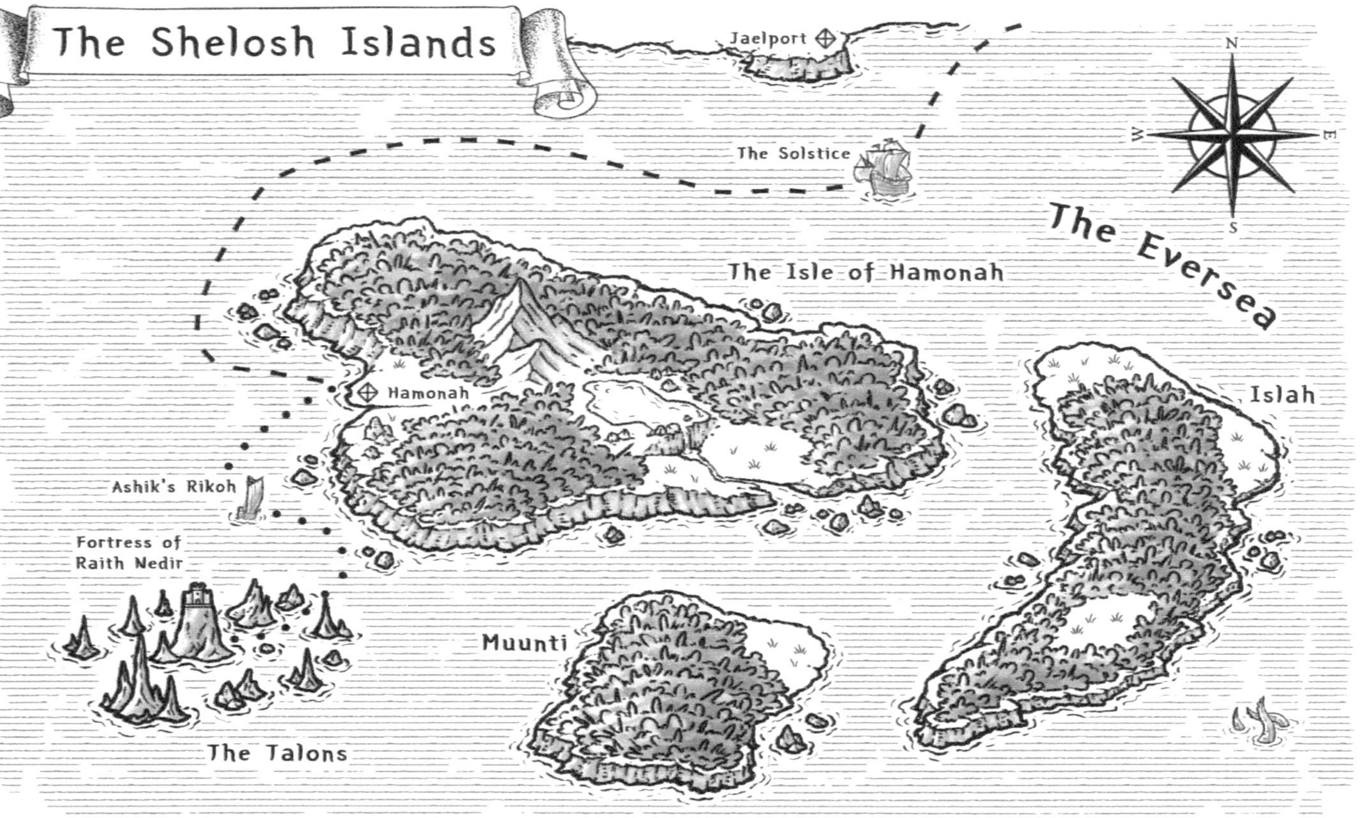

The Shelosh Islands
Jaelport
The Solstice
The Isle of Hamonah
The Eversea
Hamonah
Islah
Ashik's Rikoh
Fortress of Raith Nedir
Muunti
The Talons
N
E
S
W

"But he said to me, "My grace is sufficient for you, for my power is made perfect in weakness. Therefore I will boast all the more gladly of my weaknesses, so that the power of Christ may rest upon me."

2 CORINTHIANS 12:9 ESV

"Now the Lord is the Spirit, and where the Spirit of the Lord is, there is freedom."

2 CORINTHIANS 3:17 ESV

CHAPTER ONE

RIGIL

THERE WAS MORE TO SPY CRAFT THAN being impeccably dressed, or so Rigil had heard. Perhaps one day, he'd test that theory.

Today called for rich dyes and a good tailor.

The blue ensemble Rigil had chosen for this mission was sharp enough for a Kingsguard ambassador, yet flimsy enough that a week of travel in torrential rain had left its mark. As he stood at Lord Coble's library window, water dripping from both his hair and the sword at his waist and pooling under his boots, he squinted through the blurry glass at the ramshackle village of Land's End—a picture of desolation. Spindly trees, soupy rain, a few low buildings hunched together like old men, it was a land that still thought it was living in Darkness.

Perfect place to hide a plot against the king.

Rain pounded the glass as Coble's servant set out goblets on a table behind Rigil, humming something almost as irritating as that saltbeetle trying to bash through the window.

"Wine, Sir Rigil?"

Rigil turned to face the speaker. For a servant, the man was oddly dressed. With opulent robes, flawless pearl skin, and glossy white hair tied back with a ribbon, he would likely be considered handsome if not for those eyes. Grey as shards of foggy glass, they pierced Rigil through the dusty air as the man held the bottle over the cups.

Rigil nodded. "Thank you, Master . . . ?"

"Nedir." Wine gushed into the goblets, dark scarlet. "Raith Nedir of Har Sha'ar." An Avenis pendant around Nedir's neck jingled as he corked the wine. A servant of the god of beauty, then. Strange for a man from Har Sha'ar. Even stranger for a place like this.

If Coble's library had ever been beautiful, years of dust and abandonment had eaten at its charm. On one end of the room, a low fire added the smell of char to the musk of rotting paper. The center table was blanketed in so many maps that it resembled a four-legged parchment creature. Ghosts of students seemed to hover about, their education cut short years ago when the Kings-guard school was overtaken by black knights, then shut down altogether. Nedir, maturely handsome as he was, had an ancient, dusty aura about him that brought the room's history into sharper relief. He could have sat among the cobwebs and warped books without seeming out of place here. A relic, like them.

But a useless relic. Isemios's wit, where was Coble? Rigil had *not* crossed Er'Rets listening to his squire's endless rambling to meet with some valet.

A sharp stab burst in Rigil's temples just before his squire spoke telepathically inside his head.

Mezaedo Chevyah.

Speak of a storm, and there it stirs. As usual, the squire didn't knock to announce himself so much as pound. Rigil lowered the shields around his mind, the mental equivalent of opening a set of drapes to let light in. He usually kept his mind guarded that way, a mental trick known as *blocking* or *shielding* among bloodvoicers, basic common sense among nongifted men like Rigil. Thankfully, bloodvoicing was rare enough that he didn't expect anyone but Mez to attack his mind here.

Sirrig, I'm in, Mez bloodvoiced. *You were right about the tunnel. Straight shot to the kitchens. You wouldn't* believe *what passes for soup down here.*

Rigil crossed the room to feign interest in *A History of Sakin Mageia.* Though he had no ability to bloodvoice himself, Mezaedo could hear his thoughts while the magical connection between their minds was open. *I see you took my lecture about staying focused to heart,* Rigil thought.

Sorry, Sirrig, Mezaedo shot back. *Can't talk while I'm chewing. Lightness' sake, you* tasted *Coble's soup?*

I think you're missing the important bit. The broth. Is chewy.

"Enjoying the library, Sir Rigil?" Nedir appeared at Rigil's elbow, goblet in hand, his robe draped like a mantle against the falling dust. "I thought you might appreciate Lord Coble's collection, being from Zerah Rock."

Aye, it was all very nostalgic, down to the judgmental stare of a thousand books screaming at Rigil to read more, learn faster, work harder, be better. *There are two kinds of men in this world, boy . . .*

Strange. All these years, and books still screamed in his father's voice.

"Very thoughtful, Master Nedir." Taking his cup, Rigil pushed *A History of Sakin Mageia* back into place. "Remind me again why Lord Coble cannot join us?"

"His lordship is attending to a personal matter."

More personal than an accusation of treason from the king? "Forgive me, but what does that make you? His steward?"

Nedir laughed, an unwrinkled sound to match his unwrinkled face. "I am not a servant. Lord Coble is interested in my research. Every scholar needs a sponsor."

A gust of wind slapped wet leaves against the window as Nedir gestured for Rigil to sit. When Rigil declined, Nedir took his own suggestion.

So. A scholar. What for?

Mezaedo, Rigil thought, uncertain if the squire could still hear him, *tell me you've found the box.*

Nedir set his wine on the sideboard to wipe his hands with a kerchief from his robe. No, not a kerchief. The whiteish parchment was a little damp and more than a little crinkled. As it would be, after weeks in Rigil's pocket.

Rigil blinked. "That letter was for his lordship."

"Yes, and how very well-crafted it was." With a manicured nail, Nedir chipped the last of King Gidon's seal away. "I would like to assure you, Sir Rigil, that King Gidon has no reason to fear. Lord Coble is too prudent to attempt reopening Mageia's school for black knights. They are illegal, after all. I fear the king sent you all this way for nothing."

Sirrig. Mezaedo's bloodvoice slashed through Nedir's false decorum like a scythe. *No sign of a mirror in Coble's rooms. Maybe Prince Oren was wrong?*

Rigil kept his expression as smooth as the wine on his tongue. Rich, a tad plummy. And was that currant? *Prince Oren's informant saw the box himself,* he thought. *It's hidden behind a silver-gilded mirror.*

No gilded mirrors here, Sirrig. Coble's got all the style of a blind cabbage.

Keep searching, Rigil thought, then held his glass to Nedir, resisting the urge to rest his wrist on the pommel of his sword in warning. "This research of yours. Anything that might interest the king?"

A smile as Nedir tipped the bottle over Rigil's goblet. "I study bloodvoicing, mostly. Origins, implications, the like. I was working on my research when you arrived."

Bloodvoicing research? Almost involuntarily, Rigil snapped the mental drapes shut around his thoughts again. Mezaedo wouldn't be able to hear him think if he was blocking, but if Rigil was dealing with a bloodvoicer here . . .

Needing space to think, Rigil meandered over to a larger table in the center of the room, where a half-finished game of citadel rested beside a stack of maps. Mezaedo hadn't knocked again. Blight it all, this was supposed to be simple. Interrogate Coble, filch the mysterious weapon Prince Oren's informant had warned them of, and be back in Armonguard before anyone was the wiser. Rigil had learned the castle layout by heart. Where would a garishly ornate mirror be if not in Coble's quarters? A servant wouldn't have something so—

Wood popped in the hearth. Slowly, so as not to spill his cup, Rigil turned to face his host. Nedir, who had a study in this manor. Nedir, who worshipped the god of beauty, judging by that *garishly ornate* pendant around his neck.

"So." Rigil leaned his fingertips on the table. "Why Avenis?"

Smiling, Nedir crossed his legs. "Beauty is the muse of all great minds, Sir Rigil, and Er'Rets is full of sights that far surpass what one might find in a mirror. In my case, there is something exquisite about an ocean view that stimulates my thoughts like nothing else."

Interesting. Hoping Mezaedo had left his connection to Rigil open, he lowered his shields long enough to call out in his thoughts, the best he could do without being able to reach out and knock on the boy's mind himself. *Mezaedo?*

Look, Sirrig, the boy answered, proof that he *was* listening, *there's no moldy mirror in this—*

You're in the wrong place. Rigil bent over the map, where someone had circled Tsaftown in bloodred ink. *Try the south wing, on an upper floor. Look for a study with an ocean view.*

South wing. Ocean view. Right. The boy withdrew.

Meanwhile, Nedir was swirling his glass. "It is a pity, Sir Rigil, that you came so far for mere rumors. Not that I fault the king

for being cautious, what with that horrid business in Tsaftown."
Finger to chin, Nedir held Rigil's gaze. "Such messy things, coups.
I commend Lord Livna and, of course, Lady Viola for removing
the threat so decisively."

As usual, Viola's name bit like a gnat. Rigil covered it with a hard
sip. Decisive, clever, ambitious, advantageously married—Rigil's
dear sister was all of those things, along with extremely adept at
holding a grudge. "I must say, Master Nedir, you are surprisingly
well-informed about affairs in Tsaftown."

Nedir shrugged. "There are no secrets on this side of Er'Rets."

Somewhere in the castle, a bell chimed. Noon. Time for the
guard change. Mezaedo needed to be back in the tunnel before he
was caught nosing through the upper rooms. *Mezaedo?*

Moldy onions, Sirrig, there's a whole room *for gowzals up here.*
Mezaedo.

Hang on. I've got a good feeling about this door.

This was Rigil's reward for taking a squire who could bloodvoice. Oh, for the simple days of Bran . . .

Nedir was watching him when Rigil turned back from the table.
"Forgive me, Sir Rigil, but as we have nothing more to discuss, I
must return to my work."

Rigil straightened. Return to work. Return to his study, where
Mezaedo was currently elbow deep in Nedir's belongings and
hopefully a very incriminating box.

Rigil's cup met the table with a curt clink. "I'd hate to waste
your time."

And now for the second part of spy craft. Improvisation.

He made to follow Nedir out of the room but stopped beside
the citadel board to lay a finger on a rogue piece. This set was solid
oak. Not like his father's, which had featured one army of solid
silver, the other of dull birch. Rigil had never been permitted to
use silver. That was for future lords who had proven their worth.

Shifting the piece ever so slightly to the left, Rigil chuckled enough to be heard over the rain. "Lord Coble is not much of a citadel player, I see."

Nedir paused beside the doorway, his smile pulling taut from cheek to cheek. "Actually, that game is mine. A sort of ongoing competition with myself."

Rigil gave a laugh. Airy, with a touch of condescension. "Well, I suppose even a scholar can fall for a three-tower gambit once in a while. I did myself, when I was learning."

He tapped the rogue piece with its ruby accents. Fitting for an Avenis worshipper.

Nedir cast a cool eye on the trap Rigil had invented. A moment passed. Two.

"Oh, how right you are, Sir Rigil." Crossing to the table, Nedir tapped the board. "I don't suppose you would be willing to educate me?"

Too easy. The table was cleared, chairs pulled out, goblets forgotten. Rigil took his time moving his villager, a decoy to distract Nedir from his rogue.

"The game of lords, they call this." Nedir moved his citadel. "How *is* Lord Barak, by the way? I've always thought he must have high hopes for you, to name a second-born son his heir."

For half a heartbeat, in the rattle of the rain, Rigil was facing Lord Barak himself across a citadel board in Zerah Rock, his father's frown scalding as he shifted his paladin. *Only a fool fails the same way twice, boy. There are two kinds of men in this world . . .*

"High hopes." Rigil moved his own paladin. "I imagine he did."

The game discouraged any more talk. Between turns, Rigil spoke to Mezaedo in his thoughts, hoping the squire was listening. *Mezaedo. Are you in the study yet?*

There was no answer for a long time. Not unusual with Mezaedo. He was a spotty bloodvoicer at the best of times, even carrying Rigil's sword to strengthen the magical connection between them. Personal possessions were known to do that for bloodvoicers, but weak as he was, Mezaedo needed more than a bit of Rigil's clothes or hair to help him connect to Rigil's mind. Of course, Rigil would have cut off a limb before letting a squire wield his old sword, Keseel, but ever since he'd lost that blade in Allowntown... well, that was that. Whether the blade he carried now was his own or Mezaedo's, neither would ever be Keseel. And both would cut flesh just fine.

Still. Something in Mezaedo's silence, the keen edge of it, drew sweat to Rigil's fingertips as Nedir slid his paladin forward. He still hadn't seen Rigil's decoy. *Mezaedo?* Rigil thought. *Mez?*

This time, Mezaedo's bloodvoice carried a note of fear. *He's in the study with me, Sirrig. Coble and a few others, but Coble's is the only voice I recognize. They haven't seen me yet. Moldy onions, don't check behind the curtains . . .*

Rigil stopped seeing the board. Maybe that was why he shifted his villager, exposing it as a decoy. The saltbeetle was throwing itself at the window now, a frantic blur of wings.

"What is this?" Nedir examined Rigil's villager, then the rogue that had slowly, quietly, been sneaking across the board behind it. "Ah. You nearly had me."

With a ring of silver on silver, Nedir toppled Rigil's rogue. The piece rolled across the board, gathering speed as it neared the edge.

Mezaedo? Are you there?

The rogue hit the floor. Bounced, rolled. Went still.

Raith Nedir stood. "And that is game. Thank you for indulging me, Sir Rigil. Peyton and Kali will show you out."

Two guards appeared at the door, clad in Coble's gold and black, and Rigil nearly grabbed Mezaedo's sword before checking himself. Blight it all. Prince Oren should have known about Nedir. He should have sent Rigil in with better information, with a fellow Mârad spy instead of a half-cooked Kingsguard squire, should have—

No. This was what the Mârad had trained him for, what had

set Rigil apart as more than a soldier in Prince Oren's mind. Improvisation. *Delicacy.*

Rigil rose, pushing his chair back until it bumped the fallen rogue on the carpet. "This is farewell, then, Master Nedir."

Nedir cracked a smile. "So it would seem." And on that strange note, he swept from the room, leaving a faint musty odor behind.

The two guards, both Barthian by their ashy skin, flanked Rigil out of the library and into the dark-paneled corridor, leading him toward the foyer and the manor entrance. Nedir must have gone the other way, or else dissolved into vapor. Only the faintest mildewy scent of him remained in the corridor, and it faded as the guards led Rigil to the left.

Rigil fought to keep his hands loose at his sides. Improvise, improvise.

At the entrance to the grand foyer, the first guard slipped ahead. Rigil chose that moment to whirl on the second, bringing his foot down hard on the side of the man's knee and drawing Mezaedo's sword at the same time.

Bone cracked. The guard fell, fumbling for his sword. But Rigil reached his first.

By the time the second guard lunged back into the corridor, Rigil's sword was careening toward him. Coble's man parried; Rigil's sword skidded down his blade and embedded itself in the doorframe. He tugged to no avail, then let go, leaving the sword protruding from the wood like a misfired arrow. The guard jabbed, and Rigil jerked to miss it, his heel catching on the first guard's body. He stumbled backward as steel spliced the air where his gut had been.

Arman help him. Ducking inside the guard's next wide swing, Rigil grabbed the man's arm and wrenched until something snapped. The man's sword struck the floor in Rigil's first stroke of luck. His second stroke of luck was the knife holstered in the guard's sleeve, right under Rigil's hands.

In a moment, it was over. A quick jab, a tangle of limbs, and then Rigil was hobbling out of the melee, trying not to think of the time he'd have getting bloodstains out of his best tunic.

But first, Mezaedo.

He didn't have long. The foyer was empty, but the sleek black staircase amplified his footfalls as Rigil took the curving stairs four to a stride and charged onto the third-floor landing. All black paneling and star-gilded ceilings, Land's End was a maze, the south wing no exception.

Rigil threw open the first door he saw.

The only light in the room came from dim green lanterns on dark-papered walls. Hundreds of gowzals, feathered and rat-faced, screamed in cages as Rigil flew by. A whole room for gowzals, indeed. One door in the far wall opened onto a closet, the other into a room hung with paintings of Sakin Mageia, the man who had commandeered this school for black knights instead of the Kingsguard it had been intended for.

Only one door remained. Rigil snapped the knob sideways and charged forward into . . .

A laboratory?

It was a modest room. Modest but full, every wall of shelves laden with books and potted plants. In the middle of the room, a large desk flexed under the weight of inkpots and old maps and, at the moment, one very calm Jaelportian squire.

Mezaedo Chevyah's dark curls were dusted with cobwebs from the tunnel beneath the keep, his feet dangling over the edge of the desk as he held an apple in one hand and a sheaf of Nedir's papers in the other. Still scrawny for seventeen, he wore tight-fitting trousers and an oversized canvas shirt, the sleeves shoved past his elbows to expose the tiny scars that flecked his arms and the tops of his hands. The scars were one of many mysteries that composed Mezaedo Chevyah. Another swung on a cord around his neck in the form of a blue velvet pouch, its contents staining his apple and the corners of his lips orange.

Aye, the sky could be falling, and Mezaedo would still stop to season his last meal with his secret Jaelportian spice.

"Sirrig?" Mezaedo hopped off the table and grabbed the sword as Rigil entered. "What's wrong?"

Rigil kicked the door shut. "Where's Coble?"

"*Lord* Coble?"

"This is no time for games, boy. You said he was in the room with you." Barely bridling a curse, Rigil raked hair from his brow, scanning the room for threats. He needed to get ahold of himself. Mez was alive. Rigil hadn't failed him.

"I don't understand." Red-faced as a dawn sun, Mezaedo looked for all the world like he'd just been accused of murder. And Prince Oren thought this boy had Mârad potential?

"Never mind." Rigil jerked a thumb at the door. "I'll give you an earful later, but Nedir is on his way."

He was ready to haul the boy out by his hair, and likely would have if his eyes hadn't fallen on a blue spot on the desk. The tiniest of glints, so small he should have missed it.

It was an earring of painted blue porcelain, a common bauble in coastal towns, pinned onto a map of Er'Rets over the island of Hamonah. Someone had scrawled an inscription: *Strong Sarikar bloodlines. Descendants of Hinckdan Faluk?*

The earring was in Rigil's hand, then his pocket, almost before the porcelain could cool his skin. Around him, the room grew suddenly more vivid, from the papers on the desk to the symbols sprayed across them. The runes looked ancient Tennish, but Viola would know for certain.

So. This was Nedir's research.

"I think it's botany." Mezaedo had the decency to sound abashed, pointing at a sickly potted root on the desk. The odd scars freckling his hand—which had a different explanation every time Rigil asked—seemed starker than usual in the room's rainy light. "My third master used the same elixirs to make things sprout. And look." Grabbing a bottle off the desk, Mezaedo popped the stopper and took a whiff. "Ink from the Shelosh Islands. Poison. Worth a moldy fortune in Jaelport. *Not* friendly with fire."

So many questions. Prince Oren would have given his left hand to see this room.

"By the way, Sirrig." Mezaedo cocked his head at the empty scabbard around Rigil's waist. "Where's my sword?"

In answer, Rigil held out his hand. Reluctantly, Mezaedo returned the sword Rigil had lent him. No Keseel, this blade, but the hilt was warm and sturdy in his hand, the pommel decorated with the looped insignia of Prince Oren.

Prince Oren. The mission. The box. Rigil stepped back, scanning the room again. Sure enough, a silver-gilded mirror hung on the far wall, next to a window overlooking a moody view of the sea below the castle. But before Rigil could think of checking behind the mirror, a new voice chimed in.

"Trespassing, Sir Rigil? And here I thought you were a man of honor."

Something heavy thumped to the floor. He spun in time to watch Mezaedo's half-eaten apple lollop across the rug to stop at Raith Nedir's feet.

Rigil dropped to his knee, sparing a glance for Nedir only *after* he found Mezaedo's chest still rising and falling. Instinctively, he checked the block around his mind and found it holding strong. The scholar had dropped Mezaedo without lifting a finger.

Which meant—wonderful—he *was* a bloodvoicer.

"Don't fuss, Sir Rigil." Nedir fluttered a hand. "He is only asleep."

"He wasn't lying, then." Rigil kept a hand on Mezaedo's chest. Still rising. Still alive. "Coble *was* in this room. Mezaedo saw him. Why blot his memory?"

"To see if I could." Smoothing his hair with the same fingers that had set a goblet in Rigil's hand moments ago, Nedir gazed pensively at the unconscious Mez. "Without training, strays rarely learn even the most basic principles of shielding. Even *your* mind is better defended, Sir Rigil. Tell me, did your Jaelportian mother teach you that shielding trick?"

A dozen of Rigil's half-made plans fell to tatters when a phalanx of guards filed into the room. No, not mere guards. That sleek obsidian armor, those helmets, the stink of illegal magic . . .

Black knights.

Rigil glared at Nedir. "I want to see Coble."

"Alas, Lord Coble leaves housekeeping to me."

On cue, the black knights stepped forward, faceless in inky helmets. Rigil's urge to pray was short-lived, like every plea for mercy at his father's citadel board. If this was a test, he could not fail it. And it was always a test.

Jerking his sword from his belt, Rigil lashed out against the first knight within reach until a blow to the back of his head liquefied his bones.

Rigil's knees hit the floor, the room spinning. He could not fail. Mezaedo. He couldn't . . .

"Don't feel badly, Sir Rigil." Nedir's voice was warped, retreating. "Even the best player falls for the three-tower gambit once in a while."

CHAPTER TWO
SETHE

ROASTED, SKEWERED, COVERED IN SALT. If Sethe ever saw another gowzal, that was how she wanted it. Especially if she could do the skewering herself.

In cages along the ceiling of Coble's cavern dungeon, the rat-faced creatures screamed and fluttered as Sethe eased her cell open, triple-checking the corridor for guards. After two weeks in these sea-caves-turned-prison, the shrieks of those tides-cursed birds still shredded her nerves.

Fortunately, their bones made decent lockpicks.

Sethe squinted into the dark and inhaled a deep whiff of grime and salt and rat droppings, fingering the gash in her right ear. Ah, freedom.

The brown-and-gold owl on her shoulder bloodvoiced into her mind, *Not yet.*

The bird's unblinking golden eyes matched Sethe's one good eye perfectly, as they should: A piece of her lived inside that body right now. Curse or blessing, being able to break her mind into pieces had its definite advantages.

The dungeon corridor was lined on both sides by rusted cells, all of them empty except for some bones here and there. With the barest thought, Sethe sent the owl into the darkness, watching through its vision and adjusting her mental map of the dungeons to match what the bird saw. Six guards at the north exit, five at the west, two coming this way.

Sethe snapped back into her own senses. Sure enough, under the dripping water and screaming gowzals—footfalls.

With one last glance at the Sethe-shaped pile of hay she'd left inside her cell, Sethe closed the door, jammed her foot into the grating, and scrambled up to the narrow gap between the cell and the cavern ceiling, just wide enough for a half-starved Hamonayan.

Sethe wriggled into the space, reaching for her lucky earring out of habit, only to be reminded for the millionth time in two weeks that it was gone, the lobe ripped and blood-crusted where it had once hung. Oh well. She'd need more than luck if she was going to be the first to escape Land's End alive. How anyone could map a way out of these caves without fragments to scout, Sethe couldn't begin to guess.

The owl returned in a swoop of brown feathers to perch in the gap beside her just as two guards passed below, one of them the bottom-feeder who had spat in Sethe's gruel that morning.

After they passed, Sethe squirmed out of the gap, dropped to the floor, and followed the cells in the opposite direction. In the distance, water crashed where the sea poured into the cavern. Thankfully, Sethe's route led to higher ground. Drowning wasn't on her list today.

Escape Land's End. Find a ship. Survive.

Sethe's bare feet whispered over the floor stained with the salt she could taste on the air like a whiff of home. On her right, between gowzal cages, hanging green lanterns made shadows dance in the empty cells she passed. Her scar-sealed left eye made that side a wall of darkness.

More footsteps. Sethe ducked into an open cell, disturbing a rat from a pile of bones. Before it could dart off, she broke off a piece of her mind and thrust it into the creature.

The rodent's dull eyes turned gold, like Sethe's. It sat up, ears twitching, the fragment inside attentive to her thoughts.

Footsteps. Closer. The rat cocked its head. The piece inside it was only a fraction of Sethe, its powers of comprehension just as small, but still, she tried.

Distract the guards, she told the rat.

It chewed its tail, twitching.

Attack, Sethe added. *Distract. Dispatch.*

Another slow blink and the rat darted off, skittering through the bars into the darkness and taking a fragment of her with it. A fragment now exposed to any bloodvoicer who might stumble on it in the Veil, start asking questions.

Rotten things, questions. Raith Nedir's specialty.

Rotten man, Raith Nedir.

Sethe took off again, counting cells, searching for the staircase out of the sublevels and into the castle proper. Listening for foot-falls as she jogged, she rehearsed her list.

Escape the dungeon. Escape Land's End. Find a merchant crew that would take her on.

Never be trapped again.

Shouts from behind. That would be the two guards being at-tacked by a determined rat, but the footsteps kept coming. Cob-bled boots on stone. Echoes bouncing off salty walls.

Faster. Burrs of pain spiked up Sethe's legs as she ran between the cells, her body weak after two weeks of captivity and a meager sailor's fare before that.

She skidded to a halt at a fork in the path, her short hair blowing back in a gust of wind, the owl hovering overhead. To her right, the path spiraled down to a huge crater exploding with spray. The ocean, crashing into the cave. To her left, cells curved up toward a stone wall in the distance. A stone wall, a staircase, and at the top?

A door.

Surf pounded, retreated, letting a new sound take its place. The thunder of feet. Far too many feet.

Sethe sprinted up the path, cages rattling as gowzals caterwauled behind her, flapping at their prisons. They'd draw every guard in Land's End, every guard in *Er'Rets*, but Sethe could see the stairs now, the sconces that lit them, the beckoning door.

Green fire exploded behind her, throwing her forward. She struck the stone like a sack of seashells, then scrambled upright, one calf burning. Shouts from behind said it all.

Black knights. Close.

Just a few more steps.

Sethe was halfway up the staircase to the door when the next fireball exploded by her ear. She hadn't even heard the incantation, but then, it was hard to hear anything over the owl's shrieking. The bird dipped and swooped overhead as if caught in a hurricane, the fragment inside feeling every twitch of her terror.

Three more steps. Escape the dungeon, escape Land's End, survive.

Two more. Escape Land's End, survive.

Escape. One more. ESCAPE.

Sethe dove through the door and slammed it as the black knights reached the stairs. She dropped the deadlock, but a block of wood wouldn't hold off fireballs for long.

Dark magic. If only that were her biggest problem. As she peeled off the door, a stately foyer met her, twin ebony staircases with saffron runners curling toward a gold-gilt ceiling. Higher. Yes, higher was better. There would be no guards on the roof.

A burst of power shook the door behind her, killing the owl trapped on the other side and sending that piece of Sethe's mind back to her with a tiny shoot of warmth. No one would mourn the pile of feathers that fragment left behind.

Well, the world was full of owls.

Sethe reached the stairs and pounded up the first steps as the dungeon door behind her exploded. Near the top, the staircase curved so sharply that she had to catch the banister to keep from crashing into Coble's wall as she swung around the bend.

And slammed into Raith Nedir.

"Oh."

Only Nedir could pour so much into such a little word. Behind him, liveried guards were dragging some unconscious new plaything down the stairs like a bag of rocks, but Sethe's attention was all for the reed in Nedir's hand. The one he always carried, in case an idea struck. The one always dipped in poisoned Shelosh ink.

Sethe had no time to claw those nearsighted eyes from Nedir's bone-white head. With a prick, a tiny prick to her neck, the strength left her body. She sagged in his flabby arms. Her mind collapsed, reduced to monosyllables. *No!*

"Tedious timing, Sedhani." Nedir held her up with the same hands that had ripped the ring from her ear weeks ago in Melas, recapturing her after years and years apart. His breath still reeked of the curry he used to make when she'd survived one of his blood-voicing experiments as a child. "Today of all days, I expected better from you. I have had enough surprises to manage as it is."

Behind him, the unconscious lump stirred. One of the guards gave it a silencing kick.

Sethe barely noticed. Tides, nothing had changed. Sixteen years away from this man and not a scuddy thing had changed. Traps and more traps, always.

Nedir gripped her arm tighter. "Lord Coble expects a demonstration, and I intend to give him one. Do not disappoint me, Sedhani. Painful as today's proceedings will be for you, embarrassing me before Coble will be more so. Trust that."

Sethe tasted salt, her vision blurring, and not from the poisoned ink.

Escape the dungeon. Escape Land's End. Escape . . .

Nedir called more guards, and black-armored hands closed around her, dragging her down toward the caves where freedom never shone.

CHAPTER THREE
RIGIL

THE MEMORY CHANGED EVERY TIME Rigil dreamed it, the streets of Melas crowded one moment, quiet the next; the sky grey and then blue and then grey again as half-remembered details wrestled in his mind.

Sixteen-year-old Rigil didn't notice the weather. He had other concerns, like the ruffian tailing him through Melas like a blood-thirsty cham. He likely shouldn't have accused the man of stealing, but if he had any sense, he wouldn't be half a world from Zerah Rock either, fleeing his father's disappointment and hiding under a mule cart.

Cloth-covered merchant stalls choked his view as Rigil peered out through the wheel, savory aromas and hawkers' shouts tangling in the humid air along with the smell of salt washed in from the Gulf of Mayim. People crammed the square, people and livestock and finery and—was that a peacock?

"C'mere, boy! I'll show you robbery!"

Ducking back, Rigil didn't know what made him peer under the axle at a newly unloaded crate sitting nearby. It was likely full of spice or cloth, nothing noteworthy.

But spice and cloth usually didn't know how to open crates from the inside.

Slowly at first, then faster, more boldly, the lid rose as Rigil watched. A forehead poked out, followed by a girl's bright eyes. Or eye. Amber-gold and glaring, it was the only part of her face not obscured by choppy black hair. Something like claw marks, brutal and red, peeked out from her face between the strands as well. A stowaway?

Their gazes met. Locked.

Then she ducked. The crate snapped shut as someone neared on lopsided steps.

"You'll find the spice to your liking, sir. See for yourself. I have a crate of it here."

As the lopsided gait thudded closer, closer, the girl's eye floated in Rigil's vision, a mirage, gold as a sunset and round as a coin.

Riding pure impulse, Rigil scrambled out from under the cart and shouted at the first face he saw. "Thieves! Come quickly, sir, they're raiding the last cart!"

"Thieves?" The merchant's voice, like his face, resembled something a cart had rolled over a few too many times. "When? Which way? Dido, fetch Yehadah. We're bein' robbed!"

Playacting in Zerah Rock masquerades hadn't prepared Rigil for being so readily believed. He gaped at the merchant for a full three heartbeats before remembering that his marvelous performance was not, in fact, the most important matter at hand.

Up went the crate lid. Out sprang the girl. Older than expected, about fifteen, and wearing Hamonayan trousers over spice-coated feet. She looked at Rigil. Nodded.

And then she was running, the merchant flinging curses after her.

"Oy! Come back, thief. Someone catch that girl!"

The dream hazed. Colors and sounds whirled in a maelstrom. The girl was a blur, ducking and dodging through crowded streets as Rigil pounded after her, pulled by something nameless and formless, a need to see her face, to learn her name, a need to tell her his name and hear it roll off her Hamonayan tongue—

"Sirrig!"

Odd, Sethe's accent was certainly more chopped than he remembered it. More chopped and more . . . Jaelportian?

"Sirrig? Wake up!"

Sethe's figure dissolved, replaced by dark curls, a Jaelportian face. Shadows gridded Mezaedo's filthy skin, drawing Rigil's attention to the wall of bars between them, the crash of waves, and the reek of salt and stone. That, and the fact that he was lying in four inches of water, soaked to the skin, bound at his wrists and ankles, and—oh, joy—barefoot.

Barefoot *and* underground. Glorious.

Two black knights stood over him, likely having carried him all the way from the castle foyer. Judging by the ache in Rigil's wrists and ankles, they had not been gentle. Water crashed to Rigil's left, kicking up spray that set the black knights sputtering. They flexed their hands and rubbed their shoulders, then reclaimed his bound wrists and feet. Some of the water drained away from Rigil, like a retreating wave. Though he couldn't see over the left side of the path, instinct told him it would be a sheer drop into crashing swells. The sea had to pour into the cave somewhere down there, and as the tide rose, the swells were sloshing over the edge of the path.

On Rigil's right stretched a long row of cells built into a stone cliff, green sconces bracketed and glowing over each door. Mezaedo peered out of one of those cells, his olive skin a poisoned green in the sconce light. He, too, stood in seawater. As the black knights bent to lift Rigil again, no doubt taking him to his own cell, the crater to his left belched more water over the path and into the cells.

So. Not just underground but at sea level. That put this dungeon under Land's End.

As the guards resumed hauling him down the line, Rigil tried to catch the attention of the Barthian holding his feet. "Far be it from me to question your methods, but was taking my boots necessary?"

Seeing him awake, the Barthian dropped Rigil's feet with a splash. "Hear that, Ijo? Sir Rigil wants his boots back."

The other knight dropped Rigil's arms, and he hit the stone like a sack of bricks, the water doing little to soften the fall. His head sank below the latest swell for a split second, water shooting up his nose and down his throat. Rigil came up spluttering, his head choosing that moment to remind him loudly of the blow that had first knocked him unconscious.

The knight at his head, the Jaelportian, gave Rigil a light kick. "Too fine for bare feet?"

"I'd take his pretty shirt too, but I wouldn't be caught dead in Zerah Rock colors."

With as much dignity as his rope bindings and headache would allow, Rigil clambered to his feet, scanning the black knights up and down. They both wore yellow tunics under black leather jerkins, which had a particularly sickly effect on the ashy Barthian. Facing the latter, he winced. "With your complexion, that's likely for the best."

The Jaelportian jabbed his dagger at Rigil's gut. "Walk."

Hands tied before him, Rigil swiveled on his heel and obeyed, giving Mezaedo what he hoped was an encouraging nod as the knights pushed him down the path. Water sloshed around his shins. How far would it rise? The darkness concealed any waterlines on the cavern wall. Or was it a cliff face? Rigil couldn't see over the rim of the wall from here, but he could tell it didn't reach the cavern ceiling. How large was this cavern, then? If he managed to scale this wall, would he find a way out or another block of cells waiting for a new prisoner to swallow?

"Tell me." Rigil kept his steps goadingly small as the black knights shuffled him along the narrow, tide-soaked path beside the cells. "Is this what Coble promised when he smuggled you out of Ice Island? Hiding in his sublevels and playing prison guard?"

The Barthian sloshed a few steps ahead, keys jingling at his hip. "Better a knight playing prison guard than a prisoner playing knight."

"Besides." The Jaelportian's knife flashed. "We haven't all got titles waiting at home."

Another burst of spray shot over the path. Rigil flinched under the droplets.

"An heir who doesn't want to inherit," the Jaelportian cooed. "What's the story, Barak? My money's on illegitimate son. Harkan here thinks you ran with thieves in a past life."

"Thieves?" Mezaedo laughed, drawing Rigil's glance until Ijo turned his head forward. "What a load of mold. Sirrig's more a knight than you lot will ever be."

"That will do, Mezaedo." Rigil had to shout over the surf, but shout he did. Loyalty was one thing, misplaced praise quite another.

Three cells from Mezaedo's, the Barthian took the keys off his belt to unlock Rigil's cell.

Now!

Rigil spun, coming down hard on Ijo's foot and arm in one motion. But the black knight was ready. He caught Rigil's arm, hooked a foot around his leg, and spun him forward in time to catch Harkan's fist in his gut.

Rigil toppled, catching himself on Harkan and earning a grunt. Then it happened, almost before his mind caught up with his fingers. A flash of reflex like a fork of lightning, his fingers darting over the armor, skimming the Barthian's belt.

Ijo pulled him off. Rigil submitted, gasping.

The guards threw him, and he splash-landed ungracefully in his cell on all fours. Ijo snapped shackles around his ankles, the chain so short that Rigil could hardly take a step, let alone try to escape. Too late, he saw the swollen corpse lying next to him, bloated past all recognition.

Rigil recoiled.

Ijo slammed the door and dangled his arms through the bars. "Maybe you can borrow boots from *this* Kingsguard, eh? Not that you'll need them long."

They left laughing, the sound a rusty blade on stone until the tide overtook it.

"Sirrig?" Cross-legged a few cells down, Mezaedo was barely visible. "All right?"

Rigil was focusing on avoiding eye contact with his Kingsguard cellmate. No, not merely Kingsguard. Mârad. Who had Prince Oren's informant in Land's End been? Freyan? Kessel?

"Sirrig?"

Rigil sighed. "I am exceptional, Mezaedo. Thank you."

A long pause, followed by something that sounded suspiciously like chewing, then Mezaedo said, "You were out a long time. Moldy onions, I thought that was it."

Turning from his cellmate, Rigil sat up, praying that Mezaedo was too distant to see the body. "You suffered far worse, the way Nedir controlled you. Are *you* all right?"

Light glinted off the water and shone in the squire's irises like twin stars. "He controlled me?"

"You don't remember?"

"I remember the study, getting caught by Coble. Nedir showed up next, said something about my weak mind. Always nice to hear that now and again, you know, in case I forget." As usual, the reference to Mezaedo's stint in bloodvoicing training was glib, punctuated by a loud bite. "There's not much after that."

Rigil squinted through the bars. "What are you eating?"

"Bread, I think. Possibly potato." Mezaedo held up his ubiquitous pouch of unidentified spice, which the black knights must have missed or deemed too trivial to bother with. "With help, it's not half bad."

For all his optimism, the green light did poisonous things to the boy's face. His grin looked forced and faded too soon. "Sirrig, I think the water's rising."

Rigil peered out of his cell, straining for a glimpse of guards or gowzals as the waterline rose, soaking through his shirt. Shackled as he was, he couldn't reach the door to see the number of guards or hidden ears waiting outside. Perhaps that was the point of the shackles. Yet another way to keep prisoners off-balance.

Or perhaps they were just supposed to drown him faster.

"I'm sorry, Sirrig." Trapped between water and stone, Mezaedo's voice reverberated down the line of cells. "Sir Caleb always says I should practice blocking, and—aw, moldy *onions*. We lost your sword."

"Never mind." Rubbing the knot on the back of his head, Rigil took in the cell, the shooting spray beyond the bars, anything but the dead man beside him. That would not be his fate, and it could *not* be Mezaedo's. He wouldn't lose another one this way, not like Bran, like Tazeem . . .

Trust Arman, Eagan would say. As if it were that simple.

Perhaps for Eagan the Unfailing, it was.

Tide was rising, crashing a war rhythm in the sea caves as Mezaedo's voice trickled out of the dark. "I always thought I'd die a stray, shoveling out a hearth or doing laundry for some hired tough. But to die for the Kingsguard, and with Sir Rigil Barak?"

Rigil pulled a brass key ring from his sleeve. "Hold that thought."

Mezaedo's manic chewing stopped. "*How?*"

How, indeed. Rigil tossed the ring to his other hand. "I am no thief, Mezaedo. Remember that. I am a Kingsguard knight and a servant of Arman." And a spy, but this was hardly the time to educate Mezaedo on the secrets of the Mârad. Rigil spun a few keys aside, sizing them against his shackles.

Mezaedo whooped softly as key slipped into lock. "Did you learn that being a knight?"

No, Rigil thought. His shackles clicked open, fell away. *That* he'd learned being a thief.

He used a different key to unlock his cell, then hurried to Mezaedo's, shelving the next conundrum for now. No guards yet. They would sail that storm when they came to it.

"Do you remember the way out?" Rigil asked. "The path to higher ground?"

Mezaedo sloshed out of his cell, bread in one fist, dark curls matted to his face. "They brought me down a stairway. It was guarded."

Of course. Stepping back, Rigil examined the sheer stone cliff the cells were carved from. Not high, but slick with spray. "Can you climb?"

"Like a spotted palm spider."

Good enough. The water tugged at Rigil's calves as he jammed his foot into the cell door, seeking the place where iron bars met stone overhead. Sethe wouldn't have needed to search for handholds. She would have *made* them, an out-of-place thought that he immediately shooed off.

By the time he found a handhold, the water was tugging at Mezaedo's thighs. The boy didn't seem to notice, too busy wrinkling his nose the way he did when some new thought had struck him. "Sirrig," he whispered, "what's a seth?"

Despite his cham-grip on the stone, Rigil nearly fell off the wall. "What?"

"You said it, in your sleep. What is it? A spell? A code?"

"It's nothing. She was someone I knew once."

"*She?*"

Lightness, they didn't have time for this. "A *friend,* Mezaedo. Someone I met in Melas when I was about your age, a little over fifteen years ago. I was resourceless at the time and far from Zerah Rock. Sethe took pity on me and taught me many things a nobleman likely should not know, including how to pick pockets . . . and locks." He glanced down at the squire, who had shoved his tongue in front of his teeth to hide an expression of . . . what? Shock? Disappointment? "Yes, I was a thief. And no, it did not pay. We spent more than our share of hungry nights in the Melas jailhouse after capers gone awry."

Granted, they had never stayed in that jailhouse long, thanks to Sethe's nimble lockpicking fingers. And Rigil's charm, obviously.

"You have my permission to upbraid me later, Mez. For now, I suggest you thank that friend for the fact that you are not currently chained to a watery grave."

"Right." Mezaedo saluted to some point over Rigil's shoulder. "My thanks to Missethe and her useful tutelage."

Rigil snorted, the soles of his feet already protesting the rusty bars. He never had developed Sethe's knack for climbing barefoot. "Just climb, Mezaedo."

Grabbing his own section of the grate, Mezaedo began scaling the cell door, moving faster and more fluidly than Rigil could, presumably in imitation of a spotted palm spider. The lad had passed Rigil and nearly reached the joint where the cell met the cliff face, a flush transition of grate to stone. There, he looked back, shadows dripping down his face like his springy curls.

"What happened to her, Sirrig?" When Rigil glanced up at him, Mezaedo added, "I'm not prying, stray's honor. But you haven't mentioned her before."

Such a simple, simple question. Such a horribly complicated answer. Rigil pulled himself up another foot, jammed his toes between the next bars, and tried to imagine a scenario in which Mezaedo Chevyah wouldn't press him for answers.

He grunted, something popping in his shoulder as he stretched for the next handhold. "She was like you. An escaped slave with a bloodvoicing ability, mistreated all her life. Her old master had tortured her." The gouges on her face floated across his vision. "Though she never spoke of it, I knew she lived in fear that he would one day find her again." Rigil jammed his foot into the grate, losing himself in that mechanical motion. Grab and pull. Reach, grab, and pull. "I thought she was being paranoid about it all. Even when I suggested we leave Melas and return to Zerah Rock, somewhere she'd be safe, I never truly thought a master would go so far for one captive."

Mez waited, still hanging off the wall. The rusted bars beneath Rigil's bare feet were bleeding cold straight to his bones. Cold like that night on the road to Zerah Rock, hunched around the tiny fire Sethe had never agreed to make in the first place. He couldn't remember what they'd talked about, why her face had been so close, the fire turning her barely healed facial wounds into veins of flame on her cheek. After eight months together in Melas, he still hadn't worked up the courage to ask where the gouges had come from. Maybe he would have that night, given a few moments more.

But then—the attack. Armed men breaking out of the trees. Sparks pouring into the sky like glowing shards of broken glass. Sethe shouting as one of them grabbed her hair. The crunch of a nose breaking under Rigil's fist.

Then running, running, running. Tripping over roots and briars and his own panicked feet, listening for the sound of Sethe ahead of him, always the faster one, the best at escapes. He should have listened to her, would have to make it up to her when this was over, when the sun rose and this nightmare became just another close call, something to laugh about later.

"Sirrig?"

Mezaedo's voice nearly vanished in the boom of the tide beneath them. The light of a green lantern fixed to the stone a few feet away was flickering on his olive skin, winking in and out. There, and then gone. Like a vapor. Like a feather in a storm. Or a girl in the forest.

"She was right." Rigil dug his nails into a cleft in the wall until pain welled in his fingertips. "I had a chance to protect her, and in the end, she was right. I couldn't."

Almost before the words left his mouth, something flickered overhead.

A rat was gazing at him over the top of the wall. Small, with eyes like burnished gold, it scurried off as Rigil watched. Perhaps it had never been there.

Mezaedo, Arman bless him, asked no more questions. Putting his head down, Rigil emptied his mind of everything but reaching, heaving, pulling. Finishing this mission before it cost him more than a pair of boots.

Chapter Four

Sethe

Sethe had once thought of Nedir's fortress in Hamonah as a cage. As it turned out, she'd once been naive.

The hexagonal room at the top of the southern tower—Nedir called it the *aviary*—was unusually bright today. Lanterns glowed in all six corners, magnified by mirrors on each white-painted wall. Hanging from the vaulted ceiling in a gowzal cage, one of about a dozen, Sethe tried not to feel the bars pressing a grid into her back as she fought to breathe the foul-smelling air through her mouth. The paralysis had worn off, but she wouldn't stand straight for weeks after this.

After this.

Chin to knees, Sethe squeezed her eye shut. There would be no *after this*. Nedir had caged her again, and this time, she couldn't smuggle herself to freedom in a crate.

"...beginning to question whether Land's End is truly as *secure* as you promised."

The voice of the seer from Mirrorstone set the gowzals in the other cages shrieking and put an end to Sethe's fantasy of being the only one in this room. Under her cage, five of six seats were filled around a blackwood table. Lord Coble; a huge Eben with bone shards in his hair; the seer named Rheala of Mirrorstone; a sulky boy of about eighteen; and, of course, Raith scuddy Nedir, his hand resting on a large metal crank bolted to one wall and attached by pulley to Sethe's cage.

"Honorable Mistress Rheala." Nedir was the only one who bothered with honorifics. "I assure you, the Kingsguard disturbance has been dealt with. This location is as secure as any."

"Ah, yes, Nedir." Rheala's voice jumped an octave. "We are familiar with your *housekeeping*. I'll have you know that my god does not approve."

From up here, Nedir's glossy hair gleamed like a polished seashell. "You mean *our* god, Mistress Rheala. And you mustn't listen to everything young Erro tells you. He is . . . excitable."

No one acknowledged the dark-haired boy sitting erect beside Coble. A son or ward, he had ridiculously sharp cheekbones, polished pearl skin, and none of Coble's blunt features, though he wore Land's End's colors. The too-pretty-for-this-world type. Well, Sethe had seen prettier. And you couldn't trust a face like that as far as you could spit.

Rheala sniffed, proof that her wrinkled little beak of a nose still worked. Judging by the creaking sound she'd made settling into that chair, not to mention the way spit sprayed when she talked, that nose was one of the only parts of her that *did* work. The god of beauty didn't mind lowering his standards once in a while, then.

The aviary's one window, a tiny skylight, opened onto a cloudy evening just beginning to glow orange. Every so often, the salty smell of Land's End and fresh rain gusted through it. Without that breeze, Sethe would have been about as sane as the gowzal one cage over. The one eating its own feet.

Not that anyone around the table noticed her. Rheala and Nedir were leering at each other, Erro picking his nails, the Eben drumming the wood in an off-kilter rhythm that no one seemed to hear. For a giant, he wasn't all that frightening. Pale and knobby, he could have been a sun-bleached tree the tide had washed in.

Then there was Coble. Blockish and crisply dressed, he was just a pair of broad shoulders and black hair from Sethe's angle. He wore the colors of Land's End, gold stars on black, and moved with the slow intent of a carnivorous lizard as he set something on the table. A lacquered box, marked with some kind of cross between a crescent moon and a gowzal's ugly profile.

"As promised." Coble's voice was all granite after Nedir's reedy tenor. "I trust you will refrain from questioning me again, seer. We have lost too much time already."

Time for *what*, tides only knew. Eye closed, Sethe pressed her skull to the bars and retreated inside her head, where input from a dozen fragments fed into her mind. It was easier to ignore the meeting if she focused on that input, let it transport her anywhere but here.

Every fragment Sethe had, every rat or bird or slug in Land's End, was a window into a different view. Whatever that fragment saw or did, she saw and did in the back of her mind, existing in a dozen ways at once.

Through one fragment, Sethe saw a dank cell, tiny paws rooting through old bones. Her rat. Through another, she saw Land's End from above, the view of one of her birds wheeling around the towers. It would make its way back to her eventually. They all did, unless something happened to the host.

She *really* needed to get over that owl.

Around the table, Rheala croaked a laugh at something Coble said. "You expect a great deal of trust, Coble, after how miserably the Tsaftown operation failed."

Nedir answered, waving a hand as if spreading butter on the air. "There were too many variables in Tsaftown. Even you can appreciate that, Rheala. And I trust you remember that Lord Coble was acting entirely on our master's orders."

Five pairs of eyes darted to the box on the table, its gowzal mark, then away.

The Eben grunted something garbled, and Erro smirked. Definitely bound to break hearts.

"And what, pray, has changed?" Rheala rapped vulture fingernails on the table. "Our master expects results, but a handful of black knights stowed in a cave is hardly sufficient. Another slip like Tsaftown or that *debacle* with Othvold Myvick in Jaelport and we shall have more than one Kingsguard knight and his squire dogging us."

Did no one care that a human was swinging in a cage over their heads? Maybe Sethe could put a fragment into a gowzal, just for someone to talk to who wasn't *completely* insane.

She returned to flicking through her fragments. The castle from above. The dungeons from below. Servants in the scullery. Guards on the stairs. Waves on the beach. Flies in the study. Hundreds of vantage points, every one of them *useless*.

Fitting her mouth between her knees, Sethe choked down a throat-shredding roar.

"And what is this weapon you keep prattling about, Coble?" Rheala again. "Worth the journey from Mirrorstone, I hope. I haven't many such trips left in me."

Erro muttered something that sounded like "We can hope."

It was coming. Sethe could only hold off the dread for so long. Nedir had promised a demonstration, which meant they were all about to see her mind invaded. To see Sethe fall apart. Whatever Nedir had been saving her for these last two weeks, this *had* to be it.

Arman. The name bobbed to the surface of her mind, like it did whenever panic started to blur the edges of her world. Arman, Father God, father of Câan, freer of captives, who had walked through death's door willingly and walked out again with the key to unlock every shackle and prison. No trap could hold Him, not even the grave. Whoever He set free was free forever. Sethe's lips moved to the rhythm of those lines burned into her memory, lines that still resonated in someone else's voice from the days he'd spent teaching her to pray. Right before he had betrayed her.

The strange part? Even after scrubbing *him* from her mind, his words had stayed behind, whispering in her ear like the trapped song of a conch shell in moments like this. Sethe locked her teeth, shoving him from thought, losing herself to the words he had left behind, the last decent thing he'd done. *Arman, Father God, father of Câan, freer of captives . . .*

These days, King Gidon's words followed her too, still echoing from the Battle of Armonguard when he had bloodvoiced every mind in Er'Rets: *Arman is the One God. He created Er'Rets and everything in it. He gave each of you life and purpose. He loves all of you as His own sons and daughters . . .*

Sethe held on to those words like a beggar to his last rutah.

"You haven't answered our question, Lord Coble." As Rheala leaned forward, nose hooked over the table, the Eben stopped his drumming. The old woman looked like something death had coughed up in a wad, but she sounded worse, every word full of holes. "We have no resources, no army. What can your scholar offer that Sir Fenris Yarden and the entire network of Othvold Myvick could not?"

Coble's chair squawked back like a sawblade across steel, and when he stood, his hair nearly grazed Sethe's cage. He was a large man, large in the way the worst pirates were. A way that filled up a room to its corners and soured the air like bad wine.

Not that Sethe knew a thing about wine. Someone she'd known once—*he* had. He'd been able to tell a good batch by the smell, the color, the way it caught the Melas light.

"Mistress Rheala." Coble adjusted his black doublet in one of the mirrors. "Too much candor can be dangerous. As Avenis has not taught you this, learn it from me."

The threat stitched Rheala's lips together, and she traded glances with the Eben as Coble tucked in his chair. Nedir was watching Coble, a falcon awaiting a signal.

Sethe had no fear of Coble. Healthy respect, fine. Hatred? Scuddy right. But she had survived the streets of Hamonah too long to blink at another well-dressed tyrant.

It was the well-dressed old lunatics you had to watch for.

"Like you, seer," Coble went on, "I am impatient to see my scholar's work."

Nedir stood in a cascade of robes. If Sethe could have made herself smaller, she would have blown away.

From here, she could see the fine filigree decorating the box on the table, but she didn't need to *see* the little vial of grey powder to know it waited inside.

That powder. Nedir's secret weapon.

Time for his demonstration.

A gowzal wailed in the cage next to Sethe as Nedir set his hand on the crank. Her cage jerked. With a screech of metal, the table rushed up to meet her, forcing a gasp past her lips.

Oh, Arman, this was happening. After all these years, happening *again*.

"What is this?" Rheala jutted her lips at Sethe. "A Hamonayan?"

"A test subject." Nedir turned the crank again, jerking Sethe to a stop over the table, face-to-face with Coble. "An old one, to be precise, who escaped me as a child. I was fortunate enough to find her again in Melas some weeks ago. A gift from Avenis."

"Surely not. She's hideous."

Despite herself, Sethe snorted. The irony faded, though, when she caught Erro staring at her, his face twisted with a revulsion that made her want to bury her head in quicksand. The brat couldn't be much more than eighteen. Who had arrogance like that at *eighteen*?

Nedir pulled the vial from the box and held it up, adding a smile for Rheala, like the ones he used to give Sethe. "Dear Rheala, there is more than one kind of beauty. This woman is a bloodvoicer of rare ability, capable of splitting her mind into fragments to control multiple hosts simultaneously." He said it like she was some marvel he'd found washed up on the seashore instead of an anomaly he'd created himself. He and his experiments. "She could be of great use with the proper persuasion. This"—he held the vial higher—"is perhaps the deadliest resource in Er'Rets. A tool of world-shapers."

Tool. Not drug. Always the rhetoric with this one.

"Bloodvoicing is the enemy's strength, Nedir," Coble said.

"It *was*, my lord. But with respect, the enemy has no answer for this."

Nedir's reedy voice touched Sethe like an uninvited caress, a reminder of all those days in Hamonah, locked in his keep, counting the hours until his next experiment. There was always a silver vial, each batch more promising than the last. *Shall we try again, Sedhani? I think I very nearly took control that time.*

The room shrank, the mirrored walls crawled closer, Coble's black eyes swallowed the light. And Sethe knew the truth even before Nedir shed his robe like a snakeskin.

She was out of time.

The Eben glanced at Rheala. Turning to Nedir, she sniffed. "You explain nothing."

"It is a bloodvoicing stimulant." Nedir presented it to Rheala with a flourish of his Avenis rings, as if to remind her that they were equals, at least before their god. "Stronger than karpos or anything we have yet discovered. With it, even a mediocre bloodvoicer can enter and control the most fortified mind."

"And it works? It has been tested?"

At that, Nedir regarded Sethe. She glared back with the only eye she had left, but his perfect lips still curved up. "With promising results."

Nedir plucked the vial from the Eben, then glided across the room, robes murmuring. "This formula is the result of years of experimentation, guaranteed to multiply a bloodvoicer's ability tenfold or more. I hope, in time, to increase that effect."

"One vial?" Rheala puckered her face. "We were all promised a weapon."

"And you shall have it. This is merely a demonstration."

"Within the *fortnight*, Nedir."

A tiny crease slitted Nedir's smooth forehead. "The shipment is scheduled to leave its secure location in a matter of days. You shall have your weapon, Rheala, you and all the others, present company included. Now, may we proceed?"

Daintily, he unscrewed his vial. The last time he'd attacked Sethe with one of his dusts, her mind hadn't been the only thing scarred. Even now, he didn't have to speak to drill a message through her skin, a reminder of her role to play.

He wanted her to put on a show. He wanted her to come undone. "Arman, Father God, father of Câan, freer of captives. No trap can hold Him. Whoever Câan frees is free forever . . ."

"What is she on about?" Rheala demanded. It took Sethe a beat to realize she was mumbling one of her prayers aloud. That habit had seen her through a dozen storms at sea and twice as many near disasters on land, which had to mean Arman was listening, right?

"It is a habit of hers," she heard Nedir answer from far away, somewhere on the other side of the world. "A new one, actually. I am quite curious to know where she found this interest in the Way of Arman, but fear not, Mistress Rheala. Her prayers will not impede our demonstration."

Something tickled the back of Sethe's mind. If only to distract herself from the smile in Nedir's voice, the briny mildew smell snaking out of the vial, she shifted her focus from fragment to fragment, peering at the roof, the caves, the kitchens, the beach, back to the caves.

There, she froze. Coble was prattling about Nedir's research, what a *breakthrough* this could be, but Sethe had stopped listening. Her hands, oozing sweat, clung to the bars as she gazed into the sea caves through her rat.

Impossible. It couldn't be.

A barefooted man, in a torn tunic and jerkin, crouched over a precipice somewhere in the caves. Soaked to the skin, he was reaching down for a boy who was holding something in his teeth. Shadows and a neat beard obscured the man's face, but Sethe knew him by the set of his shoulders and the straight slope of his nose and the way he smoothed a hand over his hair when the boy found his footing.

Oh, tides.

The boy, a scrawny Jaelportian in a filthy shirt and trousers, scuffed his sopping-wet hair with both hands as the man held the keys quiet. Raith Nedir's keys. He always had been quick with his hands.

"And Mezaedo?" the man was saying. *"Leave the bread."*

His voice was deeper now, smoother than it had been in Melas. His companion took a last bite, dropped the lump over the edge, and watched it fall like he'd just surrendered his favorite thumb.

To the right, the sea crashed up with the tide, close enough to spray man and boy. They must have been in the cells down there, doomed to drown when the tide came in.

Gowzals shrieked, an alarm for the guards. If they wanted to escape, they had to act now.

Rigil. The last person in Er'Rets she'd ever wanted to see again and the last person in Er'Rets she wanted to *need*. Wrinkling his nose at the mazelike path through the cavern, he scanned the darkness until his gaze brushed Sethe's rat. Though the lanterns reflected green in his eyes, she knew what color they were.

Blue like the sky that was clear one moment, stormy the next.

Blue like the ocean that would drown her as soon as look at her.

Blue like the earring Nedir had ripped from Sethe's ear, proof that luck was like all gods, all people: full of false promises and quick to turn on her.

When the first black knight tromped around the nearest cell block, Sethe's rat scuttled under a pile of bones, cutting off her view. There were shouts. Rigil's, the black knight's, the boy's. Sethe urged her rat into the open in time to see Rigil locked in a flurry of fists and steel, more of a storm than a fight. It was him. He was here, right here, a few floors away, about to be recaptured before she could make use of this gift from the gods. No, wait—Sethe hurried to correct that old habit before Arman could change His mind—this gift from *Arman*.

Rigil always had been good at escapes. Of course, he'd also been good at leaving her behind.

Still. Reaching out, Sethe sought every fragment in the vicinity. Birds, bats, rats around the castle, hiding in dank walls and watching through golden irises. Dimly aware of the cage, aware of Nedir's voice droning in the aviary, Sethe pressed her will into them. *Attack. Attack.*

"Now, Sedhani."

Nedir's voice pulled her back to the cage, back to the aviary and the glaring light.

He saw it in her face. He had to. How could Rigil's presence *not* be written in her scars? Nedir's forehead rippled. Curiosity. But it passed, and then he was raising the vial to his lips as Rheala leaned forward in her chair and Coble watched Sethe through the bars.

The aviary door flew open then, banging against the wall. Nedir whisked the vial up his sleeve and spun to face a guard in black-and-yellow livery.

"My lord. Disturbance in the caves. The Kingsguard prisoners are loose. Permission to lock down the keep?"

Coble didn't stir. "Granted."

Rheala sat back, tilting the Avenis pendant around her neck this way and that as if disappointed that her god hadn't warned her about this. Erro's lips thinned. The knobby Eben looked confused.

"Erro, take them to the tunnel." Coble slid the gowzal-marked box toward himself. "That includes you, Nedir."

Erro, Rheala, and the giant rose as Nedir dipped his head. "As you wish, my lord."

Nedir was following the other three out of the room, moving with grace but no urgency, when Coble rapped a fingernail on the box. "Nedir. The vial."

In the doorway, the old man paused. "I would think the weapon would be safest with me. I am its creator and the bloodvoicer among us."

"You are a glorified clerk, Nedir." Coble traced the mark stamped into the box with a lazy finger. "If not for me, you would still be experimenting on potted plants in Hamonah. *I* brought you here. *I* advocated for you to the master. *I* gave you this chance to be part of something greater, and I advise you to remember that your creations are mine. I will not ask again."

Nedir hesitated, clutching the sleeve that hid the vial as if tempted to use it right then, security breach or not. *Please, no.*

Instead, he set it on the table with a kiss of glass on wood.

After Nedir filed out, Coble collected his vial but didn't crank Sethe back up to the ceiling. Instead, he leaned in to study her. A falconer, shopping for a new bird of prey.

"Nedir has high hopes for you," he said. "Care to tell me why I should?"

Sethe threaded her hands through the bars. "Care to put your face a little closer?"

His gaze traced her scars, crossing her dead eye, dipping over her face with an unsettling flatness. At least Nedir had passion, curiosity. At least you could look into Nedir's ageless face and know he was alive.

Speak of the demon. Coble scowled but didn't turn at the sound of the door creaking open, robes swishing behind him. "What now, Nedir?"

If Coble moved like a lizard, Nedir was a serpent. He glided across the room, the pen in his hand glinting like a fang. Sethe barely had time to recoil in her cage before Coble's eyes bugged. His legs crumpled beneath him, and his body hit the floor.

Sethe had never seen Nedir's poison at work from the outside. Had she looked that pathetic, a heap of useless limbs flailing useless threats?

Stopping his reed pen with a bit of wax, Nedir pressed his foot against Coble's twitching arm to still it. Coble's eyes sparked curses. Coals crackling in a fire.

"Our master had planned to make greater use of you," Nedir said. "I convinced him otherwise. Your only contribution has been failure. Not a terribly prodigious career, Coble, but what can one expect from a glorified puppet? Erro will be next, I'm sure. For all his potential, I have found him to be an underwhelming pupil."

Nedir leaned down to pluck the vial from Coble's hand, holding his robes aloft to avoid defilement. The vial vanished up one of his sleeves, replaced by another pen. Silver handled, and with a much more severe nib.

With delicate fingers, Nedir pressed the nib into Coble's neck until blood mingled with ink. "Duskroot," he said. "A lethal dose. If you survive, and some do, I suggest you make yourself very, very scarce."

Coble's only answer was a foamy gurgle. Sethe begged the tides to swallow her whole, her stomach squeezing when Nedir addressed her. "I trust you are wise enough to keep what you have seen to yourself, Sedhani."

Sethe waited a beat to clear the last cobwebs out of her voice.

"Why would I have to say anything? You were the last one in the room."

A flicker of a smile. "Leave explanations to me. If all goes well, Land's End will be mine before week's end. You would do well to make yourself comfortable here, Sedhani."

He withdrew from the room with a click of a key in the lock, leaving a vacuum not even the gowzals tried to fill. Pity. She'd prefer a bit of shrieking to the lord of Land's End's gurgling.

Only the rat in the back of her mind kept Sethe from curling up in a ball and letting the fight drain out of her. No time for shock. She still had one chance. One impossible chance, after all these years and the promises she'd made never to speak *his* name again.

But survival always came with a price. Nedir had taught her that.

Swallowing her pride, Sethe gritted her teeth and bloodvoiced the boy from Melas.

CHAPTER FIVE
RIGIL

RIGIL!

The bloodvoicer didn't knock before speaking into Rigil's mind, but that was hardly his first concern. Clashing steel filled his ears, echoing in the endless dark of the caverns as he pulled his stolen sword from a black knight's breastplate and spun to help Mezaedo.

The young squire's foe was a behemoth, thundering blows with tooth-rattling force. The first two knights had fallen quietly enough between the sea and the cavern exit, but any more of this and all of Land's End would be crashing down on Rigil and Mezaedo before they even reached the stairs. Thank *Arman* the enemy warriors hadn't started using magic.

Right on cue, Mezaedo's opponent began a guttural incantation. "Râbab rebabah râbah yârad! Rûwach âphâr mayim êsh, machmâd pârar!"

Glorious. He'd spoken too soon. Green light flashed over the knight's head like a sickly moon, soon to become a replica of him, an illusion that would make this fight oh so much harder. Mezaedo was throwing every scrap of his sword training into interrupting that spell as the bloodvoice pricked again at the back of Rigil's mind, trying to break through his shields.

Rigil!

It wasn't Mezaedo. While a person's bloodvoice rarely matched their real voice, the boy's tendency to mash words and clip syllables usually gave him away. Which could make this a trick from Nedir. That, and a distraction Rigil couldn't afford.

The knight overextended himself, and Rigil surged in, trading caution for speed. Too late, he saw the trap. The knight, still muttering his incantation, used his free hand to pull a hidden dagger from a sheath on his thigh, and suddenly all the world was a wicked edge diving for Rigil's gut.

"Sirrig!"

A winged shape—a bat?—materialized out of the darkness, diving at the black knight's chest. The knife grazed Rigil's belt and pinged off the buckle. A second bat joined the first, then a third, all shrieking and beating the air. Green light sputtered, and then a throwing knife appeared, protruding from the black knight's neck. Rigil turned to find Mezaedo's hand outstretched, cheek still bulging from that last bite of bread-or-potentially-potato.

"Well done." Breathing hard, Rigil raked his hair. "Thank you."

Mezaedo shook out his scarred hand. "Thank masters two and nine."

As the squire went to retrieve the stolen knife, something jabbed at Rigil's mind, proof that he was still shielding. The bats had already swooped away.

Only bats, then. Nothing more.

The prickle returned on the other side of the door that connected the caves to Coble's foyer. So busy leading Mezaedo along the dark-paneled walls and trying to quiet his breathing, Rigil didn't realize he'd dropped his shields until the bloodvoicer boomed in his head.

Rigil!

"Get *out*, Nedir." Strengthening the curtain around his mind, Rigil gritted his teeth against the scholar's tricks as he led Mezaedo around a wainscoted corner, wincing at the creaky floors and summoning the map in his head. The scullery was a few corridors away, along with the passage under the kitchens. So close . . .

Voices ahead. Rigil stopped before the next turn, and Mezaedo crashed into him, nearly shoving him into a hall where two guards conferred beneath a portrait of Coble. They kept their voices low, but the gist was inescapable.

Two prisoners loose . . . lock down the castle . . . no corner unsearched.

Mezaedo tugged Rigil back and pointed with tea-dark eyes at a door a few feet away. They darted inside, Rigil gingerly clicking the door shut after them.

Grey light slanted through tall windows onto a bedchamber gauzed with red. A gown draped the bed. In fashion, but barely, and opulent to the point of absurdity.

An Avenis worshipper, then. Easing off the door, Rigil scanned the room for signs of travel and found what he sought on the vanity. A small chest of cosmetics, the kind a woman would bring on a journey. An old woman, judging by those particular elixirs. The chest could have belonged to Rigil's mother if not for the moon-stamped crest of Mirrorstone on the lid.

So, Coble had a guest. An old woman from Mirrorstone, almost certainly an Avenis worshipper. Someone with political influence, no doubt. Rigil could fathom only one woman on this side of Er'Rets who fit those descriptions so neatly. Was that the business Coble had been attending to? A meeting with the seer of Mirrorstone?

RIGIL!

This time, the mystery bloodvoicer knocked hard enough to hurt. That was new. New and terribly timed. Rigil was no bloodvoicer. He could only maintain his mother's blocking trick so long before that fact caught up with him.

It had to be Nedir, attempting another ploy. Anyone else would give a name. That was how bloodvoicing was done. Everyone knew that.

Another jolt, as if someone were trying to break down a door inside his head. Rigil caught the bedpost to steady himself, gritting his teeth as his block slipped and a burst of frustration eked through.

Rigil, for tides' sake, I know you can hear m—

Rigil raised his shields. His hand skidded down the bedpost, driving a sliver through his palm.

Impossible. *Impossible.* It couldn't be her. Lightness, how often had he fantasized about Sethe bloodvoicing him like this, begging for his help, telling him that she hadn't died after all, that she didn't hate him, that she still needed him, still *wanted* him . . .

Isemios's wit, but Nedir was good. Rigil would give him that.

"Where to, Sirrig?" On his way across the room, Mezaedo grabbed a handful of dried apricots from a bedside bowl and began dusting them with spice from his pouch.

"Lightness, boy," Rigil rasped, "do you *ever* stop eating?"

Mezaedo swiveled. Pointedly indicated the dish. "They put out a *bowl*, Sirrig."

At the door, Mezaedo listened through the keyhole for a moment, then eased the door open to reveal a servant's corridor. "Look at that. Some moldy luck."

Rigil couldn't share the sentiment, not until Land's End was a shrinking speck behind them and his mind felt like his own again.

Especially that.

If only to grab at normalcy, he whisked his own apricot from the bowl as he passed. The sweetness burst like summer on his tongue, grounding him in reality, not boyhood fantasies.

Suddenly, Mezaedo stiffened in the doorway, fingering his ear as if trying to dig something out. "What did you say her name was, Sirrig? Your lockpicking friend from Melas. Sethe?"

The apricot went sour. "Not now, Mezaedo."

He had not spent sixteen years exorcising Sethe from his memory to let a dream cripple him now. A dream like running after a girl from a crate, racing through the streets of Melas until shouts faded behind them. Collapsing in an alley, breathless. Seeing her face for the first time, her scars. Wishing she would look at him so he could fall into that golden iris. *Do you have a name, Mysterious Lady of the Crate?*

Teetering on the edge of the servant's hall, one hand on the jamb and the other on his sword, Rigil found his feet frozen beneath him.

Rigil, you sandwit, listen to me!

Sethe.

Was it possible?

He dropped the shields around his mind.

Rigil, you said once that you would climb Mount Bamah and fetch a snowball from Ice Island if I asked. Well, I don't need that. I need you. I'm here in the castle. Nedir has me locked upstairs. Please, *Rigil.*

Something skittered in the dark. A mouse in the hall, perhaps. Or Rigil's pulse.

Mezaedo was rambling. "I wouldn't bother you with it, Sirrig, but how many Sethes in Er'Rets would know your name and where you're from? 'He's from Zerah Rock,' she says, 'and he owes me an escape, so get on with it. And bring the scuddy keys.'"

Rigil stepped back, snapped the door shut. The bedchamber swirled around him like a blood-colored phantasm.

Oh, Isemios's wit. Isemios's *wit.*

Mezaedo was quick to catch on. "I take it our escape just hit a snag?"

"Not a snag." Rigil spun to face the room, his back to their escape, his spine arrow straight even as the very world tilted around him. If Sethe was alive . . . Lightness. This could change everything. "It's time for your next lesson, Mezaedo. Rescuing a damsel in distress."

CHAPTER SIX
SETHE

HAMONAYAN PICKPOCKETS KNEW HOW to cut through hopes to bare-bone facts. Hopes were for the rich and sandbrained, and Sethe was neither.

Rigil wasn't coming.

Hunched in her cage, Sethe watched through the size-of-a-button skylight as the clouds turned pink outside. Her ear still throbbed where Nedir had ripped her earring out in Melas. The scabs had split open during today's escape attempt, and a new trickle of blood was oozing from the wound.

The aviary, empty now, was a cavity with no heartbeat but the chatter of starving gowzals. That and the occasional wheeze from Lord Coble the Not-Quite-Dead.

Rigil's silence filled the spaces between throbs until Sethe was one enormous pulse of pain. Now that he'd stopped shielding, she could have read his mind, *made* him answer, like Nedir would have done a hundred times in her place. Well, Sethe wasn't Nedir. Bloodvoicing was one thing, but rummaging around in a person's head? Desperate or not, that was a line she didn't care to cross. Never again.

Gowzals screeched around her, pecking each other's flesh behind steel bars. By morning, most of those cages would be lined with corpses for Nedir to discard and replace. The skylight's glow deepened to scarlet, painting a warm patch on Sethe's cheek. Despite herself, she thought of Melas, that city of bulging purses and jingling pockets. Her little shack on the shore, overlooking the Gulf of Mayim. All the time she'd spent learning the best vantage points and targets.

Those first months with Rigil. Learning to survive so far from Hamonah.

Too exhausted to know better, Sethe conjured him in her head and hated how readily he sprang up. Lean and straw-haired, too graceful to be trustworthy, with a hint of a swagger that said he didn't belong in peasant brown, no matter how fine he made it look.

And his questions. She should have known from his first shiny words that a boy so polished was too good to be true. What kind of street boy talked like that? *You are from Hamonah? Is the island as lovely as you are? Do you have a name, Mysterious Lady of the Crate?*

She shouldn't have answered the question. Shouldn't have taken the name he'd given her. Shouldn't have let him convince her that she needed the help of a silver-tongued runaway. At least, that's what he'd claimed to be: a runaway servant fleeing the tyranny of his master, the hardheaded lord of Zerah Rock.

When Sethe blinked the reverie away, every detail still hung there, layered over the aviary. The hum of the crowds. The taste of the dust, the smell of mingled salt and cypress that was Rigil, the boy in the alley. The man in Coble's dungeon.

Rigil, whose palm had pulsed warm against hers as they'd shaken on their deal.

Rigil, who'd been a half-decent survival partner, until he hadn't been.

Rigil, who was *not* coming.

Growling at herself, Sethe summoned a different memory. She and Rigil, making their way across Carm Duchy after months in Melas. Rigil assuring her again and again, *You will be safe at Zerah Rock. Trust Arman. Trust me.*

Sethe, trusting him. Her first mistake. Always the first mistake.

Her ear ached. A quick glance through one of her mice confirmed that Nedir was still in his study, rifling through his papers and waiting for someone to discover Coble's body. According to another mouse, Rheala and the Eben had already escaped through the tunnel, along with the moody one, Erro.

If all goes well, Land's End will be mine before week's end. You would do well to make yourself comfortable here, Sedhani.

Not likely. Rigil or no Rigil, she was getting out of here.

Reaching one bloody hand through the cage, Sethe tested the lock with a few hard yanks. She'd need something impossibly fine to pick it. In the next cage, a gowzal had just finished pecking its brother's bones clean.

Perfect.

Sethe clutched the bars and threw her body back and forth until her cage began to swing, gathering momentum, swooping closer to the gowzal's cage each time. If she stretched, she could almost . . . *one more swing . . .*

With a shriek of chain links, Sethe's cage plummeted. Her head slammed the bars, and she screamed, a furious roar that rattled the aviary and set the gowzals wailing.

All the other cages now hung out of reach. She'd made it worse. Just her scuddy luck, she'd found a way to make it worse.

Bare-bone facts. That was how Sethe had survived this long. By knowing that this rotten world had trapped her the day she was born.

Sethe sank against the back of her cage until only the ceiling and the gowzals hung in view. When she heard the door squeal open, she launched a wad of spit across the cage and through the bars. Let Nedir experiment with *that*.

"Sethe? Se—agh!"

Sethe crushed her face to the bars. The barefooted newcomer wiping spit from his neat red-blond beard had a black knight's sword in his belt and that Jaelportian boy at his back, the one who couldn't block worth salt and apparently had never learned not to stare.

And speaking of staring.

Face pressed to the bars, Sethe fought to tamp down the little thrill coursing through her like lightning through water. *It's about time*, she wanted to say. *Took you long enough. What, did you stop for sightseeing?*

She licked her lips and opened her mouth, but only two words squeezed out. "You're late."

"Hello, Sethe."

There was something feverish in the way Rigil's focus raced over her face, her hands, the bars between them, as if making sure everything was still in place as he remembered it. She saw the exact moment when his gaze crossed her scars, the tiny pucker between his brows as he took in the way they'd healed—in a tangle of pale, bulging threads rather than the angry red gouges they'd been when he'd known her. She'd spent enough time with her reflection to know the difference.

His eyes bore more creases now, but like back then, they didn't linger long on her scars. And like back then, she couldn't help noticing the way he spoke to her good side, his voice oddly tight as he held up the keys. "Not *too* late, I hope?"

He flourished the keys with a smirk. A *smirk*. For a beat, Sethe forgot where she was and all the reasons she hadn't expected him to come.

Then Lord Coble gurgled.

Rigil's hand flew to his sword, but the Jaelportian boy was the one to round the table and see the lord of Land's End, slowly going stiff on the carpet.

"Moldy onions!" The boy crouched and held an ear to Coble's lips. "Dead, Sirrig, but just barely." He sniffed the air like a hound, nose wrinkling. "Smells like duskroot."

"Courtesy of Nedir," Sethe said, hooking her elbows around the cage bars. "I guess he was tired of being someone else's hired brains."

As the boy frowned at the corpse, Rigil glanced up at her. "Are you all right?"

She angled the scarred half of her face to the light, gowzals cawing around her. "Why do you ask?"

The Jaelportian boy sprang back up as Rigil hopped onto the blackwood table in one sleek motion, coming to stand face-to-face with her through the bars of her cage. Behind him, the boy hurried to the aviary door and kicked it shut. Then, taking up a position inside the door, the scrawny *tiko* pulled a handful of apricots from his pocket and started sprinkling them with dust from a pouch around his neck. Snacking? Now?

"It's good to see you, Sethe."

Rigil's voice tugged her attention back to him, the bars between them dividing his face into perfectly symmetrical sections. He shuffled through the keys on his ring, sizing them against the lock. Somewhere in the castle, a door banged.

Sethe's fingers twitched. "Can you hurry that along?"

The first key failed. He set a smaller one to the lock, hair dangling over his forehead. "It's good to see you too, Rigil," he muttered. "Thank you for rescuing me, Rigil. You seem to have aged remarkably well, Rigil. And how *did* you manage to steal a set of keys?" *Click.* The door sprang open, and he stepped back with another flourish. "Just like the jailhouse in Melas."

Sethe jumped down from the cage almost before he finished, forcing him back a startled step.

"Thank the tides this isn't Melas," Sethe said. "I don't have two hours to kill watching you fumble with a jailhouse lock."

She slid down from the table before she could see what the jab did to his face, which had changed far too little in sixteen years. Well, fine. Just because she'd called on him for help didn't mean she'd let that cocked blond eyebrow reduce her to a girl from a crate again. Forget the past. Escaping Land's End was all that mattered. Escape, escape, escape.

When she made for the door, she found the Jaelportian boy propped against it, studying Sethe like a strange herb, his left eye squinting to match hers. "So. You're Missethe?"

Sethe returned his stare. "Who are you?"

"Mezaedo Chevyah," Rigil said, pocketing his stolen keys, "meet Sethe. Sethe, Mezaedo. Excellent, we are all acquainted." He jabbed a thumb at the door. "Time to go."

A flurry of questions rose in her. Why *was* Rigil in Land's End? Why the Jaelportian? What had happened to his boots? Did he really still think about Melas?

Stop thinking. As Sethe shook her head against a flock of equally useless questions, Rigil slid off the table and crossed the room to lay a hand on the doorknob.

"Right." He tossed her a glance. "On my mark."

"Wait. What?" Sethe sprang forward. "Cutting through the castle? *That's* your plan?"

"It's how we found you, isn't it?"

The words were hardly past his lips before alarm bells rang out in the keep. Great. Any moment now, black knights would flood those halls like beetles fleeing a burning log, all of them on the hunt for Nedir's two missing prisoners. And Rigil wanted to go *deeper* into the castle?

Those bells might as well have been ringing in Sethe's skull as Rigil peered into the tower stairwell. "We make for the scullery."

"The scullery?" Something warm was trickling from Sethe's wounded ear, and she clapped a hand over it. "Why there?"

"It's how I got in," Mezaedo said. "Sirrig—Sir Rigil—knows a tunnel under the kitchens that lets out on the mountain. We left our horses there."

"*Sir* Rigil?"

"Kingsguard knight extraordinaire."

Sethe took her hand off her ear, letting her gaze plunge up and down Rigil's body. So, he'd become a knight, had he? "What does the Kingsguard have against boots?"

Instead of taking the bait, Rigil shot her a flat look and threw the door wide, charging out into the narrow stone stairwell that wrapped the tower all the way down.

"Wait! *K'sil!*"

The long-unused Hamonayan word was barely past her lips before she was running after him, slipping through the door ahead of Mezaedo. She was only a step or two behind Rigil when they heard it. Boots on stairs. Shouts of command.

"Check the south tower! Secure Master Nedir's asset!"

"Sirrig!" Hanging back in the aviary doorway, the boy's whisper-yell was leaning heavily on the *yell* side. "Get back!"

Sethe grabbed Rigil's tunic to jerk him back into the room, but he moved faster, scooping a hand around her waist and yanking her up the steps to the door. Mezaedo slammed the door shut, and Sethe and Rigil fell against it. Sethe's pulse sprinted in her wrists. Which obviously had nothing to do with the arm around her waist or the fact that any chance of escaping *alone* had just flown out the window.

"Well." Blinking fast, Rigil pressed his head to the door. "This is beginning to look a great deal like the jailhouse in Melas."

Oh, just scuddy perfect.

CHAPTER SEVEN
RIGIL

SETHE. HERE. ALIVE. *REAL*. OR ELSE THE cruelest nightmare imaginable. The room at the top of the southern tower resembled a menagerie more than a prison, with its gilded mirrors on every wall and gowzal cages swinging from the ceiling by chains of varying lengths. Only a handful contained any gowzals, most of them so emaciated they did little more than croak as the bells in the castle kicked into a new rhythm of urgency.

As soon as the aviary door was locked behind them, Mezaedo and Rigil took to pushing the blackwood table against it. Sethe hung back, her face glazed in an expression Rigil remembered all too well.

"Two on the second floor," she murmured. "One on the servants' stairs. Three, no, four in the kitchens."

Her voice had changed little. Still a raspy alto, but with a darker edge than he remembered. Harder.

The table met the door, and Rigil straightened, breathing hard. As a barricade, it wouldn't hold for long. Not against a swarm of black knights with fireballs at their disposal.

He spun to face Sethe, his messy hair and water-stained tunic reflected back at him six times in the room's mirrored walls. Isemios's wit, all the care he'd taken with his appearance this morning, and he met Sethe after sixteen years looking like something dredged from the Gulf of Mayim?

"Sethe?"

Her gaze refocused, returning from her fragments to the aviary. "Forget the scullery. The kitchens are swarming with guards. Coble already knows about the tunnel. The others escaped that way."

"Others?" Rigil asked.

"The Eben and the bratty tiko and the old bat from Mirrorstone. Coble wanted them out of sight."

Now *that* was a tidbit to interest Prince Oren. Boots pounded below as guards hailed each other across the third-floor gallery. The tower connected all three floors, and they were stopping to search each in turn.

"Fine." Rigil faced the aviary door with a hand on his sword, trying to guess who might come pouring through first: normal guards or illicit black knights? How many of the latter could Coble possibly have? "You have an alternative?"

Sweeping chin-length black hair from her face, Sethe pointed up at an opening in the ceiling that was glowing with the last of the sunset. "From the aviary roof, we can climb down the cliff to the beach. The southern battlements aren't well guarded."

"How do you know all this?" Mezaedo asked.

"Fragments."

"What's a fragment?"

"No." Rigil loosened his sword. "I've seen that cliff, Sethe. It's a sheer drop."

Her gaze blurred. "Ten guards. They've almost finished searching the floor beneath us. Nedir is in his study, but that won't last long. Much as I'd love to see how he explains this corpse to Coble's men, we need to move."

Lightness, that golden eye. Those scars scoring her temples like the claw marks of some rabid beast. That way she had of staring a storm in the eye without flinching, as if it were always simply a matter of adjusting the sails.

Rigil snapped his half-sheathed sword back into place, resolving to ask what *she* was doing at Land's End as soon as they survived this disaster. "Fine. You first, Sethe."

Every line of her body stiffened, but they were not picking pockets in Melas. This was an escape, a *rescue*, even. Sir Rigil Barak, Kingsguard knight and Mârad spy, had no time for negotiations. After a beat, Sethe hopped onto the table and pulled herself on top of the closest cage. Then she wrapped her legs around the chain and began to climb toward the skylight, hand over hand. Her progress was slow, likely the result of malnourishment and confinement as Nedir's captive. She seemed to take every reminder of her own weakness as an insult, hissing curses under her breath whenever her grip slipped and sent her skidding down a few links. Still, she climbed, as under their feet, thumps and thuds abounded. Guards flipping furniture, slamming doors on lower levels.

"Now you, Mezaedo." Rigil turned to offer the boy a boost, but Mezaedo had already caught a low-hanging cage and was shimmying up the chain.

Rigil climbed onto the table, pulled a cage down, and jammed his foot between the bars. Sure enough, the whole thing, gowzals and all, came crashing down when he put his full weight on it, leaving Rigil dangling from the chain. He began climbing anyway, feathers floating in the air like black snow, gowzals shrieking at the upheaval.

Well. If the guards *hadn't* known they were here . . .

Mezaedo and Rigil reached the ceiling nearly at the same time, but Rigil's chain hung closer to the skylight. With Sethe's help, Rigil caught the lip of the window and pulled himself onto the rain-damp tower roof. Gowzals screamed, but Rigil was more concerned about the footsteps thundering outside the aviary door. That, and his squire still dangling below.

"Mezaedo!" He stretched out a hand.

Down in the room, the knob rattled. Someone barked an order to break down the door.

Mezaedo, hanging from a chain within arm's reach, froze as the door shook. Rigil recognized the look on his face a moment too late, the same look Bran Rennan had worn in the Battle of Armonguard after the tanniyn had broken through the tower, separating him from Rigil for the last time. He'd darted off to die a hero on that blighted rooftop, never to be knighted.

Bang! A guard threw his weight against the barricaded door. The frame rattled.

Mezaedo gazed up at Rigil, pulled the pouch from his pocket to dump some spice into his mouth, and spoke through orange teeth. "Meet you at the cove, Sirrig. Stray's honor."

The boy let go, hit the tabletop as the door splintered, then dove between the surprised guards like a curly-headed Jaelportian wind. The guards spun. Several peeled off to chase the squire down the stairs, their curses not quite drowning out Mezaedo's full-throated "For Arman!"

No.

Sethe yanked Rigil back from the skylight. "You heard him. He'll meet you. I'll keep watch."

Her sandy voice, the darkening sky, the crashing of waves somewhere below may as well have been someone else's sensations for all the attention Rigil gave them. He pressed his hands against the gritty roof slates.

"I'm going to kill him."

Dusk reduced Sethe to a hint of loose trousers and frizz perched on the roof's edge, where the tower and the cliff formed one sheer drop into darkness. This woman with blood-matted hair, tilted into the wind like a bird taking flight—this woman who had barely looked at him except to remark on his bare feet—was Sethe. Sethe from Melas. The Sethe he thought he'd lost.

Why Nedir wanted her, he didn't know. But if Arman had re-entwined their fates in some miraculous second chance, he wasn't about to let her make this escape alone.

If this was a test, he would not fail it. Not again.

The alarm bells in the keep sounded distant, almost unreal. Down below, rolling whitecaps slashed the dark as Sethe swung her legs over the roof's edge.

For a moment, perched on the tiles, he caught himself counting the cost. Not only of trusting Mezaedo to handle himself but of following this woman into flight, stepping into the same undertow that had drawn him to her in Melas and left him wrecked with regret.

When Rigil followed her over the edge, Sethe said nothing to acknowledge his choice. Like him, she kept her head down, immersed in each handhold, each chink in the stone. Keeping her distance as if she, too, sensed the threat of history repeating itself and what it might cost them if they let it.

On a map, Dove's Cove sat one apple seed from Land's End. Or half a blacknut, depending on what Mezaedo had been chewing when they'd gone over the plan. *This is where we meet should anything go wrong, Mezaedo. Dove's Cove. Remember it. Memorize it.*

The first principle of being Mârad: know the worst outcome and prepare for every contingency. Perhaps Rigil's mistake was expecting Mezaedo to understand that, treating him like the spy Bran had been instead of the novice Mez was.

The climb down from Land's End went more swiftly than expected. Sethe, as usual, set a breathless pace that left Rigil with bloody feet, shredded fingertips, and the distinct impression that she was trying see him plummet to his death. The tide was high when they reached the beach, leaving a narrow band of sand between the cliff and the waterline. Though Rigil was higher on the wall, he jumped down first, landing on the wet sand with burning arms and blistered fingers.

Not to be bested, Sethe jumped down the rest of the way, managing to land hard on his foot. Or as hard as Sethe landed anywhere. Lightness, she still moved like a bird.

Was that the only thing that hadn't changed? Nodding for her to lead the way south along the shoreline, Rigil tried and failed to study her face, filthy as it was. She still wore her hair short, messily cropped at her chin, but the frizzy black nest he remembered had softened into something closer to choppy waves that almost hid the scars sealing her left eye shut.

And those scars. They were dawn pale and spindly now, almost delicate compared to the angry red scabs that had marred her face back then. Wounds she'd never explained, not unlike Mezaedo's speckled knuckles.

Mezaedo. Rigil kicked up sand as he trudged over the shore, praying that Mezaedo had somehow escaped to reach Dove's Cove ahead of them.

The moon rose. Clouds rolled in. The cliff retreated, replaced by cypress trees that dangled over the water and marred the way with forbidding arms.

"He'll be fine." Splashing along in the shallows, Sethe held a strip of cloth to her ear and used her free arm to push away the fronds hanging over the water. "I'd be more worried he won't be able to find this place. Speaking of which, can you?"

Rigil let the land answer for him. A few steps ahead, the beach swerved sharply to the left. He stopped there, leaning around her to pull back a dead branch, revealing a crescent moon of dark sand, crisscrossed with piper tracks. A tiny inlet, sheltered by cypresses.

The air was so thick with the scent of them, he could have bottled it and called it home.

As Sethe brushed past him into the cove, a waft of sweat and gowzal trailed the motion, the moon emerging from behind the clouds to light her from behind.

She was dressed like a sailor, he realized. Filthy lace-up shirt tucked into billowing brown trousers, a loose canvas vest missing all its buttons and hanging open and lopsided from bony shoulders. If it weren't for the rainbow of color splashing the beaded belt around her waist, she might have passed for something other than a Hamonayan. She could not, however, have passed for anything other than a peasant. Especially not in Zerah Rock.

Which, of course, was *not* a concern right now.

"No Mezaedo." Rigil paced the full sandy crescent, as if the squire could be hiding somewhere in this tiny stretch of beach.

"He'll be here." Sethe plopped, cross-legged, onto the shore, still favoring her ear. "You've got a brave squire, *Sir* Rigil. I'll give you that."

Leave it to Sethe to turn an honorific into a barb. Rigil let it graze without piercing. Inhaling as much sea air as his lungs would take, he pivoted. "Show me your ear."

As expected, her hand tightened on the cloth. "Tell me the way to Meneton."

"So you can be recaptured?"

"I'm not staying here. If I know Nedir, he'll have all of Coble's men loyal to him by now."

"When Mezaedo arrives," Rigil said, "we'll follow the coast southeast. From there, I know a way, but you will never leave Land's End if you drop dead of infection first."

When he knelt and reached for the cloth, she recoiled as if slapped.

"Honestly, Sethe, has time made you *more* stubborn?"

"Don't call me Sethe." A weeping bird cried out in the trees, almost a wail. "If I'm still Sedhani to Nedir, I might as well be Sedhani to you too."

"Sedhani?" Rigil tested the strange word softly. "Is that your real name?"

"It's a name you didn't give me. Right now, that's good enough."

She couldn't know how hard that blow landed. Like a gauntleted fist to his gut.

Moving slowly, as if she might fly away, Rigil eased the cloth from her ear. She hissed. Or perhaps he did. "The lobe is gone. Why would he do this, Se—Sedhani?"

He refused to let his tongue trip over the name she'd kept from him in all their time together. He was Rigil of House Barak now, polished to a shine.

Speaking of which, he should probably tell her about that little aspect of his identity.

"Miss Sedhani, you clearly do not trust me, and I deserve that." Rigil tossed the blood-soaked cloth aside and dug through the lining of his tunic for the handkerchief sewn into it. It was expensive, a fact she was not likely to appreciate. "But while we are discussing *trust*, you might explain why you never told me your real name."

"What good would that have done?"

"What good?" He pressed the handkerchief to her ear—harder than necessary, judging by her grimace.

Sethe burrowed her pickpocket's fingers into the sand. "I told you I left that name in Hamonah, and I wouldn't have kept it from you if I'd thought it would make a difference. Besides, you knew everything else. Nedir was after me—"

"Wait. Back then, your old master was *Raith Nedir*?"

She shot him a slitted glare, visibly reevaluating his intelligence. Well, it did make sense. Nedir's interest in bloodvoicing, the strange emphasis on Hamonah in his study. All of it aligned with what little Rigil had known of Sethe's old captor.

He exhaled. "Of course."

"Who he is doesn't matter. It didn't back then. All that mattered was that Melas wasn't safe for me anymore. And if you recall, *Sir Rigil*, I never asked to go to Zerah Rock. You said it would be safe."

"And it would have been."

"Please." With an acid snort, Sethe shoved to her bare feet. She hadn't lost her restless grace, still moved on her toes. "Not another speech about how *protected* I'd be in Zerah Rock when we both know I was never going to get there. Nedir's men trailed us all the way from Melas, and if you'd believed me sooner when I said I was being followed—" She cut herself off with a sparrowlike jerk of her head. "Tell me this. When Nedir's men attacked that night, when you ran . . ."

"Sethe."

"Was that your plan all along? To hand me over? Tides, was everything in Melas your way of luring me in for Nedir?"

The handkerchief slipped from Rigil's fingers, fluttered to the sand like a boneless dove. "Are you serious?"

"I'm always serious."

"Sethe, you can't possibly—Lightness, I thought you were *with* me. We took off running together!" Rigil sounded about as calm as he felt, calm as a hurricane at high tide. "I went back the moment I realized you weren't there, but there was nothing left but signs of a struggle. I thought you had been—I thought—"

Calm yourself, man. She cannot make you relive it.

Too late.

"Let's say I believe you." Just like that, Sethe's golden eye found him. Unblinking and unwavering, the one part of her that all these years truly had not touched, still slashing through him like steel through cloth. "Let's say you meant everything you said about protecting me. It still left me exactly where I started: alone, surrounded, and the only one in Er'Rets who could do anything about it."

Rigil took a step toward her but stopped when the bloody handkerchief squished under his foot. "All this time, have you been Nedir's prisoner?"

She exhaled slowly, digging a knuckle into her forehead. "No. He only caught me in Melas a few weeks ago."

"So you did escape that night, when we were separated? How?"

"*You*"—she spat it like a curse—"don't get to ask me that."

"Sethe, please believe me. I combed that forest for you. For days. Prince Oren of Armonguard found me wandering the roads, half starved and fevered out of my wits. He wanted to take me back to Zerah Rock; I convinced him to help me search for you. And I did, Sethe. For a *year*. I searched all of Carm, *begged* the prince to take me to Melas, and I would have searched for years more. I would have combed all Er'Rets if Prince Oren hadn't told me to find a new purpose. He gave me a new beginning and I took it. Is that so wrong?"

Sethe's scoff was all thorns. "You think this is about the Kingsguard?"

"I think I was a young man. We were both young, and it was a long time ago."

Her jaw fell open. "Is that your *apology?*"

Lightness, no. Not any apology he was proud of. But he met Sethe's glare and channeled the Rigil of ballrooms and banquet halls. "What would you like me to say?"

Sethe opened her mouth, scars taut over her cheekbone. Then, as if a predator's shadow had just crossed the sun, she stiffened, her one good eye filming over.

"Oh, tides."

He knew that tone, the burred edge of it. It was the same tone she'd used on the rare times she'd found a lock she couldn't pick.

"Nedir has your squire."

CHAPTER EIGHT
SETHE

SETHE WOULD GIVE MEZAEDO CHEVYAH this: He had the eyes of a doe but the grit of a sandstorm. Watching through a firefly in the castle—Coble's rat catchers had taken care of her more useful fragments there—she saw exactly when the olive-skinned Jaelportian ducked into Nedir's study to hide from the guards and ran straight into the man himself.

"Master Chevyah." Nedir set down a stack of papers, glancing up without a bit of surprise. He had tucked his moon-colored robes into his belt, freeing his arms for whatever mad botanists did in their time alone. *"Auspicious timing."*

When Nedir gestured toward the closed door behind Mezaedo, the tiko's hand sprang up to open it as if on a trigger. His face had gone completely slack. *Never* a good sign.

"Come along, if you please," Nedir said, breezing into the hall.

"What's happening?" Rigil's voice tugged Sethe back to the moonlit beach, the sound of swells gossiping against the pebbled sand.

"Nedir is using him as a porter. Influencing him. They're heading for the aviary, which means Nedir is about to find me gone."

She touched her crusted ear. "Two escapes at once. It won't take him long to put them together."

When Rigil started marching for the trees, heading back *toward* Land's End, Sethe stared after him. "What are you doing?"

"Meneton is a four-day ride southeast. Follow the coast and you can't miss it."

She beat him to the tree line, but barely. His bare feet were bleeding a little from the cliff and nearly stained black around the toes. "Don't be a sandwit."

"I can't leave him."

"And I can?" The urge to jab his chest with a finger was a fleeting thing, quick to blow away. "If you think I'd abandon a child to Raith Nedir, K'sil, then you never knew me."

The moon hung behind him, a blinding halo. "I know how you like your escapes, Sethe."

He had grown since they'd last argued. Unfair, since Sethe hadn't. Refusing to crane her neck, she addressed the little divot at the base of his throat. "I can help. Just . . . let me focus."

She didn't wait for an answer before slipping back into her firefly.

Buzzing along behind Nedir, she couldn't read his face when he and the squire summited the stairs to find the aviary door open. She could have slipped into Nedir's head to taste his fury when he saw her cage empty, but no. Too risky. Not on the off chance that he might sense her.

Instead, she urged her firefly into the room and settled it on the doorframe to watch.

From here, Coble's body was almost entirely hidden by the table. Good news for Nedir: Coble hadn't been found yet.

"Into the cage," the old man said. A waste of breath when blood-voicing would work just as well, but then, Nedir had never been much of a bloodvoicer unless playing with his powders. Mezaedo

climbed into Sethe's cage and closed it on himself, face still bottomlessly blank.

After a beat, though, he blinked.

"Moldy onions," he said, knocking his head with a fist. *"Again?"*

Nedir shut the door to the room, and maybe it was the firefly's blurry vision, but was that a sheen of sweat on his face?

"He's tired," Sethe said to Rigil. "Influencing drains him. He's released your squire's mind."

Mezaedo pulled a few blacknuts out of his pocket as Nedir rounded the table toward him. *"You don't seem all that shaken,"* the squire said, *"about your dead master getting spittle all over the carpet, I mean."*

"On the contrary." Nedir prodded Coble with a foot. *"I am distraught. Tell me, how did you kill him? And was that your mission all along?"*

Mezaedo's dark brows rammed together, but then his face went slack again. *"I poisoned him,"* he murmured, *"by order of Prince Oren."*

"Good boy. That will do nicely."

Opening her eye, Sethe found Rigil pacing like a chained bear. "Nedir wants to frame your squire for Coble's murder. He's going to use him as a scapegoat."

"Isemios's wit. Tell me you have a plan."

Shifting back to Land's End, Sethe scoured her mind for something larger than a firefly, something Coble's rat catchers and fly-traps may have missed.

There. A seagull nesting in the gable of Coble's barn a half fathom off. With barely a thought, Sethe sent the bird launching into the air, watching through its vision as the skylight in the south tower grew closer, closer.

Already fantasizing about the bird's dismembering capabilities, Sethe forgot to aim. The seagull clipped the windowsill, squawked as it plummeted, caught itself, dove for Nedir. But too late. He saw it coming, had Coble's knife in one hand and a pen in the other.

With one swat, Nedir made quick work of the gull, forcing Sethe to shift back into her firefly. His voice was all composure as he stomped the dead bird into the carpet and glanced at Mezaedo. *"Friends with the local fowl, I see."*

Mezaedo cracked a nutshell between his teeth, pausing to dump something on them from that pouch around his neck. *"What can I say? Birds love me."*

Sethe scoured the castle for another host. Something deadlier, preferably diseased. A rat?

Two steps, three, and Nedir was at the cage. *"You know where she is. She, apparently, is invested in your welfare. You do realize that I could reach into your mind and take what I seek?"*

A bluff. Bloodvoicing didn't work that way, and anyway, if he could, he already would have. Tides, done in by a bit of influencing? For someone so smug, Nedir had no stamina whatsoever. That, or the boy was better at hiding his thoughts than Sethe would have guessed.

Slurp. Crunch. Swallow. Mezaedo took to licking the orange dust off his fingers, one by one. *"You can try,"* he said, *"but I'll warn you."* He flicked the side of his head. *"It's a right mess in here."*

Was the boy *trying* to get himself killed? *Use your head, tiko,* she bloodvoiced. *He's insane.* Watching through the firefly, Sethe caught only the barest tightening of Mezaedo Chevyah's lips as proof that he had heard.

Silver flashed as Nedir brandished the pen. *"Tell me where the Hamonayan is."*

Mezaedo's answer: firing a sunset-colored glob of spit through the bars to land on Nedir's cheek.

Nedir wiped his face with the pad of his finger, then raised it to his nose to sniff. Cross-legged in his cage, the boy looked downright serene, at least until Nedir reached through the bars for the pouch around his neck. Mezaedo stiffened, probably seeing that expression on Nedir's face, that distracted gleam, like he'd just thought of some new way to make the world a scuddier place . . .

Sethe sent her firefly closer as Nedir jutted his chin at Mezaedo's hands. *"Burns?"*

The boy didn't miss a beat. *"Fairy kisses."*

Nedir's smile was paper-thin. "I take it fairies are responsible for this as well." He dropped Mezaedo's pouch, letting it thud against the boy's chest. "I have never seen this particular concoction outside of Jaelport. Such a pity you are so fond of it. I'm told it is horrid for the teeth."

There had to be another bird around. Sethe felt the ghost of fingernails clawing down her temples, gouging across her cheek. Where were Coble's dogs when she needed them?

"Sethe." Rigil's voice. "I can't just stand here. I'm going after him."

"Wait." Torn between the castle and the beach, Sethe struggled to hold on to her firefly, struggled to keep eyes on the aviary. "I can do this."

Nedir was saying something. Something she'd missed, thanks to the firefly's distorted hearing. He had both pens out now and was carefully unwaxing the nibs, laying them out on the table with his orange-stained finger. Just then, Sethe sensed a pigeon in the rafters of the northern tower. Severing off a fragment, she sent it whirring into the Veil and felt the exact moment when the bird's mind became hers.

She sent the pigeon fluttering toward the aviary as fast as its wings could beat. Then faster. Nedir's pens gleamed on the table, poison welling on the nibs. *Come on, come on.*

So focused on the bird, on the window, on which part of Nedir's body she'd sink its beak into first, Sethe didn't notice the vial in Nedir's hand, on his lips, until she heard the sound.

Sedhani . . .

Sethe stiffened. That voice, *his* bloodvoice, so different from his normal reedy tenor. It was like a feather dragged across the back of her mind, leaving no trace but a vague feeling of invasion. And no one could invade her defenses, *no one*.

Not without a secret weapon.

Through her firefly, she found it in his hand. A vial of silver dust, the same dust now staining Nedir's lips. He was gazing at the ceiling, but his bloodvoice drove straight into her. Sharper this time. Not a feather. A knife.

Sedhani.

A spasm rattled Sethe's body. She lost hold of the pigeon, felt herself falling. Something caught her, and she found Rigil's face hovering over her.

And then there was pain.

Ripping, squeezing, crushing her brain, it was a pain she'd known only once before, lying on a castle floor in Hamonah while Nedir broke her mind into a thousand pieces. That had been the agony of resisting an unstoppable force, like a wall trying to stop a catapulted rock. She had sworn never to feel that pain again, never to let Nedir close enough. If she hadn't gone back to Melas weeks ago, hadn't let her guard down after all these years, she would still be sailing free instead of right back where she'd started.

Sixteen years avoiding him, and it ended here, with Rigil's arms around her and the taste of Land's End in the back of her throat.

Sethe thrashed against Rigil's arms, dimly aware of sand beneath her and water lapping nearby. She screamed against the pain threatening to split her skull along the fault lines of her scars. She bellowed against Nedir's bloodvoice driving through her. No! She was out of his cage, out of Land's End. She was *out*.

Oh, Sedhani. When will you accept that you have never left my cage? You belong to me. Return and the pain will end.

She could feel the strength in his bloodvoice, in the overpowering resonance of it. *Get out!* she screamed, aloud or by bloodvoice, she didn't know. *GET OUT!*

Blocking was a battle of wills. Hers had to be stronger. Otherwise, if she let him drive her out of her own body . . .

Come now, Nedir crooned, his hands woven before him as he gazed up at the aviary ceiling, *this is only painful because you resist. I have no intention of driving you out of your body. Your fragments make it nearly impossible to storm every last trace of you.*

Tides, the *pain.* Mezaedo was trying to bloodvoice her, an unintelligible jumble of words that couldn't cut through the chaos in her head. The pigeon was long gone, and even the firefly was barely a flicker in her mind. She couldn't focus on anything, couldn't keep hold of her eyes in the aviary or her body on the beach.

"Sethe!" Rigil was shouting now. "What is it? What's wrong?"

Words refused to connect. "N-Nedir. In . . . my head . . . the p-powder . . ."

Do you recall the last time you put up such a fight, Sedhani? All those splinters of your consciousness flying about the room? You screamed for days before you ran off and made me wait so many years to find you again. Please, do not make me break you.

You can't. Sethe fought to ground herself in the distant awareness of arms around her, sand under her, Rigil's face staring down. Faraway sensations, but there. *You broke my mind once. You can't do it again.*

She'd been a girl last time, and she'd underestimated him, but Sethe was nothing if not adaptable. If Nedir still wanted her mind, he would find it well guarded by a thousand fragments with more than a decade of practice at hating him more than anything.

Nedir laughed and the agony redoubled. Sethe felt her spine arch. Rigil's mouth was moving, saying . . . what? Her name? Did he call her Sethe or Sedhani? Did it matter? Oh, this was death. Death had found her.

Arman. Wherever the name came from, Sethe cradled it like a bird. Maybe she'd seen it on Rigil's lips. Maybe he was praying for her like he'd always said he did. *Arman, help me. Help.*

Still appealing to the Father God, Nedir bloodvoiced. *I truly am curious about that new development.*

Sethe's firefly buzzed and twitched on the doorframe, reverberating with her pain.

Arman is the Father God. She hummed the words to herself like an incantation. *Arman, father of Câan, freer of captives.* How could she still see Rigil's face as he'd taught her those words, his skin painted red by their cookfire in Melas?

Reflected six times in the aviary walls, Nedir rubbed a thumb around the mouth of his vial. *That is the trouble with gods: One day they offer shelter, the next, a cage. There is no escaping a god's whims once you have handed him your trust. Not even Arman's own son could escape His fickle will when it came to it. He died alone, tortured and killed by the very Kinsmen He had come to liberate.*

Her firefly settled on one of the walls and began to crawl toward Nedir, silent.

Get out of my head, Sethe bloodvoiced. As distractions went, it was the best she could do. *I'm still stronger. You know I am. You'll need more than one vial to break me again.*

In his sanctuary, bathed in light, Nedir closed his eyes.

Sethe launched the firefly off the wall in a whir of wings and fury, a tiny projectile soaring for Nedir's slightly parted lips. She'd send it down his windpipe, puncture his lungs, kill him from the inside. She had the firefly in her grip, a piece of her, plunging toward him.

And then she didn't.

The insect stopped in midair. She could still sense it, could still feel its life and energy, but when she asked it to move forward, it didn't respond.

Through the firefly's messy vision, she was *sure* she saw Raith Nedir smile.

You are not listening, Sedhani. The firefly veered off, flew a slow, playful circle around Nedir's head. *Don't you realize what a man could do with your fragments under his control? What that would make him?*

"Fight, Sethe." Rigil's voice came from another world. "Fight it!"

The firefly flew in a lazy loop, then landed on Nedir's palm. Suddenly, the pain meant nothing. The splitting agony in her skull, nothing.

All that mattered was this bug in Nedir's hand. Reclaiming that one piece of her.

Nails dug into Sethe's scalp. Her own. Every muscle strained against Nedir's grip on the fragment, trying to wrestle control back. The firefly went still as their wills collided, and for half an instant, Sethe felt Nedir slipping. He had the powder, but Sethe had connection. It was her fragment, *her* mind. He would not break her in pieces and then claim her bit by bit. He would *not*.

So close. She was so close. The firefly spasmed with indecision.

I have a theory, Nedir bloodvoiced, *that some people are born to be caged. Others are born to hold the keys. Shall we see which one you are?*

The firefly settled on Nedir's shoulder. She barely saw Nedir's hand come flying down toward it before her view of the aviary winked out.

That defeat, the death of a firefly, brought a wash of the worst pain yet, and Sethe screamed in her mind, in the physical world, fighting him with everything she had. Knowing it was only a matter of time before he claimed her exhausted mind and, with it, any hope of living free ever again.

Mental pain and physical sensation blurred in her like mud. Even Nedir stopped taunting, devoting all his energy to breaking through her shields. The part of Sethe that was still on the beach in Dove's Cove was aware only dimly of hours slipping by, Rigil's arms around her, his shouts growing hoarser and more desperate.

"What can I do, Sethe? Tell me what to do!"

So focused on maintaining her shields, Sethe couldn't form words. She barely saw him on the beach, barely felt time passing until, far away in the cove, Rigil's voice finally became two.

"Mezaedo! Lightness, it's been hours! How did you escape?"

"What's wrong with her, Sirrig? I can hear her screaming in the Veil."

Sethe's open eye registered little. A vague impression of Mezaedo Chevyah, dark curls matted to his head, one nostril leaking dried blood. Rigil was holding her tight to his chest, a faraway sensation that should have repelled her, but she couldn't remember why.

Pain. Nothing but pain. Nedir's silence was worse than his goading, his mind digging brutally into her shields.

"Maybe with more distance from Nedir?"

"She needs a bloodvoicer."

"I'm sorry, Sirrig. You know I can barely . . ."

"The nearest Kingsguard post is in Meneton. If we ride hard enough, and if the knight there can bloodvoice . . ."

She lost it then. The thread of the conversation, the part of her still linked to her body. Rigil's voice was the last thing she heard before agony consumed her.

CHAPTER NINE
RIGIL

IT WAS FOUR DAYS TO MENETON, THE nearest Kingsguard post, by any map in Er'Rets. Four. No more, no less.

Rigil would do it in two.

They rode through the day and night under boiling clouds, Sethe draped over Rigil's saddle astride his roan mare, Timra, Mezaedo bumping along with their provisions on the chestnut packhorse he called Wafer. When they stopped to rest the horses at twilight on the second day, the boiling clouds still hadn't broken, the sky itself hesitating to weep too soon.

They made camp that night under some twisted trees a little way from the road. Crouched beside Sethe, tightening the handkerchief restraints that kept her from gouging at her face, Rigil glanced up to see Mezaedo return from scouting. Wafer glanced up from nosing in the dirt to nicker at the boy, hoping for handouts. Timra, dozing on her picket line, only flicked her ears.

"No sign of Coble's men on the road." Dusty and sluggish with fatigue, Mezaedo had mostly stopped flinching at Sethe's screams in his head. He plopped beside their fire, the trees looming behind him like bony priests genuflecting before some uncaring god. "How is she?"

"The same." After two long days, Sethe had finally screamed herself hoarse, but watching her lips move in silent pleas with her eye open and bulging was almost worse. "She can't go on this way."

"Neither can you, Sirrig."

The sky cracked, a flash of rusty light turning the trees to silhouettes. Then gloom again. Gloom and a shiny apple bumping Rigil's foot.

"I saved it for you." Mezaedo nodded at the apple as lightning caught on the dimpled skin. "You know what they say. Last one, lucky one."

Rigil assessed it halfheartedly. "What, no spice?"

The boy's smile was just as flimsy. "Please. I know you lot like your food bland as sand."

Sethe moaned, cutting the moment short. Rigil reached for her hand, then thought better of it. Another prayer rose to his lips, fell away in ashes. Oh, Lightness. A second chance after all this time, and he was about to fail her again. "Come on, Sethe. Fight him. Fight this." *Please, Arman, let the knight in Meneton be a bloodvoicer who can help her.*

He needed her to look at him, truly look at him, the way she had the first time all those years ago. He needed that eye to rove him up and down as if measuring him for a coffin, deciding how much trusting him was worth.

He summoned her in his memory, the girl from the crate. Billowing Hamonayan trousers cuffed at her ankles. Frizzy hair strung with a few feathered braids. Her mangled face, rock hard when he asked her name. *I left my name in Hamonah. Call me whatever you want.*

He'd seen her and known. *Sethe.* After the Hamonayan owl, cunning and rarely seen.

Mezaedo's liquid eyes gleamed onyx in the firelight, no doubt seeing more than Rigil credited them for, another reason Rigil should never have taken another squire. At least Bran would have kept his questions to himself instead of thinking them so *loudly*.

"Did you know her well, Sirrig?" the squire asked.

The question pushed Rigil off-balance. He glanced at the boy, at that mop of curls, the Jaelportian fingers ripping moss from the ground and twisting it into ropes. In the firelight, the tiny scars on his arms and knuckles nearly vanished against his olive skin.

Standing stiffly, Rigil whistled Timra awake. The dappled grey snorted and swished her tail as he started toward her. "It was a long time ago and a short time together. I'm surprised she remembers it so well."

Lie.

Another tuft of moss. "Don't know if you easterners know this, Sirrig, but Hamonayans don't really go about with knights. Moldy onions, they're pirates."

"And Jaelportians, by that logic, are all traitors." Rigil grabbed his saddle from the dirt, the leather creaking in his grip as he hefted it. "Prejudice is a two-edged sword, Mezaedo."

"That's not it at all. I'm just wondering how the two of you met. You being a noble from the other side of the world."

"She never knew I was a noble."

Wait for it. "So you lied?"

"I didn't see it that way then." As Rigil approached Timra with the saddle, she shied and backed away, lamenting the too-short rest. "When I told Sethe I was from Zerah Rock, she made her own assumptions. To her, I had to be a runaway servant or stray, albeit one with a nobleman's tongue and a taste for fine wine. I thought of correcting her countless times, but the way she spoke about nobles, the way she *resented* them, it seemed simpler to let her believe what she liked." Simpler, aye, for both of them. Especially when he'd started constructing daydreams that left no room for the chasm between street urchin and heir.

Timra whistled when Rigil swung the saddle over her back, betrayal steaming from her nostrils in a huff of white vapor. He caught her bridle, ran a hand down her nose. "I promise, I will make it up to you."

As Rigil bent to tighten the girth strap, a warm wind set the trees whistling, carrying a faint scent of dust and fish and laughs stolen in alleyways. "As for *how* we met," Rigil went on, "I told you. It happened in Melas."

Melas. The place of new beginnings, where runaway heirs could disappear, where there was no one to disappoint and no tests to fail. In theory. Melas, where eight months could feel like a whole life lived in another world, until he'd brought it all crashing down.

You'll be safe in Zerah Rock, Sethe. I'll make sure of it. I'll protect you.

Zerah Rock had waited sixteen years for Rigil to keep that promise. Could it be that simple? Earn her forgiveness, pick up where they had left off, make her remember the future that had seemed so possible back then?

"You said she was like me." As usual, Mezaedo could never let Rigil stay in a reverie long. "A stray, then?"

"Something like that." Rigil paused in tightening the girth strap to stroke Timra's dappled back. "I believe she spent much of her childhood as a captive of Nedir. She spoke seldom about her past, but I always had the impression that he'd done something especially brutal right before she'd escaped him. I think her fragments may have been the result. She was learning to use them when we met."

A few feet away, Sethe gasped in the dust, a tear of strain leaking from her open eye, cutting a grime-trail down her temple.

Watching her, Rigil couldn't keep his fists from curling. "She had smuggled herself to Melas in a crate of Jaelportian sunspice. I was there . . . for reasons of my own." Aye, an adolescent tantrum that had driven Rigil halfway across the world to avoid his father. Hardly fodder for a *teaching moment*.

Timra nuzzled Rigil's tunic, sniffing at the blotchy traces of Land's End baked into the cloth. He scratched between her ears, surprised to hear himself chuckling.

"My first day in Melas, I was robbed by a cutpurse. Like a fool, I tried to confront him and nearly got my head bashed in. I was hiding from him, and Sethe was hiding from the merchants, when our paths crossed for the first time."

Mezaedo leaned back on his hands. "Sounds like fate."

"More like mutual necessity. She had experience surviving on the streets of Hamonah, but she was fleeing her old master and needed someone to watch her back. An alliance seemed pragmatic."

Pragmatic. Was that all it had been at the beginning? Rigil pushed Timra's head away.

Perhaps for Sethe.

Mezaedo closed his left eye, swirled a finger at that side of his face. "What about . . . ?"

"She never told me where they came from," Rigil answered. "The one time I asked, she nearly strangled me. But they were fresh wounds when we met. I'd wager those scars are Nedir's handiwork as well."

Of course, it was with purely clinical intentions that Rigil returned to Sethe's side to find her mouth moving in a plea so hoarse, he could only read one word on her lips.

Arman.

He pulled back, pressing her shudders into the ground with a hand on her shoulder. Had he imagined it? Willed himself to see it?

"Time to go." If Rigil's order hadn't been enough, the sawed-off bite in his voice got Mezaedo moving. Tossing his moss on the fire, the boy sprang up to help with the horses. The sky's flashings had redoubled, the air under the trees sizzling against Rigil's skin. Surely, the clouds would break tonight. No storm could simmer this long without doing *something*.

He was bending to collect Sethe, Timra's reins looped around one arm, when he heard it.

Hooves.

Leaving Sethe on the ground, Rigil threw the reins at Mezaedo and put a finger to his lips. The boy nodded, then tapped the sword at his waist. He'd stay behind to guard Sethe and the horses.

Sliding his hood over his blond hair, Rigil left the clearing on still-bare feet, testing each step for dry twigs or loose rocks. The hooves had stopped, but he could see the shape of a mounted man through the trees, hesitating on the road. Hesitating, or listening.

Rigil stilled. The cloaked figure dismounted, flowing like liquid through the motion. A flash of lightning painted horse and rider white-blue.

By the next flash, the horse stood alone.

Rigil's sword was already eased in its sheath, and when a twig snapped to his right, he whipped the blade out faster than the sky could spout lightning. "Stay where you are, stranger."

The man who stepped forward held no sword, but everything from his posture to the lazy confidence in his movements said he knew how to use one. Which Rigil could confirm.

The sword sagged in his hand. "*Eagan?*"

What was he doing here? How could he possibly have known Rigil was in need, let alone where to find him on the road? And perhaps the most important question: Of all the knights in *Er'Rets* who could be posted in Meneton, why did it have to be *this one*?

"Hello, Rigil," Sir Eagan Elk said, striding forward like a soldier into battle. "Where is the woman?"

For having spent thirteen years imprisoned on Ice Island, Rigil's older brother wore the years well, even coated in dust, wrapped in a coarse brown cloak, and stretched out on the ground beside Sethe. His mind untethered from his body, he could have been asleep as he searched for Nedir in the bloodvoicing realm, also known as the Veil.

"So this is our help in Meneton?" Mezaedo held his sword like a cane, tip down. "Sir Eagan Elk, the moldy *legend?*"

Rigil lacked the energy to chide him for his poor swordsmanship. "I knew King Gidon had a knight in Meneton. As to who it was, I am as surprised as you are. And I haven't the faintest idea how he knew to find us here." Leave it to Eagan to materialize like an angel from Shamayim's gates.

Mezaedo squinted down at the *moldy legend* stretched out on the ground beside Sethe, eyes closed. "What's he doing?"

"Bloodvoicers can't function in the Veil and physical world at once, so they have someone guard their bodies. Did no one teach you this in bloodvoicing training?"

Mezaedo scuffed his hair, spiking his curls on one side. "Sure, but Missethe can do both at once. All this time fighting Nedir and she's still awake. Not exactly *here*, but awake. And she knew where all the guards were in the castle, never had to lie down."

Rigil blinked and scratched the blurring line where his close beard met his bare cheek. Sethe's ability was unique. He'd always known that, but just *how* unique had never seemed important. Not as important as using it to pilfer coins from Melas authorities. Occasionally. In dire circumstances. And only the corrupt ones.

"I hadn't thought of it," Rigil said. "Well spotted."

Before Mezaedo could start glowing, Eagan sat up. His gaze took a moment to focus before he was rifling through an herb pouch at his hip, brows stitched together.

"Did you find him?" Rigil said. "Nedir?"

"Is that his name?" Eagan flung Rigil a distracted glance. "Yesterday, one of my informants in Meneton caught word of a message spreading among Meneton's unsavories, sent from an ally of Coble's in Land's End: A blond Kingsguard knight, his Jaelportian squire, and a scarred Hamonayan were Meneton-bound. A handsome reward awaits anyone who captures them for him. Especially the Hamonayan." Eagan glanced up again, this time long enough for a probing look. "You found what you were searching for in Land's End, I take it? The evidence of a plot against the king?"

"That depends. Can you help her?"

Sethe croaked something unintelligible and tried to rise, her good eye leaking tears of strain as Rigil pinned her arm to the ground. She wasn't unconscious, but whatever she was experiencing, the real world couldn't compete. Lightness, he'd never seen her like this. She'd always been so subtle about her gift, so private. They'd spent weeks surviving together, at first by begging and eventually by stealing, before he'd learned that she could bloodvoice at all.

Eagan finally found what he was seeking in his pouch: a small velvet bag. Sethe threw her head back, the tendons in her throat bulging, lips moving in hoarse pleas.

With a crinkle of velvet and herbs, Eagan shook two dark, shriveled shapes onto his palm, pungent with the reek of Er'Rets's best-known bloodvoicing defense.

"Karpos?" Rigil asked. "Will that stop the attack?"

"It will strengthen her shields, putting her mind beyond anyone's reach, including Nedir's, unless she chooses to open it."

"Can't you find him in the Veil? Storm him?"

Eagan dragged his wrist across his mouth, forehead wrinkling. "Trust me, Rigil. This is the best I can do."

Rigil had to turn away when Eagan forced the dried karpos fruit down Sethe's throat. He watched her bleached knuckles, her flailing feet, saw the exact moment when the fight left her body, when her fingers uncurled and her spine touched the ground again. When something *changed*.

Her eye was still open. He found it waiting, gold and red-webbed in the firelight. For the first time in days, her body was relaxed. For the first time in days, she seemed to *see* him in the old way, the all-seeing way, as only she ever had.

It lasted all of two heartbeats. A pulse, two, trying to read in her face what she saw when she looked at him after all this time.

Then her eye rolled back, taking consciousness with it.

Eagan felt her head with the back of his hand. "Her mind is safe, but she is exhausted and ill. I can treat her in Meneton." He worked the pouch in his herb-stained fingers, pulling out three more leathery bits of karpos, one for each of them. "Here. Karpos, in case Nedir makes any attempts on our minds. I hate to sacrifice what little safety bloodvoicing gives us. Meneton is not the friendliest at present. Still, it will be safer there for your friend."

"Sedhani. Her name is Sedhani."

Lie. She'd left that name behind. But what right did Rigil have to dole out the name she'd forbidden him from using?

The night flashed again, throwing the forest into relief. Meneton. Only hours away. They could regroup there, heal Sethe. Decide what in Isemios's wit came next.

"Break camp, Mezaedo," Rigil ordered, a hand on Sethe's.

They rode into Meneton at sunup.

Larger than Rigil remembered, or perhaps he saw it differently without Darkness, Meneton sat on the slopes of the Cela River valley, the Seybah River slashing through its heart. The chaos of sandstone buildings slanting down toward the river was showing signs of sun-bleaching after Darkness. Under a bank of storm clouds, a streak of sunrise painted rooftops and canvas booths scarlet. The smell of the river hung over it all like a rank brown fog.

Whispers stirred in alleys they passed as Rigil and Mezaedo followed Eagan down through the tight-packed buildings where tiny shadows moved, barefoot and vulturelike.

"New boots, sir?" A girl with rosebud lips darted in to snag Rigil's bare foot, her knuckles bruised purple where they poked from the sleeves of her sack-like dress. "Tillie can find you some for a rutah. Just a *rutah*, sir."

"No, thank you." Rigil had to repeat it twice before she seemed to hear, and even then he had to yank free. If he gave her coin, they'd be bombarded in moments, but the sight of her gazing blearily after him wouldn't leave him anytime soon. Or ever.

Meanwhile, Mezaedo was fending off another barrage from two young girls and a toddling boy who had materialized from a cloth-covered window. "No, I've got roomfuls of beaded jewelry already. Lady friend? No, that's—huh? Three for one? Moldy onions, if it's a *bargain*—"

"Mezaedo!" At Rigil's tone, the children scattered like sand in the wind, Meneton's alleys absorbing them into shadows once more.

"Where are their parents?" Mezaedo slipped a nut between his teeth, furtively, as if expecting someone to jump out and snatch it. "They can't all be strays."

"Meneton is easy prey for slave catchers," Eagan said, steering his horse down a narrow street toward the river. "Many of these children are orphans, their parents captured as slaves in the days of Darkness. Little has changed. Evil did not disappear when Darkness lifted. It simply found new holes to lurk in. For that, thank Captain Othvold Myvick."

The sunrise had been swallowed by storm clouds when Eagan finally slowed his horse before a blockish inn with an adjoining stable, both carved from sandstone. The door hung open, belching

Menetonians in various stages of inebriation into a courtyard. In red paint, the sign over the door heralded the Juggler's Inn.

Almost before Eagan dismounted, a boy in red livery darted out of the barn, a groom's brush in hand. "The usual, sir?"

Eagan tossed the boy a coin. "Rubdowns for all three, Destin. And bring the packs up when you can." To Rigil, he added, "Around the back."

Pulling a brass key from his tunic, Eagan led them around the building to a reinforced wooden door. Inside was a stairwell, the sandstone walls intricately carved with figures from too many sailors' tales to count, the imagery excessive and not entirely tasteful.

"Top floor," Eagan said.

Rigil carried Sethe up the steps, Eagan squeezing past him at the top to open the brass-inlaid door.

The room beyond made Coble's manor look like a slum.

Stained glass streamed light in fanciful patterns on the walls and across the thick Jaelportian carpets. In the corner, a ludicrously large bed was being devoured by thick drapes, all crimson dyed to match the lounging cushions on the floor. The room smelled vaguely earthy, and everything that could be gold-embroidered was, along with some things that arguably shouldn't be, like that red sailor's coat and plumed hat by the door. Not Eagan's, unless his tastes had drastically changed.

"These are your rooms?" Stooping to lay Sethe on the bed, Rigil glanced around at the half-empty brandy decanters, most of them jeweled, cluttering every flat surface. "How . . ."

"Vulgar?" Eagan offered, unclasping his cloak. "Excessive? Tasteless?"

"I was going to say expensive." That sailor's coat alone would be worth a fortune. Lightness. Rigil hadn't worn embroidery since the royal wedding.

Eagan tossed his cloak aside, revealing a wine-colored tunic with subtle green vines stitched along the collar. Tasteful, but not ostentatious. Likely the recommendation of Lady Nitsa.

Eagan turned Sethe's head to examine her ear, now a mess of scabs. "I will need water and cloths from the kitchens, Mezaedo. And broth for Miss Sedhani while you're at it."

As Mezaedo saluted and ducked out, Eagan added, "This floor belonged to a slave trader we recently arrested in Armonguard. Othvold Myvick, or Captain Myck, as he is known here. The suite is His Majesty's property now, my headquarters while I investigate Myvick's empire."

Rigil scanned the suite, pausing on the potted palms, the source of the earthy smell. Someone had been watering them. "Rather an involved mission for the king's secretary, isn't it?"

"King Gidon and Prince Oren believe Myvick's operation may be part of a larger conspiracy, perhaps the same one involving Lord Coble. I was the only man he could spare."

Rigil fingered a tassel on the canopy. "And?"

"Myvick's operation was more extensive than anyone realized. He had so many crews running slaves for him that most have never met him, and everything in this suite was no doubt purchased with those earnings." Eagan looked up from checking Sethe's pupil to give Rigil a meaningful glance. "I am glad to put the place to better use."

Rigil's fingers itched as he watched Eagan take the water basin from the bedside table, dabbing Sethe's face, pausing over her scars. Studying. Staring. Isemios's wit, if *Eagan's* was the first face she saw when she woke—

"I know you are not pleased about this, Rigil," Eagan said without looking. "But perhaps Arman willed for us to talk."

Rigil leaned on a bedpost, arms woven. "Do you have a topic in mind?"

Eagan's lips pressed, but not even Rigil's coolness would prevent a proper family reunion. "To begin with, Viola and Eric are well and expecting a baby. Hand me that cloth. Yes, that one. And you must have heard about Lady Tara and Sir Carmack?"

At that, Rigil pushed off the bedpost. "*Sir* Carmack? He's been knighted?"

"Knighted and married, praise Arman. Excellent news, yes?"

"Excellent." Rigil didn't realize he'd unfolded his arms until he found them dangling.

Eagan chuckled. "If that's how you show happiness—"

"I *am* happy," Rigil said too quickly. "Carmack has loved Tara for years. Not everyone of our—of *Tara's* station may marry below their rank. They are . . . blessed. To have that chance."

Eagan studied Rigil, pointedly *not* glancing at Sethe. Which was good, because neither was Rigil. "Your squire says you haven't slept in days."

"I'm fine."

"Rigil. Rest. I will do all I can."

"I fail to see how my staying here would interfere with that."

With a sigh, Eagan abandoned the washcloth to rifle through his pouch. "Mezaedo told me a little of your history with this woman. All I've gathered is that you met her in your hiatus from Zerah Rock."

Hiatus? Please. "Call a storm a storm, Eagan. I ran from Zerah Rock, and I've been running ever since. I met Sethe in Melas. We were both alone and penniless and decided we would fare better as allies than rivals. And before you launch into a sermon on larceny, I'm not proud of the way Sethe and I made our living in those months, but the past is the past. I'm not that boy anymore."

Eagan's tongue hit the back of his teeth. "You mistake me for your sister. I am in no position to judge a man for making poor decisions in his youth. But this woman. Sedhani."

"Sethe."

"Why have you never spoken of her before?"

This again. Fiddling with a button on his tunic, Rigil reached for words he could drain of emotion. "Believe it or not, there was a time when I had planned for her to meet you. I was returning to Zerah Rock with her when we were attacked on the road through Carm Duchy. Nedir was pursuing her even then, though I knew very little at the time, just that she had narrowly escaped his captivity once and was desperate to avoid being taken by him again."

Eagan rubbed his lower lip with a thumb, processing. "This Nedir has a special interest in her, clearly." He glanced up, as if struck by something. "As I recall, the first we heard of you after you ran from home was that Prince Oren had found you on the road to Zerah Rock. He never mentioned finding a woman with you."

It took everything in Rigil not to visibly grimace. Even so, Eagan was never fooled.

"Ah," the older man said after a moment. "I am sorry."

"Why? The fault was mine. I couldn't protect her, wasn't prepared for the ambush. All these years, I never knew whether she was taken alive that night or dragged away as a corpse. Lightness." Rigil's hand rose to his hair, digging at the roots. "Finding her at Land's End, and in Nedir's clutches no less . . . I still can't believe it. The chances of it all."

"I suspect chance has very little to do with it." Eagan paused for a satisfied hum, apparently finding what he needed in his herb pouch. "Has she been his captive all this time, then?"

"No. She escaped that night. Nedir only caught her recently, a few weeks ago."

"That is something." Eagan tossed his pouch aside, then added, as smoothly as a remark on the weather, "And you cared for her."

"Isemios's wit." Rigil turned away before he could freeze like a deer before a hunter. "We were practically children."

"You were no younger than King Gidon when he met my Averella. It is nothing to be ashamed of."

Something hooked in Rigil's chest, spun him. "I am *not* ashamed of loving Sethe."

Incredible. Such an old confession, collecting dust in his heart for all these years, and it *still* sounded so strange aloud. Strange, or simply childish.

Love? They'd been little more than youths, surviving on scraps and capers and the snatches of themselves they'd chosen to share. He hadn't even known her real name. She still didn't know his.

"Or . . . whatever it was." Trying to swallow, Rigil found his throat bone dry. "As I said, I was young. Reckless with my emotions as I was with anything else." Like his words. Particularly that one. "Eagan. I'm thankful you are here. Truly. But please, I'd rather not talk about Sethe."

People often said that Eagan took after his father, with his round face and lazy eyes and a presence that commanded obedience. Before Eagan's disinheritance, people had wondered if he would ever take on Burr Barak's ruthlessness as well.

People were fools.

"Forgive me, Rigil," Eagan said softly, gaze roving until it landed on an apple core on the rug. "Your squire seems a good lad. Eager. Though I don't know how they let such an inept bloodvoicer past training."

Mezaedo. Aye, Mezaedo he could discuss. Rigil leaned back. "He was a stray. It took him months to learn to bloodvoice with help from a token. I had to give him my sword so we could communicate in Land's End."

"Your sword? Keseel?" Eagan sounded impressed. And rightly so. Rigil had been known to speak of his old sword as more of a friend than a weapon.

Rigil grunted. "I lost Keseel in Allowntown, before the Battle of Armonguard."

"Ah, yes. I always wondered about the name."

"It was a Hamonayan word I'd heard once." Before Eagan could follow that trail back to Sethe, Rigil rushed on. "Mezaedo is still inept at shielding. Armonguard decided there was nothing more to be done, and frankly, I agree. Even so, Prince Oren expects me to recruit him to the Mârad before long."

Eagan nodded. "Why not? You recruited your last squire."

"Bran Rennan was a natural spy. He was sensible, dependable, acquainted with *subtlety*. Mezaedo Chevyah is . . ."

"Unique? That's not entirely bad." Hunched over the bedside table, Eagan began crushing herbs with a focus that seemed disproportionate to the task. "He's very attentive. Good instincts. He reminds me of someone."

Oh, *here* it was.

"He reminds you of Tazeem." The forbidden name all but *leaped* off Rigil's tongue, and just like that, he had already lost. Match and point, his rogue tumbling off the citadel board. "Go on. Say it."

"I mean no disrespect," Eagan said gently. "But the resemblance is uncanny. I thought perhaps that was why you chose him."

"Because he looks like a dead serving boy?" A crooked laugh climbed Rigil's throat. "Leave it to you to dredge up the sea-buried past."

"Rigil. You can't carry that guilt forever."

Rigil stared at him, at that face that had aged so much yet changed so little since their youth. "How long have you been waiting to discuss this?"

"It was an accident."

"It was a *mistake*. A failure, Eagan. Something I would not expect you to understand."

Eagan's pestle cracked against the mortar, crushed herbs spilling across the tabletop. "You seem to be forgetting the lapse in judgment that cost me years with the daughter I didn't know I had. Not to mention the loss of my birthright."

"Oh, aye." Rigil stood straighter against the bedpost. "How could I forget the day the great Eagan Barak was deemed unfit to inherit?"

"Now you are just being petty."

"Oh, come now. We're *talking*. Tell me, when you visited Father, did he offer you your birthright, or is there a last test he is waiting for me to fail first?"

To his surprise, Eagan didn't rise to the challenge. Just leaned forward in his chair, elbows on knees, mortar and pestle sagging. He looked tired. Almost old.

"Rigil, I know it must have been difficult after Father cast me out. I know all about his expectations, and I'm sorry—I am *truly sorry* I was not there to help you bear them." He sighed, rubbing his brow. "Arman knows, Burr Barak makes nothing easy, but I do think he has changed. Lightness, even if he hasn't, Zerah Rock *will* be yours by right. Whenever you return, *however* you return . . ." Eagan cast a meaningful glance at the brown pickpocket's hand lying next to his on the bed. "You are the rightful heir, and I will stand with you."

Rigil glanced away, letting his eyes trace the stained-glass spangles on the walls. A mirror across the room flung his face back at him, haggard and filthy and . . . No, not ready.

Was he?

Creaking stairs announced the stable boy arriving with their saddlebags. After tossing him a copper, Rigil dug out a clean tunic, blue and black in homage to Zerah Rock. A comb followed, then a lump of soap. After a moment's hesitation, he added a razor as well.

Home. It had always been inevitable. Arman knew he couldn't run from the ghosts of serving boys forever, and as for Sethe . . .

He stole a glance and felt every bit the thief for it. Time had touched her lightly, almost impossibly so, and the fresh tunic in his hand suddenly felt like hope. Like a chance to prove that he had remade himself since Melas, to succeed where he had once failed.

Eagan was weaving a thread through the head of a needle as Rigil stood with his bundle. "You never did say what you saw in the Veil," he said.

The distraction made Eagan miss the loop. Biting his lip, he tried again. "Nedir was trying to compel her to return to Land's End. She was resisting with everything she had."

That sounded like Sethe. He'd known many brilliant women, but none whose willpower could make a tempest seem weak by comparison. "And?" he prompted. "What's he after?"

This time, the thread split around the head of the needle. Blowing out a breath, Eagan set them both down and swiveled to face Rigil, his stare anything but lazy. "His strength is impossible. My strongest efforts to storm him were, at best, a nuisance. The fact that she resisted him so long is a testament to her shields, but I doubt she would have held him off much longer. Thank Arman I came when I did."

Thank Arman.

A blast of wind rattled the windows, drawing Rigil's gaze to the clouds holding dawn for ransom outside. It stormed often in Zerah Rock. All the time, in fact. But the worst squalls had a scent, a palpable energy like this.

Eagan unrolled a new skein of thread. "His bloodvoicing is not natural, Rigil, and I fear what it may mean for the Light. I must send a messenger to Armonguard. We cannot risk bloodvoicing Prince Oren or the king, not with Nedir lurking in the Veil."

"If our enemies know how dangerous he is," Rigil said, "we may not have time to wait for a messenger to reach Armonguard. The threat is here in the west."

"And?"

"And so am I. The prince sent me to investigate the weapon, Eagan." Rigil tipped his palm at the bed. "Mezaedo said Nedir took something from a vial before he attacked Se—Sedhani. If we were to remove it from his possession, perhaps the Mârad could use it before the enemy has the chance."

Looping the thread around his finger, Eagan snapped off the excess with his teeth. "We have no idea how much of this substance Nedir has. Stealing one vial—"

"Could be an asset to the Mârad, and one less vial for Nedir to use against us."

"So your plan is theft."

Rigil refused to flinch. "I'm not a common cutpurse, Eagan."

Eagan's needle stalled over Sethe's slitted ear. "As long as you are acting for the Mârad first and not acting upon your plans for Miss Sedhani."

Miss Sedhani. That name was all wrong. But then, what right did Rigil have to force her back into a past he'd left in splinters? *Don't call me Sethe.*

"What she knows could affect all Er'Rets," Rigil said. "Neutralizing this threat is my priority."

"In that case"—the needle plunged into Sethe's ear, dragging black thread with it—"I suggest you tell me everything you know about this woman's history with Raith Nedir."

CHAPTER TEN
SETHE

SETHE WOKE SLOWLY. SOFT SHEETS, A vile taste on her tongue, a sweet scent of sandstone and rum. The moan of wind rushing against glass windows. And a voice. Unfamiliar. So close she could hear his breaths.

"…means cutting ourselves off from Armonguard, I know. But we cannot risk him watching through our eyes, or worse, listening in on our reports."

When something soft and stinging-hot touched Sethe's ear, the jab of pain sprang her eye open like a pick in a lock. Mottled light nearly had it squeezing shut just as quickly.

A man was sitting beside her bed. Seeing her awake, he smiled under a fringe of dark bangs, face haloed by stained glass. "Welcome to Meneton, Miss Sedhani. How do you feel?"

Sethe barely heard. She was in a closed room. Four mosaicked walls, frescoed ceiling, floor heaped with a rich man's carpets. A stranger beside her dressed to the chin in the color of blood.

A box. Another scuddy *cage*.

Reaching out for fragments, Sethe bit back a wave of claustrophobia that tasted like phlegm. No way out. "Who are you?"

"A Kingsguard knight, and fortunately for you, a passable healer. Sir Eagan Elk at your service." The man folded into a seated bow, making his dark hair flop forward. The wet cloth in his hand was dribbling all over the coverlet. He swirled it at her ear. "I did my best, but the scar may be messy. It looked as if someone had taken a rusty fork to you."

Sethe touched her ear, fingers traveling down the aching skin until she found it, a trail of threaded bumps. "Meneton." That name was important, or had been once. "How long?"

"About a day. Before that, two days of traveling. You've been unwell. You have Sir Rigil and his squire to thank for bringing you to me when they did."

Rigil. Sethe struggled to turn her head, the world teetering even as she sought him.

"Hello, Sedhani."

Leaning against a bedpost, he would have made a decent picture of nonchalance if not for the smudges under his eyes that said he hadn't slept in, what, days? He was wearing clean clothes, had found new boots somewhere, probably from Eagan, and he'd shaved off the close-cut beard that had rimmed his mouth before. It made him look ten years younger and ten times more threatening to Sethe's escape plans.

Sethe appraised him. "Where's the squire?"

"About." Rigil's hands moved to his pockets, back to his sides. "I'm more concerned about you at present."

"I can't sense either of your minds."

"That would be the karpos fruit," Eagan said. "Apologies, Miss Sedhani, but we've all taken it now, a precaution against any further attacks from Nedir. I think it is best for us all to guard our minds, since he may watch through any one of us to locate you."

Miss Sedhani her foot. Pushing herself up on her elbows, Sethe searched for a lifeline and found it in the door behind Rigil, slightly cracked. The need to escape through that door before Nedir could catch up to her was a hammer inside her ribs, a raw, oily taste in the back of her throat. *Three days. Could Nedir have tracked me here in three days?*

This time, she managed to sit, ignoring the concerned pinch in Rigil's mouth as she did. "What," she croaked to Eagan, "do you know about Nedir?"

This man was older than Rigil, with a round face and eyes too young for their creases. At her question, he quirked one brow. "We were hoping you might help us with that."

Her laugh came out slightly frantic. "So that's what this is. An interrogation?"

Rigil's emphatic "Of course not" fell flat. Black flecks sprayed Sethe's vision as she swung her legs over the side of the bed, gripping the coverlet and trying to ignore the gnawing void in her gut.

Rigil circled the bedposts. "What are you doing?"

"I can't stay here." Now, if the pattern in the floor would only stop *swirling.* "If Nedir found me once, he can find me again."

"Yes, in the Veil," Rigil said. "Or have you forgotten that your physical location means very little to him? The moment your karpos wears off, he will find your mind wherever you go."

"I'll buy more karpos."

He arched his eyebrows. "With whose coin?"

Sethe dug her toes into the carpet. "Listen. You don't know Nedir like I do. Having my mind isn't enough. He'll want all of me. He probably already has men searching for me from here to Land's End."

Eagan Elk raised a palm. "I can confirm that."

"There. See?" Holding Rigil's gaze, Sethe jabbed a hand at the older man. "Karpos won't help me if he finds me in the physical world. I need to disappear."

"Not an option." Rigil dismissed that suggestion with a wave, then pressed the same hand against her shoulder to keep her from rising. If he thought he could comb his hair and prance about like the king of Er'Rets . . . "Seth—*Sedhani*. You haven't eaten in days. You can barely stand. Without Mezaedo and me, you would be lost in the Veil or knocking on Shamayim's gates. For Lightness' sake, think about this. You are better off with allies than without."

Their glares collided. Tides, his eyes. Not even the sea off Hamonah ever shone that blue, exactly the kind of thought her owl would have ripped to pieces.

His hand on her shoulder was hard, patronizing, not at all like the fingers she had felt brushing hair from her face in the haze of Nedir's attack. That Rigil had been a dream, then. Something conjured by the part of her that still lived in Melas. The part of her still *trapped* there.

Sethe flicked his hand aside. "You can't make me stay."

"Of course not." Eagan Elk's voice sounded different suddenly. Warmth dripped from it, oozing through Sethe, a tide of assurance that she could trust these men, that they wanted to help her.

"No!" Launching off the bed, Sethe grabbed the first thing in reach and swung. Clay connected with Sir Eagan's skull. He grunted. Rigil shouted something Sethe didn't hear.

"Stay out of my head!" she roared. "You think I don't know what tampering feels like?"

"Sedhani!" Rigil snatched the clay mug from her hand before she could give Sir Eagan another scar to match the one bleeding on his brow. "He didn't mean anything by it. It's a gift of his." Rigil's tone darkened as he aimed a glare at the other man. "*Timing* is not."

Eagan caught a drop of blood running down his temple, smiling tightly. "Forgive me, Miss Sedhani. I merely wanted to see if your karpos had worn off, but that was tactless. Here." He grabbed a velvet pouch off the bedside table, shook a couple shriveled chunks of dried something into his hand, and held them out to her. "This dose should protect you from any more intrusions for a few hours. Please, forgive me."

Chest heaving, Sethe juggled glares between the two of them before she realized her head was pounding and fell back on the bed. Hard. Eagan laid the karpos on the bed in front of her, avoiding her eye like she was some skittish animal he was trying to tame.

Glaring knives through his vine-embroidered throat, Sethe downed the karpos without chewing. Outside, thunder purred, as if someone was moving furniture in the sky.

Eagan produced a handkerchief from his pocket and dabbed his brow, chuckling. *Chuckling.* "One thing is certain, Miss Sedhani. You are not one to trifle with."

Sethe stared at the carpet. Ridiculous, this whole gaudy room. Ridiculous, like her. Rigil probably thought she had sand for wits.

Not that she cared.

"Spend years as Nedir's favorite pet," Sethe said, "and you learn how to keep people out of your head." She didn't state the obvious—that everything was temporary, that all it had taken was a handful of dust to obliterate her best efforts and shatter her mind at fifteen. Her childhood with Nedir wasn't Eagan Elk's business. Tides, it wasn't *Rigil's* business. "I learned to spot a trap almost as well as I learned to shield. And I managed to avoid Nedir for sixteen years after I escaped him in Hamonah, so yes, I'm good at it."

"And yet," Eagan said, "Rigil found you in his captivity in Land's End."

"That was my own fault. A few weeks ago, I pulled into Melas with a merchant crew and thought I'd stay awhile. I'd avoided the place for so long by then, I didn't see the harm. Why would Nedir still care about the girl who'd escaped him, after all that time?" It sounded so hollow now. So reckless. Who was she to think that running would ever have an end for her? "He must have caught wind of the ship I was on, followed me there. That was the end of it. The second I let my guard down, Nedir appeared from nowhere, drugged me, bound me, and dragged me to Land's End like the same fifteen-year-old he'd lost all those years ago. I was planning my own escape when you showed up." She shrugged. "So I improvised."

Rigil rubbed his now-smooth jaw. "The man must be obsessed. Why else would he let so much time pass just to hunt you down again?"

Sethe's laugh came out short and black. "Obsessed. Mad. Whatever you like."

"There must be more to it than that," Rigil said. "We have reason to believe that whatever Nedir wants with you is part of a plot against the king, one we know almost nothing about. You may be the only person in Er'Rets with the information we need."

"For example." Eagan used his free hand to slide a tray across the bedside table toward her. A bowl of broth sloshed on it, along with a loaf and a handful of nuts. Bribery. "Rigil tells me you witnessed a meeting?"

The ache in Sethe's gut tugged at her harder than the open door. With a glance at Eagan, she reached for the loaf, answering as she ripped it apart.

"Coble, Nedir, the seer from Mirrorstone, some tiko he called Erro, and an Eben. All interested in Nedir's powder." As silence bloomed, Sethe glanced up from the tray. "A weapon of world-shapers, he calls it. The cad. It's only a bloodvoicing stimulant."

The cut on his brow forgotten, Eagan leaned forward. "A stimulant. How potent?"

"Put it this way." Sethe reached for the bowl of nuts, only to have Rigil tug it away.

"Mezaedo's," he whispered with a grimace, drawing Sethe's attention to the bright orange spice coating the nuts. "Trust me."

Retracting her hand, Sethe went on. "Without that powder, Nedir would have as much chance of breaking through my shields as you would have of buying that Magosian tapestry over there on a knight's wages. But with it . . ." A tide of memory washed over her from that first time, in Hamonah. Writhing on the floor of her fortress prison, trying to claw Nedir out of her head . . .

Eagan's lips bunched. "So he is not a strong bloodvoicer?"

"Without the powder? Average at best."

When Rigil's head sprang up, not a single straw-colored hair shifted. "Average? He used Mezaedo like a broken toy, and to my knowledge, that was without powder."

Sethe stopped licking crumbs off her fingers long enough to slide him a glance. "Your squire's mind is weak as milk, K'sil. Didn't you think to teach him that blocking trick of yours?"

Rigil folded his arms, watching Eagan. "Am I the only one concerned that this man can make puppets of whomever he likes?"

"That is not so novel, Brother," Eagan said, something flickering in the corner of his mouth. "Influencing is frowned upon, but memory alteration takes very little skill. For instance, do you remember the time I made you wade through the bloodsucker's pond?"

Rigil's chin tipped up. "No."

"Exactly. All you need is a weak enough mind without shields. That, and no scruples."

Well, well, Sethe had never seen Rigil's eye twitch like *that*. And then it struck her, halfway through tossing back the satin sheets. "Wait. *Brother?*"

"Half brother." Rigil was too busy aggressively rolling his cuffs to catch Eagan's wink.

"Are you both from Zerah Rock, then?" Eagan nodded, and Sethe studied him. "Don't tell me you're a runaway servant too."

The older man blinked as if struck on the nose. "A runaway what?"

But then Rigil was there, speaking fast enough to jumble words like crabs in a barrel. "That is a tale for another time. We must decide what to do about Nedir."

Must decide? *We?* Sethe pressed her toes into the carpet. "I've told you everything. Nedir is a lunatic with a bloodvoicing obsession. Always has been, always will be."

Even to herself, she sounded manic. Were the walls getting closer?

Come on, Sethe. Pull yourself together.

"I understand wanting to put as much distance between yourself and Nedir as possible," Eagan said, moving to the mirror on the wall to tend his cut. "But if he was willing to hunt you down after sixteen years apart, what is to stop him from hunting you again? Unless, of course, he got what he wanted from you this time, in Land's End."

"He didn't."

"It would be helpful," Rigil said, "if we knew what that was."

Eagan watched her in the mirror. "Miss Sedhani, Rigil has told me what little he knows of your ability. Tell me, are your fragments infinite? That is, can you make an infinite number?"

Sethe leaned back on her hands. "I haven't found a limit."

"And you invest them into living things?"

"Mostly birds. Sometimes rats. I use them as my eyes and ears."

"You mean you watch through their eyes?"

"I control them—where they go, what they do. Most of the time, I keep the fragments in the back of my head until I need them." She plucked at her vest. "It keeps me sane."

Eagan's brows rose. "So you've been doing all of this awake? Influencing multiple creatures at once and still functioning in your own body without going unconscious?"

"For as long as I've been able to fragment," Sethe answered. Which was about as much information as she cared to share on *that*.

A gust of wind slammed the windows on one side of the room, making Rigil's lips tighten. "If you have a theory, Eagan, then by all means, enlighten us."

In the tinted mirror, Eagan's face was the color of pirate gold as he gingerly pressed the handkerchief to the edges of his wound. "Nedir wants to control men. To influence them with your fragments as you influence animals. Just think. He could maneuver legions of black knights on the other side of Er'Rets. Destruction from afar. All he needs is your mind and your fragments at his disposal. If that is true, then protecting your thoughts, Miss Sedhani, may be a matter of life and death for more people than yourself."

Turning from the mirror, he let his thoughtful gaze fall heavily on her. "That might explain the timing as well. Perhaps he has spent the last sixteen years perfecting this weapon with your ability in mind. Now that he's mastered the stimulant, all he needs is a bloodvoicer who can split her mind as you can. It's only natural that he would think of you, perhaps the only bloodvoicer in Er'Rets with such a unique skill. *You're* the weapon as much as his powder is."

When Sethe didn't say anything, Eagan plowed on. "Perhaps I could test your defenses, to be sure that the karpos is working as it should? Only with your permission, of course."

Sethe hesitated. A tiny bead of blood welled in the gash on Eagan's head, and he left it, waiting for her choice.

"It's all right," Rigil said. "I would trust Eagan with my life."

Oh, in *that* case. Rolling her lips together, Sethe nodded. After a beat, she felt Eagan's consciousness hovering on the outside of her mental defenses. Even seeing him there, standing at a safe distance with his hands in view, she nearly jumped when he knocked on her karpos-infused shields and bloodvoiced his name. *Sir Eagan Elk.*

Sethe held his stare. She also held her shields up.

Eagan nodded as if satisfied. Then, "I'm going to try invading without permission this time. Don't be alarmed, Miss Sedhani, but this is what Nedir will try."

He waited for her tiny nod, then brought the full weight of his mind down on her shields like a hammer. Sethe felt it happening, but her defenses held. He tried again. Still nothing.

Tides, where had karpos been all her life?

"Now see if you are able to let me in," Eagan said. "Just me and no one else. Like opening a door and closing it behind me."

Yes, she knew how to use her own bloodvoicing ability. Pulling her feet up onto the bed, Sethe gripped her ankles, held his stare, and opened a crack in her shields wide enough for Eagan Elk's voice to leak through.

You know your way around your gift, clearly, he bloodvoiced. *Have you had any formal training?*

Sethe chuffed. *As a sailor for a merchant crew?*

Across the room, Eagan smiled a little as Rigil glanced back and forth between them, trying to read their thoughts through their skin. *I can see why my brother was so concerned for your welfare, Miss Sedhani,* Eagan added. *You are certainly a formidable woman. As for your ability to fragment, I hope you realize that Arman has given you a rare gift.*

Sethe bit her cheek. Should she make it harder for him? *Why would Arman have anything to do with me?*

The question, only half sincere, drew a fine, sharp line between Eagan's eyebrows. Only when his pause went on long enough to be irritating did Sethe realize she wanted an answer. Maybe needed one.

You may not remember, Eagan bloodvoiced, *but you were calling to Arman during Nedir's attack, reciting words from the Book of Life that had the ring of a prayer to them. Are you not a child of Arman?*

Rigil seemed ready to burst from curiosity, burning on the edge of her vision like a blue-clad star. His presence was a whole other net of fish, one she planned to leave behind as soon as she could, before it could snare her too. But right now, that question . . .

Sethe? A child of Arman? Why did that sound like a sailor's *land ahoy!* after a long voyage at sea?

I didn't know it was that simple, Sethe replied. Even in her bloodvoice, caution tinted every word. *Is that all it takes? Knowing a few lines from the Book of Life?*

At that, Eagan's face changed, relaxing into something curious and kind. *In this case, I think that may depend on whether or not you believe them.*

"Ahem." The conversation ended when Rigil inserted himself between them, snipping Sethe's train of thought like a loose thread. "I assume the test was successful? The karpos is working?"

Sethe licked her lips against the fruit's tart aftertaste. "It works."

"But only as a temporary solution," Eagan put in, all traces of their conversation wiped from his face as he turned back to his mirror. "Nedir is too great a threat to trust karpos alone."

Rigil dragged a hand down his mouth and didn't seem to notice Eagan doing the same. Yes, definitely brothers. But where had two former servants learned to carry themselves so grandly?

"Without the dust," Rigil said, "Nedir is an ordinary blood-voicer, no? Just one man with a vial."

"Not for long." Sethe pushed herself to standing. "Nedir mentioned a shipment going out in the next few days to everyone at that meeting. Coble, Rheala, the Eben. He didn't mention where it was sailing from, but—"

"Wait." Eagan's face hardened, and he hurried across the room to an ornate desk piled with feather plumes. "Myvick kept a log of his voyages. I'm sure I saw somewhere here . . ."

"Myvick?" Sethe whirled on Rigil. "*Othvold* Myvick lives *here*?"

She kept forgetting how much taller he was now. Spinning to face him put her eye level with his chin. Closer than expected. Close enough to notice, again, that he'd shaved since Land's End. Shame.

"You know Myvick?" he asked.

Sethe refused to step away. Refused to tip her head back. "I know his type. A man like him owned the ship that got me off Hamonah."

A tiny flex of his mouth. "You shipped yourself to freedom on a slaver's vessel?"

"A smuggler. And relax. No one checked my crate."

Rigil's mouth stayed stubbornly fixed, but there was a grudging smile in there somewhere. Probably.

Eagan, leaning backward on the desk, was flipping through a red leather journal faster than Sethe could have dreamed of reading it. He finally stopped with his thumb on one entry, spun it for her and Rigil to see.

"Here. Myvick has a shipment scheduled for three mornings from now. Delivery stops in Mirrorstone, Land's End, and the Cela coast afterward."

"From where?" Rigil stepped forward and took the book from Eagan, rubbing at a smudge. A draft inched the door behind him a little wider. "It just says the *Talons.*"

Sethe had been creeping for the door when that word, that *name*, yanked her to a halt as hard as any shackle. Stormy light moved over the carpet in blood-colored speckles, wind moaning against the windows like the cries of the sea-buried dead.

The Talons. How long had it been since she'd last heard that name? Seeing Nedir's operation in Land's End, she'd assumed he'd moved his headquarters to Coble's castle and that his *secure location* would be somewhere nearby, like Barth.

She should have known better. With Nedir, it always came back to Hamonah.

"The Talons. I've never heard of them." Returning to the desk, Eagan began unrolling a map of Er'Rets. "Perhaps in Jaelport?"

"A shipment of powder?" Rigil said. "It would make sense."

This close, Sethe could pick out the grain of the door, the dents where Othvold Myvick's blade had nicked it coming and going.

Kingsguard business. That was all this was. She'd done her part, told them everything she knew. Time to go.

"We cannot afford to guess," Rigil was saying. "With only three days—"

"It's on Hamonah."

Part of Sethe hoped she'd said that in her head, or that the thunder rolling outside had drowned her out. The silence in the room said otherwise.

Turning, Sethe found them both watching her, Rigil's gaze darting from her to the door and back. Reading her like a scuddy map.

"Hamonah," he said, fingertips pressing down on Myvick's desk. "You're sure?"

So, they were going to pretend she hadn't been running for it. Fine. "They're rock formations off the coast," she said. "So full of caves you could run an inn out of any one of them."

"Or hide a year's worth of smuggled cargo, I take it," Eagan deadpanned. "How do we know which cave Myvick was referring to?"

Sethe spoke only to Rigil. "There's an old sea fortress in the middle of it all. Centuries old, but Nedir uses it now. The cave underneath it is legend among smugglers, big enough to hide ten ships and their cargo. No city lord or navy would risk the rocks, so some of the elites on Hamonah pay Nedir to use it. Keeps the other riffraff in the Talons from cutting in on their shipments, I guess."

Eagan rubbed his jaw. "So. Myvick was planning a personal visit to Nedir's fortress."

"He's one of the few who'd risk it. The Talons are hard to navigate, even harder to sail out of." The scars over Sethe's eye itched. "I would know."

Rigil's chest caved a little, like he'd been holding his breath. An unspoken question was rolling from him, gathering speed, breaking as it neared.

Sethe took a step back. "No."

"Sedhani, listen."

"No, *you* listen. That island will eat you alive and drink your blood like rum. And the Talons? I escaped those caves in a *box.*

Sandwits who go there *don't come out*, not without Nedir's permission." Sethe's tongue tripped over that last bit, her old accent cropping up, a sign she was losing control. "And if you think I'll help you find it, if you think I would ever, ever go back—"

"You saw what Nedir can do." Rigil could sound so annoyingly sincere when it suited him. "As long as he has this powder, you will never be free. They'll find you, Sethe, *use* you. I can't let that happen."

Which part? she wanted to ask. The threat to Er'Rets or the threat to her?

Stupid question. So many stupid questions, like how badly did he want to try on that embroidered-to-the-hilt sailor's coat on the wall, just to see if he could pull off the disguise as easily as he had countless costumes in Melas? Had he thought about it? Even noticed it?

Maybe *Sir* Rigil, Kingsguard knight, didn't do that sort of thing anymore.

"It doesn't matter," she said. To herself, not him. But of course, he misunderstood.

"Doesn't matter?" he echoed. "An army in the hands of Raith Nedir doesn't *matter*?"

Sethe dug her nails into her sides, spoke so calmly she shocked even herself. "Myvick's man is collecting the shipment in three days. Even if you reach the Talons before that ship does, what then? You think Nedir's guards will let you prance in and out with his goods?"

His lips twitched, a hint at something she couldn't place. "That never used to stop you."

Foul play. "Hamonah is for pirates, K'sil, not knights. If you know what's good for you, you'll stay away from Nedir. I can't go back."

"Can't? Or won't go with me?"

He had abandoned his *Kingsguard* voice for something more

familiar, something with the dust and seagull cries of Melas dancing between words. And that curve in his lips, falling somewhere between a plea and a challenge . . .

Did he still keep that one secret grin in the corner of his mouth, she wondered, or had he left that behind like he'd left her?

Anyway, he wasn't wrong. As long as Nedir had that powder, she *would* never be free.

The door banged open before Sethe heard footsteps on the stairs, before she could flee the sucking sand trap that was this man, this room, this whole scuddy nightmare. Back to Hamonah? Back to the *Talons?*

"Moldy *onions.*"

Scrawny as ever and top-heavy with curls, Mezaedo Chevyah looked like he'd just outswum a tanniyn as he snapped the door shut behind him and collapsed against it, panting. His dark irises hung on Sethe, a tangy-smelling bag clutched to his chest. "Oh, good. She's awake. That'll make things a moldy heap easier."

"Mezaedo?" One word and Rigil slid back into his Kingsguard persona, perfect posture and all. "What is it?"

"The good news?" Mezaedo hoisted the bag. "I bought the karpos. The bad news . . ." He glanced at Sethe. "Half of Meneton is on my tail. And thanks to Nedir, they're all after her."

CHAPTER ELEVEN
RIGIL

I SEMIOS'S WIT, IT NEVER PAID TO THINK you were one step ahead. Hurrying to Myvick's window, Rigil found a boiling sky and a swarm of men moving down the valley toward the inn. How many men composed that swarm was nearly impossible to make out, but more than one blade flashed in the crowd as they trickled through the narrow streets.

Just glorious.

"I told you." Sethe jounced on her heels, simmering with anxious energy. So, she still did that. "Tides, I *told* you."

Glass crashed in the inn beneath them, making Mezaedo jump. Then fists pounding the door at the bottom of the stairs. Myvick's private entrance.

Rigil turned from the window. "We need to leave Meneton."

"The gates will be locked," Eagan said. "By now, the river is your best hope."

Blight it all. "Will any ship give us passage?"

"Yes." With a sweep of his arm, Eagan cleared Myvick's desk and began tugging it in front of the door. "Straight to Land's End."

Sethe was standing on a creaky floorboard. Every time her heels rose and fell, a wooden whine joined the melee. *Squee-aak, squee-aak.* "There are other ways to get passage," she said, pressing a hand to one wall as if trying to hold it away from her. Her gaze, slightly wild, swerved to Rigil.

His spine locked. "No."

"We have no choice, K'sil."

"*No.*"

"They're in the stairwell!" Mezaedo dug his heels into the carpet, braced against the desk, a one-man defense against all Meneton. "Sirrig?"

Rigil made for the eastern wall, grabbing Myvick's sailor's coat as he passed. He wadded it around his hand, then seized one of the half-empty brandy decanters on the sill and proceeded to smash the stained-glass window into a thousand gem-colored shards.

Hot wind poured in, billowing in Myvick's tasseled curtains. "After you, Sedha—"

Sethe had a foot on the sill almost before he turned from the window. A snow of fine glass crunched beneath her heels as he grabbed her arm, rooting her in place. "We are all in this now, Sedhani. Do you understand that? If you wish to make certain no one can use that powder against you, joining us, *helping* us, is your best chance."

A fine line appeared between her brows. She tugged free, spoke to Mezaedo over her shoulder. "Try to keep up, tiko."

When she swung out of the room onto the ledge that rimmed the upper floor, Mezaedo was quick to follow—after snatching the remains of Sethe's bread from the bed.

"You next, Eagan." Rigil hurried to the pile of packs in the corner. His coin pouch was buried under his extra tunics, none of which, blight it all, would be coming with him. By the time he dug out his purse, the door was rattling, banging against the desk.

Someone cursed outside. "What are you waiting for? Fire and ash, break it down!"

Eagan tossed Rigil the sword belt he'd stolen off a black knight. Rigil was swinging it around his waist when an especially forceful blast shook the door off its hinges. The door toppled inward, then slid, scraping along Myvick's desk to land with a thud.

Two men stared at Rigil over the desk, half shadowed by the stairwell. Eagan pressed against the wall beside the door, out of sight, something cudgel-like in one hand.

To keep their attention on him, Rigil drew his sword. "Stay where you are, men. We haven't time for pleasantries today."

To his immense shock, the foremost man took one look at Rigil and stepped back.

"Yer forgiveness, Captain Myck." He dropped into a sloppy half bow. "We didn't know you were—I mean, eel's breath, we was told you was in Armonguard!"

Captain Myck, eh? How serendipitous.

Rigil tipped an imaginary hat. "Aye, well. Surprise."

Eagan took the cue. Launching off the wall, he swung his weapon, a stone vase, at the newcomer. It connected with a crack that drove Rigil's teeth together. The first man dropped in a leaden heap, toppling into his companion. The last Rigil saw of the latter was a set of pinwheeling arms as the man crashed backward down the stairs.

Back at the window, Eagan nodded at the coat in Rigil's hand. "You do resemble him, especially now, without the beard. A little more bowing and flourishing and I might ship you to Armonguard myself."

Slinging his arms into the coat, Rigil debated bowing. He also debated taking Myvick's garish hat to complete the ensemble. Naturally, that debate was brief, and he clambered out the window behind Eagan with Othvold Myvick's feather-plumed monstrosity on his head.

Sethe and Mezaedo were waiting on the roof, ready to pull Eagan and Rigil over the balustrade as they clung to the decorative ledge that topped the building. And not a moment too soon. Around the corner, the street belched voices of at least a dozen Meneton men scrambling up Myvick's private stairs.

"This way." Sethe hopped the narrow gap between the inn and the stables, landing on the thatched roof with only the slightest crunch. One by one, under a brooding evening sky, they followed her across the stable and onto the wall that encircled the courtyard. There, they ducked between the ramparts, Eagan watching the courtyard, Mezaedo scouting ahead.

"There's the harbor." Peering over the far balustrade, Mezaedo would have been just a mop of hair to anyone gazing up from the street. Behind him, the Seybah River was a stripe of darkness reflecting occasional flashes of lightning. The storm was about to break. "Any chance someone's left a boat unattended?"

A drop of rain splattered the wall beside Rigil. "*No one* is stealing a ship," he snapped.

Sethe led the climb down the other side of the wall. She moved like a feather, finding footholds where none existed, gliding over sandstone. Once on the ground, Eagan took the lead, cutting a path down the valley to the river and changing direction every time the sounds of pursuit came too close. So focused on avoiding people in the streets, Rigil almost jumped when Sethe appeared beside him.

"Desperate times call for desperate measures," she said softly as they hurried down a mule path. "Didn't you used to say that?"

Pausing against a wall to let Mezaedo pass between them, Rigil kept a hand on his coin purse. "We are not talking about bread crusts, Sedhani. Any one of those ships could mean life or death for some honest merchant."

Overhearing, Eagan wobbled a hand. "*Honest* may be generous for Meneton."

Rigil ignored him. Packed between the narrow stone walls, gull cries in one direction and crowded streets in another, it felt like a rift in time. Melas, Meneton, was there a difference?

Yes.

"I am a Kingsguard knight." He kept his voice steady, as empty as he could. "Not a petty thief, Sedhani, and *not* a pirate."

Dusk cast deepening shadows in the hollows of her face. "I don't like this costume of yours," she said. "And I don't mean the coat."

Lightning exploded over Meneton, making Mezaedo jump. The crack of thunder that followed was not loud enough to drown out the voices echoing down the valley.

"This way, men!"

"Cut 'em off at the square!"

Eagan, peering out into the next street, jerked back into the alley. "It's as if they know our every move."

He hesitated in the alley mouth, thumbing his sword while Mezaedo offered Sethe some of his spice. When she shook her head, he dumped a handful into his own palm with a shrug that said, quite clearly, *Your loss.*

"This way," Eagan said.

He led them out into an open market. Bells in the upper city were ringing down the valley as hawkers darted every which way, clogging streets already crammed with carts, covered booths, and dogs worked to frenzy by the tension in the air. Something was happening. The people could sense it.

As they hurried across the thoroughfare, a young boy with an armful of oranges tripped in front of Rigil. Sunset-colored fruits rolled like heads at an execution, and the boy glanced up with a panic that told Rigil his master must not be far behind.

"Two rutahs for the lot, sir?"

Rigil dropped three into the boy's hand. "Find a safe place, lad. Away from the streets."

The child scurried off, tangy-smelling oranges tumbling behind him. As they passed, Mezaedo stooped to collect two of them, stuffing one in each pocket of his trousers without breaking stride.

Following Eagan's lead, Rigil, Sethe, and Mezaedo ducked into a covered portico as a burst of cries and screeching steel cascaded down the valley.

Sethe jolted. "Are they fighting each *other*?"

"They are competing for the same prize, Miss Sedhani," Eagan said. "You. Myvick is no longer here to keep the city in check."

Something crashed behind them. A woman screamed. Then an accented shout as men broke into the square.

"Oy! There she is!"

"Run." Eagan pushed Sethe, jostling her forward. "Run!"

They sprinted down the portico in a pack, Eagan hollering directions, Mezaedo yelping course corrections whenever he found a path blocked. Meneton was a maze of half-clogged alleys stinking with dead fish and sleeping urchins, but Eagan seemed to know it well. Unfortunately, the men of Meneton knew it better. Every time Rigil thought the shouts had died down, a new bout rose from another direction, herding them down the valley toward the river. And straight into a dead end.

Mezaedo met the wall first and spun with a hand on his sword, the other on his spice pouch. Sweat had carved tracks through days of travel grime on his face, making him look like a Poroo in war paint. "Back! Back, back!"

Too late. Shouts filled the alley behind them, closing off their retreat. Fish skeletons and chamber pot leavings littered the dead end, and the stink of the river here was potent enough to burn Rigil's lungs.

Sethe was already searching for handholds in the wall when Rigil seized her arm. "Do you remember what I said when you first took me pickpocketing?"

She flinched at his touch but didn't hesitate. "*Stay with me.*

Lucky for you, my answer is the same now as then. Where would I go?"

In answer, Rigil slapped his coin purse into her hand. "For a ship. Take Mez and wait for us."

She bounced the pouch in her hand, coins grating between her fingers. "How does a runaway servant turned soldier come by coin like this?"

When Rigil didn't answer—Lightness, he really needed to address that little misconception of hers—she snorted, pocketed the purse, and dug her toes into the wall. When Rigil retracted his hand and turned to Mezaedo, the boy was ready for him.

"I'll look after her, Sirrig."

Mezaedo scrambled after Sethe and nearly caught her. They went over the wall together.

Rigil turned to find Eagan's lips slanted with irony. "So. You're a runaway servant now?" Eagan said.

"Isemios's wit, don't start." Rigil ripped Myvick's hat off. A few fat drops of rain splattered on the ground, kicking up a peaty scent. "I was sixteen. She jumped to that conclusion when we met, and I allowed it. Foolishly, granted, but I certainly never intended for it to carry on this long."

Eagan chuckled. "Would that I could be with you when you tell her." When Rigil didn't answer, too busy staring at the wall she'd disappeared over, Eagan added, "She will be fine. Trust Arman."

"I gave Arman reason to take her from me once. I won't do it again."

Rigil felt Eagan's gaze hanging on him, almost black in the dusk. "Remarkable," his brother said. "I've heard you preach Arman's grace to countless broken men, Rigil, always with just the right words. Why, then, do you still talk of Arman as if He's leering at *you* over a citadel board?"

Rigil had no time to reply before a spray of pebbles burst out from around the corner, followed by four men marked with that combination of scars, ale stains, and steel that typefied Meneton's unsavory class.

He had never been more grateful for an interruption.

Rigil took in faces, weighing builds and weapons and tics. That one with the cruel slash of a grin had to be a slaver. That one with the twitching hands, a pickpocket. That one with the broad shoulders and flat, passionless face, a thug for hire.

"Not much to look at, this lot." The lead man, a weedy creature with protruding front teeth, stepped forward in a doublet that may once have been deep blue. With almost reptilian slowness, he slid a cutlass from his belt. "But if Nedir wants a knight, I don't mind giving him two. And an ugly Hamonayan while I'm about it." He grinned, his teeth shooting in different directions as if trying to escape him. "That's right, Kingsguard. We know all about your scarred friend, and I'd bet my weight in silvers she can't be far."

The sky over the alley flickered white with bursts of lightning, there and gone. There again, then gone, like the prayer flickering in Rigil's head. *Arman, do not let me fail.*

"Since when do the men of Meneton bow and scrape for scribblers from Har Sha'ar?" Rigil asked.

The twitchy pickpocket was tossing his knife from hand to hand, but the buck-toothed leader only chuckled, digging something from between his incisors with a blackened fingernail. He turned to his thug. "Nearly to the harbor now. Go. Cut her off."

Odd. The way he spoke, as if he were tracking Sethe's location in real time.

How could he know?

As the broad-shouldered mercenary darted back the way they'd come, the leader added to Rigil, "Come easy or come half dead. Your choice."

In reply, Rigil drew his sword, falling into a fighting stance beside Eagan and checking that his mental shields were up. Karpos or no karpos, if this man was some kind of bloodvoicer capable of watching Sethe in the Veil, Rigil would use every defense he had.

Cutlasses *shing*ed. Cudgels thumped scar-knotted hands. The pickpocket fluttered his thumb and ring finger together as if preparing to pluck the heart from Rigil's chest.

There was no first strike. No true beginning. One moment, it was a standoff, and then with a whistle of steel through dusk, the sons of Zerah Rock were battling for their lives.

The slaver swung a cudgel at Rigil's head, and he blocked it with one arm, producing a shoot of pain he didn't have time to feel. He grabbed the cudgel, smashed it into the man's face, and spun to block a wild swing from the skinny leader's dagger. Strangely, not until he had kicked that man back a step and caught his balance on the wall did he realize that most of his maneuvers had come not from the Kingsguard or the Mârad but from the man beside him. Sir Eagan Elk.

Eagan fought like a cornered lion, thrusting and darting and cutting as he held his ground against the jittery pickpocket's spastic maneuvers. But when a feint drew him in, he left his side unguarded. Rigil lunged too late to stop the sneering leader from piercing Eagan above one knee. Eagan grunted, staggering a little as his leg threatened to buckle, but recovering quickly. His attacker's buck-toothed sneer became a curse as he found Eagan ready for what should have been a finishing blow.

By the time Eagan managed to fend off that attack, Rigil was backed into a corner, sliding on old fishbones and trying to hold off the slaver's explosive swings. Othvold Myvick's coat had taken a gash along the shoulder, spewing threads like broken sinews as rain bled down the alley walls.

"Rigil!" Eagan had let the wiry ringleader slip behind him and was now facing blows on both sides. Rigil blocked the slaver's next blow with his sword hand and punched with his left, buying enough time to lunge sideways and slit the hamstrings of Eagan's attacker from behind.

The man went down with a scream, leaving Rigil and Eagan with an open route to the alley.

They took it.

They hadn't reached the first bend when a dozen men poured out of an alley ahead of them. More blades. More fists. A solid wall of men, with the twitchy pickpocket and the slaver closing in behind.

Nowhere to go. Nothing but chaos, a shout of recognition, three weapons diving toward Rigil's chest in the hands of three Menetonians.

Rigil had his sword up to meet whichever blade found him first, but the blow never fell. Rabid shouts had melted into silence.

A very eerie silence.

Sword hanging lamely in midair, Rigil found himself staring not at a swarm of angry mercenaries but at a sea of blank faces. Some were smiling, some slack-faced; all stood eerily still. Two dozen rabid bounty hunters gazed into nothing.

Eagan released a long, shaky breath.

Rigil stared at him. "Are you—"

"Later." Eagan spoke through gritted teeth. "Need to concentrate."

No one stirred or even blinked as Rigil wove after Eagan through the half-lowered blades, passing close enough to smell ale on many a thug's greasy clothes. He had to forcibly shove past some of them, all but holding his breath until they broke onto the other side and backpedaled to the next thoroughfare, then the next.

Only then, five streets and two squares later, did Eagan break their silence. "That," he panted as they collapsed against a sandstone arch, "felt wrong. Far too much like what Nedir might have done."

Rigil sagged against the arch, a meager shelter from the rain. "How long can you hold them like that?"

"Tired as I am, not long. Some of them may already be coming to their senses, which means this is where I must leave you. Someone must bring news of Nedir's plans to Armonguard, and I know Meneton well enough to lead the hunters off." Eagan paused, hair dangling over his forehead. Blood had seeped through the puncture above his knee, and more was darkening a small slit along his ribs, almost invisible against his crimson tunic. "We have more than enough to warrant Nedir's arrest, but not before that shipment goes out. I know three days seems like a great deal of time, but—"

"Don't dally." Rigil wiped his sword on his tunic, sheathed it. "Understood."

"I gave the dried karpos to Mezaedo. Don't forget to take it daily, all of you. Knowing what Miss Sedhani can do, Nedir will not let her slip away easily."

Sethe. Lightness, what were the odds that she hadn't already run off with his coin?

"She is right, you know." Smiling, Eagan rested his head on the arch. "Hamonah is a place of pirates, not knights."

Rigil blinked. "Are you advising me to steal a boat?"

"I am suggesting that this mission may require you to shed Sir Rigil Barak the Irreproachable for something slightly less ostentatious. And, dare I say it, more genuine."

"Ah." Rigil gritted his teeth. "I'm being disingenuous."

"You are afraid to fail a woman you care for," Eagan said. "That, I understand. Oh, admit it, Rigil. All these years as the heir of Zerah Rock, few visits home and even fewer serious courtships—such things don't go unnoticed in Er'Rets and you know it. You are becoming quite the source of gossip among the noble ladies. All this time, I thought Tazeem was the reason you had stayed away, but there is more to it, isn't there? Your history with this woman . . ."

"Eagan."

"Fine." Eagan bunched his lips. "Let's say it is Tazeem. Rigil, you cannot keep letting guilt rule you like this. Zerah Rock is yours by right, and one foolish boyhood mistake will not change that."

"Father has made it abundantly clear that I am his heir in name alone," Rigil said. "Until I can return to Zerah Rock a worthier man than when I left, I see no point in wasting his time."

Eagan's blue eyes rounded for a too-innocent expression, all at odds with the signs of battle on his face. "And what exactly would make you a worthier man? Righting a past wrong? Reconciliation with the woman who seems to see through you even better than I can?"

Rigil tipped his head back to growl at the dripping arch overhead. "For the last time, this is not about Sethe." Half true. "Once, it may have been different, but I am not the same person I was then. Besides—" He chewed the words for a moment, reluctant to make them real. "She doesn't know Arman."

"I wouldn't be so sure," Eagan said. "Suffering has hardened her mind, but I think her heart is reaching for Him. I didn't mention this before, but when I visited her in the Veil, she was reciting a hymn based on the Book of Life in her battle against Nedir. Appealing to the Father God and Câan, His son, freer of captives, *who had walked through death's door willingly and walked out with the key to unlock every shackle.* Or something of that kind."

All Rigil's poise melted in the time it took to recall those words, exactly where he'd heard them before. "I taught her that. When we were young and she asked about . . . Lightness, I thought she was teasing me."

He'd taught her to pray once, told her of Câan the son of Arman, who had laid down His life for Er'Rets and risen to free her from all the cages she so feared. He had littered Arman's gates with petitions for her scarred and skittish heart. But that was before he'd lost her on the road from Melas to Zerah Rock as a boy. Before he'd failed to protect her, broken her trust, and left her with more scars to bear alone.

Was it possible? Could this be more than a chance to right his long-ago wrong? Oh, Arman, if there was any hope of a future with Sethe in it . . .

Eagan's face remained thoughtful, reflecting the last of the light. "Whatever you taught her, she has not forgotten, the mark of a heart that *wants* to believe, if nothing else. Either way, Arman knew what He was doing when He brought you two together after all this time." He held out an arm, a tired grin lifting one half of his face. "I like her, Rigil. Arman could do great things with that fierce heart of hers in Zerah Rock. Trust Him. And for Lightness' sake, *tell her* who you are."

Trust Arman. With a lame smile, Rigil clasped his brother's forearm, the world tilting momentarily with the realization that for once, they were on equal footing. Brother to brother, not man to boy. "The harbor is close, I take it?"

"Just follow the slope. And Rigil?" Eagan's grip tightened on Rigil's arm. Rain dripped from the arch. "Our father did his best. You know that, don't you?"

Rigil pulled free. "I know I've never been on the right side of the way he sees the world."

"*Two kinds of men*, yes." Strange how when Eagan spoke their father's words, something noble almost seemed to glimmer behind them. "In fairness, though, he was right about life. It *is* a test. His only mistake was convincing us we could pass it on our own merit."

"Aye, well," Rigil said, "Father never did quite grasp the concept of grace, did he?"

Half open and all-seeing, Eagan's eyes drilled through him. "Do any of us?"

Thunder drummed on Meneton like boots on polished manor floors. Rigil sighed. "I have missed your words of wisdom, Brother."

"No, you haven't."

"True. I haven't. But I'm grateful all the same." Rigil bowed with a flourish.

"Lightness." Eagan whistled. "Are you certain you never met Myvick?"

As Rigil stepped out into the drizzle, sword swinging at his side, Eagan clapped his palm to his fist, a last salute that made Rigil's skin prickle as he walked away. It was a Zerah Rock salute. Unique to the family, generations old, and never aimed at equals.

Only lords.

CHAPTER TWELVE
SETHE

HAMONAYANS CALLED THESE BOATS *rikohs*. Light-hulled, single-sail knives that sliced through waves, they were built for no more than six or seven crewmen, stretching twenty paces from bow to stern with a short ladder separating the quarterdeck from the main. No galley, no bunks, just a tiny captain's cabin and a hold made for bending all the rules of maritime law. A dozen of the little smuggling boats had clogged Sethe's home port, some wrecks, some seaworthy, all someone else's. So this was nothing new.

Hidden by twilight and drizzling rain, Sethe treaded water in the Seybah River, ducking every time a searching lantern swung on the nearby docks. How Nedir's men had managed to arrive *ahead* of her was a mystery. Was he tracking her in the Veil somehow, despite the karpos? Men called to one another across the dark docks, checking each boat for stowaways. Sinking to her nose in the water, Sethe edged along the hull of the rikoh, watching for a handhold.

"How many times have you done this?" a voice chimed in suddenly.

And here she'd almost managed to forget about her Jaelportian *nanny*.

"What part of *not a sound* did you miss?" Sethe snapped to Mezaedo.

Neck-deep in the river beside her, the scrawny Jaelportian frowned. "What was wrong with the first two ships we checked?"

"They were fishing boats."

"So?"

"So they belong to honest men trying to make an honest living." And Sethe would rather avoid *that* lecture from Sir Rigil the Saint.

The stealing part, he'd just have to live with. Any chance of *paying* for passage to Hamonah had flickered out the moment Sethe and Mezaedo had arrived at the teeming docks to find that every captain on this river was already looking out for a scarred Hamonayan. That left two options: wait to be caught and shipped to Nedir, or offend *Sir* Rigil's delicate sensibilities with some unavoidable piracy.

The third possibility—taking off with Rigil's coin and lying low until things settled down—had crossed her mind once and only once before she'd dismissed it out of hand. Call it a thief's honor, but there was some trust a person shouldn't break. Ugh. As usual, he wasn't playing fair. Treating her like an ally instead of a flight risk, almost like he *knew* she wouldn't betray him.

"This is a Hamonayan boat," she said at last. "Most likely stolen to begin with and almost certainly a smuggling vessel, which makes this a crown-sanctioned confiscation, not a theft."

Confiscation. One of Rigil's favorite words back in Melas, along with *repossession* and *redistribution of goods*.

"So you've never done this before?" Mezaedo whispered as the rain began to fall harder, hammering the water around them. "I thought you were from Hamonah."

"Which makes me a pirate?"

"Which makes you a pirate *expert*." Swimming with one hand,

Mezaedo shoved hair off his forehead. "Like how I'm an expert on climbing ships. My eleventh mistress used to make me scrape hulls for one of her powders. Laughing dust, I think, which, ironically, is not *nearly* as fun as it sounds." He reached up to point out a spot on the hull, droplets from his arm making soft metallic plinks in the river. "See that crack in the pitch? Catchable as it gets."

Sethe squinted at the spot, then at the squire, all shadows and shimmers off too-big eyes. What was he, fifteen? "You were a slave?"

Still treading with one arm, he plunged the other hand underwater and brought up a palmful of blacknuts. He'd tied his spice pouch tight around his neck to keep it above water, but still, the spice he'd dumped over the nuts now had to be at least a little damp. He ate a seasoned nut, then held the rest out to her. A peace offering?

Fine. Taking one, Sethe caught sight of the white marks dotting his knuckles, the ones Nedir had noticed. "What are the scars from?" she asked before slipping the wet blacknut between her lips.

He dumped the rest of the nuts into his mouth and answered offhandedly, like a reflex, "Raving monkey disease."

A secret, then. Fair enough. The spice on the blacknut hit the back of her throat, sharper than Hamonayan curry and not nearly as sweet. She winced, the river sliding between her treading fingers. "Ugh. What *is* that?"

Mezaedo licked his teeth clean, the water lapping at his throat. "My eleventh mistress liked to experiment. Pretty sure this stuff was supposed to make me taller."

Sethe snorted, reached for the chink in the hull and caught it with one hand. As she pulled herself out of the river, water rushed noisily to fill the space she'd left behind. She signed for Mezaedo to wait. Taking the cue, he sank lower, holding his pouch above water.

No sound on deck. A good sign. Or maybe a very bad one.

Catching the decorative border beneath the rail, Sethe reached up to grab the rail itself, careful to peer onto the deck before she dared swing a leg over. Under the mast, a seagull was waddling about. That would come in handy when it came time to tell Rigil where they were.

In any plan, there were bound to be variables. Screeching cats. Keys that didn't fit their locks. Even one crewman too many could mean the difference between success and failure. But the deck of the rikoh was empty. Finally, a bit of *luck*.

First stop, the helmsman's quarters.

Sethe's bare feet touched the deck like the wind. Silent, leaving nothing behind. The rikoh was too small for a full stern passage, which meant that the door to the helmsman's quarters was barely taller than Sethe. She pressed her ear to it, listening for life inside. Two boats over, someone shouted that another vessel was clear.

Sethe eased the door open and found a tiny cabin flickering in the light of a single candle on a desk. Next to it, the sleeping captain looked dead, cheek to desk, mouth open, rum steaming on his breath. His filthy beard and matted hair matched the map he was slobbering on—dull, greasy white. Not Hamonayan, then. From the east, most likely. Or the north.

Not important. What mattered was the red-and-gold eel tattooed into the flesh between the man's right thumb and forefinger. The same red eel entwined the knife lying next to his hand. Not just a tattoo, then, but a signature. A very powerful man's very permanent mark.

This man belonged to Othvold Myvick.

Sethe had slipped the captain's dagger into her belt almost before she felt her fingers move, but when she turned to leave, she nearly crashed into Mezaedo Chevyah.

"Scuddy—" Sethe bit down on a shout, shoving him out of the cabin as the captain moaned in his sleep. "I told you to wait!"

"Sirrig would want me to stay close." Mezaedo's drenched hair could have been a pile of seaweed on his head as he squinted at her, a spindly little dustbeetle sent to . . . what? Protect her?

Gripping the knife, Sethe shoved the squire toward the hatch. "Keep watch. I'm going below."

The companionway ladder was somewhere between a true ladder and a staircase, lethally steep on a small vessel like this, where every bit of space belowdecks had to count. Experienced as she was, Sethe didn't need to hold the hatch opening for balance as she made her way down, the rungs creaking like the bones of old men.

The cramped space below held four hammocks—none occupied—and nearly a dozen battered crates of what could only be contraband. Squinting in the light of the lanterns swinging from the ceiling, Sethe left the ladder to wander among the cargo and found herself lingering with the crates, a hand resting on the largest one. Old wood, slightly red stained. Just large enough for a fifteen-year-old girl, just small enough to make her spine ache with memory.

Lightning flashed through the hatch. Between the creaking hull and the rain dribbling from the ceiling through the deck, Sethe didn't hear the footsteps until shadows crossed the grate overhead. Shadows with voices, slurred and Hamonayan.

". . . enough to pay off Myvick, to buy our own ship!"

"That much for an ugly 'amonayan?"

"Who cares? Go below and check."

Sethe spun, putting her back to the crates as shadows moved toward the hatch. The box beneath her hands was scabbed with rough splinters. Easy enough to open. She'd done it once.

Sweat sprang to her fingertips, seeping through the wood. *Four walls. No light. No air.*

No choice.

Locking her teeth, Sethe pried her fingers under the lid. A waft of spice rose from the slats, and she covered her mouth against a gag. Why did it have to be a crate?

Then a hand seized Sethe's wrist. She nearly hacked it off with one swing of the captain's knife until she saw who it was.

Mezaedo Chevyah drew a finger across his lips, then tugged her behind the crates as the first pirate's boots struck the hold.

The rikoh whispered and crooned around them, rank with the musk of the cargo and Mezaedo's spice, still gritty on her tongue from the nut she'd eaten. Hunkered between crates, the boy kept a hand on his sword and an eye on the smuggler rummaging near the hammocks.

"Well, tiko," Sethe whispered, "you're stealthy. I'll give you that."

Hand wrapped around his spice pouch, he darted a summer-bright grin at her and whispered so softly she barely caught the tails of his voice, "My sixth master used me to spy on his wife. She had moldy good ears, but I've got moldy soft feet."

The sailor lurched his way through the cargo, edging nearer. Mezaedo reached for his belt and the bag of karpos tied there. But when he handed Sethe a handful of karpos bits, they went straight into her pocket.

Not yet, she mouthed. Reaching out for possible hosts, she found the unclaimed mind of the seagull on the deck above her head. By the time she managed to send the gull flapping across the docks, the pirate had wended his way to their corner and was prying open crates one by one.

Sethe glanced at Mezaedo and mouthed, *Stay down.*

As the sailor lifted the lid of the crate she was hiding behind, Sethe adjusted her grip on the knife and jumped up swinging.

The first thud was a jeweled eel meeting the man's temple. The second, that same man hitting the deck.

Sethe vaulted the crate and landed hard atop the sailor, a knee on his throat as he struggled to rise, lashes fluttering over dark-gold irises. For a second, she snagged on those eyes, the long nose, and the lazy eyelids now springing open with something like recognition. That expression, like he *knew* her from somewhere. And why did he seem familiar?

All the more reason.

His canvas belt would work well enough as a binding, but Sethe had barely managed to rip it off his waist when a heavy hand fell on the back of her neck.

"Look what the tide washed in."

If they'd been slightly more drunk, Sethe might have been able to put the knife to use before one of them yanked it away.

"Oy! Isn't this the captain's knife?" One Hamonayan handed the blade to another, who fumbled it in clumsy hands. It struck the deck, useless.

Three pairs of hands tore her off the lazy-eyed sailor, but only one man held her hands behind her back and wrapped rope around them. He held her close, his mouth in her hair.

"You're a pretty stroke of luck, aren't you?"

One of the others, a short Hamonayan with a black ring through his nose, laughed around the mouth of a bottle. "She ain't a pretty anything. Drown and drag me, look at that *face*."

Four of them. Three Hamonayans and, judging by the accent behind her, one Jaelportian. In the lanternlight, amber irises and dark skin took on an orange flush. Glancing at the stack of crates she'd leaped out from behind, Sethe caught two pinpricks of light bouncing off another set of eyes. Mezaedo.

Stay where you are, tiko, she commanded, though he wouldn't hear her through the karpos unless he consciously opened his mind to her, the way Sethe had with Eagan. Like normal shielding, but much stronger. And considering Mezaedo Chevyah's lack of skill in that department, the karpos was definitely for the best.

The pinpricks disappeared. Shifting to her seagull's view, Sethe watched a blond figure stride across the darkening docks, torchlight licking like flames at the hem of his ridiculous red coat. A streak of something white and wet had dripped down one of his shoulders, and the coat barely hid the Land's End sword in his belt. The red cloth was ripped in places, like he'd come from a knife fight.

Still, he was here. Sethe's next breath came out shaky with relief. It wasn't too late. They could still save this.

Back in the hold, one of the other Hamonayans, thin as a bottleneck but holding much more rum, ran sweaty fingers along Sethe's scars. She barely kept from shivering. Or spitting in his face. "What's Nedir want with her?"

The Jaelportian finished tying Sethe's hands with a whorl knot, of all things. "Don't know," he said. "But for a price like this, she's got to be something special."

Sethe kept her face flat as she dug her thumbs into the weakest point of the knot around her wrists. When the Jaelportian's hands began sliding down her waist, she swallowed the bile gushing up her throat and poured herself into her fingers, the hemp around her hands. *So close.*

With the karpos in her blood, her thoughts were well protected. It would take a bloodvoicer more skilled than Mezaedo to break through without her permission, but if she could be selective, open her mind just to him like she had with Eagan . . .

Tentatively easing up the wall around her mind, she found his consciousness waiting there, jittery as a candlewick.

Missethe? Mezaedo's thoughts sounded shaky. *Missethe, can you hear me?*

Sethe's bloodvoice was rock solid. *Stay down, tiko.*

Bottleneck waved a hand in front of her face. "She got sand for wits or what?"

"Keep it down." The one with the nose ring watched the hatch. "Half of Meneton's hunting for her. We want the reward, we gotta slip out quiet-like. Someone oughtta wake the captain."

"Why?" The Jaelportian's nose was in Sethe's hair now, his

breath warm on her neck. "Goras go further with four men than five. Anyway, what Laban don't know won't kill us."

The idea swelled between them like Sethe's lungs when the Jaelportian's lips touched her jaw. Mezaedo's mind was a white-hot jumble. Sethe focused on the knot. Two more loops . . .

"Ho, on board!" A new voice cut through the pattering rain, a new shadow crossing the hold through the slats in the deck. Through her seagull, Sethe had a bird's-eye view of the blond figure vaulting over the gunwale from the gangplank with a flash of red cloth and gold embroidery. No hat, though. And was that blood on his coat? "Is this the welcome a generous patron can expect from his beneficiaries?"

The smugglers froze, gazing up as rain dripped from the hold ceiling. Nose Ring reached for his belt knife. "Who's there?"

Sethe mentally begged Rigil to keep his voice down. Waking Captain Laban was the *last* thing they needed.

Rigil's shadow stopped over the hatch. "Whose city do you think you are moored in, men?"

That got them moving. The Jaelportian hissed for the first sailor with the droopy eyelids to hide Sethe, then hurried to the ladder. Obediently, that sailor grabbed Sethe's arm. He seemed to have recovered from Sethe's attempt to jump him, smiling through those sleepy eyes as he tugged her behind his back and doused her in another whiff of sweat and Hamonayan rum. Was that why he seemed familiar? Just another Hamonayan pirate?

"Captain Myck!" the Jaelportian said. "We thought you'd been taken at Armonguard. Trial, prison, all that."

Before the man could scramble up the steep stairway, Rigil's boot appeared on the top step.

"Trial, perhaps. Prison? Please. Not even Ice Island could hold me." With a flourish, Rigil descended another few steps, then hopped down the rest of the way, his coat flaring behind him as lightning lit up the hold.

Their eyes connected across the space. His, orange in the lanternlight but blue in the centers, like the hottest part of a flame.

For his first two steps toward her, Rigil was still a knight, his posture rigid and his steps a march. The next two steps were Rigil from Melas—the Rigil who wore confidence in the loose slope of his shoulders and the smart heel-toe of his boots on deck.

By step five, his gait morphed into a swaggering glide adorned with something extra, a flourish so subtle she couldn't place where he was adding it. He wore embroidery like a king, the rakish sweep of his hair sharpening the clean-shaven half smile on his lips.

That smile. Smugger than usual, and part of an act, but still. *That* smile.

So. He hadn't left everything in Melas.

"What is this?" Rigil stopped before her, rain dripping from his hair.

"She's the one Nedir's after, Captain. The ugly Hamonayan."

It took a moment, but Sethe caught it—a danger in the set of his jaw, the too-wide curve of his nostrils. He leaned in, pretending to study her, and set one finger under her chin to raise her face to the light. The lazy-eyed sailor was still holding her arm, and the ghost of the Jaelportian's lips still clung to her neck, but at that touch from Rigil, just a knuckle under her chin, Sethe's gaze snapped up to meet his like it had a will of its own.

His gaze pinned questions to her skin, one hand brushing her arm as if to secretly steady her. Only when Sethe gave the tiniest of nods did he pivot on one heel to face the others.

"Well, I suppose you are not entirely useless, then." Rigil tugged grandly on his cuffs, probably to distract them from the rip in one shoulder. Was he hurt? "Tribute received, men. Now, off my boat."

The smugglers blinked. "What? But, Captain, that bounty—"

"Was for an ugly Hamonayan." Rigil flicked a hand at her as if he couldn't be bothered with a grander gesture. "If I were you, I'd take a look in the glass and lie low for a good long while." To Sethe's surprise, the Hamonayan holding her arm made a tiny whiffling sound, like a stifled laugh. Rigil went on. "Now, be off, unless you'd rather join your usual cargo. Slave labor sells for a premium, and I could use another coat."

A ripple of mutters passed between them, too low for Sethe to hear. Apparently, none of them had ever met their sponsor. That, or Rigil was making one *scud* of a performance.

"Still no?" Rigil smoothed his rain-dappled lapels. "Allow me to sail it straight. I've known that you lot haven't been performing to my standards for some time, but did I cut you loose? Nay, I gave Laban the benefit of the doubt. I continued sponsoring your voyages, paying your wages." Rigil pressed a hand to his chest. "I'm a generous man. Benevolent, even."

"'Course you are, Captain."

"Zitheos bless you for it!"

Rigil's face remained stone. "To be sure, for skimming profits, I could cut out your tongues and feed them to a tanniyn." He tilted his head, weighing that option on invisible scales. "I could also skin you alive. Less efficient, more entertaining."

Bottleneck's knees actually wobbled. "Captain?"

"Chin up. You'll keep your lives. I shall even make it worth your while. Here." Rigil produced a coin purse from up his sleeve and tossed it at the Jaelportian's feet. Gold skittered out, rolling across the planks.

Sethe's jaw slacked, and she glanced down at her pocket, suddenly sure it was empty. When had he taken that coin purse off her? Unless . . . oh. The touch. The knuckle under her chin, the steadying hand on her elbow and hovering by her waist. Had she really fallen for such basic sleight of hand?

Leave it to him to see *this* as a good time to show off. "Now it's a matter of business," Rigil said. "If you're still on deck after I count ten heartbeats, I shall be forced to show my less generous side."

Shock pulsed through the foursome. "But what about Captain Laban?"

"Leave Laban to me."

Take the bait, Sethe begged. *Just go.*

The Jaelportian didn't look convinced, his lips pursed in a way that made Sethe's throat itch where he'd kissed her. But he picked up the coins and edged toward the ladder, the others following suit, including Lazy Eyes. *That* one gave Sethe a backward glance before he left, and there it was again. That twinge of recognition.

Rigil followed them up, taking the steps two at a time and hardly seeming to notice the steep incline. "Swiftly, men. I've been known to change my mind on a whim, and wouldn't you know it? I'm feeling unpredictable just now."

Not until the hold emptied did Sethe slip the ropes from her wrists, flitting to her seagull's point of view to follow the men on deck. Mezaedo popped up from behind the crate but had no chance to speak.

Up on deck, unnoticed by Rigil or the rest of the crew, the door to the captain's cabin was creaking open.

Captain Laban had rejoined the world of the living.

Rigil had his hands full herding the sailors off the deck, so Sethe scooped up the red eel knife and scurried up the steps and into the quarterdeck passage, blade out. She met Captain Laban as he stepped out of his quarters, the front of his reddish-brown doublet soaked through with something sourer and lumpier than rum. He blinked at her, bloodshot eyes dipping to the knife. *His* knife.

"Oy, girl." He gave her a rank smile. "Didn't that face of yours teach you not to play with sharp things?"

Sethe set the dagger above his belt. "Don't move. Don't talk."

"That's right," Rigil crowed out on deck, making Sethe glance through her seagull's eyes. "Enjoy Meneton. Oh, and drinks on me." A metallic flash, then a white splash in dark water. That would be Rigil's signature coin toss, usually saved for those he outwitted. "Let no one say that Captain Myck isn't generous."

Sethe all but *felt* Laban's blood heat through the knife, and she hurried to shift back into her own senses before he roared, "Myck, my rotting teeth!"

The punch came from nowhere. A meaty fist to her temple, a burst of pain. Sethe saw stars and tasted blood and took a long moment to realize she had crumpled to the deck, the captain's shadow crossing above her as he ran into the rain.

"Liar!" Laban shouted. "Myck's in prison, boy, and you ain't him!"

"No?" That was Rigil.

Peeling herself off the deck, Sethe could picture him even without her seagull's help. Unruffled, unshakable, unfairly striking in that red coat.

"That's quite the accusation, Captain," he said. "Willing to wager your life on it?"

"I'm willing to wager yours."

By the time Sethe stepped out of the cramped stern passage and onto the open deck, the sky was pelting rain in steel-colored shards, wind drowning out the clash of blades. Under the mast, Rigil was trading violent blows with Laban, still using the sword from Land's End. He ducked the captain's swinging cutlass and repaid it with a hard combination of his own, a graceful specter in stolen clothes. Tides, he really had become a Kingsguard knight.

"Mezaedo!" she shouted.

The boy's sodden head popped up through the hatch. Gulls screeched, wheeling around the mast like vultures, underwings lit by the harbor lights and the torches of six Menetonians pounding down the docks toward them. Six Menetonians led by four smugglers: Lazy Eyes. Bottleneck. Nose Ring. Jaelport.

Sethe severed off as many fragments as she could, then thrust them into the Veil just as the men reached the gangway.

The world exploded with seagulls.

Screeching, diving, tearing, gouging, the birds converged on Laban, on the Meneton men and the pirates, on Mezaedo and Rigil fighting for their lives as the rain fell like tacks. Sethe stood in the center of it all, a bird in the eye of a storm, wielding every beak, wing, and talon. Splashes announced several of their opponents diving over the rail, Lazy Eyes among them. Lightning struck nearby. Someone shouted, but not Sethe.

She didn't flinch. Not when a gull hit the deck in pieces. Not when Nose Ring fought through the birds, cutlass outstretched, snarl rabid. Sethe was a feather in a hurricane. No, she *was* the hurricane.

The man's curses were lost in the downpour, but steel still flashed in his hand.

A hundred beaks dove for him, scrabbling and tearing, shredding flesh wherever they found it. Until he fell and didn't rise.

Unexpectedly, the boat heaved beneath Sethe. She staggered back and squinted at the riverbank. Were they moving?

Mezaedo stood with the sliced mooring line in hand, bleeding from one shoulder, rain running down his face in grimy rivers. Nose Ring lay at his feet, torn to shreds by gulls. Pity. It was so hard to lift bloodstains from wood.

"Mezaedo!" A blur in a red coat was already hauling up the anchor, hand over hand. Rigil gestured at the unmanned helm, Laban nowhere to be seen. Her gulls must have driven him to jump off with the others. "Starboard tack!"

The squire tossed the severed line aside. "Starfish *what?*"

So much for that. Sethe hurried up another short ladder to the quarterdeck. Onshore, some Menetonians were commandeering another ship, throwing sailors overboard and drawing up the anchor to give chase. Or to try.

Sethe seized the helm and slid the wheel notch by notch to the right.

Rigil and Mezaedo had the anchor up and set to unfurling the sails—dangerous in this wind, but they needed all the speed they could get. Wind caught the half-reefed canvas. A rush of momentum tugged the rikoh toward the sea waiting beyond the river mouth. So close, Sethe could smell it. Salt. Salvation. Open water.

A flash of lightning illuminated Rigil on the main deck, hair plastered to his head, his grip on the sheet confident and almost violent as he hauled the sail into position. Darkness followed. The Menetonians were pulling from shore, but Sethe had a hundred pairs of wings at her command. She felt like she'd regained a lost limb.

And yet, there was a wrongness. A prickle behind her temples, a gentle pressure in the back of her mind, a whisper growing by the moment.

Sedhani . . .

Nedir? *Now*? Sethe dug a piece of dried karpos from her pocket, the pressure on her mind rushing toward pain. Nedir was quickly oozing across the surface of her thoughts, testing her defenses.

Sedhani . . .

She set the leathery wedge on her tongue, embracing the sourness as she bent the seagulls' will to hers.

It didn't take much to ruin a sail. Sethe didn't release the gulls until the enemy's canvas hung in tatters. By then, the karpos was already clogging her mind. She felt a burst of something from Nedir. Frustration?

"All right, Missethe!" Mezaedo was halfway up to the quarterdeck, climbing the steep, short staircase with his hands *and* feet, ladder-style. He let go of the top rung to punch the air. "Why couldn't you do that sooner?"

Sagging against the helm, Sethe shoved two more pieces of karpos into her mouth, begging the fruit to work faster, begging that poisonous whisper to retreat. "Arman, if you're listening, if you've *ever* been listening . . ."

Sedhani.

The prayer had more desperation than faith behind it, but the pressure of Nedir's mind began to fade as the karpos took hold.

Safe. For now.

"Sedhani?"

Sethe jolted at the name that somehow seemed to belong to Nedir more than her. But no. Nedir was gone. It was Rigil this time.

Rigil. He seemed mostly unhurt except for another cut on his arm, splitting Myvick's coat right through a swath of flowery embroidery. Maroon stains had seeped through the fabric, and one of his sleeves was torn from the rest of the coat, sagging down one arm and exposing another shallow cut on his shoulder. He might even have brought that gash with him to the docks.

Following her gaze, Rigil winced at his shoulder, the ripped tunic, and even more ripped skin showing through the coat's broken seam. "I'll have to stitch it," he said sadly. Talking about the wound probably. Maybe.

Moon shadows traced every crease of his face as he bent to touch her shoulder with slightly bloody fingers.

Sethe grabbed the spokes of the helm. "Did we just . . . ?"

"Steal a boat?" He chuckled wearily. "If Kingsguard knights have diplomatic immunity, I believe I just used the last of ours. Thank you for saving my life, by the way. Laban very nearly had me before your birds drove him overboard."

"How did you know where to find us?" Sethe asked.

He flicked a streak of white droppings off one shoulder, wrinkling his nose. "I got your bird. Please tell me you've taken more karpos."

"I'm fine." And she was. Now. Shouting over the gale hid the tremor in her voice. "But you were right. Nedir was waiting in the Veil when the karpos wore off. His men were ready for us at the docks too. How did he know where we would be and when?"

Rigil combed a hand through his tangled hair. "An educated guess?"

"Or he was watching us through someone's eyes."

"Possible. His men did seem to have information they shouldn't, almost as if someone were feeding it to them." Again, he touched her arm. Again, she noticed. Here he was, bleeding from half a dozen places, but someone else always mattered more. "But are you *all right?*" he asked.

The boat rocked and creaked, drawn by the lure of the sea. As storms went, it could be a bad one. Maybe she shouldn't be smiling. "Are you?"

His smile was too strained for Othvold Myvick but didn't belong on a Kingsguard knight either, not even a drenched one with gull feathers in his hair.

"If I didn't know better, Miss Sedhani," he said, "I would think you rather enjoyed that."

Sethe looped an arm over the helm, something almost smile-like tugging on the scars around her bad eye. All these years out of their rhythm, and all of a second to find it again? "Think whatever you like." She stepped back, leaving the wheel to him. "And for tides' sake, call me Sethe."

CHAPTER THIRTEEN
RIGIL

THE SOFT PINK OF DAWN WAS CREEPING down the rikoh's sail when Rigil coaxed the vessel through the Cela Inlet, the coast visible off the starboard bow now that the storm had passed. To port, there was nothing but grey waves and moody clouds, a horizon holding a grudge.

If the sky wanted to best a son of Zerah Rock, it would have to try harder than that.

"So. Sir Rigil can sail."

As usual, Sethe alighted soundlessly beside him, her palms raw from the rigging and her chin-length hair windblown. Her voice still carried traces of the shift she'd taken sleeping, a shift Rigil had spent patching up his few wounds and expelling a seagull-torn corpse from the boat as respectfully as he could. Fatigue, however, was no reason to waste one of her good moods.

"You're quite the sailor yourself," he said as she put the helm between them. She had traces of karpos on her chapped lips. Seeing it brought back the tart aftertaste of the fruit he'd eaten that morning to protect his own mind.

She shrugged. "I've made a decent living of it. There's always a merchant willing to take on another sailor, so work at sea is easy to find. I stay with one merchant until the route gets dull, then I find another. Not a bad way to see the world, if you don't mind the stares. And making a pittance."

She must have seen something in his face—surprise, perhaps, or confusion—because her smirk turned jagged as she leaned back against the quarterdeck rail. "What, did you think I'd spent all this time cutting purses for crumbs?"

"Well, until you mentioned sailing with merchants in Meneton, I suppose I assumed . . ."

"That my life stopped when you left it? Hardly. By the time I found my way to Sitna after escaping Nedir's men that night, I was too starved to *think* of stealing. I begged every merchant in that harbor to hire me as a cabin girl, finally wore one of them down enough to take on a half-dead fifteen-year-old with no skills and a face full of scars." Sethe hopped onto the rail, her smile turning sharkish. "Turns out, I was born for sailing. Still, if I had kept cutting purses instead of trying to *better* myself with an honest living at sea, maybe Nedir wouldn't have caught wind of the last ship I was on and followed me to Melas."

Well, if she could joke about it, so could he. "So you admit that I have bettered myself?"

She pulled a face at him, her unmarred side twisting to match her scars. "Please. For all I know, you learned to sail in your secret life as a smuggler for the mantics of Cherem."

On his father's personal skiff, more like, attended by servants and with a valet standing by. "I think you'll find I'm a man of many talents," Rigil said. "Jousting, for instance."

"How practical."

"No less practical than a comprehensive knowledge of Tsaftown's precipitation patterns." When Sethe snorted, he added, "I had a tediously thorough education."

"Ah, right. Zerah Rock, where even servants learn their letters."

Servants. Isemios's wit, he could almost *feel* Eagan prodding at him from leagues away. A weak lie back then, it never should have dragged on this long. But here he was, reaching for a way out of it. *That reminds me, Sethe, I was never a runaway servant. I'm the heir of a noble house and lied to you about it. Care to be the next Lady Barak?*

Sethe had her eye closed, the cloudy dawn playing on her face. The same face in most ways, but harder, leaner, far less forgiving. Even more perfect than he remembered it.

The silence Rigil had barely noticed before took on substance now, wrapping his throat, squeezing. Urging him to say something that *wouldn't* send them spinning in opposite directions.

"I'm sorry," he heard himself say at last.

Her golden eye cracked. "For what?"

For failing you on the road to Zerah Rock. For leaving you to escape Nedir's men alone.

For lying to you.

"For asking the question you told me not to ask." Rigil clenched the helm, squeezing dread into the bone-smooth wood. "That night, on the road to Zerah Rock, how *did* you escape Nedir's men? I thought for certain they must have dragged you off, but I couldn't find their tracks in the dark, and then the rain . . ."

She let him trail away, let the silence drip like wax, let him begin to doubt whether he'd ever know the answer.

Finally, *finally*, Sethe let out a breath, running her tongue over the points of her teeth as if bracing herself for a taste she'd rather avoid. "By the time I realized you were gone," she began, "I had all six men on my tail. One grabbed me, the rest closed in like vultures, and I thought, *This is it. Back to Nedir.*" She let go of the rail to rub one arm, as if the touch of one of Nedir's hunters still lingered on her skin. "I didn't understand what my fragments could do then, how to control them, and when that rat grabbed me and I felt the trap snap shut, I . . . *ugh*." She scrubbed her face.

"I don't even know what I did. Next thing I knew, there were six men on the ground, their minds floating into the Veil and leaving their bodies to rot."

Rigil blinked. "You stormed them? Pushed the souls out of six men at once?"

"I told myself it would be the first and last time." Sethe shoved her hair off her face, exposing her scars in all their tangled glory. "Nedir might have no problem turning people's minds to weapons, but I'm not him. I *won't* be like him. My freedom isn't worth that much."

That pulled something from Rigil's chest, a sound that fell somewhere between a sigh and a chuckle. She frowned at him. "What?"

"Just you, Miss Sethe." He smiled, if dimly. "I'm glad to see you are still entirely ignorant of your own selflessness."

Hooking her feet through the pickets, Sethe spoke to the top button on his coat—Myvick's coat. "Not selfless. Realistic. I stopped expecting this world to care about my freedom the day my mother sold me to Nedir for pocket coin."

Rigil blinked. "Your mother *sold* you? To Nedir? Lightness, is *that* how you first became his captive as a child?" Was she really telling him all this? It was about time.

She stretched her neck back and forth, choppy hair spilling first one way, then the other. "Don't sound so shocked. Desperate people do worse all the time. Nedir wanted bloodvoicers, my mother had one on hand. She gave me over to him, and he kept me locked up as a subject for his bloodvoicing experiments until I was fifteen."

Fifteen. "That was when you escaped to Melas. In the crate."

"Now the *crate*," Sethe went on, "was the easy bit. All I had to do was wait for some smuggler to make use of the cave beneath Nedir's fortress. The hardest part was trying not to starve on the journey to Melas, but one of the ship's boys, the surgeon's apprentice, I think, put out food and water for the cat every night. I *think* he did it for the cat. Part of me always wondered if he knew I was there and left it out for me." She lifted one shoulder, let it drop. "It got me to Melas. You know the rest."

What could he say to that? What could *anyone* say to that?

"I wasn't sure you'd remember how it was done, you know," she said suddenly, changing the subject so abruptly he nearly broke his neck trying to follow. "I imagine being a better Othvold Myvick than Othvold Myvick himself isn't something they teach in the Kingsguard."

Ah. His performance in Meneton. Rigil cocked his head. "Was that a compliment?"

"A question." Deftly avoiding Eagan's stitches, she touched her wounded ear. "You know what I've been doing all this time. What has *Sir* Rigil been up to since Melas? Other than earning a title, I mean."

"Sir Rigil." The deck pitched a little beneath him. "Not Keseel? Calling me that always used to amuse you."

"K'sil," she corrected, changing the emphasis slightly.

"You never did tell me what it means."

"You never earned the right to know."

For all the edge in her voice, this was a conversation, not a war, and any interest in the Kingsguard was progress. Now, if he could only find out how she felt about nobility.

Rigil leaned on the wheel, hooking his elbows on the spokes. His face itched where his beard was resurrecting with a vengeance, but he resisted the urge to scratch it, like he resisted the urge to look too closely at why he'd shaved it clean. "I have been with the Kingsguard since Prince Oren recruited me. When Darkness fell after King Axel's assassination, many knights sold their loyalties elsewhere, but I stayed on, mostly out of loyalty to the prince. In truth, I would have fought a war to put Oren on the throne long before the true heir came along, but King Gidon has my allegiance now. All the blood I can spare belongs to him."

"I can't see it." Sethe put her head off-kilter to study him. "You, fighting a war to put a spoiled heir on a throne."

"I happen to have some sympathy for heirs, *Miss Sethe*, and King Gidon hasn't been spoiled since before his parents were killed. Besides, my part in his ascension was somewhat clandestine. Prince Oren had special uses for those of us with a *delicate* political touch."

"Ah." At the oblique mention of the Mârad, Sethe actually smiled. "So. You became a spy."

"I did my part."

"The tiko too?"

Rigil shook his head. "Mezaedo came along after Gidon emancipated the strays. For now, he knows only what he must. I will admit, though . . ." He let his gaze drift to the hatch that had swallowed Mezaedo some time ago. "He did impress me in Meneton. King Gidon may make use of him yet."

Sethe followed his gaze until a new thought seemed to strike her. "Did you fight in the Battle of Armonguard?"

Pain shot under the calluses on Rigil's right palm. He'd found the only splinter left on the spokes. "I did. And my then squire, Bran Rennan, fought alongside the king until the end."

Sethe leaned in. "And he's a knight now?"

"I never saw him knighted."

Rigil stopped there, words sticking in his throat like hot ashes. Sethe's knowing silence could have out-boomed last night's storm, and he rushed to circumvent the questions he saw brimming behind her thoughtful frown. "I lost my sword around that time. Keseel. A fine blade I loved like a fifth limb."

A flagrant obfuscation, but one she didn't press. She was too busy raising an eyebrow at him. "Keseel? Really?"

"I liked the sound of it," he said.

"You don't know what it means."

"*Dashingly heroic master of disguise?*"

Her smile was close-lipped, secretive. But still. It *was* a smile.

Aye, this was definitely progress. Best to capitalize on it now, before the wind changed and took her fair mood with it. "I'm curious," Rigil said. "Where were you at the time? During the Battle of Armonguard, that is."

Sethe swept a fraying braid off her face, exposing the nest of scars that marred the skin. "Off the coast of Nesos," she answered, "collecting a shipment of herbs from the Poroo. I heard King Gidon in my head, saw Darkness lift, same as everyone else."

"Did you sing?" Rigil asked.

She glanced at him. "What?"

"When the king spoke into our minds, called the faithful of Er'Rets to sing praise to Arman. Did you sing?"

Another sixteen years seemed to pass in the time it took her to answer. He felt her gaze raking him, stripping him down to his secret motives as only she could. He supposed he could have been subtler, but that moment on the way to Meneton, watching her lips form Arman's name. If there was even a chance . . .

"Yes," Sethe said finally, tone cool enough to chill wine. Cool and cautious. "I sang."

She gave him no time for follow-up questions. Shifting on her perch, she went on, "Speaking of Darkness, I've been thinking. What if Laban *is* the man Myvick planned to send to Hamonah?"

Rigil considered, tucking Sethe's new interest in Arman aside for later. "Laban escaped."

"With at least two of his men. Which means he'll report back to Nedir or find another boat. He could be racing us to Hamonah now." She began tying knots in the tails of her corded belt, her fingers never stalling, never missing a loop. Rigil couldn't look away.

"Then we arrive first," he said. "If it means cutting my way through all of Hamonah, if I must tear the island apart stone by stone to keep Nedir from using you that way again, I will."

One of Sethe's fingers slipped, producing a half knot that resembled a nest of snakes. She slid a finger through one loop and pulled it all apart. "Ever the poet. I suppose you kept that much from Melas."

A question wrapped in a statement. No amount of knotting and reknotting would convince him that she wasn't hanging on his words, waiting to know how much he remembered.

"I kept many things from Melas," Rigil said. "Just because I earn my living these days hardly means I've forgotten what you taught me. You've made it clear that Hamonah is no place for knights, and I know how to play a part."

Overhead, the sail gave a sudden snap, like breaking bone. "So that's all this is. A part."

"Well, I certainly have no intention of becoming a pirate."

A gold glance. "You know that isn't what I meant."

"Honestly, Sethe, I wish I did." He gripped the helm, feeling every sway and slap of water on the hull. "I'm beginning to wonder if you'd prefer me as a thief."

"Tides." She slid off the rail, landing hard enough to make a sound this time. "You talk about it like we were nothing but vultures. Like we had *options*."

"Sethe—"

"Do you think I've forgotten your rules?" she said. "The days you went hungry trying to *earn* your living before you became desperate enough to do things my way? The way you kept lists of whoever we robbed in the hope of paying them back? The way you insisted on giving half our earnings to that blind old cripple by the docks? The targets you picked—dodgy merchants, tax collectors, rotten clerks who had it coming—why do you think I decided to steal from *pirates* last night instead of some fisherman? For the pleasure of it?"

The collar of Myvick's coat rasped like hemp around Rigil's neck. "You remember that?"

"Having a saint for a thieving partner? Yes, K'sil, I remember.

And where a runaway *servant* gets principles like that, I'll never know."

Her eye turned dark when she got this way, molten amber rimmed with stolen-coin gold.

Tell her. "I don't regret becoming something more than a runaway, Sethe." Rigil's voice came out more strained than he'd hoped as he tugged the coat off sleeve by sleeve and tossed it onto the deck. "Try to understand. Is there nothing from Melas you'd rather leave there?"

What a dangerous, dangerous question.

With clawlike hands, Sethe wrapped her vest tighter around her. He could all but *see* her defenses rising, triggered by that fragile moment of almost normal they'd shared.

"What do you think I've been trying to do?" The wind whipped at her sleeves as she held her ground. "But some of us don't have a Kingsguard to give us a new beginning, can't strut about without fear of being shipped back where we came from. Some of us can't shed the past like a coat. We just have to live with it. So that's what I did. I lived with it, I learned from it, and then I moved on."

The heap of scarlet and gold at Rigil's feet seemed to emanate heat as she turned toward the inclined ladder that connected the quarterdeck to the main deck. Her heels slammed the planks like battle drums.

"Sethe." Holding the helm with one hand, he lunged to catch her arm, barely managing to lock her there, close enough to see the mess where her earring had once been. Something else she thought he'd forgotten, no doubt. It still burned in his pocket like a hot porcelain coal, yet another secret waiting its turn. "There are things from Melas I could never forget. I need you to know that. You *must* know that."

Her chest rose and fell, rose and fell. He had a hand on her arm, and she glanced down at it as if seeing it for the first time. "What am I supposed to say to that?" she rasped.

Her arm was a taut rope, coated in gooseflesh. From the cold, perhaps. Or something else.

"Say I'm not one of the things you left behind." He traced her scars with his gaze, begged her to feel his meaning through his fingers on her arm. "Say that I am not the only one who still hears Melas in the cry of a peacock at night or a gilded carriage rattling by. Say you still remember the names of the stars we claimed as ours." When her face remained a wall, something in his gut clenched tight. "Isemios's wit, Sethe, say I'm not mad for seeing you in the flash of every coin since I lost you on the road to Zerah Rock."

At that, her eye sprang up, searching his face. Scouring for lies, for the catch, the costume. Rigil's other hand slipped off the helm, itching to find out how the pale ridges of her scars would feel under his palm.

The boat lurched.

Rigil released Sethe's arm to crank the vessel back on course, hoping Mezaedo hadn't noticed the shudder down in the hold. Leaving a helm unmanned? Lightness, Rigil's father would have skinned him alive.

Busy righting the vessel, he couldn't stop Sethe from hopping down the ladder to the main deck and striding off. He did, however, hear her parting words, so soft he almost missed them.

"I kept the name, didn't I?"

He let her go, listening to the slap of her feet on the main deck, not bothering to bridle his smile.

Chapter Fourteen
Sethe

H e could smile all he wanted. Sethe wasn't going to apologize for keeping a perfectly good name that served its perfectly practical purpose. *Sethe* made sense. It was functional, gritty, apologized for nothing, and wasted no time. It didn't pretend to be something it wasn't, unlike *Sedhani*, with all its lilts and curves. So why change it?

And what in the tides was that grin supposed to *mean*?

Don't look back, she ordered herself as she marched away from the quarterdeck, her arm prickling where he had held her in place like an anchor, where he'd all but confessed to something she'd only ever dreamed about. *Don't you dare look back.*

This wasn't about Rigil's nostalgia or the way he could still make the simplest, most forgettable things seem beautiful just by deciding they would be. It was about freedom. Freedom so close she could taste it like karpos. One last heist to keep Nedir's powder from spreading across Er'Rets like a rash, to buy Rigil's knight friends enough time to stop this conspiracy before it began. If it worked, it would end with Nedir behind bars, never to cage her again. *That* was all she'd come for. The *only scuddy thing.*

"Wad'jer shtep, Mishethe!"

The warning came just in time for Sethe to see a lumpy potato rolling across the deck toward her. Pinning it under one foot, she glanced at the hatch, where half of Mezaedo Chevyah had risen from the hold with at least a dozen potatoes in his arms and one locked between his teeth. Seeing her, he spat that one onto the deck.

Sethe jutted her chin at his cargo. "Is this some kind of Jaelportian ritual?"

He blinked, all innocence. "Potatoes?"

"Right, tiko. I want to know if *potatoes* are a Jaelportian ritual."

When he grinned, flashing a set of dimples she hadn't noticed before, Sethe's impression of Mezaedo Chevyah shifted from a shapeless tangle to something like a sailor's knot. So. He wasn't only good in a fight; he was also sharper than he looked. Even had a sense of sarcasm.

Sethe kicked the wayward potato back toward the others, which were already rolling in different directions with every pitch of the boat. Hopping up onto the deck, Mezaedo corralled them between his legs and began inspecting them for blemishes, one by one.

Catching Sethe's stare, he explained, "There isn't much in the way of provisions down there. Most of it's gone to rot, and these would have too if I hadn't saved them." He held one out to her. "Hungry?"

"That depends." Sethe plopped down beside him, completing the corral before the rest of the potatoes could roll too far. "Any teeth marks?"

"Always a possibility."

His dimples showed again as he picked a potato from the batch and rolled it a few times in his hands, running his fingers over the spores. Obviously, he knew what he was doing. Had probably worked as a kitchen slave; or maybe a farmhand.

"Master number four," he said, reading her mind. "He had a

vegetable stall in the bazaar, used to have me sort his rotten stock so I could hide it under the good stuff people bought. Decent fellow, believe it or not. Always thought I would have liked to stay with him a little longer. But you know how it is. Strays are useful until they aren't, and then there's always someone else willing to take you if you're eager enough."

Sethe grabbed a potato. "How many masters have you had?"

"Eleven. Although, the one who talked to herself could probably count as two."

Sethe snorted. The potato in her hand was gnarled and knobby as a figurehead left too long to the wind and salt. Tiny spores and creases crisscrossed it like scars. "So that makes Rigil number twelve?"

His head shot up, sending glossy curls flying. "It's not like that. I'm a squire now, not a slave, thanks to King Gidon and Sirrig. Especially Sirrig." He set a potato aside, nodding to himself. "If not for him, I'd still be back in Armonguard, begging some knight to give me a chance. I wasn't exactly what most of them were after." He said it lightly, which Sethe saw through like glass. "Being Jaelportian doesn't do me any favors."

"So." She tried to sound like she was following an idle trail of thought. "Rigil picked you?"

Mezaedo smiled, one dimple showing. Suddenly, she saw it. This gangly, good-natured, newly freed slave with half a normal bloodvoicer's skill and twice a normal human's quirks, passed over by every Kingsguard in Armonguard. All except one. The one who wouldn't think of what a Kingsguard knight needed when he saw a need *he* could fill.

Just her luck. Rigil was getting *more* gallant with age.

"Is he good to you?" Sethe asked. A strange question, probably.

The tiko didn't seem to think so. "He made a Kingsguard squire of me, Missethe. More than anyone else would do. I just wish I could do more to thank him." He tossed another potato onto his growing pile. "Him and Arman."

Maybe it was his story, or his unexplained scars, but Sethe had taken for granted that this tiko was her mirror, the one person on this boat who might understand her doubts. So much for that.

"You believe in Arman?" she asked. "After all that? A slave to eleven masters in, what, fourteen years?"

"Seventeen." He glanced up at her through thick, dark lashes. Older than expected. "And they weren't all bad."

"You were a slave."

"I'm not anymore. The way I see it, it's like Light and Darkness." He swooped a hand at the sea around them, the pale, cloudy sky overhead. "Until Arman raised up King Gidon, my world was black as ink. And then one day, it wasn't. Once Arman gives you a blue sky, the dark before it stops feeling so heavy." He paused, cocked his head. "Was it me, or did that sound like moldy *wisdom*?"

Sethe tossed her potato aside and grabbed another, this one even more gnarled than the first, like it had been tortured. "But isn't Arman just another master? Aren't you worried He might get tired of you, toss you aside like all the others? He let His own son die."

"Don't know if you've heard, but Arman brought Câan back to life."

"But He still let him *die*. What kind of a master is that? Why couldn't He turn on you too?"

Wherever that last bit had come from, it had the ring of Raith Nedir to it. An ugly thought that didn't change how badly Sethe needed an answer.

Rigil used to talk about Câan all the time, the warrior God who had come to Er'Rets to fight for the Kinsmen, only to be murdered by the same people He'd come to free. Arman had breathed life back into Him a few days later, all fine and good, but what about the night of His death? What about the torture, the loneliness? All the stories said Câan trusted the Father God completely, but was there ever any fear, even the *tiniest* bit, that Arman would leave Him in the dirt?

Mezaedo didn't reply right away, and Sethe found herself leaning in, hanging—actually *hanging*—on this bizarre tiko's verdict, as if he could make sense of the twisted wishes that lived where her faith should be. Well, fine. Rigil the Flawless wouldn't understand, and Eagan Elk was a near stranger. She didn't exactly have options.

Which was why, when Mezaedo finally tore his gaze from the sky, Sethe was nearly faint from holding her breath.

"He won't," he said finally.

"What?"

"You asked if I worry that Arman might cast me off like all the others." He scratched the back of one hand as he spoke, scraping his nails over the white-flecked scars. "I do worry about it. All the moldy time. What if He decides He doesn't need me, shuffles me off like everyone else?" He shrugged, curls dancing and bouncing like candlewicks in wind. "But that's the thing, Missethe. I've had enough bad masters to know a good one when I see it. If Câan could go to the grave believing His Father was still good, that Arman's love could bring Him back again, I figure I can trust that too, you know? Thanks to Arman, I'm with Sirrig now. I saw Darkness lift, heard a herald in Jaelport telling me I was *free*, got to walk away from a mistress on my own two feet. Sure, sometimes I worry He'll turn out to be too good to be true, but I've got a lot of good things to go on." He shrugged. "And they all say He won't."

Sethe leaned back. "That's it? You just believe? Do you know how sandwitted that sounds?"

He laced his hands and stretched them out in front of him until his knuckles cracked. "As sandwitted as praying like mad to a God you don't believe in?"

Praying like . . . ? Oh. The road to Meneton. "You heard that?"

"To be fair, Missethe, you *were* sort of screaming in my head."

Before Sethe could grill him on exactly who had overheard exactly *what* while she'd been half conscious, Mezaedo's gaze drifted over her shoulder and locked on something there. He jumped up, scattering potatoes.

"Sirrig!"

If not for that warning, Sethe would have missed the mast on the horizon until too late. As it was, even with Mezaedo pointing over the gunwale, all she saw was a smudge against the coast.

A smudge flying Jaelport's colors.

"Friends?" Mezaedo called up to Rigil, gripping his bag of spice. He'd probably reach for that pouch before his sword if things turned sour. "Can we outrun them?"

"Mezaedo, take the helm," Rigil answered from the quarterdeck. "Hold her straight. We'll let them come to us."

Rigil, still coatless, waited for Mezaedo to relieve him at the helm before he descended from the quarterdeck with *maddening* grace and ducked into the helmsman's quarters. He returned with a spyglass, face tight as he squinted into the lens. "Jaelportian royal navy. I'll handle this."

This, Sethe had to see.

At Rigil's command, Mezaedo held the vessel steady, letting the wind lead as Rigil and Sethe fixed the sail to cut speed. Turning themselves into sitting gulls. The Jaelportian ship was gaining fast, too fast for comfort. The sun seemed to stand still as Sethe hauled lines and climbed the shrouds to cut down the little rikoh's sail, throwing glances at the olive-green colors growing closer, closer, *closer*. Before an hour had passed, the goatlike head of Zitheos was stark against the newcomer's mainsail, sending a sheen to Sethe's palms that turned the rigging greasy in her grip.

For tides' sake, it was just the Jaelportian navy. Nedir had no ties to the Jaelportian navy.

A change came over Rigil as the Jaelportian ship approached, the lines of his body and the planes of his face hardening into something more rigid than usual. The voice he'd used to order Mezaedo to the helm was one she'd never heard. A part he knew well, then.

As long as it worked better than his last performance. Grand entrance or not, Rigil's Myvick trick last night had ended in chaos, and Sethe didn't have an army of seagulls on hand.

Though modest in size, twin-masted and probably crewed by no more than twenty men, the Jaelportian ship still dwarfed Myvick's minnow, drawing up beside them in minutes and tossing hooked lines across their starboard rail.

From the rail of the other ship, a bald Jaelportian stared them down and bellowed into the wind. "You are encroaching on Jaelportian waters in an uncleared vessel. State your business."

"The vessel is a gift," Rigil called back. "For Her Highness, Queen Mandzee Hamartano. Confiscated from the fleet of Captain Othvold Myvick."

A stir rippled through the sailors but didn't touch the captain. A hard man, then. No sandwit. His face barely moved when he said, "Prepare to be boarded."

Sailors dropped a plank across the gap and accompanied the captain over. Once on deck, they fanned out, searching for threats with daggers drawn.

Sethe shifted her weight. "K'sil?"

Rigil curled his thumb over one empty finger, as if feeling for a ring that wasn't there. "Trust me."

"How many aboard?" the captain asked, his skin a deep olive like the others. "Any passengers?"

"It's only the three of us. We sailed from Meneton last night."

"In the gale?"

"*Gale* is a tad excessive."

"And on a stolen vessel?"

Rigil raised his chin. "A confiscated vessel. Myvick is an enemy of Er'Rets, and his slaving network is being disbanded. Consider this an investment in the good of Jaelport and a sign of goodwill for Queen Mandzee. In exchange for the boat and the removal of a threat to Jaelportian commerce, we request passage through your waters."

The captain appraised Sethe, then Mezaedo, lips jutting. "Kingsguard?"

Rigil stood straighter. "I am Sir Rigil Barak."

Barak. A nobleman's name?

"This is my squire, Mezaedo Chevyah, and my . . . associate, Miss Sethe of Hamonah."

Miss Sethe. Still sounded like a bad joke.

Rigil's latest false name didn't seem to impress the sailors, but one or two of them regarded Sethe like she might sprout claws and rip them all to shreds.

The captain, meanwhile, scoured Rigil's dirty uniform as if trying to peel back a disguise. "Barak, hmm? Your story will need testing. I'm inclined to believe that you aren't running slaves, as you have no cargo and nowhere near enough crew. But until we can confirm the rest, you and your companions are under arrest. You will appear before House Hamartano within the fortnight, perhaps within the month. I promise nothing."

Arrest? A flow of multicolored horrors poured through Sethe's head. Bars and locks and tiny rooms where wind couldn't reach. *Tides, no.*

She expected Rigil to change tactics. Try a bribe, slide into another character, claim to be the long-lost prince of the sea people. *Something.*

Instead, he sighed. "I understand."

Before Sethe could shoot him a glance, he went on in a bolder voice.

"I assume that a man of your rank can get a message to the throne room. If so, then you can confirm my identity with Queen

Mandzee. Please tell her that the wine her mother served at our last meeting took two weeks to scrape off my tongue and another two years to forget."

"Sir?"

Rigil clasped his hands behind his back. "And if that is not enough, please inform her that her cousin, Sir Rigil Barak, heir of Zerah Rock, invokes the Treaty of Barak–Hamartano to demand an audience. Immediately."

CHAPTER FIFTEEN
RIGIL

RIGIL FELT SETHE'S SILENCE LIKE A PALpable force with every rock and swell of the passage to the coast. He stood on Captain Iago's ship, the *Solstice*, under the drum of that silence, hardly aware of the steely waves cruising by. Too busy choking on the fumes of Sethe's fury.

Iago's crew gave them all a wide berth, but they were especially leery of Sethe, the only woman among them in a duchy ruled by the female population. She didn't seem to notice and planted herself at the rail, gazing back the way they'd come as if expecting something to rise out of the water and swallow her.

Rigil didn't *try* to mute his approach, but one did not accost a hungry cham without caution. The same rule applied to a Sethe of Hamonah who'd just discovered she'd been lied to for sixteen years.

"Sethe." Standing behind her, Rigil watched the breeze swirl in the chopped-off hair at the base of her neck. A sailor called across the deck, reporting a change in the wind. "I know you're surprised, but I can explain. Yes, I'm a Barak, but I am also a Kingsguard knight. Intercepting Nedir's powder shipment before it reaches the other traitors is what matters here, and my status does not change that. Nothing will change that."

"Should you be talking to a commoner?" she said without turning. Her shoulders were relaxed, but he could see her hands on the rail, her knuckles blooming white from gripping the wood too hard.

Isemios's wit. "I never actually claimed to be a servant. You assumed as much when we met."

"Ah." She spun to face him, leaning backward on the rail with a casual grace that nearly had him feeling his neck. "So it's *my* mistake."

She dismissed him by turning her back again. This time, the wind blew back enough of her hair to expose the pulpy mess where her earlobe had been. Scars upon scars. Betrayals upon betrayals. And for what? A flimsy lie that never should have lasted so long?

They spoke no more after that. Upon reaching the harbor in Jaelport, Rigil strode ashore to the rhythm of Sethe's silence and rode the velvet-lined carriage to Queen Mandzee's summer estate, choking on sour guilt. Whenever he looked at her through the bumps and rattles of the carriage, her eye darted off. Not angry, then. Angry Sethe would never look away first.

No, this was worse. She was *wounded*.

Sir Eagan Elk, right again. But no surprise there.

Jaelport had been in Darkness for a long time, but the vestiges of that era were fast disappearing. The view outside the carriage was all budding desert flowers and drooping palms, almost fragrant enough to overwhelm the distant tang of the sea as they wended up the coast toward a secluded summer estate nestled between two low hills. Strange how a bit of sunlight could almost make one forget the dangers of this land. But perhaps that was the view talking.

Standing proudly on the Cela coast on a modest garden estate—modest by Jaelport's standards, at least—the summer palace was more secluded than Tenma Palace, the official seat of the royal family. Rigil had always seen something idyllic in the manor-like building, if only because reaching it did not require braving the chaos of Jaelport proper. There was a dangerous sense of security in that. Security, because Jaelportian politics felt further away. Dangerous, because nowhere in Jaelport was truly safe, no matter how far one was from the court.

The carriage finally slowed to a stop before a manicured lawn, where a bald, middle-aged eunuch, marked by his maroon skirt and black-lined eyes, stepped up to the door. Unlike Rigil, whose hair was already wilting around his ears from the humidity, the man's pristine eye paint showed no sign of melting.

"Sir Rigil. Her Highness regrets that she could not greet you herself. We do not often receive unexpected visitors at the summer palace, and she is preparing for your arrival as we speak."

Rigil waved the apology away as he climbed down from the carriage. "Her Highness should not trouble herself."

The eunuch bowed, holding the door for Mezaedo and finally, Sethe. Seeing her, his posture shifted slightly, adjusting to the presence of a woman. The formality was a compliment of sorts. Hamonayan or not, she was a woman, and that meant power in Jaelport.

"This way, sir."

As the eunuch turned to lead them up the gravel walk toward the summer palace ahead, Rigil clapped Mezaedo on the shoulder, trying to pretend he wasn't watching Sethe trail behind in his peripheral vision.

"How does it feel to be in Jaelport again, Mez?"

As he watched the eunuch, Mezaedo's steps grew almost ginger. "Oh, just moldy *brilliant*."

Stifling summer heat shimmered over the paving stones as they approached the palace through a lush garden path, Rigil and Mezaedo in the lead, Sethe meandering behind them. Without the breeze off the sea, the flower-sweetened air felt thick and close, each breath like a mouthful of warm milk. Orchids and blossoms bloomed along the path in full splendor, filling the air with tempting floral notes of jasmine, lily, desert rose.

Half tempting. Smelling anything in Jaelport was a sure way to find yourself signing away your inheritance to a woman you'd never met—or worse, waking up to discover you'd married her. Stranger things had happened here.

"Don't smell anything," Rigil whispered to Mez. "No flowers, no powders. Be on guard."

Mezaedo shot him a long-suffering look. "I know my way around mage powder, Sirrig."

The palace swelled before them, a masterpiece of arabesque arches, scrollwork, and stone towers, each a work of art. Tenma Palace in Jaelport proper would have dwarfed it, of course. As the duchy's seat of power, it was designed to intimidate, a threat in stone and scrollwork and a blatant display of Jaelport's power in the city and the greater area. As for the summer palace . . .

Rigil winced, his tongue crawling with the memory of bad wine, worse conversation, and long walks in these very gardens with Queen Torrezia's daughters. Lightness, how long had it been since his mother's last attempt to wrangle a marriage alliance with Jaelport? Six years? Eight?

Not nearly long enough.

As they passed through an arch in the stone wall that separated the palace garden from the grounds, Mezaedo nudged Rigil's arm. "Sirrig, how did you know Queen Mandzee would be here and not at Tenma Palace?"

"I didn't," Rigil said. "I was braced for a detour to Jaelport proper, but I'm not surprised. Queen Torrezia used to come here for respite on occasion, especially at this time of year. It is something of a tradition in House Hamartano, though for the queen's safety it is rarely advertised."

Mezaedo rolled his bottom lip out, impressed. "Why would a noble from Zerah Rock know the Hamartanos' secret summer plans?"

The simple answer? Rigil was a spy. He knew things. The more accurate answer? "House Barak has ties to Jaelport, however seldom we may speak of it. The late Queen Torrezia Hamartano was my aunt. That makes Queen Mandzee and Lady Jaira my first cousins."

Mezaedo didn't seem to know what to do with the revelation that Rigil was tied by blood to Er'Rets's most treacherous duchy. Fair enough. Most days, Rigil tried to forget it himself.

After a beat, though, the squire shrugged. "How about that. We could be related."

Surprising himself with a laugh, Rigil gave the boy a shove.

Moving deeper into the garden toward the palace courtyard, they passed beneath a four-legged flowering trellis that arched over the path like a spider, Sethe drifting behind them like a slow-moving shadow. When Rigil glanced back, he found her leaning over an ailing orchid, tracing the shriveled brown spots with one finger. Her expression was so focused, so intent, as if she saw something in that struggling flower that meant more than all the gardens combined.

"Sirrig." Mezaedo stopped a few steps ahead. "You coming?"

Sethe's head snapped up, and Rigil swerved to follow Mezaedo, burning under her hot scrutiny.

The eunuch brought them to a stone courtyard veined with lush green creepers, a two-tiered fountain burbling in the center.

"Her Highness will arrive presently. Wait here."

He bowed and left through an archway as Mezaedo dropped beside the fountain to wash his face, proof that he hadn't discarded his awe of Jaelportian nobility along with his orange stray's tunic. Watching him, Sethe kept her face deliberately blank, arms crossed over her tattered vest, still bearing the marks and scents of her captivity in Land's End. If Rigil was as filthy as she was, he could hardly blame Captain Iago for wanting to confirm his identity. Perhaps he should join Mezaedo at the fountain.

"Cousin."

Too late. Queen Mandzee Hamartano swept into the courtyard on a cloud of grace and perfume.

Years of etiquette training bent Rigil's knee by reflex. "Your Majesty. Exquisite as always."

Mandzee curtsied, her hair piled atop her head in black braids, the arrangement offset by a shimmering olive-green gown. Taller than her infamous sister, Jaira, she cut an imposing figure against the stone courtyard. The gown accented her olive skin and dark eyes, but the ensemble was surprisingly modest. Perhaps becoming queen had dashed her hopes of a marriage alliance after all these years.

The queen's smile was calculating. "Did your mother send you, Cousin?"

Then again, perhaps the sky was yellow.

"No, Your Highness," Rigil said. "I am not on Lady Zora's business this time." If one could call enforced courting *business*. "In fact, she doesn't know I'm here."

To his surprise, Mandzee visibly relaxed. "Then we can dispense with any pretense of a marriage alliance. I trust that is a relief to both of us."

Rigil's grin broke out on its own. "A relief indeed. No disrespect intended."

"None taken. You know, that was entirely our mothers' scheme. I only went along because Jaira would have been *madly* jealous, always a reward unto itself."

Mezaedo jumped to his feet with a shower of droplets, likely giving himself vertigo and certainly making himself seen.

"Forgive my rudeness," Rigil said, straightening. "Your Highness, allow me to introduce my squire Mezaedo Chevyah and Miss Sethe of Hamonah."

Mezaedo bowed nearly low enough to brush the ground with his nose as Sethe unfolded her arms and lowered her gaze, as close to a curtsey as Mandzee was likely to get.

Rigil watched the queen's Jaelportian eyes snag on Sethe's scars. Her smile showed no teeth. "Friends of Sir Rigil's are friends of mine. I trust you will all join me for dinner after you have washed and rested. That is, you *will* stay here as my guests."

Sethe mumbled something that Rigil hastened to drown out. "Of course we will, Your Highness, at least for the night. I'm afraid that's all we can spare."

Mandzee's gaze shone. "Tonight it is."

A clap of her hands brought a gaggle of maidservants through the archway, and Rigil could practically hear Sethe disdaining the aristocratic luxury. *What, so she has troops of maids just waiting around to be* clapped *for?*

"Miss Sethe will have a guest chamber in the ladies' wing. Dinner attire will be provided, of course." A flutter of the queen's fingers ushered the maidservants toward Sethe, most of them younger than Mezaedo and wearing enough eye paint to coat Othvold Myvick's apartment twice over. "The young man of Jaelportian blood shall be an honored guest. Master Chevyah, if you would follow Jakeen . . ."

The eunuch reappeared to usher Mezaedo away, and then Sethe was there, clutching Rigil's arm against the maidservants trying to herd her toward an awning. The hair around her face was frizzing in the humidity, the halo only making her look wilder.

"I can't stay here," Sethe said. Isemios's wit, was that a rattle in her voice? "You and your lady friend can discuss noble life when the powder is dealt with, but banquets and *dinner attire*? Rigil, we both know I don't belong here. I have no business being in a place like this."

"You're a guest, Sethe."

"I'm a *sailor*." She growled the last word, grip tightening with meaning. "A former *thief*."

He cringed and glanced at Mandzee, who didn't seem to have heard.

Apparently taking the hint, Sethe lowered her voice. "We don't have time for rest."

"The shipment doesn't go out until the morning after next. We have time, Sethe. Calling this meeting was the only way to avoid arrest for trespassing, and even if I could hire another ship today, we need permission to sail from Jaelport. That will require some diplomacy."

"What if Nedir knows where we're headed?" she demanded. "He knows we left Hamonah on one of Myvick's boats. What if he puts the pieces together, figures out what we're trying to do?" A maid bowed hesitantly in Sethe's direction, and Sethe hissed at her—actually *hissed*—before turning back to him. "Rigil, we *need* to get there first."

The queen was watching them, tall and resplendent in green silk. Rigil angled his head for only Sethe to see his lips. "This is Jaelport. They won't let us sail through on a smuggler's vessel without permission."

"Say it's a Kingsguard mission."

"That does not carry weight here."

Her lips twisted. "But being a Barak does?"

Before Rigil could compliment that impossibly skilled segue, a maidservant touched Sethe's arm. She flinched, and this time he saw it in her face: fear.

Palace or prison—there was no difference to Sethe. She wouldn't see finery, just walls.

Well, what better chance to change her mind?

"Sethe." He laid a hand over hers. "I know that I kept my identity from you, but my name changes nothing. I still escaped Land's

End with you. I stole a *boat* with you. We need Mandzee's support, and this is the key. Trust me. For one night."

"If Nedir finds us here—"

"*One* night, Sethe."

He stepped away, letting the maidservants swarm between them. The panic in Sethe's face as they ushered her away was enough to twist his windpipe, but Lightness, she had to trust him. This was his world, like the streets were hers. She had to see that for herself.

"You look weary, Cousin." As the courtyard cleared, Mandzee drew close to his side, emerald stones dangling from her earlobes to match the pendant around her neck.

"I'm fine." Time to focus. He needed to be Rigil Barak now, heir of Zerah Rock. "A day's rest is all I need, Your Majesty. Thank you for your hospitality."

"Mandzee will do." As usual, she moved like a coiled serpent. Beautiful and watchful, slow-moving only until she needed to be swift. "Shall we walk?"

Rigil offered his arm, and she accepted, far more relaxed now than in the past with both their mothers breathing marriage plots down their necks. That, he supposed, was one thing they could both appreciate: the trials of living with Jaelportian women.

Not that he would ever say as much.

"I was surprised when Captain Iago contacted us," Mandzee said as they passed through another archway into a garden colonnade below the palace windows. "Kingsguard business has never brought you to Jaelport before, and certainly not on one of Myvick's boats." She slid him a glance. "I would like to see that man's empire crumble to dust before the year is through."

Rigil tipped his head. "Consider the vessel my investment in that mission."

"After Myvick, the only person in Er'Rets more deserving of imprisonment is my sister. I suppose you heard about Jaira's recent attempt to throw off the yoke of King Gidon?" The last words dripped irony. "I always knew Jaira would go too far. I'm half surprised she didn't toss me into the sea the day our mother died."

Rigil opted not to comment on Jaira. "My condolences for the loss of your mother."

She waved a hand. "I'm just sorry for what Lady Tara suffered at my sister's hand. Think of it, Sir Rigil. Guests of Jaelport, bewitched and abducted like common slaves, as if King Gidon would ever be *bullied* into granting Jaelport sovereignty." With a quiet growl, she checked herself and faced him with forced composure. "Lady Tara is well, I hope? Recovering from it all? Have you word from Viola?"

A smirk lifted one half of Rigil's mouth. "More than recovering, I should say. She and Sir Carmack married recently." When Mandzee nodded, Rigil waited a moment, then ventured, "It must have been a difficult transition after your mother's passing, but if I may say so, the crown seems to suit you."

"Does it?" Mandzee stopped to pluck a flower from a vine, her jade-ringed fingers somehow both ruthless and gentle as they ripped the stem at its base. "Truthfully, it unnerves me."

Rigil blinked. An admission like that from a Jaelportian woman, and one as guarded as Mandzee? "You don't want to be queen?"

The flower fluttered to the path, a delicate corpse. "I am tired of being feared. Jaelportians manipulate, destroy, use our magic to turn men into slaves." She wrinkled her nose, the effect decidedly unpretty. "I must change that. Which is why I was thankful to hear from you. I was hoping you might counsel me on my plans for a new Jaelport."

"New Jaelport? A tad ambitious, don't you think?"

Her lips tightened. "No more ambitious than placing a new king on the throne."

Rigil slowed his steps to match hers. "How can I be of help?"

She stopped in the middle of the path and gazed at the far side of the garden, where a shrine to Zitheos was slowly being digested by an unkempt fern. "I was thinking of building a small shrine as a tribute to Arman, but it occurred to me that the Father God may have preferences about this sort of thing. So?"

Rigil stared. "A *shrine?* For Arman?"

"Why not? All the other gods have at least a monument within my city. I imagined something small to begin with. I will have to tread carefully, of course, and not usurp old traditions." She fluttered a hand at the garden, the palace, the burning Cela sky. "But I have plans beyond that. Importing priests from Armonguard, mandatory tributes, anything to draw Arman's favor. This is why I need you. You are a follower of the Way, yes? Tell me what King Gidon did to secure Arman's favor, and I shall do no less."

Sincerity strengthened her grip on his arm. Sincerity or desperation.

"This is about power, then," Rigil said.

"It is about changing history. I want to do well by my people, Cousin, to change Jaelport the way your King Gidon has changed Er'Rets. I intend to make your kind see mine anew."

"And that is admirable." A hawk swooped down in front of them, rose with something limp in its talons. "But you cannot expect the world to forget Jaelport's legacy overnight."

"Then that is it?" Retracting her hand, Mandzee drew herself to full, formidable height. "Arman has no grace left for Jaelport? Hardly what I expected from a follower of the Way."

Well, Rigil hadn't exactly expected a request for spiritual counsel from the mage-queen of Jaelport either. Isemios's wit, who was he to advise her on trusting Arman?

"Your Highness, what you are proposing—shrines and imported priests—it is well meant, but misguided. Arman's grace cannot be bought."

Mandzee blinked. "So I simply let the country go on as it always has, trapped in a cycle of ruin?"

Knotting his hands behind his back, Rigil channeled Eagan

Elk with every bit of poise he had left. "If I may, Your Majesty—Mandzee—perhaps Arman wishes to change your heart before He does your city."

A cool "What could He want with my heart?" was her only reply as they finished their turn of the colonnade. Before Rigil could fill the silence that followed, a maidservant emerged from the palace with a bundle of silk in her arms.

"Your pardon, my lady." She curtseyed hurriedly. "This is the gown you requested."

Mandzee released Rigil's arm to study the garment, holding up a swath of violet silk. "This will do nicely, I think. Cousin, do you approve?"

Rigil bunched his lips. "I tend to look better in blue."

Her smile turned dead-eyed. "Not for *you*. It will look becoming on your Hamonayan friend. Reeja, alter it for dinner. Use whatever jewelry of mine you think would be suitable. Go."

If Sethe hadn't planned to strangle Rigil before, she certainly would now. With violet silk. And jewels.

Rigil, we both know I don't belong here.

"Very kind of you," Rigil said. It came out as more of a cough, but Mandzee didn't seem to notice. Sethe? In that gown? *Willingly?* What had seemed possible for the Sethe of his hopes—a Sethe who could stand beside him at Zerah Rock and deflect every one of his father's doubts with a lady's poise—appeared as flimsy as that pale silk next to the woman inside right now. The one likely fighting like a half-drowned cat against the serving staff's attempt to make a lady of her.

No. Rigil inhaled sharply. They were the same Sethe. They *could* be. He just had to be strategic.

Mandzee gazed after the maid, fingers tented over her lips, imagining more tortures to inflict on Sethe, no doubt. Silk, jewels, and what next? Stays? "Anything for my dear cousin's . . . friend."

The word wasn't nearly strong enough to warrant a reaction.

But then, Rigil supposed *friend* was better than *liar,* which was no doubt his current standing with Sethe.

Aye, something had to be done about that.

"I look forward to dining with you, Your Highness." Rigil poured a touch more polish into his voice. "You have already been so hospitable, I hesitate to make more requests."

"Nonsense. Request away." Mandzee's smirk reminded him how dangerous she could be if she chose. Mage powders seemed to be Jaira's specialty, but Rigil could not drop his guard. The less Mandzee knew about Nedir's powder, the better.

"Meneton was not kind to us," Rigil said. "We must be on our way as soon as possible—Kingsguard business, you understand—but we need passage to Hamonah."

"That can be arranged." Mandzee settled her hands before her, every drop the queen. "But let us discuss it after dinner."

After dinner. Dinner with the queen of Jaelport and *Sethe*—frank, barefooted, defiant-of-pretenses Sethe—wrapped in *violet silk.*

Lightness, she was going to kill him.

Rigil bowed again, more subtly than Myvick but with a touch more finesse than a knight. Aye, earning her forgiveness would take more than a few well-meant words this time. What fabric would complement violet best? Grey? Gold perhaps?

"Speaking of dinner, Your Highness," Rigil said, mentally parsing patterns and fabrics, "I am woefully underdressed."

Mandzee smiled, jeweled rings glinting on her lithe hands, fine golden threads wound around her fingers.

And just like that, Rigil decided.

Yes. Gold. For Sethe's eye and new coins and the sunset off the ocean—all the things that lived in his memory of her. All the reasons to spare her a night of misery, if he could. And if that required help from a local tailor, so be it.

"Sir Rigil?" Mandzee was assessing him with pursed lips. "Are you all right?"

Focus, man. Rigil cleared his throat. "Of course, Your Majesty. Now, where might I find a bazaar?"

CHAPTER SIXTEEN
SETHE

As if being imprisoned in the palace for a whole night wasn't enough, now this Queen Mandzee wanted to turn Sethe into her personal doll? Well, Sethe didn't care how expensive the gown was. The queen could take her whale-boned cage and—

"Ah!" Sethe gasped, gripping the bedpost. "Enough! I said take it *off*."

Reeja, the Jaelportian maidservant, *tsked*, fingers tangled in Sethe's stays. Stays: the noblewoman's equivalent of a cell, like all the frills and lace Sethe had no business being wrapped in.

"Apologies, Miss Sethe," Reeja said, "but Her Highness selected this gown especially for you, and I'm afraid you simply must wear the stays. And the slippers."

"Must, my foot!" Tides, Sethe couldn't breathe. Too much fabric, too much perfume, too much gloss in her hair, now done up in braids. The bath she'd tolerated, but there were slippers on her feet. *Slippers.* Were they mocking her? Was this all some kind of game? *How much finery does it take to make a lady out of a Hamonayan?*

A knock at the door saved Reeja from replying. Poor woman.

Just doing her job. But if Rigil expected Sethe to play noblewoman just because he was the heir of Zerah Rock . . .

One of Sethe's fingernails broke on the bedpost as she tried to wring sap from the wood.

Rigil. Rigil from Melas. A noble.

An *heir*.

She should be angry. She *had* been *livid* when she'd first seen Captain Iago's reaction on the *Solstice*, first realized that this time, Rigil didn't seem to be playacting. After all, didn't it explain why he'd always seemed too polished for a servant?

Even then, though, a part of her had hoped it would all turn out to be another one of his brilliant tricks. But all her denial had died the moment Queen Mandzee had floated into the courtyard and greeted him like a long-lost brother. No, like *royalty*.

Still clutching the bedpost, Sethe pressed her forehead to the wood and exhaled long.

The worst part of all this? She couldn't even hate him for the secrets, not after keeping as much from him. All those months in Melas, she'd never even told him her real name.

As for his secrets, all she wanted to know was *why*. She knew her own excuse for keeping her past quiet. What was his?

"Miss Sethe?" A new maid, this one dressed all in red with her hair plaited like a dozen snakes, pushed the bedchamber door open with her back. A large gold box filled her arms. More tools of torture, no doubt.

"No." Sethe struggled to breathe through the half-tied stays. "No more gifts. Tell Her Highness that I refuse—um, decline. Respectfully. I *respectfully* decline."

And *this* was why Hamonayans didn't go to court.

The maid smiled, her painted eyelids marking her as a servant with some minor mage training. "But Miss Sethe, this isn't from her ladyship."

Sethe reached for the box, but Reeja propped the lid for her, revealing a mass of amber cloth. When Sethe pulled the garment out, it spilled across her arms like molten gold.

A blue bodice embroidered with amber. Capped sleeves in sheer saffron. Where the skirt should be, two billowing gold legs that ended in blue-beaded cuffs.

A *shikana*. No, more than that. The most expensive scuddy shikana Sethe had ever seen.

"It's beautiful." Reeja studied it sideways like it was a two-headed animal. All one piece, meant to be stepped into, like a gown, the garment buttoned up the back with tiny blue pearls. "Who sent it?"

Better not to answer that. Better not to speak.

"Sir Rigil sent it with strict instructions." The maid clasped now-empty hands. "He says it is Miss Sethe's to wear or not, as she wishes. But if she *does* choose to wear it, slippers and stays would 'most certainly spoil the effect.'"

That was how Sethe arrived at the banquet hall both barefoot and breathing, and as beautiful as a woman with her face was ever going to be.

The shikana fit perfectly, snug around her body, loose in the legs, cuffing at her ankles and accenting the toenails that now shone with Reeja's frantic polishing. Honestly, it was like the woman had never seen a barefoot Hamonayan.

Still, painfully aware of the polished floor beneath her unworthy feet, Sethe stood before the doors like a counterfeit coin. Mezaedo had divvied out Eagan's dried karpos during the carriage ride to the palace, and her personal bundle rested inside her bodice, a knot against her hammering chest.

"What in *Er'Rets* am I doing?" she mumbled.

"Waiting for me, I hope."

Sethe turned.

The heir of Zerah Rock cleaned up well, as always. She now recognized the little lightning bolts on Rigil's belt as a tribute to his home, like the newly washed black jerkin and blue shirt underneath. His old clothes. Cleaned and mended where swords had slashed them in Meneton and Land's End, but still. Had he really wasted good coin on a shikana without buying anything for himself?

Nothing could be done for Rigil's sunburn, but the color on his face only made his blue eyes bolder. Shame about the scruff, though. He'd gone and shaved again.

"We shouldn't be staying." Sethe spoke before he could say something about her shikana or before she could accidentally tell him that he looked . . . Well, never mind how he looked. "If Nedir knows our plan, staying in one place could mean letting him or his smuggler reach Hamonah first. What if he's already on his way? What if he has spies *here*?"

"We will sail that storm if we come to it." Rigil eyed her sideways, adjusting one of his cuffs. "Mandzee will not keep us here. Frankly, I'm hoping she'll let us take Laban's rikoh. If Arman is with us, we'll reach the Talons tomorrow."

"And if Arman isn't with us?"

He frowned. He'd tried to sweep the hair back from his head, but his bangs curled across his brow like a defiant tidal wave. It struck her that he'd never faced this question, like he'd rarely thought of his words as more than a figure of speech.

"Of course He is," he said finally. "We're doing this in His name. For all Er'Rets."

Glasses clinked beyond the door. Inside, Mandzee laughed at something Sethe didn't catch as music began, a series of twinkling notes held up by a complicated lute harmony.

Rigil offered his arm, the perfect nobleman. "Shall we, Miss Sethe?"

The hand she used to take his arm felt wooden, totally numb. But it was just one dinner. She could tamp down her flight instincts for one little dinner, pretend this palace didn't feel like a cage, pretend she wasn't an impostor.

Rigil opened the door. Mandzee sat at a round table lit with enough candles to chase away a Hamonayan fog. Tall windows on the eastern wall, propped open to let a cloying breeze in, showed a dark green mass where Mandzee's manicured gardens met the jungle at the edge of the palace grounds. Mimicking the foliage, the tablecloth was patterned in green and gold, the whole room decorated with tapestries in warm colors to match the rugs. Servants swirled around with chargers of steaming meat while a few minstrels played in a frescoed corner. They were surprisingly good. As Jaelportian entertainment went. Even if only rich sandwits would *pay* for Jaelportian entertainment.

One dinner. Tides, but Sethe missed her owl. Talking to herself was nearly pointless without it. *You're safe. It's just one night.*

The bird would have made that sound so much more convincing.

Rigil moved toward the table where his squire sat with a gaggle of Jaelportian ladies. Mages too, judging by the prickle on the back of Sethe's neck. Predators.

Sethe squeezed Rigil's arm. "Stay with me," she hissed. A command, not a request. If he abandoned her to go strolling with the queen or fall under some love spell . . .

Rigil brushed a thumb over her knuckles. Barely a touch. "Where would I go?"

Sethe cursed her pulse for beating through her fingertips. Did he think pretending they were still in Melas, just Rigil and Sethe, would make up for his lies?

But if he felt her heartbeat, he misunderstood. Right before they reached the table, he leaned in to whisper in her ear.

"One exit in the north wall, one in the south. Stairs to the upper rooms just outside the southern door. From there, an easy climb from the gallery to the roof, then a leap to the grounds."

"You think we'll need an escape route?"

"No." Rigil grabbed her chair, still whispering. "But I know you like to have one."

Definitely trying to make up for the lies. Sethe accepted the seat he pulled out and braced for the longest meal of her life.

Queen Mandzee, regal in deep-sea indigo, showed a touch of curiosity at Sethe's clothes, saying something about Hamonah's endless surprises that landed somewhere between polite and patronizing. Beside Sethe, Mezaedo sat with hair still wet from bathing, his old clothes washed like Rigil's. He had sprinkled some of his spice on a steaming roll and offered her some as she sat.

Sethe stared at him. "I thought you'd like Jaelportian food."

"I do," he whispered with an orange-stained grin. "That's why I'm making it *more* Jaelportian."

As Rigil took his place at the table, the queen's three companions pinned Sethe to her chair with black-as-ink eyes. None greeted her. The one in green actually scooted away.

So, no small talk, then?

Pity.

She was counting on Mezaedo to be her ally. A former street thief and a former stray weren't all that different, and at least they could struggle through the arsenal of utensils together. But the tiko was annoyingly skilled. He didn't spill a drop of soup or pick the wrong spoon even once. While Rigil held the ladies captive with an elaborate toast to the hostess, Sethe leaned over to jab the squire with her spoon under the table.

"Let me guess. You learned table manners from your eighth master, the *prince of Magos*."

Mezaedo's brows curled as he reached for another roll. "My eighth master raised prizewinning goats, so, wrong. Except for the table manners bit. That actually was him."

Jaelportians. You couldn't count on them for anything.

". . . found Meneton quite pleasant, didn't we, Sethe?"

Sethe glanced up from her ridiculously intricate salad—honestly, was it art or food?—and found herself the center of attention.

"Oh." She swallowed a mouthful of greens. "Meneton? Right. Very pleasant."

Bored eyes returned to Rigil.

It was hard to navigate conversation and courses at the same time. Hard for Sethe, at least. Rigil didn't seem to have any trouble winning laughs from the long-nosed woman in green, coaxing gasps from the fawning one with the freckles, and even finding something praiseworthy in the sour-faced one beside him, the one holding Er'Rets's ugliest cat. As servants came and went, replacing old dishes with steaming new ones, he deflected inquiries, skirted specifics, and somehow managed to make Meneton sound like a routine mission. Nothing to bore them with.

Tides, he was brilliant. Now, if he would just stop trying to drag Sethe into it.

"And what of court?" The sour-faced one leaned close to Rigil, lashes lowered demurely as her cat ate something from her hand. She must have *bathed* in perfume. The reek was making Sethe's nostrils burn from here. "Surely you've found a bride by now, Sir Rigil? Some noblewoman, perhaps?"

Sethe set down her fork. The shikana was suddenly too constricting, or maybe that was the room shrinking. What had Rigil said about that escape? *Stairs to the upper rooms . . . easy climb to the roof . . .*

"Lady Fateema." Mezaedo murmured the name to Sethe between spoonfuls of pudding. "Daughter of the Patron Mother of the Grand Bazaar. Lots of status, but no scruples about skimming the coffers when she collects rent for her mother. Paranoid about bloodvoicers too, but don't ask why. All I know is, she never goes without karpos and has about a dozen hired toughs in her service. My seventh master was one of them."

Sethe grabbed her wine and held it to her lips so hard that her teeth nearly cracked the glass. "Which made you what? A tough-in-training?" she whispered.

Mezaedo shrugged. "I was just the one who scrubbed the blood out of his clothes."

"I'm afraid I have no news of a bride, Lady Fateema," Rigil was saying. Was that a bite in his voice? "In truth, I do not believe such a noblewoman exists."

Setting her elbows on the table, Fateema laced her hands together and settled her chin on her knuckles. "And what kind of woman would that be, Sir Rigil? An intelligent one, I suppose?"

"Intelligent, aye," Rigil said. "Wise, even better. I believe Arman gifts some people with the wisdom to see the world as it is and the courage to face what they find. You don't come upon such wisdom in books. I would know."

That seemed to amuse Fateema. She tittered into her fingers before adding, "And she must be beautiful?"

"Of course."

Sethe's knife slipped halfway through her potato, screeching against her plate like a cat on fire. She did not look up as Rigil went on. "I seek the most elusive kind of beauty, Lady Fateema. Sincerity." Sethe glanced up, surprised, but found Rigil intent on the Jaelportians, calm and straight-backed, not a hair out of place. "Without sincerity, a woman can be beautiful at best. With it . . ." His eyes darted to Sethe, blue and unruffled. "She is radiant."

Caught staring, Sethe could do nothing but grip her fork and hold her breath and wait for those eyes to stop *spearing* her to the back of her chair.

What game was he playing? First, all that talk of stars on the rikoh, then the shikana, and now this. One little flirtation would be nostalgic, but three?

Three was bait.

Fateema sat back as if spurned, but Sethe knew better. This time, when the Jaelportian leaned toward Rigil, face set, Sethe glimpsed the little grains of powder in her hair.

"You must forgive me, Sir Rigil, but I confess I would be envious if some other noblewoman stole you away. You would be so very welcome in Jaelport, and there is truly no realm like it." She smiled, leaning closer until one of her powdered braids nearly brushed his shoulder. "Just breathe that air. Isn't it marvelous?"

"No!"

Chair legs screeched back from the table. A wine glass toppled and broke. Not until Sethe found herself standing, her chair fallen behind her and her wine glugging onto the green and gold carpet, did she realize—oh. *She* had shouted.

Six stares pierced her from around the table, seven if she counted that witch's hairless cat. The queen looked torn between surprise and fascination. The two Jaelportians on her left seemed more interested in glaring at Fateema than Sethe, probably because they'd hoped to enchant Rigil themselves. How much powder were *they* wearing?

Rigil. Was it too late? With love dust, all it took was one whiff. Fateema was watching him, her gaze as hungry as her feline's, waiting for signs that Rigil was hers.

He wiped his hands, took a slow sip of wine, his movements even. Relaxed. Too relaxed?

"Thank you, Lady Mandzee, for the fine meal." He spoke past Fateema to their hostess. "The wine was an especially considerate touch. Who would have thought that innophoria would pair so well with Carm grapes?"

Innophoria. Still standing, Sethe felt her lips flail around the strange word. Reaching past her for a gravy dish, Mezaedo stopped to whisper out of the corner of his mouth, "Love dust."

Innophoria. Love dust. So Rigil *had* inhaled it?

The queen smiled, also speaking past Fateema. "The versatility of our plant continues to amaze. And think nothing of the wine, Sir Rigil. I would never place my guests at risk."

Confusion must have been tattooed across Sethe's face, because Mezaedo flicked the side of his goblet and mouthed, *Antidote.*

Oh. The innophoria antidote, probably made from the same plant as the love dust. Mandzee had put it in the wine as a precaution. As one did in Jaelport. Obviously.

"Miss Sethe." The queen turned her smoky gaze on Sethe now, as if just noticing that one of her guests had forgotten how to use a chair. "Are you all right?"

In her rush to stand, Sethe had planted her hand on her plate. Gravy was squelching between her fingers. "No," she managed. "No, Your Highness, not since I was *arrested* at sea. Either this is how you treat your company, luring them into a den of powdered lions, or we really are captives here, not guests."

Rigil's eyes went round. "*Sethe.*"

But Queen Mandzee only laid her fork on the table beside her knife, perfectly parallel. "Miss Sethe, I apologize if I have given you the impression that you are anything less than an honored guest. Truly, it was not my intention. Do tell me how I can make it right."

"Grant us passage out of Jaelport." The words were out of Sethe's mouth before any of the reasons to sit down and be quiet could assert themselves. "We have a boat. Let us take it through the Shelosh Channel at first light."

"If you will excuse us." Rigil stood abruptly, gesturing for his squire to follow. "Your Highness, perhaps you and I can discuss this further after—"

"Granted," Queen Mandzee said.

Rigil froze with his elbow crooked awkwardly in the air, like he'd forgotten who he was holding it out for. A grinning Mezaedo wagged his eyebrows at Sethe.

Whatever Sethe stammered out next was half gratitude, half apology, but Rigil's lips were curving up as he came and claimed her arm, furtively slipping a napkin over her gravy-coated fingers as he made some polished excuses to the table. Her Highness was too generous. They'd depart at dawn. Truly a pleasure, as always.

"That," he whispered, as he led her toward the doors, "is why *you* are the master, and I the apprentice."

Sethe held her smile and his arm only until the banquet doors closed behind them.

Then she fled, burning and exposed and the only sandwit in this palace who really was in danger of enchantment.

CHAPTER SEVENTEEN
SETHE

THIS WAS WHAT SETHE GOT FOR PLAY-ing nice with Jaelportians: a torn shikana, bruised pride, and a downright *mediocre* rooftop view.

Rigil had been right about the escape route. It had taken Sethe all of five minutes to flee from the banquet hall to the upper rooms, then out the gallery window. Now, stretched out on the palace roof, the bronze tiles still warm from the sun that had already set, Sethe ripped out her braids and let her chin-length frizz fall over her scars. She'd torn the shikana climbing out the window, and balmy night wind was pouring in through the gash along one calf. Beneath her, Mandzee's gardens unfurled around the palace like a map.

Lying on her back, one arm under her head, Sethe tried to put herself on a rooftop in merchant-crowded Melas instead. A simpler time, when all she'd cared about was watching the sunset from her seaside shack, searching for the fattest purse to be her next target.

Or *their* next target.

"Sethe?"

Like ashes, the memory blew away. In reality, perched on a

Hamartano roof in finery she didn't deserve, Sethe hadn't even heard the footsteps of the one man in Er'Rets she least wanted to see. Teeth gritted, she pressed her head to the roof, focused on the buzz of cicadas and the deepening blue of the sky. Maybe if she kept still . . .

"Sethe, if you think I won't join you up there, I will happily disappoint you."

Well, she might as well get it over with. Sethe slid her legs over the roof and dropped to the balcony.

Rigil was waiting there, leaning backward against the alabaster rail. Creepers climbed the palace wall beside him, framing the double doors and twining around the spindles of the rail. Moths rustling in the leaves made the whole balcony feel alive somehow, like it was breathing around them. Breathing and listening.

"I'm fine." Sethe jerked on the bodice of her shikana, twisting the waist and legs back into place after her landing. "If that's what you came to ask."

"I came to thank you," he said. "My mother taught me never to dine with Jaelportians without an antidote. Mandzee saw to that, but if I *had* been in danger . . ." He winced, probably thinking of Fateema. "Well. You would have saved me a great deal of embarrassment. Perhaps worse. And that aside, I believe Fateema was rather jealous."

Sethe slicked oily hands down her beaded bodice. Beads. On her *bodice*. She should never have let the gods trick her into trying for beautiful, even for one night.

Still. Fateema, jealous? Of Sethe? Why would—

He was smiling at her. Or half smiling, but with something in the tilt of his head, the knowing curl of his lips, that was pulling heat to her face like steam.

Sethe swallowed hard. Better not to finish that thought about Fateema. Better to leave now, before the stars lit his eyes and made her forget how dangerous it was to be with him. A regret waiting to happen—that was all Rigil could be to her. And Rigil *Barak*? Even worse.

Her feet refused to move. A flicker lit the night as a firefly burned across the balcony.

"You lied about Zerah Rock," Sethe said. "I might have guessed wrong, but you could have corrected me. You could have told me what you are."

He was worrying one of his cuffs, but he flinched then, as if bitten. "I was rather hoping we could work up to that."

"Is that what you were doing in Melas for, what, eight months? Working up to it?" All the air in her body left her in a mirthless laugh. "I guess that's what rich men do to entertain themselves, is it? Dress up in rags and see how many filthy street urchins you can fool?"

"Sethe."

"Why didn't you tell me? Why did you *lie*?"

He'd missed a patch of blondish hair under his chin. She only noticed because his throat bobbed for an oh-so-guilty swallow right before he said, "I was fleeing Zerah Rock when we met. My father had disinherited Eagan for joining the Kingsguard, and I felt I couldn't replace him. So I ran." A ghost smile touched that corner of his lips. "In Melas, when you met me, a fool with no plan, you were satisfied with so little. I thought you would think less of me if you knew."

Sethe snorted. "That you're rich?"

"That I'm a failure and a runaway." He sagged against the rail. "And a liar."

He looked tired. Tired, and for the first time since she'd known him, so unsure, it put the world off its axis. For a heartbeat, looking at him almost hurt.

A hot wind raked the balcony, whipping the shikana around her legs. Typical. The one time he expected anger, and she had none left. Not a drop.

Incredible. All his jokes about fleeing his hardheaded master at Zerah Rock. All his attempts to convince her that he'd learned his accent from the family he'd served. The pieces had been there, begging to be put together. She'd just liked the illusion too much.

A man of many talents. Sethe hugged her arms against a snort. "You should have been a bard. You scuddy well had me convinced." He blinked, gauging her mood, and didn't relax until Sethe perched on the rail beside him. Probably a mistake. "Your father must be a tyrant to make Melas seem better than Zerah Rock," she said.

He didn't answer at first, just raked his hair, ruining whatever neatness was left. There wasn't much to begin with, and that unruly lock of blond hair was only getting unrulier. And more distracting.

Then, deepening his voice, Rigil murmured, "*There are two kinds of men in this world, boy: those who see life for the test that it is, and those who still manage to fail it.*"

Sethe watched his face. "Gave that speech often, did he?"

"Every time I lost a game of citadel."

"What about the games you won?"

He cast her a smirk, probably unaware that he was rubbing his finger where a noble's signet ring should be. "I suppose I should give the man some grace. It can't have been easy for him, all his hopes resting on the disappointing shoulders of his second-born son."

By the flex of his jaw, there was more to that story, but she'd need a lockpick to pry it out of him. "And that's when you came to Melas?"

"No. That came later. After I learned the hard way that life is not a game of citadel." He dragged a hand over his eyes as if scrubbing something from them, a memory painted inside his head. "I thought I could begin again in Melas. No one to disappoint. To fail."

He smiled, then, a spider-silk version of the smile she knew, tucked in that corner of his mouth that was always so quick to give him away. He had a scar there now. Tiny and pearl-colored and so thin she couldn't help wondering what could have left a nick like that.

"And the Kingsguard?" she ventured. "Another new beginning?"

A cicada buzzed in the vines climbing the wall behind her. It nearly masked the sound of his sigh. "We can hope. I'm not certain it will be enough. My father does not forget failure."

A Barak family trait, apparently.

"I don't see what Eagan has that you don't," Sethe said. "You both give orders and wear fancy clothes."

Rigil's tilted glance said *I know what you're doing,* but he took the escape. "Frankly, I wear them better."

"And I watched you at dinner. You were born for this. Nobility, politics. It suits you."

He went still, his entire mien bending to her. "To hear you say that, Sethe . . ." Then he growled. "But I shouldn't have put you through that tonight. I just wanted you to see that I *am* good at it, that this is my future, whether I like it or not. Arman knows I can't avoid it forever."

Wind whistled between the towers, waves crashing somewhere to the east as Sethe gripped the rail against the force of that statement.

This was his future. It always had been. He was Sir Rigil Barak, heir of Zerah Rock, and there was no other road for him. When this was over and he had finished his Kingsguard work, they would part again, Rigil for nobility, Sethe for freedom. That had always been the plan.

Whether she liked it or not.

"Your father will accept you." Sethe didn't know where that confidence had come from, but if it would take some of the invisible weight from his shoulders, fine. "Any sandwit can see you're every bit an heir and as worthy as Eagan."

His smile, a phantom, barely existed before it didn't.

Normally, Sethe wouldn't mind the silence that pooled between them, but tonight, she didn't want to fill it with the fragments in her head. Tonight, there was only the stillness in her mind and Rigil in pain beside her.

"It's funny." Two more fireflies crossed Sethe's sight, blinking in time. "My mother wasn't exactly the nurturing sort either."

"It isn't the same." He tugged at one sleeve as if bent on ripping the worn cloth to shreds. "I shouldn't bemoan my life after what you suffered from—Lightness, from your own mother. It's no wonder you never mentioned her."

"Not never. What about when I taught you how to spot a false wagon bed?"

"She taught you everything you know, I imagine."

The way he said it. Like it was a compliment, like they weren't talking about digging through the pockets of drunks after dark. She'd forgotten how easily he could do that. Make her feel like a pearl instead of the grit pearls were made of.

"She taught me to survive. On Hamonah, that's as good as love." With a dry laugh, Sethe pushed her hair aside, exposing the line of stitches where an earring had once hung. For some reason, Rigil's hand moved toward his pocket as if to fish something out, but his hand dropped as she went on. "Our last night together, she gave me that earring. Something to remember her by, she said. The next day, she took me down to the docks."

Breathing in, Sethe tasted it, *lived* it. Brine and fish guts, tar and curry, jungle flowers and crates that smelled of sunbaked wood. A handsome, mildew-smelling man with bone-white hair, waiting for them at the harbor.

"I thought we were leaving the island. She said we'd go to Jaelport, start a new life where we wouldn't need to steal. All I had to do was get in the box."

Stars began poking through the velvet sky as Rigil's gaze brushed her, seafoam soft.

Nose stinging, she tipped her head back. "Nedir gave her five golds for me. Five. Used to say he had the better end of the deal. To his credit, he took care of me. Taught me my letters, kept me fed." Sethe worked her thumbnail into the railing, the grooves like the halls she'd once known as surely as her own palms. Her world had been so small then, orbiting a few inescapable constants. The halls that smelled of incense. The guards who trailed her everywhere. The sound of the sea crashing against the fortress walls. Vials and vials of silver dust.

"There were always tests," she said. "*Experiments*. He was obsessed with strengthening his bloodvoice, breaking through my shields. After a few years, I took it for granted that he never would, but . . ."

Rigil exhaled. Sand rushing through an hourglass. "But then he broke in."

Sethe shivered. "I thought he'd kill me with his bloodvoicing, just his voice in my head. I *felt* myself splitting open until I thought there would be nothing left when it was over, nothing but a hole for Nedir to fill. That *pain* . . ."

Crushing her good eye shut, Sethe tried not to remember and nearly jolted when Rigil's fingertips brushed her face, pulling the hair from her scarred side.

"Did he do this?"

He was close. Probably close enough to see the gooseflesh that broke out on her bare arms when he touched her. Close enough to see every drop of her pain. That should have terrified her.

It didn't.

Sethe stayed perfectly still, her silence its own answer as Rigil studied the scars around her eye, down her cheek, up to her temple. His gaze followed them, and Sethe followed his gaze. Even now, he looked so much like the boy from Melas. Older, more burdened, but still. *Him.*

"I did it," she whispered, her voice sand. Rigil's gaze snapped up, shocked, and a sob cracked her throat. "I just needed him out of my head, and if I had to rip him out with my bare hands, if I had to tear myself apart to do it . . ."

So this was what ugliness felt like. Clawing hair back over her scars, Sethe ached when his touch fell away. "I was fifteen. Smuggled myself out of the Talons before Nedir could put my fragments to use. I learned how to use them, how different they made me from other bloodvoicers. I'll admit, it was an advantage, being able to do so much at once and even use the Veil without going unconscious because of what Nedir had done to me. But I decided never to use my ability the way he would. And I swore never to be trapped again."

Had he ever stood so close before, ever touched her face with his breath before? Did it matter?

No. It didn't. It couldn't. Sethe fisted her hands, made one last desperate attempt to remind herself why this could not happen. It could *not.* She would not give this man her heart again just to find herself alone with a broken heart that would never heal quite right. Not again. His future was nobility, and hers was . . . whatever it was. Even dreams could be traps, if she let them.

But were they always?

Did they *have* to be?

Rigil's face hung so close that if they were only two cutpurses in Melas, two simple nothings, she might have wanted him to kiss her. She might have wanted it more than anything in the sea and sky, the universe made of nothing but blue eyes. *So close.*

For the second time in moments, he brushed her hair aside, exposing her in all her misery, a shattered, ruined thing that had never left that first crate despite the strength she'd found while she'd known him. But he didn't pull away. His thumb trickled along her scars, along her jaw, then to her mouth, and he seemed surprised to find it there, like he had never fully lingered on her lips until that moment.

Sethe's first instinct to run warred with a jittery something in her gut that was rooting her feet to the floor. *Remember,* she commanded herself, *he's a noble, bound for a world you have no place in. Letting him lure you in now will only hurt more when he has to leave you behind.*

She forced the words past her lips: "What are you doing?"

He tensed, fingers freezing on her cheek, and she felt the shift like a hammer to her heart. Proof that she'd been hoping for something else, something that would have broken her walls past all rebuilding.

His face pulled tight, like the skin of a drum, his hand sliding down until the tips of his fingers barely rested on her jaw. Hesitant, but not pulling away. The question seemed to surprise him, but something determined laced his voice when he answered. "Don't tell me you don't know."

"You're an heir, Rigil."

"I was an heir when we met."

"And you don't think that makes a difference?" Sethe grabbed his wrist but stopped shy of yanking his hand off her face. "You don't think I know there are a dozen Lady Fateemas out there for every one of me?"

A tiny tick on one side of his mouth. "But there is only one of you."

Tides. She couldn't do this. This was everything she was afraid of, and she wasn't strong enough to keep her barriers from crumbling. Before she could second-guess herself, tumble sixteen years into the past on a landslide of regret and what-ifs, Sethe pried his hand away and pushed it back at him. "What. Are. You. Doing?"

He gazed down at his hand, now hanging limp between them. "There is no one else, Sethe. There has never been anyone else."

"Liar," she rasped. "In all this time? A smarter man would have moved on."

His mouth hardened into a thin line. "Do you think I didn't try? I know my duties as heir, Sethe, know precisely what is expected of me, but that doesn't change the fact that for every woman I met, not one of them ever saw through me the way you always could. None of them challenged my foolishness or made me laugh at unexpected times or saw the world in all its rawness but still stopped to be captivated by a wilted orchid. None of them could be all those things and still think so little of themselves. None of them were *you*, Sethe."

Her fingers found her beaded belt, began tying the cords in knots. "I didn't know you were an heir. You fooled me, same as anyone else."

"Did I? Truly?"

She glanced up at him, Rigil Barak in all his splendor, pristine hair and razor-straight spine and all. So different from the ragged boy who had chased her through the streets of Melas and gaped like a loon the first time he'd seen her slit a guard's purse without a sound. A runaway servant, she'd thought. Helpless as a beached fish, but so strange about some things. The way he'd moved as if *expecting* the air to bow for him. The way he'd met every stare without flinching and refused to back down first, no matter who it was. The way his words had flowed from him like silver from a crucible.

No. He hadn't fooled her. Not completely. Some part of her had always known.

Sethe set her teeth and turned away.

"I knew it," he said. "I always thought you were humoring me by not asking more questions. It was a relief, somehow, to know that I had never fully deceived you. Lightness, if you only knew how *free* I felt not having to pretend to be better than I was, you would understand why, when I saw you in Land's End . . ." He sipped a breath. "You're laughing at me."

She scoffed weakly, studying the sky. "Because this is ridiculous."

"Is it? I had deserted my father's house when I met you, Sethe. Even so, I was prepared to return to Zerah Rock with you, to face my punishment, if it meant bringing you to a safe haven Nedir could never touch. Does that mean nothing?" He stepped closer, cutting off whatever limp response was crawling up her throat. "I know you felt something for me. You never said it, perhaps you still would not admit it, but I know our time together meant something. I was more than *useful* to you."

Sethe's foot slid backward. "Of course you were." When he blinked in surprise, his mouth still wrapped around some silver-gilded plea, she put another step between them, lungs burning for air that didn't taste like him. "I'd been a caged pet for half my life. You were the first boy I'd talked to in years, let alone the first to make me feel like I was worth half a rutah. Those months I spent teaching you to survive in Melas were the only days I stopped thinking of life as a cage."

He opened his mouth to interject, but she held up a hand.

"I'm not looking for pity. Yes, I cared about you. I was too young to know better. But I'm not that scared little girl anymore. I know you think we can pick up on the road to Zerah Rock, finish whatever story you've written in your head for the girl you remember, but that girl, Rigil? She's gone. She disappeared a long time ago, and I won't be backed into some glittering cage just so you can return to Zerah Rock having fixed a blot on your ledger."

Her voice buckled before she could go on. Probably for the best. Whatever pollen filled the air above the gardens, it was burning murder on her eye.

He still held her gaze, his face hooded by shadows, guilt dripping off his sagging shoulders like rain. Anyone else would have looked away, but not Rigil. He liked punishing himself too much for that.

Oh, tides. She'd said too much. Or not enough. Or both.

"I just got away from that night," she said. "The road to Zerah Rock, believing you'd abandoned me, having to start all over again, alone. I was finally starting to believe I'd left all that behind, and I can't go back, Rigil. I can't be trapped like that again." *I can't be the woman you're waiting for,* she almost added. *The beautiful, wise one with no scuddy doubts.*

Never mind that just now, she'd give her good eye to stand in that woman's skin. Apparently, he wasn't the only one who liked torturing himself.

Rigil crushed his lips together, gaze falling to their feet, his silence so thick that Sethe rushed to fill the void with the first pathetic lie she found in reach. "Anyway, I don't even believe in your God."

To her surprise, he laughed. A short, brittle bark that shot through her like a splinter. "Your honesty is brutal enough, Sethe, but I never thought I'd see the day you hid behind lies."

How did he always know? "I guess I'm not as *sincere* as you thought," she snapped.

That did it. The moment shattered. A peacock wailed somewhere in the garden. Rigil took a step back, then another, and once again he was the Kingsguard noble with perfect posture and manners to match. The lamplight from inside the balcony doors warmed one side of his face, shaved clean as the day she'd met him. Was that why he'd done it? All part of his ploy to convince her they could still go back to the way things had *almost* been?

"I believe that is the third time I've managed to distress you today, Miss Sethe," he said, his voice suddenly as dark and dry as the Jaelportian wine they'd had at dinner. "Please, forgive me. I forgot myself." And the quiet subtext: *Apparently, you did too.*

Sethe clung to the balcony rail, willing the stone to seep some of the fever out of her.

He tipped his head back, shoulders squaring in the glow shining through the glass-paned balcony doors. "Shall I walk you to the ladies' wing?"

Sethe forced herself to perch on the rail again, feet dangling, the night wind playing carelessly in her hair. "You go ahead." She tried for nonchalant. It came out strangled. "I'd like to stay awhile."

For once, he didn't protest, his "good night" cordial and sickeningly flat. After he slipped through the doors, Sethe made herself count to fifty, sixty, a hundred before she even thought of following him inside. A hundred came and passed. She slid off her perch to sit on the balcony floor, chin propped on her gold-clad knees that shimmered in the lamplight. When she lost count somewhere after three hundred and thirty, she started again, determined not to leave this balcony until she'd done at least that much right.

CHAPTER EIGHTEEN
RIGIL

FOOL BOY. HOW MANY TIMES HAD RIGIL heard that in his childhood? How had it taken thirty-two blighted years to realize it was true?

Fool. Fool. Hollow-headed *fool*.

Brassy sconce light pooled on the floor of Mandzee's corridor as Rigil stalked down the hall like a hound off its chain, passing window after tall window shining indigo with nightfall. Potted palms rustled in his draft. His wrist still tingled where Sethe's shaking hand had pried his touch away.

Sethe.

Lightness, she had seen right through him. Only she could lay bare her soul like that and leave *him* flayed and bleeding.

But he deserved that, silver-tongued halfwit that he was. Playing the nobleman, wrapping Sethe in silk and beads, trying to write a new history in which he hadn't abandoned her or Zerah Rock and was somehow worthy of both. What had he expected?

Boots clipping on tiles, Rigil swung around the corner and came face-to-face with Queen Mandzee herself. If there was irony here, he refused to see it.

Mandzee's face registered only the slightest surprise at finding him alone in her halls, her bemused "Cousin" even drier than usual as she glided past him, leaving a jasmine trail behind. Her entourage, minus Lady Fateema, trickled behind her, Lady Halia passing close enough to brush Rigil with her skirts.

"I do hope Miss Sethe is all right," Halia whispered, smiling, as she passed. To that, Rigil managed a bow so shallow it likely fell short of the word.

Isemios's wit, he hated Jaelport.

With no destination in mind, he continued down the hall, slowing slightly as he passed a large oil painting of the late Queen Torrezia in all her sharkish glory. A space had been cleared on the saffron-and-amber-frescoed wall for Mandzee's portrait, but either it hadn't been painted yet, or else Mandzee had refrained from hanging her likeness next to her dead mother's legacy.

Here, the hall forked again, the forward path winding back toward the dining hall and the rightmost path leading to the women's wing. Forbidden to men, of course. He could almost smell Jaelportian treachery wafting from that corridor.

Which was why the female shout of distress took him utterly by surprise.

Throwing Jaelportian etiquette to the wind, he darted down the women's hall, scanning for something other than a porcelain pot that might serve as a weapon. Rooms lined the hall on either side, most of them closed and bleeding shadow into the hall from the cracks beneath their doors. Up ahead and to the right, however, one door hung slightly open, orange light glowing in the gap like the last stripe of sunset before the sun vanished under the ocean.

Rigil did not announce himself before pushing through the palm-etched door, but the moment he stepped in, he almost wished he had.

Lady Fateema stood in a large sitting room decorated in deep green and gold, her back to Rigil, hairless cat wrapped about her scarlet-gowned shoulders like a stole. The room was windowless, but an archway in the southern wall opened onto what must have been a private study or bedchamber. The dim light from the lamp on Fateema's parlor table made it difficult to make out anything beyond the vaguest shapes.

For a moment, he thought she was alone and that he had just committed the gravest cultural infraction imaginable, until he heard a voice behind her. Low, a gritty whisper, as if pushed through the wrong throat.

"I know everything about you, Lady Fateema. All of your secrets. Remember that."

Rigil hesitated. That was Mezaedo's voice.

One fist balled at her side, Fateema stood straight as one of the palace spires. "You are on dangerous footing. Do you know what happens to men caught in a Jaelportian woman's quarters? This little meeting could be messy for both of us."

"We both know I had no choice," Mezaedo's voice answered. "Now, to be sure you were paying attention . . ."

Before the unseen speaker could finish that thought, Fateema bent toward him, raising her balled fist until her body blocked it from Rigil's view. A puff of breath, followed by a choked cough from the speaker, his last few words hanging in the air like a broken song.

Too late, Rigil sidestepped to see around her and found—sure enough—Mezaedo Chevyah, his lips slightly parted for a smile of sudden, bewildered delight.

No. Bewildered *enchantment*.

As Rigil watched, Fateema reached up to stroke Mez's cheek with a red-painted fingernail, tucking a small pouch into the folds of her dress as she did. The beaded hem tinkled when she moved.

"I do not appreciate being bullied," Fateema crooned. "I work best without threats, but I must say, I like the package this one came in."

Mezaedo shuddered under her touch, oozing adoration. "You are beautiful," he rasped, in his own voice this time. "You're perfect. You're a moldy *goddess*."

"And that will be *quite* enough of that." Rigil strode forward, ignoring Fateema's little jolt of surprise, as Mezaedo dropped to his knees, breathing hard. "Lady Fateema, I hope you realize that the queen will hear of this."

Fateema laughed, but the sound was strained, the square of her shoulders too stiff to be quite casual. Rigil saw fear in the tense skin around her mouth as her gaze flitted to the door, then back to him.

"Oh, I do hope you will tell her, Sir Rigil," she said. "And be sure to include that he was threatening *me*. I did only what was necessary to protect myself from a strange man *intruding* in my chambers. Do you realize how grave this transgression is?"

On his knees, gazing up at her, Mezaedo pawed at Fateema's hand. "Marry me, Fateema. Marry me and I'll make you the happiest woman in all moldy Er'Rets."

Oh, Isemios's wit. Rigil planted a hand on Mezaedo's shoulder to keep him on the ground, but never turned his back on Fateema. Her perfume was obnoxiously thick, designed to fuddle the senses. "Protect yourself. From Mezaedo? I heard him say that he didn't have a choice in coming here. If compelling him to your chambers was your way of getting my attention, I would ask that you leave my squire out of your games."

She flung her shoulders back, her cat mewling with the sudden motion. "So he was forced, was he? Well, that sounds like your word against mine, and I don't advise challenging a woman's testimony in Jaelport, Sir Rigil." She tipped her chin up. "I would be well within my rights to bring this matter to the queen with a request for a, shall we say, *proportionate* form of discipline?"

As a eunuch's maroon skirt flashed across Rigil's mind, Fateema made for the door, her slippers soundless on the rug, the beads crisscrossed down her back catching the light like a thousand tiny eyes. She turned back with one hand on the knob, her sharp features set in stone. "You really ought to keep a closer watch on your squire, Sir Rigil. Anyone might make use of him."

After the doors had closed behind Fateema's slithering skirts, Rigil counted ten heartbeats, then he hauled the boy to his feet, stumbling when Mezaedo sagged against him as if his knees had forgotten their functions. "Isemios's wit, Mezaedo. You got yourself enchanted?"

Mezaedo sighed with all the theatrics of a bad bard. "Call me enchanted, Sirrig. That's what I am, moldy enchanted with the beautifullest, cleverest, gracefullest, beautifullest—"

"Aye, you said that."

Rigil could have been gentler tugging Mezaedo out of the women's wing and back up the corridor toward his rooms. But then again, Mezaedo could have been wiser.

The world was not what it could be tonight.

"What were you doing in the women's wing?" Rigil asked as they passed beneath Queen Torrezia's secretive smile once more. "Fateema claimed that you were threatening her."

"Fateema." Mezaedo tripped a little, letting Rigil hold him up. "Fateema, Fateema, Fateema. Have you ever heard a more beautiful name?"

Right. Mezaedo Chevyah was many things, but threatening was not one of them. Lightness, just when Rigil had been warming to the idea of recruiting him to the Mârad. Had Fateema truly lured him there to capture Rigil?

To Rigil's surprise and relief, he arrived at his bedchamber door to find Jakeen the eunuch waiting, his hand on the filigreed knob.

"Sir Rigil, Her Majesty wished me to ensure that you are well after—" The eunuch cut off at the sight of Mezaedo, rapidly assessing symptoms. "Oh."

"I need an antidote, Jakeen. Quickly." Thank Arman, Fateema hadn't sounded the alarm. Yet.

With the briskness of a servant entirely at peace with his place in the world, Jakeen bowed once and clipped down the hall as Rigil pushed Mezaedo into a large bedchamber with a vaulted ceiling, crown molding, and an adjoining parlor, both rooms aglow with drowsing fires. No sense in sending the boy to his own room. He would need watching.

"All right, Mez. We're off for Hamonah tomorrow, and I need a squire, not a lovesick puppy."

"Leave? I can't leave!" Mezaedo flung himself onto a long divan, arms dangling, face sheened with sweat. "What if she marries someone else?"

Oh, Lightness. "Over the great Mezaedo Chevyah? Not likely."

"She's perfect, Sirrig. She's everything. I won't ever be happy without her."

Better this than bolting for the exit, he supposed. Rigil folded his arms and leaned on the door. "And the Kingsguard?"

"Forget the Kingsguard. I'm telling you, there's nothing without Fateema. If I can't have her, I'll—I'll—"

Isemios's wit. And people thought Arman had no sense of humor.

"I know it feels that way now, Mez." Trying to sap some of the sting from his voice, Rigil rubbed his brow against a mounting headache. "And I'm sure you mean it. But there are more important things." He tried not to see the gravy stain on the sleeve of his tunic, tried not to remember the way his pulse had stammered when he'd first seen Sethe in that shikana, when she'd let him close enough to cup her face, trace her scars, see the spray of tiny freckles on her nose as she'd pushed him away. "What of Arman, Mezaedo? If Fateema is not part of His will for you, are you willing to accept that?"

The question hung in the room like fog. A choking, choking fog.

When the boy began reciting Jaelportian poetry, one arm still over his face, Rigil began praying for another knock at the door and nearly thanked Arman when it came.

"Efficiency." He swung the door wide, gesturing Jakeen inside. "I see many promotions in your future, Jakeen."

The eunuch swept into the room, holding a slender root between his fingers like a goblet stem. "If you would be so kind as to fetch a bowl, Sir Rigil?"

Nullifying innophoria was done easily enough, but the process was far from pleasant. By the time they convinced Mezaedo to eat the root, Rigil had six lines of a Jaelportian love sonnet burned into his memory. They cycled in his head while he held a vase under Mezaedo's mouth, watching the boy vomit course after course of Jaelportian delicacies into the porcelain.

"Stuffed moldy onions." Perched on the side of the divan, gripping the cushions for balance, Mezaedo's first unenchanted words came out in a groan. "What did . . . ?"

"You were bewitched," Rigil said. "By Lady Fateema."

Mezaedo fell backward onto the divan. "Stuffed moldy onions, anything but that."

Propping one foot on the chair next to his, Rigil tried to smile. "It has happened to the best, Mezaedo. Even King Gidon."

"Not *you*."

"If you're suggesting that no woman has ever enchanted me, you would be wrong." That came out more sharply than intended. Standing, Rigil stretched his laced fingers until his shoulders cracked, keenly aware of watchful Jakeen. "And if it comforts you, my enchantress needed no powder."

Before Mezaedo could comment on that little confession, Rigil grabbed the nearest nonlethal projectile—a bolster—and threw it at the boy. It struck with a dull thud. "Get some sleep, lad. We leave at dawn." To Jakeen: "You have my thanks."

When the eunuch didn't move, Rigil added, "Was there something else?" If Fateema were going to demand Mezaedo's manhood as punishment for intruding, it *would* happen tonight of all nights.

Jakeen gestured to the neighboring room. "A moment, Sir Rigil?"

Leaving Mezaedo to mutter about his humiliation in peace, they passed into the candle-spiced air of the parlor. It was so dim that Jakeen's features all but disappeared when he faced Rigil in the doorway. "Lady Fateema is claiming that your squire stole into her chambers tonight," he said. "She is telling the queen that she used her powder to protect herself. I'm sure I do not need to inform you that this is a serious offense."

Rigil reached for the door to their side room, clicked it shut between him and Mezaedo's listening ears. "With respect, Jakeen, I know my squire, and he is not capable of what Lady Fateema is claiming. From what I heard, it's entirely possible that she may have lured him there. You may not be aware that she attempted to enchant me this very night, before the queen herself. Forgive me if I don't take her at her word."

Jakeen's brows arched. "You do not require my forgiveness, Sir Rigil. I have no particular loyalty to Lady Fateema."

"Then I can count on your support if it comes to a conflict of testimonies?"

"I do not think it will come to that. Lady Fateema treads shaky ground with the queen, and you are Her Majesty's family. I simply wished to keep you informed."

Rigil exhaled long. A lock of hair fell across his brow, but he couldn't find the energy to sweep it aside. "I appreciate it, Jakeen. Now, is that all?" Half a moment. If he could just have *half a moment* to himself to determine where this night had gone so utterly wrong . . .

Jakeen's mien brightened slightly, as if the conversation had moved into smoother waters. "Her Highness noted that you did not purchase anything for yourself at the bazaar." He waved a hand at the room's one window, currently obscured by something draped from the frame. "She commissioned this for you. The tailors produced it in record time."

Tailors? Commissioned? Rigil turned to study the mysterious window-hanging with equal parts interest and dread.

As expected, it was a tunic in Zerah Rock blue, all fine satin and gold embroidery, lightning stitched over the heart. A statement more than a garment.

"Her Highness feels that a future lord should represent his house," Jakeen said, as if sensing the need for an explanation.

"I'm already wearing blue and black," Rigil replied. Was Sethe still on the balcony? Perhaps he could still salvage the night, explain himself, make her see the life he'd built for them in his mind.

"Sir Rigil, are you listening?"

"Hmm?" Rigil blinked back into the cinnamon-scented room, firelight dancing on the walls. "Forgive me, Jakeen. Do you happen to know if Miss Sethe is still outside?"

Jakeen's face went carefully blank. "If I may be so bold, Sir Rigil, we have an expression in Jaelport: *The goat in the henhouse lays no eggs.*"

Rigil sat down on the arm of the nearest chair. "Meaning?"

"There are some boundaries that cannot be traversed. Some worlds that cannot meld." Jakeen looked prepared to go on, but catching Rigil's stare, he closed his mouth instead. The paint around his eyes made the expression almost feline.

"I see," Rigil said. "So this ensemble is not a gift. It's a message. Her Highness wishes to remind me of my *familial obligations*."

Jakeen folded his hands. "I cannot speak for Her Highness."

"Odd. I rather thought that was your job."

Before Jakeen could respond with infuriating composure, Rigil shoved to his feet and spun toward the window, the perfectly tailored tunic blurring and fuzzing in his vision—or perhaps that was just anger. He shoved the garment aside. Outside the window, fireflies bobbed over a maze of manicured orchids and flowering bushes, most of them carved in whimsical patterns to match the scrollwork on the palace walls. Garden paths wended like rivers through the shrubbery, flowing toward the distant prick of light that marked the garden gate. A single lantern, burning low. Flickering stolen-coin gold.

Who was Mandzee to intrude on his personal affairs? Who was Mandzee to decide whom he could and could not love? That was between him and Sethe.

Sethe who was currently hiding on the balcony. Or worse, halfway back to the coast. *I know you think we can pick up on the road to Zerah Rock . . .*

Because she hadn't come on this journey for him. It was about freedom for her, about escaping Nedir, when for Rigil, it had never been about the Mârad or the mission or saving Er'Rets.

Lightness, Eagan had been right. This whole venture had been about Sethe from the beginning.

Before he knew it, Rigil had a hand on the tunic, the fine silk and gold embroidery grating like sand between his fingers. The anger was leaving him, bleeding away like rich blue dye. "I suppose this is fitting, isn't it?"

"Sir Rigil?"

"This is what I do, Jakeen. I dress old failures in new clothes in the hope that all Er'Rets will forget what lies beneath. Even Sethe."

The eunuch shifted his feet, black-lined eyes pinched as he grappled for a response to something Rigil likely should not have said to a servant.

Well, decorum be blighted. He had no one to impress.

New clothes. Isemios's wit, but that *was* what he did—wrapped the same failures in new colors, pretending he was better this time, worthier. He'd found a talented Bran Rennan to atone for dead Tazeem, and Mezaedo Chevyah to atone for both of them. He'd found the Kingsguard, then the Mârad to counter the tests he'd failed at Zerah Rock. Now, he'd thought a golden shikana and a fancy meal with Mandzee could convince Sethe that he wasn't the same boy who had abandoned her. The failure *still* running from his place in the world. The one who had missed his chance.

Same man. Same failure. Just new clothes.

"You're right," Rigil said. "I've been a fool. Wishing her into a life she doesn't want, another cage. She despises this world." He flung an arm to encompass the room, the palace, every noble house in Er'Rets. "And here I am, an heir, expecting her to take it in stride, forcing her to play a noblewoman's part, and *surprised* when being near me causes her pain."

That last part nearly shredded his throat.

"If I may," Jakeen began in the vocal equivalent of the way a deer moved among wolves, "how do you know Miss Sethe, sir?"

The question of the night. "Perhaps I don't."

Lightness, what a fool he was. Not only for thinking he could change Sethe's mind but for hinging his future on a woman who had lived an entire life without him, a woman he hardly knew. He'd go back to Zerah Rock if he could go back with *her*. He'd feel worthier before his father, perhaps even Arman, if he could prove worthy of *her*. But the Sethe he'd been chasing, who was she really? A face from a few boyhood capers, a raspy laugh cutting through the Melas bustle, a regret that had tailed him through life like a storm head, a will that nothing could break and an intuition no mask could fool and a heart that no amount of suffering had ever managed to harden completely.

That girl, Rigil? She's gone. She disappeared a long time ago.

He didn't believe it for a moment, and watching mist move through Mandzee's garden below his window, Rigil caught himself praying. *Arman, You are supposed to change men, make them better. Why, then, am I no better than I was while stealing bread in Melas? Why return her to me if I still cannot deserve her?*

"Sir Rigil?" Jakeen's golden-brown forehead was buckling. "If the gift has caused you distress, the fault is entirely mine. Her Highness intended no such thing."

"Jakeen, I need a favor." Turning his back on the tunic in the window, Rigil faced the eunuch, his vision slow to adjust to the dimness in the parlor. "I must contact Zerah Rock. Could you have a message sent?"

Firelight pooled in the dips and hollows of Jakeen's face. "To whom?"

"To my father, Lord Burr Barak."

"I shall send for parchment and ink."

The eunuch departed on silent sandals, easing the door shut behind him and sealing Rigil within the tomblike silence of privacy. He reached for the tunic, already envisioning the words unspooling under his pen: *Father, I have one last mission to complete. You can expect my return within the month.*

One last mission. That meant Nedir behind bars and Sethe free to go wherever the wind took her, even if that was away from Rigil. Aye, even then.

Rigil wasted little time in shedding his old tunic, letting the fabric pool at his feet. Enough running. Enough waiting for something to change, for the past to give him *permission* to go back to the people he'd failed. Every stitch here, every thread, every embroidered lightning bolt was a tribute to the home he *would* be worthy of, with or without Sethe.

He had been a runaway and a failure long enough.

It was about time he started acting like an heir.

SETHE

Sconce lit, frescoed, and studded with potted orchids, the palace halls flung sound back at Sethe no matter how quietly she tried to move. Scuddy crinkling shikana and aristocrats and their determination to complicate *everything*.

Even after hiding on the balcony for nearly an hour, her head was still spinning and her face *still* burning when she stopped at her door, braced for a maidservant ambush. So Rigil thought she'd spent the past sixteen years just *waiting* for him, did he? Thought he'd give her a shikana and one of his smiles and, what, she'd scamper off to Zerah Rock with him like the fool girl she'd been back then?

Sethe froze with her hand halfway to the door handle, muscles fusing to her bones.

The door was closed but not locked, the handle gleaming in the lanternlight, the brass around the lock gouged with scratches as if it had been attacked by a cham. Or a set of lockpicks.

Sethe eased the handle down, then nudged the door open with one bare foot, watching an arc of orange light pour into the room from the hall. Her shadow stretched before her, falling on the bed like a spindly black ghost.

Sethe took a cautious step into the room, kicked the door open wider to let more light in.

And cursed.

Embroidered pillows had been thrown everywhere, sheets torn off the low daybed as if someone had expected to find her wrapped in them.

Reflex sent Sethe's hands to her bodice, where the small bundle still hid, crushed to her chest under the fabric. Her karpos. Tides, she'd told Rigil. She'd *told* him it wasn't safe here. Stumbling back a step, she groped for the doorframe, wetting her lips to shout for the guards.

That was when a meaty arm plucked her off the floor.

Sethe thrashed, screamed, but a thick hand clamped over her mouth. She kicked with everything she had, but her attacker's grip never wavered. He reeked of ale and *kajash* leaf and something else. Something faint and sharp and familiar.

The man's breath ruffled her hair. "Play nice, girl, and I'll let you sleep through the long sail back."

Something slender and sharp plunged for Sethe's neck, and suddenly, the smell made sense. Nedir's poison.

Back to Land's End? Drugged and bound and smuggled back to Nedir in a sack?

"NO!"

Her head came back; her teeth came out. This time, something crackled beneath her thrashing foot, and the attacker dropped the pin in shock. Hooking her hands under his arm and one foot around the back of his knee, Sethe dropped, popping his arm over her head as she did. The pin rolled across the floor. The man, a Jaelportian with a sprawling tattoo on his neck, spat something in the local dialect nearly as potent as Nedir's ink.

She sprinted for the door.

She must have done more damage to the man's knee than she thought. By the time she reached the door, she'd gained ground. Catching the jamb, Sethe swung out into the hall, where the eunuch Jakeen was running around a corner, Mandzee close behind.

"Miss Sethe! What is the matter?"

Sethe grabbed a potted fern from an alcove in the wall and pivoted back to the door of her room, swinging the porcelain monstrosity down on the head of the Jaelportian man careening through the door.

Porcelain exploded in Sethe's hands, slicing her palms and skittering across the floor in shards. *THUD.* The goon hit the tiles, blood welling from his scalp.

Sethe collapsed against the frescoed wall and pushed hair from her face, remembering the blood on her hands too late.

That was when Rigil arrived, his hair messier now, like he'd been worrying it since the balcony. Sword out, he planted a hand on Mandzee's shoulder and forcibly *shoved* the queen of Jaelport aside. "Sethe!"

"I'm fine." Blood tracked down Sethe's palms, tiny rivers emptying onto the floor. "He was in my room. Tried to take me to a ship. Nedir must have sent him."

The unconscious attacker could have been a sack of potatoes to Rigil as he stepped over him to reach Sethe. "Are you hurt?"

He'd somehow found time to replace his old tunic with fine blue satin, gold-embroidered cuffs, and a Zerah Rock mark stitched over his heart in amber. He couldn't have looked more noble if he'd tattooed it across his forehead.

"He came for me," Sethe said. "The room was ransacked when I came in."

"Moldy onions." Mezaedo, apparently here too, stepped out from behind Rigil, studying the unconscious man. He seemed a bit wobbly. "That's Ishka Ravan. A mercenary. One of Lady Fateema's."

And the tiko's seventh master, no doubt.

Rigil whirled on Mandzee, his sword not nearly as low as it should have been. "Your Highness, I trust you are as shocked as I to hear of mercenaries in Fateema's employ?"

For all her elegance, Mandzee looked more like a scolded child than a monarch. "Rigil, will you truly assume the worst of Lady Fateema simply on the word of your squire?"

"I have plenty of reason to assume the worst of Lady Fateema, and my squire's word is not in question here."

Tides, but Sethe could get used to this side of Rigil Barak.

"Isemios's wit," he said, "I trusted you, Your Highness. How many of your *guests* belong to Nedir?"

"I have never heard that name in my life." The queen was slowly regaining her poise, like a lizard changing color in the sun. "You are rightfully shaken, but I assure you by Zitheos, by *Arman*, if this man belongs to Lady Fateema, then she has deceived us both. And if you think I would do this, betray my own kin without cause . . ."

Her chin inched upward. "You must truly think me no different from my sister."

Rigil looked ready to spit venom until Sethe stepped on his boot. "Rigil. I believe her."

It took a moment for the fury to drain from his face as he stood there, framed by ferns and orange tiles, painting every inch of her with his eyes, especially her bloodied hands. He could have been a royal in that new tunic. *Drip, drip, drip* went Sethe's blood on the tiles.

"He knows where we are." Sethe focused on the bags under Rigil's eyes, bridling her voice for only him. "We've been stuffed with karpos since Meneton, and somehow Nedir is *still* one step ahead."

Rigil jammed his sword back into its sheath. Still facing Sethe, he spoke to Mandzee. "I suggest having your palace scoured for more unsavories, Your Highness. For your own safety."

His voice was bowstring tight, and Mandzee matched it. "So I shall. Jakeen?"

The eunuch padded away. Mezaedo started chewing his lip like it was his last meal.

"You must have suspected this, Mezaedo," Rigil said suddenly, turning to the boy. "Is that why you approached her after dinner? Why she enchanted you?"

"He was enchanted?" Sethe asked.

The tiko hesitated. "I don't remember a thing after dinner, Sirrig. The dust, you know. But I wouldn't put it past Lady Fateema to throw her peppers in Nedir's pot."

"Who cares?" Forgetting herself, Sethe wiped her hands on the legs of her shikana. She left streaks of blood down the fabric, a fitting end for her one night of almost beauty. Seeing it, Rigil's hands moved toward her but stopped halfway, so Sethe put another much-needed step between them. "We can't afford to wait until dawn. Hamonah is just hours away."

"I will have Captain Iago ready the *Solstice*," the queen said.

"Master Chevyah, while I cannot forget your transgression this night, it seems that I cannot condemn you either—not without more information than I have. If you would join me for a moment? I would like to hear more about this Ishka Ravan and how you know him."

She glided off with a reluctant and somewhat green Mezaedo in tow. And just like that, it was happening again. Here they were. Sethe and Rigil, alone. She looked like a vagabond. He looked like a king.

"You look beautiful," he said finally, wearily. "Did I say that earlier?"

She drew a shaky breath. "Please, don't."

"Sethe." Rigil broke the strangling silence with all the intensity of a man finished talking in riddles. "This is all kinds of improper, but I won't insult you by pretending that I asked you to join me on this mission simply to navigate the Talons."

"Rigil, please."

"Let me finish." He studied his hands, knotted and white. "I can't make up for the trust I've broken or how cornered I must have made you feel these last days, but I want you to know that tonight . . . that won't happen again. You were right. I've had far too much time to imagine a different ending to our story, but I see now that the Sethe of that dream no longer exists. Perhaps she never did except as someone I created to chase across Er'Rets. And to help me avoid going home a little longer." His limp smile drove through her like a sharpened stake. "But that is my battle to fight, Sethe, not yours. I can find my own way through the Talons. I never should have asked it of you, and I hope that, in time, you can forgive me. Perhaps . . ." His mouth made a lame effort to climb higher on one side. "Perhaps one day your travels will bring you to Zerah Rock."

"What are you saying?" Commotion rustled down the hall. Mandzee's guards, eunuchs, probably an army of maidservants to help Sethe out of the torn shikana. "Are you sending me away? Rigil Barak, heir of Zerah Rock, has no more use for me?"

"I'm giving you what you want, Sethe. I'm letting you go. You never wished to be part of this. You said it yourself, in Meneton. And whatever I may have said to persuade you, I *will* find a way through the Talons. I'll leave you in peace, if that's what you want."

So. He would let their past fade like a sunset if she wanted that. Which she did. Of course she did.

Didn't she?

Sethe's silences weren't always answers, but he seemed to take this for one. He stepped back. Then again. Started to say something, gave an awkward laugh. His smile was faint. But still perfect.

"I understand." Flawlessly, he bowed. "I will speak to Mandzee, arrange your passage back to Melas. I believe she owes you that."

Hold on. "This is my freedom at stake, K'sil. You can't expect me to walk away."

K'sil. Why use that name now? Now, when she was *so close* to escaping the maelstrom that was Rigil Barak?

"Sethe, I may not know you as I once did," Rigil said. "But you've been one step shy of panic ever since we left Meneton, ever since you agreed to return to Hamonah. You simply didn't trust me to thwart Nedir's plans. You never could leave a heist in anyone's hands but your own."

He was right, in a way. That *was* why she had come. But, oh, *tides.*

It wasn't why she was staying.

Sethe's hand lurched toward her chest, toward her heart, but too late. She'd already gone and done it. She'd dropped her guard. She'd broken her own rules.

Two guards arrived to haul Nedir's spy away, maids close behind. One maid called Sethe's name, trying to coax her into the bedroom, saying something about blood on her hands, a journey to prepare for, leaving at first light. They were edging Rigil out of the women's hall; helpless, he was letting them. In the melee of dark tresses and flapping skirts, he was a flash of blue satin, a blond curl that refused to lie flat across his brow, shoulders pulled straight as a yard on a mast, a soft "Farewell, Miss Sethe" that couldn't drown out the words in her head.

I'm giving you what you want, Sethe. I'm letting you go.

Doing the noble thing even now. Putting his own dreams and fears and pride last *even now.*

Dropping her hand from her racing heartbeat, Sethe charged toward him, wincing when she tripped on the broken urn and sent porcelain shards dancing across the floor. "Rigil, wait."

He glanced up from the maid he was placating, and oh, there he was. The future lord of Zerah Rock, poised and austere and elegant and perfect, so *obvious* now that she knew. He wasn't the boy she'd met in Melas. He was something far more dangerous.

"I'm coming," Sethe said. Actually, she almost growled it. "I've never left a job in someone else's hands. I'm not about to start now, not with my freedom at risk."

Never mind that she'd lost her freedom somewhere between dinner and a caress on the balcony. Never mind that she would swim to the Talons a dozen times, step into a dozen cages, if it would keep him from being snapped to bits by the ruthless rattrap that was Hamonah. Him. Rigil. The mistake she was still making.

Look at that. She'd wasted so much breath convincing him that she'd moved on, grown up. But she hadn't changed at all.

Rigil studied her for a moment, until a maidservant managed to snag his attention. He bowed to her, then to Sethe. It was a reserved bow, a reminder of what awaited him after Hamonah.

"As you wish, Miss Sethe." His face softened, hands curling at his sides. "You truly do look beautiful."

Do. Not *did.* Ripped shikana and bloody palms and tattered hair and all.

He left the hall with Sethe's heart tucked in the same hand

that had touched her face just an hour before. That had been the distraction, then, the trademark of any good pickpocket. Sethe hadn't even felt the telltale tug of her heart leaving her chest.

She felt it now, and it wasn't quite pain. No, what should have been an empty cavity in her chest was filled instead with breath and heat and an impossible urge to laugh as the maids ushered her into the bedroom, tittering about the state of her clothes.

So she laughed. Quietly, madly, with no one but Arman and the maids to hear it. Because nobleman or not, the boy from Melas was still a scuddy good thief.

CHAPTER NINETEEN
RIGIL

THWACK!

Rigil ducked as Mezaedo's blade embedded itself in the mast of the *Solstice*, Captain Iago's pride and joy. As if protesting the assault, the crimson sail snapped overhead, glowing in the noonday sun as Rigil waited for Mezaedo to free his weapon. Courtesy was not dead. Not even this close to Hamonah.

When Mezaedo reclaimed his sword, a cheer rose from Iago's gathered sailors: doe-eyed Paydo, toothless Yash, Fabian the eunuch navigator, and nearly ten others all clad in loose trousers and, in some cases, little else. Watching from the forecastle, bald head gleaming like a dark pearl, Captain Iago gave Rigil a nod. Sethe stood beside the captain, arms crossed, hair blowing in the wind. Keeping her distance. She was back in her worn linen shirt, vest, and oversized sailor's trousers, her beaded Hamonayan belt wrapped double around her waist. He didn't dare ask what she'd done with the shikana. It likely involved fire. Or the claws of a wild beast.

Free now, Mezaedo darted in with renewed vigor, gripping his bottom lip in his teeth. Rigil parried a cut, feigned right, then swooped into an offensive combination that threw the boy stumbling. He met three of Mezaedo's hard blows, then a fourth. A fifth. Steel screeched as Rigil's blade skidded nearly to Mezaedo's hilt, and fear touched the boy's face in a flicker that came too late. In a smooth motion Rigil knew like a dance, he grabbed Mezaedo's blade with a gloved hand and hooked the squire's crosspiece with his own.

A quick twist, a flash of metal, a round of cheers from the sailors. Even Iago laughed.

Rigil stepped back, holding both swords, then dropped one at the boy's feet. "And that, Mezaedo, is why you avoid catching such an attack with the strong of your bla—"

A blow to Rigil's back sent him stumbling forward. He managed to catch himself before he fell, but barely, and he hadn't fully turned before a foot flashed from nowhere and connected with his fingers. His sword fell from his hand, skidded across the deck.

Sethe flew in like a hurricane.

Her first punch caught Rigil across the cheek, but he caught her second strike and threw her arm back at her, face throbbing. "What are you doing?"

She shook out her hand, knuckles cracking. "Do you really think Hamonah will be as polite as the Kingsguard?"

Falling into a defensive stance, Rigil blocked her next kick, causing one of the Meneton wounds on his arm to throb, but failed to snag her foot before she was on both feet again. She danced out of reach, fists up.

Rigil scoffed. "You hit like a street brawler."

"And *you* hit like a street performer. This isn't a tournament, *Sir* Rigil. You've forgotten how to fight like a survivor."

Jaelportian sailors spotted Rigil's peripheral vision as he locked his molars. "I would rather not do this, Sethe."

A near kiss on a balcony, last night's attack, hours of brooding, and now, brawling like urchins? Lightness, this *woman*.

Tossing hair from her face, Sethe bounced forward in a sloppy but recognizable fighting stance, her bare feet skimming the deck. She *wanted* this.

Fine.

The next time she swung, Rigil caught her arm and twisted, locking it behind her back. She threw her head back, connected with his chin, and slipped from his grip like an oiled eel.

You've forgotten how to fight like a survivor.

Shaking his head, Rigil watched her drop into another stance. Sweat salted his lips, and the deck rolled beneath him, reminding him of the time they used to spend on rattling Melas rooftops, watching targets pass in the streets. Fighting to survive another day.

He beat Sethe to the next attack, grabbed a loose swabbing brush and threw it at her. She had to bat it away, dropping her guard for half a beat, all the time it took for Rigil to throw his weight into a leg sweep that would have, *should* have worked.

Sethe jumped just in time and didn't come back down. Too late, Rigil realized she had caught the boom overhead, her bare feet already flying toward his chest.

He landed on his back, chest aching, staring upside down at a Jaelportian sailor whose frown resembled a grin from this unflattering angle. Basha, Rigil recalled from their introductions earlier. Born in Cherem.

Sethe dropped from the boom and bowed. "And *that* is how to fight like a Hamonayan."

He sat up, rubbing his chest as coins traded hands amidst mingled grunts and chuckles. "The force was a tad excessive, don't you think?"

"Be thankful I don't wear boots."

Rigil caught himself stashing away her smile like a coin for a stormy day. And why shouldn't he?

"That was moldy brilliant." Mezaedo stepped between them,

sheathing his sword. "She knocked the wind right out of you, Sirrig."

Rigil grunted. "It wasn't quite what I would call fair play." To Sethe, he added, "Where did you learn that?"

"The merchant crew I sailed with kept a few Hamonayans on board in case of raids." Sethe sat down in front of him, rubbing the back of her head. "They taught me enough to be of use. You've got to use every advantage against Hamonayans. Fight with instinct, not style." When Mezaedo pulled a cluster of apricots from his pocket and handed them to her, she paused to frown. "Have you seasoned these?"

He gazed at her, flat-eyed.

"Never mind. Give them here."

Despite Mandzee's attempt at a hospitable send-off that morning, Sethe had none too politely declined anything made by Jaelportian hands. Apparently, Mezaedo was an exception. She didn't even grimace at his spice as she downed the apricots one by one, Mezaedo watching with a surprised smile he tried and failed to hide.

It was almost sweet. Nearly enough to make a man jealous. Not that Sethe would ever take credit for the glow in Mezaedo's face as she accepted his offering without a word, proof that the cynical girl from Melas had grown into something kinder than most noble-mannered ladies Rigil knew. A bittersweet thought.

As Captain Iago's twelve-man crew scuttled back to their stations, Paydo flipped a coin to Yash, who grinned toothlessly at Sethe. She raised one of her apricots to him.

"What?" she said when she caught Rigil staring. "He bet on the Hamonayan."

Leaning back against the foremast with a rueful smile, Rigil took in the *Solstice*. It was a well-wrought work of art, three times the size of Laban's little rikoh, with two masts, a galley, a full forecastle and quarterdeck, and enough bunks belowdecks for a twenty-man crew. Mandzee's colors had been tucked away as soon as they'd entered the channel between Jaelport and Hamonah, but there was no mistaking the figurehead as anything but a mage. The woman's wood-carved hands were outstretched toward the sea as if to claim it. Actually, she looked remarkably like Jaira.

Difficult to unsee, that.

"You don't have to worry about Sirrig in Hamonah, Missethe," Mezaedo said suddenly. "Prettiest swordplay in the Kingsguard."

"Thank you, Mezaedo." Rigil propped his elbow on his knee, pushing a hand through his sweaty hair. The Jaelportian heat had been intense, but the wind had changed since then, carrying a suffocating weight of humidity that only Sethe seemed immune to. The island of Hamonah filled their view to port, the coast of Jaelport gliding by on the starboard side. "I'm afraid Sethe has never appreciated my finesse. Or my planning."

The jibe was halfhearted. Sethe had been more than clear about her unwillingness to discuss the past last night.

Which was why it threw him completely off-balance when Sethe cocked a playful eyebrow, slinging an arm over one propped knee. "Oh, really? I seem to remember going along with a great many of your plans. Lord Neuma's carriage, for example."

Mezaedo scoffed. "You robbed the Duke of Melas?"

"Stripped the gilding off his carriage right under his nose, and Rigil here did the bulk of it. Cost us a night in the jailhouse eventually, but he never saw his gold again."

So *now* they were reminiscing about old times? Fine. He'd play along. Rigil waved the compliment away. "I was only the distraction. Without Sethe's birds keeping watch—"

"Or your ridiculous hat."

"I like hats." He sniffed. "Arrest me."

"It was distracting."

"Aye, Sethe, that was rather the point."

"Sir!" Basha, now on his knees with a bucket, hailed Rigil with a wave of his brush. "Nearly to Hamonah now. Captain wants you in his quarters."

Sure enough, Iago stood in the quarterdeck passage, his eyes on Rigil hard, and even harder when they flitted to Sethe. Twin chips of flint.

"I take it that means all of us," Rigil said. "Mezaedo, you too."

The sailors eddied around them as they stood and started toward the quarterdeck. Some of them still gave Sethe a wide berth, watching the jungle island to port as if expecting Hamonah to leap up and swallow the *Solstice* whole. With the mainland on their starboard side, the ship was following the coast of the island southwest, away from Jaelport and toward Hamonah proper, though the harbor town wasn't yet in view around the curve of the island.

Before following Iago into the cabin, Rigil touched Sethe's arm. "You've taken karpos?"

She gave him a flat look. "Stuffed to the teeth."

"Mezaedo?"

The squire made a face, but nodded.

The inside of Iago's cabin was flooded with daylight from the stern windows, but a bank of clouds in the distance prophesied that he'd need his lanterns before long. Rigil ducked to avoid one as he joined the captain at a low oak table. A map of Hamonah and the surrounding sea lay on it, held down by a jar of incense that smelled like pine, and a glassy blue carving of a tanniyn, albeit not a terribly realistic one. Hopefully the map was better scaled.

Glancing up, Iago gestured for Mezaedo to close the door. "Sir Rigil, I will be frank. Her Highness has commanded me to extend you all the deference that she would expect aboard the *Solstice*. This I have done, despite knowing little of your *Kingsguard business* in Hamonah."

"For that, I thank you, Captain," Rigil said. "Queen Mandzee is generous."

"Generous, yes, but no sailor. Any captain worth a rutah knows better than to sail a royal vessel into a Hamonayan port without at least two dozen armed men. Lord Sigul does not take kindly to Jaelportians. Nor do we take kindly to his kind."

This, Iago punctuated with an especially acidic glance at Sethe. "I will not lead my men into smugglers' waters, Sir Rigil. Not without more information."

Rigil caught himself wondering what this man had to go home to, what playful children or doting wife had etched those laugh lines into his sun-spotted skin.

"Fair enough," he said after a beat, settling his fingertips on the map. "In truth, Captain, we intend to best a particular smuggler at his own game, and for that, we need more than passage to Hamonah. We need your cargo hold."

Rigil hadn't realized Iago *had* eyebrows until they appeared in the middle of his forehead, dark and fine and arching. "The *Solstice* is no pirate craft."

"And we, Captain, are not pirates."

In answer, Iago pulled a bundle of scarlet and gold from the back of his chair and threw it onto the table. "Convince me."

Othvold Myvick's coat spilled across the table, the shoulder torn from the battle in Meneton and stained nearly black with Rigil's blood. Rigil dismissed his first thought—it really would be better in blue—in favor of something more helpful. "This proves nothing, Captain. We confiscated Myvick's boat in Meneton. I told you as much."

"Confiscated. Commandeered. The difference is negligible."

"Sirrig is no pirate." This from Mezaedo, who had left his place at the door to see the map, face flushed. "If you knew the danger Jaelport is in thanks to Raith moldy Nedir—"

"Tiko!"

At Sethe's cry, Mezaedo faltered. "What? I say we tell him our plan. See if he calls us pirates then. Go on, Sirrig. Tell him."

Iago knuckled the table, thoughtful. "Raith Nedir. I know this name." The table creaked under his fists. Out on deck, someone shouted that the port town of Hamonah had finally appeared on the island's coast. "What business has a Kingsguard knight with him?"

"Tell him, Sirrig." Mezaedo leaned over the map, his fingernails bright orange from the same spice that laced his breath. "Tell him what we've come to do."

Sethe shook her head. Captain Iago watched, expectant, but something felt very wrong. Off-kilter, as if the deck had pitched for a wave but never rolled back.

If there was one thing Rigil knew intimately well, it was the voice and mannerisms of Mezaedo Chevyah. Always eager, certainly loyal, but never this insistent. Never this obnoxious.

Tell him, Sirrig.

"Mezaedo is right," he said, his voice too loud for the small cabin. "Captain Iago has every right to know what we intend to do in Hamonah. Go on, Mezaedo. Tell him."

Even as he spoke, Rigil watched the boy's face brighten with triumph, then turn confused. He felt the deck pitch as Mezaedo said slowly, "We're going to Hamonah to stop Nedir. That's all I know, Sirrig. You never told me the rest."

There was hunger in his face, in the dark pools of his eyes, and though he was pinned by three scrutinizing gazes, the boy showed no sign of anxiety. He wasn't even eating.

You never told me the rest, Sirrig.

Tell him the plan, Sirrig.

"Rigil?" When Rigil's hand found his sword, Sethe was the first to notice. "What is it?"

Praying he was wrong, Rigil spun to face the boy. "Mezaedo, what do you remember from last night?"

Mezaedo sighed. "I told you, Sirrig. Nothing after dinner."

"What is this about?" Iago asked.

Rigil ignored him. "You conducted an entire conversation with

Lady Fateema before she used innophoria dust. That much you should know, yet you claim to remember nothing. Why?"

Sethe's gaze flickered between Rigil and Mezaedo, never settling long.

Mezaedo frowned. "I . . . don't understand."

"Sometime last night, one of Fateema's mercenaries attempted to capture Sethe. We were not expected in Jaelport, so Fateema could not have had orders to do so before that night. That night, I found *you* alone with her, making a demand she didn't take kindly to, but now that I think of it, she also didn't refuse. *I work best without threats,* I believe, were her words. Sethe was attacked not two hours later."

It took a while, but understanding dawned in Mez's face as someone gave a rowdy laugh outside. The dissonance was nearly as jarring as what Rigil was suggesting.

And yet.

"Nedir is a bloodvoicer." Rigil realized he was gripping the tanniyn figurine and set it down hard on the table. "One who has followed us every step of the way. His men tailed you to Myvick's suite in Meneton, Mezaedo, and they tracked Sethe's every move down to the harbor, while she was with *you*. He also knew we were in Jaelport, or he would not have sicced Lady Fateema on Sethe."

"Lady Fateema is known for her aversion to bloodvoicers," Iago said. "She thinks magic in a man's hands is an abomination and takes karpos religiously by all accounts. This Nedir, if he is a bloodvoicer, could not have contacted her from outside Jaelport."

"But he could have done it through me." Mezaedo took a step back, one hand tangled in his pouch as if to anchor him against the accusation. "That's what you're saying. That I threatened Fateema into sending that man to Missethe's room, scared her into enchanting me. You think I've been Nedir's mole. His puppet."

Sethe winced. "Tiko, no one said that."

Mezaedo jerked back a step. "Sirrig, you can't think I'd betray you like that. You can't think I'd take Nedir's side."

"Not intentionally," Rigil said. "But we both know how he manipulated you in Land's End. If he has been watching through you . . ."

"How?" Mezaedo cried. "My head's stuffed full of karpos, same as you." A gust of wind slammed Iago's window, and Mezaedo gave a ragged laugh. "Moldy onions, Sirrig, is this why no one tells me anything?"

For some reason, Rigil nearly flinched at that. Lightness, how long had the boy known that Rigil was keeping things from him? Long enough to suspect that Rigil was more than a mere soldier?

Blight it all, this was why he hadn't recruited Mez to the Mârad. What use was a spy who couldn't keep enemies out of his own head?

"I know how it feels to be used, Sirrig." Drawing himself to full height under the swaying lanterns, Mezaedo had, ironically, never seemed smaller. "If I thought I was a danger, I'd ship *myself* back to Armonguard. I would, Sirrig. You've got to believe me, I—"

He cut off at a sharp inhale from Sethe. It was a tiny sound, softer than a crackling wick, but it drew their attention to where she stood, gripping the table with both hands.

"Sethe?"

She jerked, knocking over Iago's jar of incense. Half-burnt sticks skidded across the table, filling the room with the smell of scorched pine. Rigil waited for Iago to curse her clumsiness, but he couldn't tear his eyes from Sethe.

She had her arms braced over her ribs, as if trying to hold herself together.

"I *just* took karpos," she rasped. "He can't have found me this quickly. He *can't*."

Her whisper seemed to echo on and on. Deafening, but not as loud as the sound of steel leaving its sheath.

"Sirrig! Look out!"

Turning, Rigil was too late to draw his own blade before Captain Iago, face blank, lunged at him with cutlass outstretched.

243

CHAPTER TWENTY
SETHE

THE TIKO GOT THERE FIRST. DIVING IN front of Rigil, he knocked the cutlass aside with a sword Sethe hadn't seen him draw, too busy gritting her teeth against the sudden pressure in her temples. Squinting against the pain, she watched Iago's blade spin off, sparking off one of the lanterns. The distraction gave Rigil time to draw his own weapon and push Mezaedo toward the door.

Mezaedo. The mole. But no. That was wrong. Rigil was wrong. He had to be.

Like steam, Nedir's voice curled through her thoughts, searching for the cracks in her shields. Sethe staggered back from the table, jolting when her back hit the cabin wall. *Sedhani . . .*

"Go!" Rigil shouted at Mezaedo or Sethe, maybe both. She heard him, spine soldered to the wall, but the crushing in her skull made it hard to focus on anything but the growl coming from the captain of the *Solstice*.

Iago swung again, but this time Rigil seemed ready, putting the table between them. Mezaedo joined him there, and the next time Iago lunged, they flipped the table together, pinning the captain against the far wall. The impact toppled a few trinkets off a shelf. Glass broke. Ink glugged, pooled across the deck, lapping at Sethe's bare toes.

Rigil shoved Mezaedo out the cabin door. He turned to Sethe, hand out. "Sethe!"

She barely heard him.

It was the pits of Iago's eyes that gave him away. Hollow, unseeing, as if someone else had taken control.

Right on cue, Nedir's bloodvoice poured through her, finding every weakness in her shields. *Making* cracks where none should have existed. Like a thousand tiny chisels driving down all at once.

Save us both some trouble, Sedhani, and don't resist me this time. Karpos is hardly a permanent solution. It can be lost, misplaced. Overpowered.

How? Sethe's bloodvoice roared in her own ears, but maybe that was the distant crash of Rigil shouting her name. Iago was struggling to rise, doublet soaked dark with spilled ink. *How can you find me through the karpos? How are you using my fragments?*

You have your secrets, Sedhani, and I have mine.

She was still standing. That, at least, was an improvement from his first attack. Maybe the karpos in her blood *was* slowing him down a little.

"Sethe, come on." Rigil gripped her arm, tugged her through the door. When he slammed it shut and fell against it, she could sense Iago on the other side, stumbling toward the door.

BANG. The slam of the captain's body against the door nearly launched Rigil across the deck. With a grunt, he anchored himself, shouted for Mezaedo to find a brace. He was still gripping Sethe's arm.

"Is it Nedir?"

Sethe wheezed for breath. Who did he *think* was controlling the captain's mind?

Oh, tides, this pain, this red-hot knife inside her skull. All the blocking in the world couldn't stop it from carving her mind apart.

Sethe tore free of Rigil's grip, caught the bulkhead, and dragged herself along the passage toward the open deck. Her open eye registered little, the world around her just a crash of surf, all thunder and lurching chaos and the green mound of Hamonah looming over it all.

I'm not your plaything, she bloodvoiced, teetering out onto the main deck, trying to make sense of the sailors who stood frozen at their posts, watching her.

Oh, no, Sedhani, Nedir bloodvoiced. *One does not play with weapons. One* tests *weapons for strength, versatility, effectiveness. Let's begin.*

Nedir's consciousness drove down like a chisel, breaking off a piece of her. She felt it shoot into the Veil, an invisible image of her, and felt a prickle as it traveled toward one of the Jaelportian sailors. Paydo. The man's gaze hung on her, full of fear ingrained in him by a lifetime of servitude to powerful women.

That face slackened as Sethe's fragment settled into his body. Sethe felt his gaze become hers. His hands and feet, his mind, all hers.

No. Nedir's.

Interesting, the old man bloodvoiced.

Paydo's face lost all expression. It was a forgettable face, square and small featured, but with eyes like hot tea on a cold night. His clothes looked too small, as if he'd grown a lot recently. Someone had patched the knees of his trousers.

As Sethe watched, trying to reclaim the fragment inside him, Paydo drew a sheepsfoot knife from his belt, the kind meant for cutting through hemp. Slowly, almost languidly, he turned on the man next to him. Yash.

"What are you doing?" Yash's lip curled in confusion, exposing one toothless gum. "Zitheos' sake, Paydo, what are you about? Put it down!"

"Sethe!" Rigil again, grunting when Iago threw himself against the cabin door. Helping to brace, Mezaedo was nearly tossed across the deck by the impact. "Sethe, stop this!"

Sethe couldn't stop watching, couldn't make herself move. She watched Yash stumble back, hands raised. He shouted for help and others came running. Basha. Fabian. The ferret-nosed cook. Their shouts joined Rigil's, but Paydo's limp face locked their feet beneath them. Fabian lunged to grab Paydo, but too late.

The knife swung. Fabian jumped back.

Yash didn't.

The impact of blade on flesh rattled Sethe's bones, but the gurgle of blood in a dying sailor's throat was worse, oh, *so much* worse.

No. *No!*

In a blink, Rigil was there. Tackling Paydo, wrestling him to the ground, wrenching the sheepsfoot knife aside. It landed in a blooming pool of sailor's blood.

Panting, Rigil wheezed a prayer. "Arman, help us."

Arman. Maybe this time the Father God was listening. Maybe this time . . .

Not likely, Nedir bloodvoiced. *Now, Sedhani, to test your limits.*

Again, he bored down, chiseling off fragments of Sethe's mind. Invisible pieces of herself burst in all directions, shooting through the Veil so fast that Sethe felt the severing like a dozen cords tugging her every way at once. She raged against Nedir's grip on her, tried to summon every lesson she'd learned as a child, resisting his experiments for all those years in the Talons. Blocking was a battle of wills. Her will just had to be stronger.

One by one, the sailors' faces deadened. Jaws went slack. Cutlasses slid from sheaths, cutlasses and knives and wooden pegs and rusty nails. Rigil was shouting, trying to reason with a dozen men turning weapons on each other. On their shipmates, their *brothers*, all at Sethe's command.

"No!" she screamed. "I don't want this! Stop this!"

Pointless. She was a weapon in Nedir's hands, like all her fragments, like everyone here. She sought Rigil and found him close, something stricken in his face as he lurched toward her, cutlass in hand. "I am sorry for this, Sethe."

He swung, pommel-first, aiming for her head. *Yes!* Sethe waited for the strike, bent to meet it, prayed that it would only take one hit to knock her unconscious.

The blow never fell. Sethe opened her eye to find Rigil wrestling with a manic Captain Iago. She hadn't even noticed the captain escaping the cabin, but there he was, clawing at Rigil's face, fighting savagely to keep him from getting to her, from ending this.

She had to end this.

The *Solstice* moaned and banked as Basha left his post to attack the captain. Fabian swung for a sailor's throat and went down with a dagger in his back. He didn't scream. No one did. Their actions were Nedir's, but so was their silence. The air reeked of blood, tasted of vomit.

"Fight it, you sandwits!" Sethe roared. "*This isn't you!*"

She dropped to her knees to pound her skull against the deck, anything to hammer herself into unconsciousness, but Nedir slipped into her muscles and stopped her before she could. Truly a puppet now, she could only watch as horrors piled up around her.

"Sethe!" Rigil wrestled a cutlass away from a burly Jaelportian with a bloodstained apron. He tossed the cutlass overboard and ducked to avoid a punch, but when he lurched toward Sethe, Iago jumped on his back again, trying to choke him. "Sethe!"

Another Jaelportian fell, gripping a cutlass that protruded from his gut. Sethe felt him die. She felt all of them. Not the pain—she rarely felt a host's physical pain. But she felt the emotions, the frenzy, the shock, then the stillness. Another fell. Rigil had his sword out now and was fending off three sailors whose dead shark eyes had all locked on him at once.

No. Not him.

She strained against Nedir with everything she had. Sweat matted Rigil's hair, his sword whirling like he'd been born this way, with a blade in hand and a battle before him.

Just as long as he didn't die this way.

Rigil *could not* die.

Interesting, Nedir bloodvoiced. *Your strength just increased. I wonder, is it simply a matter of finding the right motivation?*

He released her suddenly, and Sethe slumped forward, exhausted. Cutlasses hit the deck as sailors blinked awake, slowly taking in the blood on their blades. Fitting the pieces together.

"The Hamonayan!"

"Mage!"

"She'll kill us all!"

Cheek pressed to the rocking deck, Sethe tried to focus on the waves beyond the gunwale, on anything but the smell of blood. She could still feel Nedir in her head. Why had he stopped?

Then a shaky voice came out of the haze. Soft. Familiar.

"Sethe."

She pushed herself up. The sails snapped as wind rolled over the *Solstice*. The last few sailors stood watching, expressions ranging from murderous to petrified, but all the men remained locked in place. Nedir hadn't released their bodies.

Of course not, Nedir bloodvoiced. *The key to any experiment is a controlled environment.*

"Please, Sethe." That voice again. Rigil. Exhausted. "Please."

He stood with his hands in the air, pleading with her over Iago's shoulder. The tip of the captain's cutlass rested beneath the bulb of Rigil's throat, perfectly still. *Too* still.

"No." Sethe shuddered. *Nedir. Please. Not him.*

Stop me, Sedhani.

Rigil sucked in as the cutlass tilted, began to dig.

"*No!*" Sethe shouted. "Stop it!"

"Arman." Rigil's voice remained steady. Had the pain started yet? Was he fighting it? "Sethe, He can free you. Where Arman is, there is freedom. I told you that once. Do you remember?"

Lies, Nedir bloodvoiced. *Arman put you here.*

"Arman put me here," Sethe whispered. She tried to reach for her prayer but found it lost somewhere, blown away like every chance she had of ever escaping Nedir.

He won't free you, Nedir bloodvoiced.

"He won't free me."

That is the trouble with Arman, Sedhani. He demands your trust, but only so that He may own you. That is not love. It is a trap, Sedhani. A cage. But I suppose that is true for all love, isn't it?

Sethe trembled, the words seeping through her like venom. She couldn't fight this, not even for Rigil. She would live inside the bars of this memory for every moment of the rest of her life.

I'll come back to you, Nedir, she bloodvoiced. *I'll be your weapon. I'll stay in your cage. Just let him live. Please. Leave him, and I'll come back to Land's End. You have my word.*

A pause. *Your word. And what is that worth, Sedhani?*

She watched Rigil's throat flex against the blade. *Everything. It's worth everything.*

Rigil's gaze leaned on her. So calm. Filled with things unsaid. Why hadn't she kissed him on the balcony? Why hadn't she taught him what *k'sil* meant, or told him he was the reason she'd given up thieving all those years ago and never looked back? Why hadn't she told him that if she saw beauty in a withering orchid, it was only because he had taught her how?

As romantic as this is, Nedir bloodvoiced, *I am more interested in where you are going. Land's End is of no further use to me, but tell me where you are and I will consider sparing him.*

The Eversea. Sethe tried to stand. Couldn't. *I'm in the Shelosh Channel, nearly to Hamonah. Now let him go.*

Hamonah? Whatever for?

I'm trying to find my mother. Sethe gritted her teeth, struggling to guard her thoughts. *Who else would I come back to this sinkhole for? There, Nedir. I've told you what you wanted to know. Now end this. Let him go.*

A tiny bead of blood trickled down Rigil's throat, vanishing beneath his collar.

I accept your first offer. Nedir's bloodvoice had a physical heft, pressing on the insides of her temples. *Your return in exchange for this man's life. But not to Land's End. Meet me in Hamonah. And come alone.*

Iago's hand trembled, jostling the blade against Rigil's throat. Somewhere behind Sethe, Mezaedo cried out and was silenced.

I'll be there, Sethe bloodvoiced. *Just name the place.*

I have many hands and eyes on the Hamonayan docks, Nedir bloodvoiced. *Find the crates marked with Avenis's symbol. My men will meet you there. I trust, Sedhani, that you will be cooperative. I will not hesitate to exploit this new weakness of yours.*

He didn't wait for more promises, just vanished from her mind. Gone, like that.

As her fragments slid back into her control, Sethe barely found the strength to grab one of the topgallant backstays and pull herself upright. Captain Iago dropped his cutlass with a loud oath, and Rigil sagged back against the gunwale, white as a gull's wing.

She stumbled toward him, sure her voice would come out three octaves too high if she asked any of the questions tearing through her. *What did I do to you? What did I just do?*

As if reading her mind, he ran a thumb over his neck, where the blood had run down his throat, toward his heart.

His heart. Stopping in front of him, Sethe smothered the urge to press her hands to his chest, just to feel the beat, to be sure he was still there, still alive, still with her. *Stay with me.*

Instead, she reached for his neck, the needle-fine wound where Iago's blade had rested.

"I'm all right," he said, catching her hand halfway. But judging by the way he squeezed and didn't let go, Sethe's grip was probably the only thing keeping him from shaking.

With the throng of sailors gathering around them, Rigil began scanning faces. "Mezaedo?" he asked one sailor. "Please. My squire. Where is he?"

"Murderer."

Sethe hadn't even known Basha could speak Kinsman until he rasped that word.

"She'll kill us all. Zitheos demands blood for blood."

"That was *not* Sethe," Rigil snapped. "She was attacked, like you, by a bloodvoicer named Nedir. *He* is responsible for this."

"We are not blind, Barak." This from Captain Iago, whose face had turned from wax to granite in the time it took him to survey the damage. His weapon hand flexed and unflexed with battle residue. "There are five men dead on this deck. *My* men. You repay my queen's generosity with a curse? With bloodshed?"

"Did Armonguard send you?" another man asked. "A punishment for Lady Jaira's conspiracy?"

"The war is over!"

"We want no trouble with Gidon!"

"*Listen* to me." Something animal lurked in Rigil's voice, low and long out of patience. "Raith Nedir caused this by bloodvoicing through Sethe to control all of you, and if he can turn men and women against each other here on this ship, do you not think he can do it in Jaelport? In your villages? In your homes? That attack was only a *glimpse* of this man's capacity for bloodshed. If you keep us from our mission in Hamonah, rest assured, he *will* do worse."

"We'll be cursed if we keep you." Grey-faced Basha spat to the side. "I say we let Zitheos decide their fates."

"Overboard!"

Rigil flung an arm at the island, the ribbons of smoke rising from the port town on the coast. "Hamonah is in *sight*."

Before anyone could logic his way around that observation, a head of glossy hair lurched out of the quarterdeck passage. "Sirrig!"

Mezaedo barely made it two steps before they seized him.

"Let him go!" Rigil took a half step forward. "The boy did nothing!"

The sailors shoved Mezaedo, and he tripped into Sethe. She barely caught him, but his attention was all for Rigil. Blood matted the curls to his scalp on one side of his head, and a bruise was forming around one of his eyes.

"You saw, Sirrig." His gaze was bright, desperately bright, like Melas coppers. "Nedir can get through Missethe's karpos. He could've been spying through her, not me."

Rigil's mouth pinched. After a beat, he turned to Iago and added, "At least take the lad with you to Jaelport."

Sethe felt the tiko's arm go rigid under her hand. *No,* she tried to say, but her voice was flayed raw. All it gave her was a wheeze that everyone seemed to ignore, including Rigil.

"What?" Mezaedo shoved Sethe's steadying hands away. "Sirrig! I promise, Sirrig, I didn't do this! I would never help him!"

"Captain, this boy is one of you. If you wish to punish me for withholding the full danger of this voyage from you, then be my guest. But please, have mercy on your kinsman."

Mezaedo sputtered protests, but Iago was already considering, taking in the boy's Jaelportian skin and accent, acknowledging Mezaedo as one of his own. Nodding.

This is wrong, Sethe thought, willing Rigil to hear it, even though the karpos in *his* blood still seemed to be doing its job. *Rigil, this is wrong. You can't leave him behind.* Tides, she was so tired.

Paydo, his soft eyes now bloodshot to match the red on his hands, seized Mezaedo's shoulder. "We'll return him to Jaelport."

"Safely," Rigil said. "I must have your word. By Zitheos, Queen Mandzee, and the blood of Jaelport in your veins. You *will* protect him."

"Sirrig, I can *help*. I'll prove it, I'll moldy prove it!"

Sour wind blew across the deck, snapping in the sails. Captain Iago nodded once.

The sailors began pulling Mezaedo away.

"No! *No!* Sirrig, you need me!"

"K'sil." Exhaustion frayed Sethe's voice like a broken thread. "Don't do this. He's loyal. I know he is."

"Sirrig, wait! Rot the lot of you, let me go! Sirrig!"

"I do need you." Rigil's face had gone frighteningly hard, and he caught Sethe's hand again like a brace against some internal pain. A little damp patch was darkening his shoulder. One of his Meneton wounds, reopened in the fight. "I need you alive, Mezaedo Chevyah. Wait in Jaelport. I will find you when this is over."

"*No*, Sirrig!"

Sethe couldn't watch. Too drained to stand on her own, let alone stop this, she looked away as three sailors dragged Mezaedo toward the hatch. He fought them at first, but by the time they reached the opening, he wasn't struggling, just staring, dull-faced and still.

That expression. It was somehow practiced *and* surprised, like he'd been through this a dozen times before, but never expected it here. Not from Rigil. Master number twelve.

Sethe was almost glad when Paydo put a hand on the back of Mezaedo's head and pushed him below.

No. Not glad. Scuddy sick to her stomach.

"Ready the skiff," Iago barked as new cloud shadows swept over the deck.

As men scurried to obey, Iago turned to Sethe, his lips pressed thin as the blade he'd nearly put through Rigil's neck. "In the name of Queen Mandzee and the men whose blood you have spilled, I wash my hands of you, mage. Zitheos will be your judge."

CHAPTER TWENTY-ONE
RIGIL

AS IF THE ATTACK HADN'T BEEN SICKening enough, now Mezaedo's last stricken expression haunted Rigil's thoughts with every heave of the oars, nearly as gut-wrenching as the torture on Sethe's face as Nedir had slaughtered the crew before her. Mezaedo's face, Sethe's, back to Mezaedo's. Memories, constant as the waves against the little boat or the mound of green and gold that was Hamonah, swelling before them. The heat seemed to swell with it, the air like a smothering wet cloth pressed to his skin.

I left him. The thought resurged for the thirtieth time since he'd climbed into the rowboat with Sethe and left the *Solstice* behind. A small pouch of coins in the bottom of the boat made up the whole of their meager possessions, along with Myvick's coat, a passive-aggressive parting gift from Iago. *I called him a traitor. I abandoned him.*

"You didn't abandon him." Sethe sat curled in the bow, knees to chest, her vest discarded on the bottom of the boat alongside Myvick's coat. "Keeping him from Hamonah might well save his life."

Rigil pulled back on the oars. "I know my karpos is wearing off, but you shouldn't read my thoughts."

"You can't really think he's a traitor." She said it without feeling, a bite with no teeth, but with it came images of the two of them sorting potatoes on the deck of Laban's rikoh, or bending toward each other around Mandzee's table. Mezaedo sitting a little straighter when Sethe accepted his offerings. Sethe defending him on the *Solstice* with what little strength she had.

Lightness. She truly cared about him. Rigil scraped the back of his hand across his mouth, unsure whether to be pleased or depressed that the woman sitting across from him had a nurturing side he'd never see again after this mission.

"I trust Mezaedo Chevyah's heart," he said, "but that doesn't change the fact that until he can control his magic, he is a liability."

Sethe snorted into her knees. Or was that a sob?

Blight it all, he was usually better at this.

"If karpos is really useless against Nedir," she said, "he could have been watching through *your* eyes all along. You have no idea what that eel is capable of."

A cloud crossed the sun, throwing shade over the water, the isle ahead, and the landmass of Jaelport they'd left across the channel. Rigil dragged the oars back. "You know it wasn't your fault, Sethe. You didn't kill those men."

When she didn't answer, he jutted his chin at her pockets. "We'll buy more karpos in Hamonah. Perhaps some protection is still better than none."

"Waste of time." Sethe tipped her face back to the sky, her hair damp from the spray and hanging around her face in dark strands. "Nedir and I have an understanding. I'm going to meet him on Hamonah. If I do, no one else will die."

Rigil nearly dropped an oar. Forget rowing. Forget everything. "You made a *bargain* with him? Sethe, why in all Er'Rets would you agree to that?"

"People were dying. And before you have a conniption, we'll still get your shipment. Nedir needs at least two days to sail from Land's End, plenty of time to send his powder on its way to Armonguard." She peered over her shoulder at the island, a mound of jungle and rickety buildings, the occasional column of smoke. "I can't let him hurt anyone else."

Remarkable. Did she have any idea how very selfless she sounded? How different from the jaded young girl who had never learned how to see beyond her own survival?

Hamonah consumed the horizon now. What did she see in those docks, the masts like bobbing spires, the mass of jungle trying to swallow the mass of buildings, the pinwheeling gulls over the beach?

Not home. That much he knew.

Rigil lifted the oars above the water and let the blades rest on the gunwales, dripping. "We could have found another way."

"Would that have been before or after I ran you through?"

"That wasn't you, Sethe. It was *him*. All the more reason not to go about making deals with the man. I don't like this. You of all people should know a trap when you see one."

Sethe's palm hit the gunwale. "He was about to *kill you*."

"So you sold yourself into slavery? To a man who could wield your fragments like an army for Light knows what? I know you had good intentions, but this could affect all Er'Rets. More people could be harmed *because* you return to him. If Arman—"

"Arman is your God, not mine." A wave rocked the hull, stippling them both. The sea tasted different here than in Zerah Rock. Sharper, almost sour, like the warble in Sethe's tone as she went on. "I'm not like you, Rigil. I can't trust like you, but just because I'm not ready to hand my life to the Father God doesn't mean I'll stand by and watch Nedir destroy everyone I love."

The oars liquefied in Rigil's hands. "Love?"

"What?"

"You said . . . who did—"

This time, her fist struck the seat hard enough to set them swaying. "Rigil Barak, for tides' sake, did you learn *nothing* from the jailhouse in Melas?"

Waves drummed the hull. Rhythmic. Jarring. Jailhouse in Melas? What did that have to do with—

Oh.

Oh, the *jailhouse* in *Melas*. The one where every inmate had served double duty as the jailer's eyes and ears. Any whisper of an escape attempt and some wretch in the next cell over would holler like a wounded dog, bringing the jailer running faster than Sethe could pick a lock. Well. *Almost* faster.

That prison was where Sethe had first revealed her bloodvoicing ability to Rigil, speaking her plans into his head for fear of who might be listening behind the next set of bars. And someone was always listening.

Lightness, but she was brilliant. Too brilliant to trust Nedir, promise or no promise. Leaning back, Rigil checked that he was still shielding his thoughts, silently thanking his mother for the lessons that had kept his defenses in place since Land's End. Light knew he was a moderate blocker at best. If Nedir *did* try watching through one of them, it would almost certainly be him.

Something tickled his thoughts, and Rigil concentrated on fortifying his mind against it.

Across the boat, Sethe pressed her lips together. "It's me, sandwit. Let me in."

As there was nothing at all terrifying about letting this woman into his *innermost being*, Rigil lowered his shields and Sethe's bloodvoice poured in.

You're better at blocking than you used to be. That's something.

Rigil shoved his tongue over his teeth. *You might try knocking first.*

It's me. Sethe. Requesting permission to bloodvoice. She fluttered her lashes. *Better?*

His flat stare was returned in kind.

I'm going to leave a fragment to watch through your eyes, she bloodvoiced. *That way, you can keep shielding, but I'll be able to bloodvoice you from* inside *your shields. Think of it like a personal guard. If anyone tries to break in, my fragment will know.*

Rigil scratched his jaw. *I'm not terribly fond of having you in my thoughts, Sethe.*

Why? The boat shot up with a swell, and she cracked a smile. *Keeping secrets, K'sil?*

The smile didn't last nearly long enough before she slumped against the bow. "He isn't watching through you. Not that you would feel it. Watching is nearly impossible to detect. But Nedir . . ." She rubbed her arms as if she felt something crawling there. "Nedir is different. Him, I can sense like a bad smell. That's why I left a fragment in your head. I'll be able to sense him even if you can't, as safe as we can be without karpos."

More clouds joined the first, darkening the afternoon sun. "And if he uses powder?"

"Why would he bother?" Sethe pulled up her feet. "I've promised to go back to him, and he has every reason to believe I'll keep that promise."

She was avoiding his eyes now. That had to mean something. And the way her voice had caught around the word *love* a moment ago . . .

He glanced at her for a reaction, some hint that she'd heard the prodding thought and might actually respond to it. But her gaze was on the sea, glazed and far away. Arman knew she had enough to distract her without following every stray thought of his.

Rigil's knee started bouncing. "Sethe. I meant what I said last night."

That caught her attention. "Don't."

"Wherever you go after this," he said, "wherever you *want* to go, I will wish you well with all my heart. Truly. So long as it is not back to Nedir."

She sniffed, her face granite under all that flailing hair. "Why?"

"Why not Nedir?"

"Why do you want me free so badly? I already told you I can't be your Lady Barak."

At that, he actually snorted. "Isemios's wit, Sethe. Give me some credit, would you? I promised to accept your answer, and I intend to keep my word, but I can hardly stop caring whether you live or die, and I will not sit back and watch you throw your life away like this. I can't do it, Sethe. Believe me when I say that if you return to him, it will be over my dead body."

She regarded him for a long moment. A windy, salty, cloud-shadowed moment.

"What do you think I'm trying to avoid?" she asked. Then, before he could jam a word in, she jabbed at the oars. "My turn."

Rigil knew better than to protest.

Sethe rowed for a while, but Rigil was back on the oars when the bustling Hamonayan harbor was close enough to taste. Ships clogged the docks, mostly cargo vessels undoubtedly crewed by smugglers, but a few sun-bleached fishing boats bobbed among the galleons. Fishermen paused their work to watch the rowboat pass, checking the horizon for the vessel Sethe and Rigil must have left behind. But the *Solstice* was long gone.

Sethe kept her head down and her hair over her face until they reached the pier, where Rigil leaned out to grab the dock. Water sloshed over the side as he did, as warm as it was blue, shocking after the colder tides he'd grown up sailing. A warm ocean. How novel.

"What now?" Rigil held the boat steady against the pier. "We stroll in?"

Trailing a hand in the water, Sethe surveyed the docks and the town behind, all crooked beams and cockeyed canopies, not a single straight line in sight. The town teetered on the very edge of the land, and by the way the dark jungle rose up behind it, the island was actively attempting to push it into the sea.

"Keep your head down," Sethe said. "Don't meet anyone's eye. Do *not* try to charm anyone. Hamonayans will see through that faster than you can take a bow."

Rigil began rolling up his sleeves. "In my experience, Hamonayans respond rather well to my charm."

Ignoring him, she pointed at the nearest cargo ship bobbing a short way out, a galleon flying the mark of Hamonah, a wheel on a bed of blue and white. "Lord Sigul's ship. Runs mostly stolen goods, sometimes slaves. He raids coastal villages on the Shelosh Islands, but I'd wager most of his wealth comes from Nedir. Payment for Nedir's free rein on the island."

On the next pier, presumably where the water was deeper, a large vessel was being unloaded next to a smaller one. Both bore Lord Sigul's mark. Blight it all, the lord of Hamonah, raiding towns and running slaves like a common pirate? Small wonder so much of his citizenry saw smuggling as a valid profession. Even smaller wonder Barth and Jaelport were the only duchies treacherous enough to forge alliances with these people.

"I heard that." Sethe flicked water at him.

Rigil rifled for the mooring line in the bottom of the boat. "*Stop reading my thoughts.*"

When he had gathered it, Sethe grabbed the line and began looping it around the nearest post. Behind her, Hamonayan sailors were unloading cargo from the larger ship, stacking crates and casks on the dock until Rigil could hardly see the guards patrolling the shoreline.

Wait. Rigil jerked his chin at one Hamonayan pacing the dock. "Isn't he one of Laban's?"

Sethe glanced up, taking in the harbor, the workers. Ah. There.

The Hamonayan appeared again, shirtless, with billowing trousers dyed a deep royal purple. Something glinted in his ear when he moved.

"Lazy Eyes," Sethe confirmed. "From Meneton. So, Laban does serve Nedir. He must have found another ship."

"Which means that Nedir is expecting us."

"He's expecting *me*. By now, he's probably bloodvoiced every spy he has on the island with instructions to watch for an *ugly Hamonayan*."

"Well, good." Scooping Myvick's sopping coat from the bottom of the boat, Rigil turned it inside out before slipping it on, wincing as he instantly began to sweat under the extra layer. "They'll be too busy watching for whoever that is to notice *us*."

Sliding back into the rowboat, she gave him nothing. Unless… was that a smile? A shred of one? Her fingers drummed the top of the pier. "We can't row to the Talons. We need a ship, especially if you hope to make it out with the powder. I know where to find captains for hire, but it'll mean slipping past that guard."

"We," Rigil said. "If *we* hope to make it out."

She gave him her scarred side, a mass of untraceable lines. Down the pier, the sailors unloading Lord Sigul's galleon traded curses with every trip up the gangway, rubbing their backs the moment each box hit the pier. Sooner or later, that cargo would be transported inland, likely on a wagon. Most certainly past the guards.

Watching the plan forming behind her expression, Rigil raised a brow. "It's almost poetic."

If she was thinking of the crate her mother had once closed over her head or the one that had borne her, alone and frightened, out of the Talons, the grid of scars over her left side gave no sign. She was all metal beside him, every muscle tight under her skin. Lightness. All the years he'd wasted on the run from Zerah Rock, terrified to face everything he'd left there, and here she was, marching back into the jaws of her own personal beast just because it needed to be done.

And people wondered why the women of Er'Rets's glittering gentry had never held Rigil's attention.

They waited until the sailors dropped their loads and retreated back up their gangway. Then Rigil climbed onto the pier and reached back for Sethe. It was reflex, a thing of ballrooms and banquets, like so many of the mismatched trappings that composed the man he was.

Amazingly, she accepted his hand, letting him pull her up beside him. She followed him to the stack of cargo, then began darting from crate to crate, studying the brands burned into each lid. They were all unintelligible to him, but she seemed to be after something specific. Finally, she paused over the largest crate.

"This one. Emberfruit."

They worked together to pry the box open, but Rigil hardly glimpsed the bright red fruits inside before a jet of fire-colored steam burst from the crate. He jerked back with a hiss, eyes stinging from the tangy-sweet heat. "Isemios's wit!"

Fanning the air, Sethe leaned over and began shoveling fruit out of the crate. "The steam is hot, but the fruit isn't. The steam might keep them from looking too closely. If not . . ."

He nodded—no need to dwell on that—and climbed into the crate to help her with the emberfruits, tossing them out in armfuls and ducking whenever a sailor passed too near. Sethe was straddling the side of the box, keeping watch while Rigil made room, so focused that she actually jumped when he held his hand out to her.

"Shall we, Lady of the Crate?"

Her smile was tight-lipped. Of course it was. Holding the lid with one hand, Rigil caught her fingers with the other. *We can find another way,* he thought for her to hear. It felt more respectful than speaking her fears aloud. *You don't have to do this, Sethe.*

She was watching their hands, her fingertips cold and her nails all jagged-bitten edges. The crate smelled of fermentation and the trace of spice that clung to her wind-matted hair, and if he hadn't been studying her lips, he would never have caught her whisper.

"It means shiny."

"What?"

She brushed her thumb along his finger, tracing the red-stained edge. "K'sil. It's what cutpurses here call a coin that still catches light, hasn't gone to grime like everything else in Hamonah. Some think they're blessed, keep them around . . . for luck."

A sliver of sunlight speared the clouds, glowing warm on her face and in the little hollow of her throat where her pulse was flickering fast.

In fairness, Rigil's pulse wasn't exactly plodding either. "Why are you telling me this now? I thought I hadn't earned an explanation."

She laughed a little, a vanishing sound. "You earned it the first day we met. And every day after for as long as I've known you." A flush was rising to her cheeks, making her faint laugh sweeter for its uncertainty. "I always thought you were showing off. You and your rules, your honor, the lines you wouldn't cross. But it's just you. You live for something more than survival. For Arman, I guess. I don't know. I only know that you made me want that." She swallowed so hard that he heard it, and then she took her sandy voice and drove it through his soul. "You still make me want that."

"Sethe—"

"What I said about Arman earlier. I didn't mean it. Most people only hold a real k'sil in their hands once in their lives, so why I got a second chance . . ." Her voice thickened even as her lips tipped up in a smile as thin as the horizon. "That's my proof, I guess. That Arman does hear prayers. That He really must be good."

Before he could even think of asking what in Lightness she was trying to say, her head shot up like a startled bird's, sensing something he couldn't. Her pulse rammed his fingers. Too fast. *Much* too fast.

And then it happened.

Ripping her hand free, Sethe splayed it on his chest instead. The white of her eye gleamed veiny red, damp strands of hair zagging across her face like black lightning. "I'm sorry for this."

Rigil's knees buckled without warning, plunging him up to his chest in emberfruit as the crate lid snapped shut over his head. Darkness enveloped him, clouded with emberfruit stink and hot, humid air so close each breath felt like drinking through his lungs. He tried to shout but found his tongue useless. And not only his tongue but his arms, his legs, every limb and tendon and bone and breath caught in a vise.

I'm sorry, Sethe bloodvoiced through the fragment she'd left in his head. The fragment now clamping his mouth shut as he tried to roar her name. She toppled a few smaller crates on his, locking him inside. *I'm sorry,* she bloodvoiced. *I'm sorry, I'm sorry.*

SETHE! he thought in a roar, hoping to rattle her brain with the force of it. *Whatever this is—*

"Well, look at that." At a new voice, Rigil's thoughts cut out even as his body continued to strain against Sethe's hold. "Nedir thought you might not show."

An emberfruit exploded near Rigil's ear, splattering warm pulp down his neck.

Outside, Sethe's voice was smooth and cool, a seashell washed up by the tide. "Captain Laban, wasn't it? Found another ship, I see."

"Don't get cheeky, girl. You haven't got your knight to fight your battles for you now."

Laban. Rigil's breaths were deafening in the box, more like the chuffs of a bear. He no longer cared if she heard his thoughts. Isemios's wit, if this was her blighted attempt to *protect* him . . .

"Where is he?" Laban asked Sethe.

"Gone," she answered. "Nedir told me to come alone. I've got to say, I'm impressed. Myvick's smuggler, Nedir's spy. What else are you, queen of the mages?"

Laban laughed. Down the pier, some sailors struck up a shanty that sounded undecided between a jig and a dirge. "Myvick had his time," he said, "and as for Nedir, he made a mistake showing his hand. All this trouble for one Hamonayan? Makes a body wonder just *how* much he'd pay to have you."

The dock creaked beneath a heavy boot, followed by the thunk and groan of a blade prying open a crate.

"Into the box," Laban said. "While I'm still young and pretty, eh?"

"No need." Was it the crate distorting things, or did Sethe's voice sound like a lyre string pulled too tight? "I'll go along without trouble. I gave Nedir my word."

"Promises don't buy me a new ship, love. But the bounty on you might. I can't risk that face of yours drawing attention. Get in."

Even as Sethe held Rigil's body hostage, something seemed to bloom between his temples. An emotion. Warm and jittery, but not his own. Maybe it was bleeding from the fragment she'd left in his head. More likely, it was just what he knew he would find in her mind, if he could read it.

Fear.

"Into the crate," Laban said again. "I know you know how it's done."

Rigil's palms went slick with secondhand panic, a sign that Sethe was losing control. Locking his teeth, he threw every ounce of willpower into regaining his own strength as another emberfruit exploded somewhere in the darkness. Hot seeds spattered his jerkin, seeping through Myvick's coat. Every breath tasted somehow both sweet and rotten, and his lungs spasmed against the steamy air cloying his skin. *Sethe, don't do this. Don't sell yourself back to him. Run. Forget me, forget the powder and run.*

She could hear him. He knew that much. *Arman, let her listen.*

"Into the box, girl," Laban said again. "It's a long way to the Talons, and I won't have another of Nedir's men intruding on my catch. There you go. That's it, nice and—oy!"

Even knowing it was coming, Rigil felt the heat spike at the sound of Sethe taking flight. A chaos of sounds exploded outside the crate. Bare feet slapping the wet pier, Laban's boots hammering after them, the *shing* of a cutlass leaving his belt. And shouts, so many shouts, some Kinsman, some Hamonayan. A nearby shanty cut off abruptly in a string of sour notes.

"Get back here, rat!"

Sethe's emotions bled through Rigil's mind in serrated spikes of panic, adrenaline like a tide, regret that burst like sparks only to disappear into the dark inside his head. Either she was intentionally opening her mind to him, or she was too panicked to bother controlling the fragment she'd left in his head.

Run, Sethe, he thought, willing her to hear it. *Run.*

He felt the precise moment when she ceased influencing his body. In the meager threads of light between the slats, Rigil began patting walls, seeking the weakest joints. When he finally found a partially rotten board, gulping air in hot, moist lungfuls, Rigil forgot everything but the prison around him. Bracing his feet on the wall, sinking nearly to his shoulders in fuming emberfruit, he kicked at the gap with everything he had.

Emberfruits burst around him. A passing sailor would have heard not the hiss of steam but the thump of boots and roars of a caged lion, and still, the crate held.

Until it didn't.

Rigil's foot broke through, sudden light bursting in. He scrambled onto the pier as a fisherman was finishing his hitch knot at the next post. The man swore, dropped his line.

Rigil ignored him. Pushing to his feet and slipping on emberfruit guts, he vowed never to touch the blighted things as long as he lived as he searched for Sethe in the swirl of sailors and fish stench and rattling wagons. A woman in a tattered green shikana whistled at him from the next pier, inviting him to give his attention to someone with more to offer. The shrill edge of her laughter sawed at him like a rusted blade. Breathing hard and squinting harder against the glaring sun, he scanned the dockyards for any flash of movement, any sign of—

There. A dark figure hopping between wagons, sending kegs and vegetables tumbling every which way. She was trailed by a man in a doublet the color of dried blood who was keeping up far too well for his girth. When Sethe vanished under a tattered canvas tacked between shacks, Laban was mere steps behind.

Life was strange. If this town had been a touch less crooked, the air a little less saturated with ale and fish, the crate behind him filled with spice instead of emberfruit, this could have been Melas. A beginning. *Their* beginning.

Rigil took off running.

CHAPTER TWENTY-TWO
SETHE

IT TOOK RACING THROUGH NEARLY EVERY alley in Hamonah, hitching rides on wagons, mule carts, back to wagons, clambering over rooftops, jumping piles of tides knew what—but when Sethe finally stopped to catch her breath in an alley barely shoulder wide, she couldn't remember the last time she'd seen Laban.

Which was why it took her completely by surprise when someone dropped on top of her.

The impact buckled Sethe's legs, and she hit the dust, pinned under her attacker's weight. Wheezing, she bellowed a war cry with all the breath she had, which wasn't much. And it didn't stop him from clamping an elbow around her neck and squeezing. Hard.

Sethe thrashed. She swung her head back, hoping to connect with the stranger's face, kicking and slashing and grappling for any weakness. *Rigil!* Even as she bloodvoiced, she scanned for anything living nearby. A rat, an osprey, something she could shove a fragment into.

A hand gripped the back of her head. The ground whooshed up to meet her skull.

Blackness, stars, blots of colorless pain. Sethe lost her grip on time, reality. Spots floated in her vision, expanding and shrinking as she tasted blood, smelled Hamonayan spices. Someone had arms around her. Her mother? Rigil?

Sethe woke in utter darkness, her head full of wool.

Dark. Why so dark? The only light came through chinks in the walls. A closet instead of a crate, but not much bigger. The hot, close jungle air clung to her skin, reeking of long-dead fish and sweat. The sour, all-wrong kind.

". . . told you, I had her."

Sethe didn't recognize the voice, but Laban's reply had her pressing an ear to the wall: "Let me see."

"What?" The first voice again. "You think I'm trying to put one over on you?"

"Just open the door," Laban snapped.

A rectangle of light bloomed on one wall. Framed against the open door stood Sethe's captor, bare-chested and clad in billowing plum-colored trousers, something glinting in one ear.

Lazy Eyes. The guard from the docks, who had found her in the cargo hold in Meneton. The one whose amber irises and faint curry smell were washing her in nostalgia even now. Laban stood behind him, smiling.

Sethe lunged for him. For the door. For the light. She would rip these bilge rats limb from limb if they thought they could cage her so easily.

The door slammed shut. Sethe crashed into it, heard Laban laugh. And then . . .

And then.

Sethe had smuggled herself off Hamonah in a crate. Six confining walls much closer than these, in darkness much more total. She had survived a cell at Land's End, survived a *birdcage*, for tides' sake.

So why couldn't she think?

Why couldn't she breathe?

"Keep her here," Laban ordered. "Until Nedir pays, she doesn't leave this rock."

Lazy Eyes's reply was mocking. "You're the captain."

Panic closed around Sethe's throat, and she heard nothing more after that.

Four walls. A ceiling. A hard-packed floor. Alone in the darkness. Alone. Alone.

For the first few minutes after Laban left, Sethe did nothing but wheeze in the hot, pressing dark. By the time her shirt was soaked through with sweat, she had lost her hold on time completely. There was no sound outside, not so much as a sigh from Lazy Eyes. How long had it been? Minutes? Hours?

Years?

It didn't matter. She couldn't make her lungs expand, was fairly sure she had blacked out more than once already. Out, she had to get *out.* With a monumental effort, she lurched back, gathered herself, slammed against the door. The throbbing in her shoulder told her she must have tried it a dozen times already.

Nothing. Everything else in Hamonah was falling apart, but not this scuddy closet.

Rigil!

But bloodvoicing wouldn't help. She couldn't guide him to her if she didn't know where she was.

Sethe had already probed outside her closet for insects or birds a dozen times. She didn't know what made her try again, but when she sensed the owl nearby, she nearly wilted. From its point of view, she saw the closet, its wooden door, the rusted lock hanging from the outside. It was some kind of barn. No sign of Lazy Eyes. Maybe he was lurking out of sight.

Find Rigil, she urged the fragment. She already felt faint from lack of air. About to black out again, probably. *Bring him here.*

The part of her tuned to the owl's senses felt remote, impossible to focus on. Would she even notice if it found Rigil? Would she be conscious when it did?

Tides, this place. The way the Hamonayan air pushed on her lungs until breathing felt like drowning, heat clapping to her skin like her mother's last touch. This panic. She'd been trying to tamp it down since the *Solstice,* when the first steamy wind had blown in from the south, spiced with the jungle scent of this island she hated. This town that had taught her to trust no one, fear everything, never let anyone back her into a corner.

Close and getting closer. The walls, the roof, all of it shrinking, a cage with no up or down, no time, no air in her lungs, an eternity, in a cage for eternity . . .

Sethe had aged a hundred years when something banged outside. She had been drifting, but at least some part of her mind was still functioning. She looked through her owl's eyes and found Rigil. Rigil, wild-haired and drenched in sweat, emberfruit staining one side of his face as he stumbled into the barn, tearing aside cobwebs, ripping open stalls, kicking up a hay-dust cloud.

"Sethe!"

Sethe somehow found enough air to fill her lungs and keep her mind from fuzzing. *Rigil. I'm in here. The closet. I'm—*

The door exploded into splinters. In blasted Rigil Barak, nearly crushing Sethe in the process as light spilled into the space. Light. Air. Wind.

Him.

"What happened?" He dropped before her. "Are you all right? Where is Laban?"

When she didn't answer, he charged out into the barn again, lit orange by sunbeams slanting through a gap-toothed roof. She watched him glance both ways and rip a hand through his sweat-soaked hair, his other hand on his sword, a viper searching for a reason to strike. In another world, she might have worried about Lazy Eyes. Where he was. If he was close enough to hear them.

In another world, she might have been doing a lot of things. Like breathing.

"He can't be far." Dust swirled around him. "Did you see any-thing? Which way he left?" Then spinning back to her. "What were you thinking, Sethe? What in *Light* were you thinking?"

His eyes took a long moment to focus through a glaze of wild blue fury Sethe didn't, *couldn't* understand. She tried to rise, gave up. Bracing for a sermon, she nearly dissolved when Rigil's voice softened to the gentlest of whispers.

"Oh, Sethe."

She didn't realize she was hyperventilating until her face was in his hands, his thumbs catching tears as they poured from her in the dark that had nearly been her unwinding. Falling apart. But no, *no*, she couldn't do this in front of Rigil.

"It's all right." He was breathing hard, like her. From breaking down the door, probably. He still had Myvick's coat on inside out, but his fancy new Zerah Rock tunic was gone, leaving a thin layer of his black undertunic between Sethe's hand and his heart. "It's all right. You're safe. Lightness, I ran in circles for hours, but your bird found me, thank Arman . . ."

He stopped talking. Pulled her against his chest, one hand in her hair and the other firm against her spine, holding her steady, cradling her. But she was supposed to be a survivor. She had to be stronger than this, *so much stronger* than this.

And yet, she clung to his tunic, to the smell of Mandzee's palace and of Rigil. Salt and sweat and cypress. "It was your idea," she rasped. "What you did to Mezaedo."

"Mezaedo was a liability. But you had no right to make that choice for *me*, Sethe. And what did you expect me to do, turn around and sail home? Didn't you think—"

"No, I didn't." She pushed off his chest, cheeks flaming. "I didn't think, *Sir* Rigil, because I'm not you. I'm not the man who never makes a scuddy mistake."

His heartbeat hadn't slowed. And the hand in her hair—tides, why was *he* shaking?

The urge to put more distance between them was a hazy, slippery thing, sliding through her fingers like wind when Sethe tried to grab hold of it, to remember why she *had* to. This couldn't happen. She couldn't let him hold her like this, couldn't let him brush the sweaty hair from her face like this, tucking it behind her good ear even as his eyes trailed down to her lips and lingered, flickering through emotions like a stormy sky. Regret, worry, hope, something else that was turning his hand on her back to fire.

His mouth hung so close that Sethe could have reached out and touched the tiny scar on one corner of his frown. So close that she could have pressed her lips to his and tasted for herself every promise she hadn't let him make on the balcony in Jaelport.

When Rigil leaned in, the swath of light from the door fell over his nose, the rim of his ear, the dirty blond curl he'd forgotten to tame. Sethe didn't realize she was watching his lips until he pushed rasping words through them. "We should go, before your captor returns."

When he pulled away and offered a hand to help her up, Sethe felt the polish on his skin. She felt him becoming Sir Rigil Barak, the knight who was never unhinged, never vulnerable, never wrong. Only then did she notice that the light filtering into the storehouse had turned the crimson of freshly spilled blood. It matched the emberfruit stain down his neck.

"Laban doesn't strike me as a man who would leave a prize unguarded," he said as they stepped out of the closet. He smoothed his hair with a hand that was mostly steady, if not perfectly. "We should put some distance between us and this place before he returns."

All business. Running her hands down her sides, Sethe followed him past a row of empty barrels toward a hole in the storehouse wall. The packed-dirt floor was marred with snakelike tracks where Lazy Eyes must have dragged her through the opening. That would explain the torn skin on her heels, stinging with every step as she followed Rigil under a lacework of cobwebs and into a narrow gap between this building and the next.

"Sunset?" Sethe breathed, blinking in the mellow evening light. "It really has been hours."

Rigil didn't answer. The knuckles resting on the pommel of his sword were stained from emberfruit as he studied the alley in both directions, chose one, and marched with a purpose that belonged at the Battle of Armonguard, not here.

It took him a few steps to notice that Sethe hadn't moved. He glanced back, face streaked with so much dust he nearly looked Hamonayan himself.

"You're angry," Sethe said.

His smile was a jagged gash. "Well, it has been a prodigiously trying day."

"I would have found a way to handle the shipment alone, I just couldn't risk letting Laban see you."

"I understand, Sethe."

He wouldn't look at her. Wouldn't even *look*. Did he expect her to stand here and pretend that she hadn't just felt his pulse against her cheek, his hand in her hair, his shuddering breath against her ear?

Shifting her weight, Sethe flinched as a mouse scuttled across the alley, vanished into a heap of bricks. "Are you going to forgive me?"

"There is nothing to forgive."

"Then why—"

"Lightness, Sethe." Rolling his head back, he whirled on her. "I thought someone had killed you. You didn't bloodvoice, I couldn't see you, I was certain . . ." His throat tightened, each tendon pronounced in sharp vertical lines. "I failed you once, Sethe, and I swore it would not happen again. Not with you. Not ever with you. I am *not* that man anymore."

It was the closest he'd come to a true apology for the road to Zerah Rock. The closest he'd come to showing her the raw regret beneath his Kingsguard armor, a regret that ran much deeper than the two of them.

"K'sil." She tried to sound gentle. Tides, but she tried. "Tell me honestly, why did you leave Zerah Rock in the first place?"

She would have fled like low tide if he'd tried to corner *her* that way. But after a long beat, he leaned against the alley wall, as exhausted as Sethe had ever seen him.

"You and Eagan." He folded his arms tightly over his ribs, as if to keep something from leaking out. "Both of you, determined to dredge that up. I'm half surprised he didn't tell you himself, the way he went on about Mezaedo."

"Mezaedo?"

He spoke to the wall, chest swelling with a not-quite-steady breath. "He took me by surprise, you know. I never dreamed I'd take on a second squire, certainly not one as *special* as Mez. But when I saw him in Armonguard"—he cringed a smile—"this odd young Jaelportian, a reject from bloodvoicing training, so *eager* to be of service. Call me a fool, Sethe, but I took it as a sign. Even Eagan saw the resemblance."

Sethe shook her head. "I'm not following."

Rigil's eyes slipped shut. "There was a Jaelportian serving boy at Zerah Rock. Tazeem. My sister adored his family, practically adopted them as the parents and siblings she'd always wanted." He paused. "I suppose I cannot blame her for that."

The strain of this confession sharpened every angle of his face. This was something Sir Rigil Barak didn't talk about, which meant that right now, he wasn't a knight. He was the Rigil she'd known in Melas. The one running from something as far as he could go, as fast as he could trade one mask for another.

"It was a Barak rite of passage," he said softly. "Sailing a skiff around the point in a Zerah Rock storm. Every heir for generations has earned his birthright that way. Eagan did it at fourteen. Exceptional, as always. I was sixteen. Sixteen, next in line, and inferior in every way, as my father reminded me almost daily.

"If I'd waited for his permission, he would never have granted it. I believe a part of him was still hoping for some way to reinstate Eagan, some way to avoid acknowledging me. So I didn't wait. I took my skiff and Tazeem, hardly more than a boy himself. Viola told me I was mad, told me what failure could cost." He swallowed, jaw tightening. "I told her I wouldn't fail."

He was living in the memory, his face sun-washed and filthy and, for a moment, decades younger. "He had Mezaedo's stare, you know, that way of soaking everything in. And so loyal." His smile was like lightning, quick to go dark. "Loyal, but no sailor. And couldn't swim worth an Eben's breath. Neither of us saw the rock until it was too late, and when I found him in the water . . ."

Rigil pressed the back of his head to the wall, squeezing his eyes tighter.

"He looked all wrong on the shore. I remember thinking that. Sixteen years old and thinking, *This isn't him. This* thing *is not Tazeem.* His father, Rayado, wept like a child at the funeral. A part of me wished my father would do as much. Light knew I deserved every tirade he could unleash. But he just looked through me, *over* me, as if I had simply ceased to exist." His shoulders rose and fell again. "Weeks later, I met you in Melas."

Shadows creeping down his face made it longer, sadder, and when he faced her then, the strange time warp they'd been existing in seemed to dissolve. Boy and man, urchin and woman, they were and they weren't what they had been once. Time had altered them, made something new from the bleached bones of who they had always been, like coral transforming sunken ships, bit by bit, into works of art.

"You didn't know the truth, Sethe," he said. "Until I made the same mistake with you. I failed you on the road to Zerah Rock, exactly as I did Tazeem. And then there was Bran, killed defending his prince with his knight nowhere in sight, to say nothing of Mezaedo."

"Rigil, enough."

"You were right in Meneton. The Kingsguard knight? He's a costume. An act. This life is a test, and when it matters most, I fail. That's the truth. Now you know."

Now she knew.

One moment, they were divided by too many impossible steps, and the next Sethe was close enough to see the pain behind his not-so-seamless Kingsguard mask. She hadn't even felt herself move. "You were a boy."

"Bah." He swiveled away. "You sound like Eagan."

"I'm talking about us. You and me on the road to Zerah Rock, when we were young and afraid and you ran, like I would have in your place. Only I might not have gone back for you the way you did for me. I might not have been brave enough." He looked ready to argue, but she didn't let him. "And even when I'd lost you and told myself it had all been some lie, I couldn't go back to what I was, sapping someone else's survival to feed mine. You'd done something to me, you and your principles and the Father God who meant more to you than your own survival." Sethe rose onto the balls of her feet, trying to bring herself level with him. "Whatever I am now, if I'm even a *feather's weight* better than I was, I owe it to you. You and Arman."

On a burst of reckless courage, Sethe grabbed his hand and didn't flinch when their fingers slid together, lock and key.

He looked down at them, Sethe's deep brown against his, his voice all rust and calluses. "Everywhere the Kingsguard took me,

Sethe, I was searching for you. Always. I never stopped hoping to find you."

Sweet wood dust swirled around them as Sethe stepped closer, an insurmountable distance suddenly surmounted. She could feel every ticking muscle in his fingers, feel her inhibitions dissolving like footprints in wet sand. The only view she had was her own. No fragments, no extra eyes. She refused to acknowledge them in the back of her mind or his.

No, right now, it was just Sethe and this man whose shaky breath was mingling with hers, his free hand settling on her neck, sliding toward her jaw.

"If I were to kiss you," Rigil Barak whispered suddenly, "would you allow it?"

Sethe dropped his hand. Grabbed his coat.

And kissed the boy from Melas.

It was terrifying at first, like being in the eye of a storm, crashing up and down with the swells, losing all sense of direction. He tasted like emberfruit, like salt and risk and freedom, his hand on her jaw both a question and a promise as, just like that, he was kissing her back.

Sixteen years crumbled. She was Sethe and he was Rigil, and her pickpocket's hands were tangled in embroidery, and maybe she was imagining it, but he still smelled of Zerah Rock cypress and Eversea salt, exactly like he had on those rooftops in Melas a thousand lifetimes ago.

He kissed her like that boy, that runaway with no sense of the future beyond this moment. He kissed her like he was lost at sea and she was the light guiding him home. His fingers slid into her hair as he cradled her face, this man who could have anyone, *anyone* in Er'Rets.

But he wanted her.

He wanted *her*.

Rigil drew back and pressed his forehead to hers as Sethe took a few burning breaths, for practice. Just to make sure her lungs and heart and brain still remembered their functions. Dusty light filtered down into their alley through the clouds, painting the world rose gold.

Someone had to say something. Something sparkling and perfect, like this moment.

"Well," he said, still breathing unevenly, "if I'd known I had only to *ask*."

Sethe laughed, let her fingertips trickle along his jaw, where dust masked the reddish-blond stubble he hadn't shaved since Jaelport. He leaned into her touch, tracing her wounded ear with his thumb. *I love him. Tides. I love Rigil Barak.*

She should have said it. She was *going* to say it, until she studied him again. His eyes closed, his fingers exploring her scars as if committing her to memory. As if this was not a beginning but an end.

"Lightness, Sethe."

The way he exhaled her name, heavy and drawn out, felt wrong, all at odds with the sparks under Sethe's skin.

Of course. He was still an heir, bound to return to a world she had no place in. But what did that make the kiss? A mistake? A goodbye?

"No," Sethe growled. Rigil stiffened, misunderstanding, but when he tried to pull away, she trapped his hands against her face. "This isn't goodbye. *I* decide when it's goodbye."

He smiled grimly. "You picked an odd time to stop reading my mind."

"So you aren't thinking about Zerah Rock?"

"I was *thinking*," he said, "of all the years I might have saved us, had I been brave enough to kiss you then." The sad smile returned. "And now I'm thinking that I've already broken my promise to you in Jaelport. I'm sorry, Sethe. I know my place is in Zerah Rock, and I know what that means to you, how impossible this is . . ."

When he sucked in a breath, Sethe almost felt it, the cord that bound him to his duty, a noose around them both.

"Forgive me," he whispered. "I know what I promised, and I know I can't ask you to choose a noble life for my sake, but more than that, I know that I can't let you go." He looked up, something ferocious in the set of his jaw that turned all of Sethe's doubts to sawdust. "It appears, Sethe of Hamonah, that I am desperately and chronically in love with you."

She was still holding his hands to her face, his knuckles warm as a Melas rooftop in the sun, and she felt the absence of that heat when she let her hands drop to her sides.

The silence had gone on long enough to be painful when Rigil winced, letting his hands slide down to her shoulders. "Lightness, Sethe. Say something."

Oh, right. Just give her a moment to compose a scuddy *ballad*. "I was going to," she snapped. "But then you went and waxed poetic, and now anything I say will sound like wet sand."

For a beat, he only stared at her. She stared back. Awkwardness curled her fingers at her sides. "As for Zerah Rock, we can sail that storm when we have what we came for. The *brooding heir* act won't get us to the Talons." Her attempt to put off the inevitable question of their future would never have worked, except, of course, that he was every bit as desperate to live in *this* moment as she was. Tides. Imagine *that*.

Smiling with one corner of his mouth, he reached up and touched her face once more. A light touch this time, but it felt like a promise. "And who would you prefer I be, Miss Sethe?"

"Nothing you can't handle." She hooked his gold-embroidered lapel. "Just a pirate."

CHAPTER TWENTY-THREE
RIGIL

IN DAYLIGHT, HAMONAH WAS A CARCASS of a town, disintegrating inside a sun-bleached ribcage of bobbing masts and sails. For all Rigil's dreams of finding Sethe here one day, he saw little romance in the tight-packed shacks, the reek of unwashed bodies crammed into too little space, or the sound of obscenities hurled from windows as he wended along the waterfront.

The sun had dipped below the horizon, but the Hamonayan humidity remained, air parting like steam around Rigil, sticking his clothes to his skin. To his right, the narrow dock dropped into a murky cove, one of the island's quieter inlets. To his left, door after slanted door belched sounds and smells and siren calls, each entry glowing orange like the maw of some fire-breathing beast as he passed.

Rigil kept his head down, the scarlet coat slung over one arm. It was still damp from the sea and permanently stained by sweat. In this humidity, it never would dry completely.

A bare-shouldered woman leaned out of an alehouse to hail Rigil as he walked by, but her lewd remark slid past him like rain off oilskin. It was the figure behind him whose attention burned through his shirt. The patter of feet threatening to tug him back to a hazy alley, sweet sawdust, a lacework of scars beneath his palm.

Why the smile? Sethe bloodvoiced as Rigil quickened his pace. Her feet whispered over the planks as she darted from shadow to shadow behind him.

He hiked the coat up his arm as a swinging sign came into view a short way up the dock. Someone was laughing inside. *Just preparing my character,* he thought.

He didn't see the gap in the dock until he was tripping over it. And then Sethe was there, darting forward to catch his arm right before his foot splashed into the cove below.

There she paused, a hand on his elbow, her face a swamp of shadows. "Watch yourself, K'sil. You're in Hamonah now. Less *you*, more Myvick."

"As you wish."

Sliding a hand behind her back, Rigil dipped her low. She gasped, clutching his arms for balance, her face mere breaths from his. A kiss away. It was strange: Anywhere else in Er'Rets, the scars that crisscrossed her sun-dark face would mark her as a victim. But here in Hamonah, in this stitched-together place of ragged edges and crooked backs, those scars seemed to vanish in the light of who she was. A treasure with the soul of a survivor.

He flashed a grin that held nothing of a knight, but an ample dose of Captain Othvold Myvick. "Better?"

"What, no kiss?"

"*That* would make me a scoundrel."

"Well, if the stolen coat fits."

It was tempting. Lightness, he'd never felt more sympathy for the young Eagan Elk and his wayward desire. For an instant back in that alley, more than an instant, even Rigil had begun to fabricate a future in which Sethe and Zerah Rock weren't utter opposites.

Which returned him to the unanswerable question.

Had he been wrong to kiss her, knowing how much lay between

them and the future they both wanted? Knowing that no amount of *wanting* could forge a path from Hamonah to Zerah Rock if that path didn't exist for them?

Righting Sethe gently, Rigil stepped back, watching as she melted into the dark between one building and the next. No, he didn't have the answer yet. But he would. Arman willing, tonight would not be their farewell.

Slipping into Myvick's coat, Rigil willed himself to focus and turned his attention to the inn at the end of the rickety dock.

At the entrance to their chosen inn, a bleary-eyed Hamonayan sat against the door, his head rolling back to track Rigil's approach. What remained of his shirt was marbled with a blend of drink and vomit. Several days' worth, by the smell.

"My daughter." The man wrung an empty bottle as he spoke. "You seen my Kiah?"

Keenly aware of the thug leaning against a pillar a few paces away, Rigil flipped the wretch a coin from his pocket. It landed in the man's lap, unnoticed.

As Rigil passed, he bent to touch the man's shoulder, keeping his voice low. "May Arman return her to you, my friend."

Inside, the dregs of Hamonah, perhaps all Er'Rets, waited in a low room of mismatched tables. Only a dozen or so patrons sat about, some nursing tankards or tossing weighted coins on the floor in some kind of game of chance. Tapered candles lit the tables, dripping fragrant wax into even more pungent bowls of fish stew. A few crooked windows were opened to the dock Rigil had entered from, admitting a slight draft that did little to cool the sticky air. At the bar, one man sat with his back to Rigil, etching something into the wood with a fingernail while an orange cat strutted between tables.

The cat paused to stare at Rigil in the doorway, its eyes gleaming lustrous gold.

Captain Othvold Myvick stepped into the room with a smart

click of boots on planks. He did not announce himself, merely chose a seat and strode for it, but he was sure to embellish every step, flick his coat at every turn, draw every glance he could before he settled at the bar.

In short, Rigil milked those six steps for every rutah they were worth.

Behind him, murmurs trailed like the faint scent of brandy still cloying Myvick's coat. Eyes darted at Rigil, darted away. One or two patrons stood swiftly and left. Murmurs abounded.

"... couldn't be ..."

"I heard he was taken at Armonguard."

"... bet he spat in the king's face and walked right out ..."

"Brine and bones, don't *look*."

"Pardon me." The cat hopped onto the counter at Rigil's side as he hailed the barmaid, flashing a smile befitting any man who would commission this coat.

The barmaid, her curly black hair knotted tightly at her neck, glanced up from polishing tankards with a glower that crystallized swiftly into recognition. Recognition and perhaps something more, judging by the flush climbing her beaded neck. "*You.*"

"Alas, an accusation against which I have no defense." Rigil quirked a brow, unsure how to tread. "Have we met?"

"Just once." Her smile turned coquettish, and she leaned toward him, necklaces rattling over her dirty white blouse right before she dumped a tankard of soap water on his head.

A few stools down, the other man at the bar chuckled without turning from his drink.

Wiping suds from his jaw and trying not to think of the havoc this would wreak on satin, Rigil propped his chin on curled fingers. *Sethe?*

Osla, she answered. *Someone called her that earlier.*

"Ah, Osla." Rigil flicked his sopping cuffs. "The fairest face in Hamonah, made fairer still by your prodigious capacity to hold a grudge." He leaned forward, and despite the hard curl of her lip, she mimicked him, a blush climbing her cheeks that matched the dirty scarlet of her skirt. "I would not have shown my face again, my lady, but I find myself in need of an ally. Naturally, I thought of you."

Rigil ignored the vicious tail lashing of the cat next to him, instead watching the glow seeping into Osla's cheeks. Lightness, this was far too easy.

"Out with it, then." Osla planted both elbows on the ledge, exposing the fine thread of grime that lined each of her fingernails. She smelled of the jungle flowers growing out of the cracks in the tavern floor.

"I have an appointment with a helmsman," Rigil replied.

"Aye? And who's that?"

Rigil slipped a hand into the lining of Myvick's coat and produced one glimmering gold, only a few shades lighter than Osla's wide eyes. "Anyone willing to fatten his purse tonight. A time-sensitive offer, and one that demands discretion." He slipped the gold into her palm and curled her fingers around it, well aware that the sight would be like blood in water to the sharks in here. He forced himself to let the touch linger. "I would be most indebted, Osla, if you would procure one for me. Under normal circumstances I would manage it myself, but Armonguard and I did not part amiably, and I hear the Kingsguard may be about."

Her smile was secretive and not a little insinuating as she tucked the gold into a pouch on her belt, then sidestepped the counter. "You owe me, Captain."

She took the cat with her, slipping out onto the dock with a swish of skirts and a mewling hiss of indignation.

Well, great, Sethe bloodvoiced. *That was the best spy I had.* Although she had put another fragment in Rigil's mind, promising not to read his thoughts, that only let her sense attacks from Nedir. It wouldn't help her watch his back.

"Neatly done," said the man a few seats down. Younger than Rigil had first thought, perhaps twenty-five, he wore a moth-eaten coat over a bare chest, his hair plaited in dozens of long black braids tied back in a tail. His voice carried the burred timbre of a hard life lived in a short time. "You must know Myvick well."

Rigil swiveled. "I should hope so, friend. Who can a man know but himself?"

The stranger chuckled. "You've briny near got the accent too."

A tankard cracked against a table, coins dropping and rolling and dropping again. Rigil struggled to find his footing. This man clearly didn't believe his act, but was it a test? A trap?

Before he could consult Sethe, the Hamonayan turned to face him, a ruby-crusted ring glinting in his right ear. He lifted his tankard to his lips, keeping his voice to a murmur.

"I take it you found her, then."

Rigil's first thought was of the drunken man at the door. *Have you seen my Kiah?*

Then clarity struck. Sethe. This man was talking about *Sethe*.

Rigil propped one elbow on the bar, an illusion of control for the sake of the onlookers in the room. His other hand, he draped over his lap, where his fingers could hang close to his sword.

"Who are you?" he asked.

The Hamonayan blinked, his hands cloth-wrapped for hauling sheets, as if he'd just come from the sea and couldn't be bothered removing them. The trousers peering out from his sailor's coat looked suddenly wine-colored in the tavern light.

Purple trousers. The earring. In an instant, Rigil was back at the Hamonayan docks, peeking over the pier at the bare-chested man standing guard in the distance. Lazy Eyes, Sethe had called him. One of the men from Laban's crew. And now that Rigil saw him up close, the man did look half asleep.

Did the recognition go both ways? And why hadn't Sethe

jumped in to identify the man when Rigil had first noticed him? Unless she was preoccupied with some other threat he couldn't see.

"Who are you?" Rigil asked again.

The man ran his tongue over his teeth. "I've got a boat."

"That hardly answers my question."

"You can call me Ashik."

Before Rigil could answer, Sethe's bloodvoice shot through his head. *Rigil! Laban—*

She had hardly finished the name when voices on the docks crowded out the chatter in the room. Thumping boots, a plaintive cry from the drunk at the door—"You seen my girl?"—and then a string of curses as Laban charged in, nearly toppling a table.

Candles flickered on their wicks. Frightened by the noise, a moth bashed against the window. It fluttered to the sill and lay there, upside down, legs working feebly.

"Othvold Myvick my foot!" Two of Laban's men, the Jaelportian and the skinny one from the skirmish in Meneton, flanked him with knives drawn. "If you lot took this puddle of bilge to be Myck, you haven't got the sense Barthos gave a flea."

"Now, now, Laban." Rigil slid from his stool with the languor of a sunning snake. "I cannot advise slandering your captain."

The others in the room were squinting at him now, weighing Laban's claim against the angles of Rigil's face, the gash in his coat, his conspicuously unbejeweled fingers.

"Drown and drag me." A swollen-eared man with a pocked left cheek leaned back to see Rigil more clearly, then slammed a hand on his cutlass. "It ain't him."

Floorboards tugged and lurched beneath Rigil's feet—the tide, turning against him. Behind Laban, a figure in filthy red skirts slipped through the door, rolling a gold over her knuckles as she smirked up at Rigil through her lashes. Osla.

Get out. Sethe sounded urgent, but not panicked. This was his theater, and she knew it.

Time to put on a show.

Before he could lose the room, Rigil swung the coat off with a clink. When his hand appeared next, it was weighted by a sack of coins. All eyes trailed it. Rigil jingled the pouch, the ring of metal playing out in their twitching fingers.

Blood in the water indeed.

"I see you require some convincing," Rigil said. "How much to see Captain Othvold Myvick in place of a knight?"

Laban spat to the side, nearly hitting Osla's toes. "Keep your money, king's boy."

"I don't know, Laban." This from Ashik, who had spun to face the room and was now lounging with both elbows on the bar. His trousers, albeit worn-out around the knees, were luxurious purple under the coat. "For ten golds, he looks a briny deal like Myvick to me."

"Twenty," Rigil said.

Even Osla's breath caught at that sum. Ashik, meanwhile, was holding Laban's glare through the candle smoke.

"Rat," Laban hissed at Ashik. "That's the last time I trust you to watch my cargo."

Rigil glanced at the young Hamonayan to find him worrying the eel ring in his ear. "It's like you said, Captain. Myvick's had his time, and I don't fancy being Nedir's errand boy any more than I fancied being yours."

The pieces slid together like one of Viola's prized puzzle boxes. Ashik had been involved in locking Sethe in that closet. Even if he had turned on Laban and let her escape, he was too steep a risk.

At a grunt from Laban, his two sailors edged forward, knives catching candlelight.

"I've still got a boat, mate," Ashik muttered at Rigil's side. "Room enough for three, if you take my meaning."

Rigil reached for his sword. "How do I know you don't belong to Nedir?"

"Fair question. You don't."

In any other circumstances, Rigil would sooner have trusted Lord Coble. But even as he stood here, the night was bleeding out from the wound no sutures could close. Time.

Nedir's shipment was scheduled to leave the Talons at dawn, and once his bloodvoicing stimulant was dispersed into Er'Rets's most treacherous hands, there would be no stopping it. Perhaps Laban was the smuggler assigned to it. Or Nedir had someone else on the way.

Rigil needed to reach the Talons first, and a ship was a ship. Wasn't it?

"Where is she?" Laban slid his own cutlass free, a slow grind of rust on leather. "Play along, king's boy, and I might gut you here, merciful-like, before Nedir does worse."

Just then, the striped cat slipped back into the room, hopped onto a table, and stretched with feeling. Her slitted pupils glowed as Rigil trained the point of his sword on Laban's nose.

"I respectfully decline."

Laban swung for Rigil's gut with all the force of a hurricane and about as much aim. Rigil parried, but Laban's men were already surging forward, the Jaelportian armed with a knife as long as his forearm, the other wearing bloodstained knuckle braces.

Neither ever reached Rigil.

The cat launched itself at the Jaelportian, cutting his attack mid-swing. There was a wild caterwaul, a glint of claws as they tore at Jaelportian cheeks. A scream and a clatter as knife met floor and Osla stumbled back, both hands clapped over her mouth.

As the Jaelportian went down writhing, fighting to rip Sethe—the cat—from his face, Laban attempted to meet Rigil's next combination. Tripping over the Jaelportian's legs, Laban stumbled against a table, upsetting it. Rum sloshed, billowing its woody fragrance through the room.

Two down. Rigil whirled to his left, already on guard, only to find the last of Laban's men immobilized, one arm crooked behind his back, well past the breaking point.

Ashik finished whispering something in the man's ear, then released his arm and nodded to Rigil as his opponent slumped to the floor. "Shall we, then?"

A trail of rum prints followed them out of the inn, along with the sobs of a Jaelportian who was not likely to see again.

"This way." Ashik checked the dock in both directions before leading Rigil left down a short staircase to another walkway, this one left-flanked not by buildings but by thick green foliage. Even Hamonah's flora was not immune to the Light. Before long, the town would be swallowed by jungle.

"Wait." Rigil hesitated, half turning toward the inn they'd left behind.

A liquid shadow stirred the leaves beside him, and then a very solid hand slipped into his.

"I'm here," Sethe said. "And fairly sure I just blinded a man."

"Can't make him uglier," Ashik said brightly.

Sethe took one look at the Hamonayan and frowned. "You do realize this one nearly bashed my head in today, K'sil." Her voice held the rattle of a cornered snake. "Remind me why we'd trust him?"

Ashik raised empty hands. "Sorry about earlier, but this is Hamonah. A body does what he must. I served Myvick a long time before he assigned me to Laban. Never thought of making my own way until, well, a few blinks ago. Right about when Sir Kingsguard here flashed that gold."

His halfhearted grin went unanswered, vanishing like a gleam on water.

"All right." The Hamonayan settled his hands in his trouser pockets. "I don't know what business a knight's got with Nedir, but anything that drives a hook into that eel's gut is well and good to me. You need a boat, and I'd say you need it quick, or you wouldn't have risked that spectacle back there." He freed his hands to crack his knuckles one by one, a gesture Sethe marked with the slightest crimp of her brow. She was watching him closely, as if trying to see through him.

"What?" Ashik demanded, recoiling from her.

"I can't read your thoughts. Karpos?"

"Can't be too careful." He flashed a hand. "And no, I don't have any more."

Sethe scowled. "Pity. I might need to bloodvoice you."

That earned her a whip-thin, lazy-eyed smile. "So. I'm hired?"

"We need passage to the Talons," she said. "In and out, with cargo, no questions asked."

"Betray us," Rigil added, "and you shall find yourself reunited with Othvold Myvick in the dungeons of Armonguard."

"There's the knight." Ashik's grin was all pirate. Flashy, gold-tinged, lacking nothing but embroidery. His voice softened, though, as it curled toward Sethe. "I suppose you'll just have to trust me."

Chapter Twenty-Four
Rigil

Call it his Zerah Rock upbringing, but *ship* struck Rigil as a generous term for the rikoh Ashik dragged from the jungle under a starless sky. The lights of Hamonah shone along the coastline behind them, each window and torch a firefly against the curve of the land. The town was distant enough that only the odd dog's bark or burst of drunken laughter carried over the water, which did not stop Rigil from glancing over his shoulder every five heartbeats.

"I take it Laban doesn't know you've got your own boat," Sethe said dryly, watching Rigil and Ashik heave the single-masted vessel down the beach and settle the keel in the water. The rikoh couldn't be more than fifteen paces long, if that. It made Laban's little minnow look like a whale.

"What Laban doesn't know," Ashik said, "might just kill him one day."

Remarkably, even miraculously, the rikoh not only held water but responded to Ashik's commands with all the austerity of a well-trained warhorse. Before long, the single yellow sail was swollen with moist jungle wind, pushing them toward the mouth of the cove to the tune of chirruping flies and lapping waves.

Only when the town lights had been replaced by the coastline did Rigil dare hope that Ashik was not another sour gamble. Sethe seemed relaxed around him, falling into an easy rhythm as they tended the sail and watched for the rocks that made this coast so perilous. A choppy wind was blowing, dispelling some of the humidity, but only in fits and starts.

Rigil stayed out of the way. They had enough expertise between the two of them. And besides, on a boat this small, under a boiling black sky . . . it all felt far too familiar.

"A rutah for your thoughts?" Ashik was at the helm when Sethe stepped up to the rail beside Rigil. Only the lantern hanging on the stem could pierce the jungle of shadows that made up her face as she hung her wrists on the rail. "Nedir will be suspicious by now. If Laban hasn't already told him we've left the island, I wouldn't be surprised if one of his other spies has. Maybe Osla."

"They know we're leaving the island, not where we're going." Rigil licked his lips against a shoot of foam that slapped up the hull. It tasted of seaweed, dying things. "Nedir has no reason to think we would try to smuggle his shipment out from under him."

"Unless he really has been in my head all along." Sethe threaded her fingers together, flexing until her knuckles paled. "All that time, choking down karpos . . ."

"It makes no difference," Rigil said. "Even if he set out from Land's End the moment he broke his connection with you, he could never reach the Talons before we do, and his smugglers aren't scheduled to arrive until tomorrow. We have tonight to take the powder and sail east."

The hull scraped a shallow rock, jostling Sethe against him. Shockingly, she lingered there, arm to arm with him. "We have tonight," she echoed, as if dropping a wish in the water.

"You say it as if it's our last," Rigil said. When she didn't answer, staring over the water with tight lips, something in her silence made Rigil stiffen. With disbelief, partly, and the other part dread.

"Wait. Sethe. You can't really intend to keep your bargain with him. Back in Hamonah, on the docks, you ran. I thought that meant you had given up on turning yourself in."

Sethe's features twitched in the facial equivalent of a shudder, but turned bitter just as quickly. "He was trying to put me in a box. I lost my mind a little is all. But nothing has changed, except that now, I *know* I couldn't live with myself if anything happened to you. My bargain with Nedir is still the only way to make sure you walk away from this, and I'm going to keep my side of it."

Rigil gripped the rail until slivers chipped off in his hands. "You chose a strange time to develop an honest streak."

"Honesty has nothing to do with it. Some deals are worth keeping."

"But there's another option." He caught her hand and felt the ease of it like a bloom of warmth. Once, she would have slapped him for a touch. Now, she ran her fingers over his knuckles as if trying to sculpt them in her memory.

"Let's take the powder to Armonguard. After that…" He pulled in a breath. "After that, come with me to Zerah Rock."

"Zerah Rock again?"

"Or anywhere else you wish to go. But think of it, Sethe. My duchy would grant you protection, a personal guard, and with the king on our side, as many bloodvoicing allies as you could hope for. We can find a way to make certain Nedir never touches your mind again. You won't have to risk your life."

Sethe sniffed. "He still knows who you are. He can make good on his threats just as well with assassins as he can with powder."

"What, then? You return to Nedir and give your freedom for mine? You can't honestly think I would let that happen."

She slid him a dry look. "I'm not opposed to rescue."

So *that* was her plan. "I see. So this is a ploy to buy the Kingsguard time to rally against him? Rest assured, Sethe, I would rescue you whether you were opposed to it or not. But just think. Even if you stay behind while I raise an attack force, what could happen to you between now and then, the things he could do to you . . ." He blinked long. "He'll *torture* you, Sethe. You know he will, especially when he learns that his powder hasn't reached the other traitors."

"He'll have no reason to think I had anything to do with that." Sethe toyed with her broken ear. "And I've survived his torture before."

Behind the helm, Ashik began whistling, owllike, to himself. Sethe watched the island, a hard gold rim to her gaze that made her last smile hard to remember.

But no, he could remember. That moment in the dusty light, the air steeped in the emberfruit scent of her, their heads pressed together as she laughed for him. *Laughed.*

"No," he said, staring hard at her until she glanced up, starting a little. "No, Sethe, I'm not leaving you this time. This time, we stop him. I don't care what it takes."

The promise hardened between them like cooling steel, and the quiet over the water suddenly felt purposeful. Divine, even. Clouds were amassing overhead, drowning the stars, but something was billowing just as thickly in Rigil's chest, turning each wet breath to brimstone.

And then Sethe nodded. A tiny dip of her chin, but it meant that he had won. No, they'd *both* win. Tonight.

Nedir would never own her again.

"So quiet." Sethe craned to study the sky. "Feels like we should be praying."

When he didn't answer, he felt her surprise. Shadows distilled her face to a glinting eye, sliding toward him. "Nothing? The Rigil from Melas would never have missed a chance to talk about Arman."

"You were hardly the most receptive audience."

"Maybe you weren't paying attention."

Rigil hesitated, unsure how deep to let the jab sink, but then Sethe curled in on herself. Fog was rolling over the water now, hanging over the deck like a spirit. In the distance, thunder pealed.

"I know you never wanted to be a thief," she said. "I didn't know you were a noble, but I knew you had principles, and I hated watching you become desperate enough to set them aside. I hated what it did to you, the way you always had to give something away, *atone* somehow, just to look yourself in the eye. I hated that you stopped praying. I couldn't imagine someone as good as you carrying so much guilt."

Rigil winced, his silver tongue a lump of slag. "I was never as good as you seemed to think me, Sethe. Most of what you saw— the rules I made, the coins I gave away—was the desperation of a boy who feared how far from *good* he'd fallen. And it wasn't entirely the stealing either. It's like you said. I couldn't meet my own eyes after what I'd done in Zerah Rock, all the ways I'd fallen short. How could I meet Arman's?"

Flickering lamplight cupped the curve of her cheek as she watched him. "I see. *Everything is a test*, right?"

"Arman is nothing like my father." It seemed like the right thing to say. Even if it fell flat in his own ears.

"If you really believe that," Sethe said, clutching the rail until her knuckles bleached, "then start acting like it. Say a prayer for us. For me." The last of her tiny braids had fallen out since the *Solstice*, and damp hair hung around her face in loose black ribbons now. "Because if you can't, Rigil, if He won't hear *you*, then, tides, I have no chance in the world."

Somewhere in Er'Rets was a perfect response to that, and Sir Rigil Barak the Kingsguard knight might once have been able to conjure it. All around the rikoh, night had turned the sea to ink. The fog was so thick now that it seemed to rise from the water in banks, like claws.

"Brine and bones!"

Ashik shouted a belated warning as the mist parted to reveal one shadow as a massive rock outcropping in the rikoh's path. The Hamonayan cranked the wheel just in time, and the little boat listed hard, juddering along the rock until it broke into open water.

No. Not open water.

The Talons.

Rocky spires jutted out of the sea around them, like the claws of some massive beast reaching for the sky. They towered over the rikoh, some nearly twice its height, and Ashik spun the helm back in time to avoid what looked at first glance like a whale carcass and at second glance, a shipwreck strung between two stones. Likely one of many.

That put an end to talk. Sethe climbed the rigging with Ashik's spyglass and called out rocks as she saw them. The sky was only darkening and the wind only mounting. Gliding past the towering stones felt like sailing into another world.

That was when Rigil saw it.

From this distance, the mound of rock could have been another claw of the Talons. Then a distant flash of lightning caught on two turrets, a balustrade lit with sconces, balconies and promenades carved from the rock, following its edges as if they had grown out of it.

Nedir's fortress. A keep carved from stone.

At the keep's base, two stony arms curved around a small cove with a cavern at its back. As Rigil watched, a ship was cruising between the spurs. It was so far ahead of them that they'd never met it or even seen it on the open water. Perhaps it was arriving from a different direction entirely, like Jaelport.

"Well, that's just briny." Ashik slammed a palm down on the wheel. "You didn't say he'd be *home*. Oy, Kingsguard. Kill the light."

Rigil hurried to the stem to douse their lantern, throwing them into darkness. Even with the cloud cover, though, the night was strangely bright, the clouds rimmed with moonlight and flashes of lightning that seemed to multiply in the mist.

"Could they have seen us?" Rigil asked.

Ashik was breathing hard but still patted the helm with fatherly pride. "Tides bless her, she's small and quiet, and there's a few dozen rocks between us. At this distance, no chance."

Heels slammed the deck. Sethe, dropping from the rigging. She was gripping the spyglass like a weapon, but didn't protest when Rigil tugged it away.

He raised the glass and peered through it. The ship had crossed into the lagoon now, midsized, Jaelportian, a light burning on the stem. Figurehead of a beautiful mage reaching for the sea.

"Rigil?"

"I see it."

The *Solstice* was sailing on a skeleton crew of six men. Four sailors working the rigging, a broad-shouldered Iago at the helm, and a lone figure now stepping into the lanternlight. Small, white-haired. Dressed in flowing robes that shimmered like opal when he moved. "Those men look Hamonayan," Rigil said. "Wherever Iago found Nedir, he must have traded out his crew there."

Sethe dug her fingers into the rail until it creaked like splitting bones. "Nedir couldn't have come from Land's End so soon. We're supposed to have *two days*."

A spattering of rain hit the deck as, for a moment, the man's face almost seemed to find them across the mist. Even at this distance, knowing they were invisible, Rigil had never felt more exposed.

Raith Nedir, it seemed, was still one step ahead.

Chapter Twenty-Five

Sethe

So much for all Sethe's hopes of a simple heist. So much for *We have tonight.*

A light rain started falling as she helped Ashik coax the rikoh into the shadows of a towering rock, one of the few not decorated with ship guts, and dropped anchor in the thickening drizzle. Mist still swirled about them, obscuring everything but the crags and the towers guarding Nedir's harbor. *Those* were new. New and problematic.

"I'm sorry, mate," Ashik was saying over the rain. "But no one said a thing about robbing Raith Nedir right under his scuddy nose. He's got your shipment and a fortress of guards to keep it that way. Whatever you came for, it's not worth the price."

Rigil crossed his arms, his damp hair curling around his neck and ears. "And here I thought I was hiring a smuggler."

"He's right." Perched on the rail, Sethe jolted at the way her voice carried over the rain, bouncing off the stones of the Talons. "I know you planned to bring the shipment to Armonguard, but maybe we need to settle for making sure it never leaves that rock."

"How?" Ashik jabbed a hand at the cavern that had swallowed the *Solstice*. "I can hardly cozy up next to him."

"We won't enter through the harbor." Sethe let her eye rise to the mound of rock that had once been her prison. In a poisonous way, her home. "Do you trust me, K'sil?"

Rigil's lips parted, but it was Ashik who spoke, face glued to the spyglass.

"However you get in, you've got an hour at most before this wind becomes a squall." He lowered the glass, his trousers snapping in a breeze that was suddenly sharp enough to cut. "I can wait that long. No longer."

"Can you get us closer to the north wall?" she asked. "We can swim part of the way before the chop gets worse."

Ashik sniffed and rubbed his nose, Hamonayan for yes, he *could*, but did he *want* to? As he sauntered past Sethe toward the helm, she half expected him to back out right then, decide he wasn't keen on risking his neck for two strangers he'd just met at a tavern.

Instead, he paused beside her, reaching for his belt. Something metallic flashed between them, and then he was setting the wooden hilt of a Hamonayan knife in her hand.

"The pointy end goes in Raith Nedir," he said. "Now pull up the anchor, will you?"

That was how Sethe found herself dangling off the side of Nedir's keep, sopping wet and half deaf from the thunder pounding overhead. Rigil waited below, treading water in the dark where two rocky spurs sheltered him from the chop, watching her move from ledge to ledge. If she shifted to the fragment she kept in his head, she could see herself from his point of view—a splash of cloth against black water.

This feels familiar, he thought, making Sethe glance down. She had promised not to pay attention to his emotions or wayward thoughts, but it was hard to ignore him when he addressed her directly. *The farrier's house, wasn't it?*

Sethe snorted. *The clerk of the guard.*

Now more than ever, the keep seemed part of the sea, carved by water over centuries and left to the ocean's pleasure until Nedir had claimed it. When Sethe finally found herself flush with one oh-so-familiar window, the glass was opaque with crusted barnacles.

All the better.

She'd found a rat inside the keep, and a peek through its head confirmed that the closest guard was circling an upper floor. Hopefully he didn't hear the glass shatter under the handle of Sethe's knife.

Time flexing and contorting around her, she climbed through the opening.

Her first breath was all sourness and salt and candle wax and things that gathered in dark corners. The stone floor felt smoother than she remembered, and when wet wind poured in through the window, it snapped in the tattered curtain.

Tides, this room. That door that had never budged, no matter how hard she'd yanked. The bed, draped in moth-eaten purple and gold. The ceiling, painted with frescoes of Avenis, who was—look at that—*still* laughing at her. Even now.

Four walls, a ceiling, a closed door. Close and shrinking closer.

No. Turning her back, Sethe unwound the coil of rope she'd tied around her waist, another gift from Ashik. She anchored the rope on the bedpost, then dropped the end out the window.

She counted to three hundred before Rigil's head appeared in the opening.

"Are you certain it was the clerk?" he said. "I recall breaking into an upper floor only once, and I could have sworn it was the farrier's."

"It was the clerk." Sethe's voice came out in tatters. The walls were *not* getting closer. "He was filching wages from the guards and nearly put your eye out when you confronted him about it.

We stole the guards' wages back for them ourselves. Trust me, it *was* the clerk."

Air stirred behind her. Rigil, coming to her side. "A bedchamber?"

"Yes." A flake of plaster fell from the smiling Avenis on the ceiling. "Mine."

Typical. Nedir had left the room to collect dust like a shrine, as if he'd always seen her childhood escape as temporary. A sixteen-year hiatus. Another gust of wind blew the curtain up, and this time, moths flew out in a cloud. Sethe nearly slid into one of them and flew away, across the Eversea, leaving her body and past behind.

Instead, she crossed the room and tested the doorknob. Locked, of course. Nedir had no reason to come in here anymore. If she could find something small and sharp—

A pair of lockpicks appeared inches from her face, glinting as Rigil dropped them into her hand with a flourish. "It's astounding what our friend Ashik carries in his pockets," he said.

He was trying to make her smile, to loosen the knots in her hands, but she knew as soon as she set pick to lock that it wasn't working. Yes, the room had stopped shrinking, but tremors? Now?

Sethe tried again, failed again. Her shaky fingers couldn't resist as Rigil knelt beside her, gently pried the lockpicks away, and set them to the slot. It would have been sweet, but locks had never been his strength. Tides, she needed to be better than this. She needed to be—

Click.

The picks returned to Rigil's pocket with another elaborate flourish and a smirk that actually did make her smile.

She stood. "You've been practicing."

"Well, I had someone to impress."

A quick glance through her rat's senses confirmed that the hall outside was clear. Sethe reached for the doorknob again, but a wet blue arm jutted out in front of her.

"I remember now." Rigil stood with his arm in her way and his breath in her ear. "It *was* the clerk. He beat me within a breath of my life when I tried to make him repay the guards. Afterward, you complimented my eyes."

"Eye," Sethe said. A reflex. "At the time, you could only see through one. And I only noticed because I was the one putting your face back together."

"Did I ever thank you for that?"

She blinked at him. Were they doing this here? "I think we should—"

He opened his hand, revealing an earring. Blue lacquer. Hamonayan made. The last gift her mother had ever given her.

With no warning, Sethe's throat closed. "How?"

"I found it in Land's End, even before I knew you were there. I should have given it to you then, I know, but I wanted to wait for the right moment."

"And that's . . . now? Here?"

He pressed the earring into her palm. "You had a life before this place, Sethe, and you will have a life after it. Whatever the cost, I will pay it. Believe that."

And he thought his brother had poor timing. She flipped their hands and pressed his against his chest, the earring still folded in his fingers.

"Tell me again when we survive."

He grinned. Kissed her knuckles. Tucked the earring back into his pocket. Then crept out into the hall before her, a knight and a scoundrel all at once.

Whatever that made him, Sethe loved it.

She followed Rigil down the hall Nedir called the gallery, hung with paintings of his ancestors in gold-gilt frames. Their stares seemed to follow Sethe's every move. She was trying not to imagine Nedir's great-grandmother leering at her when Rigil flattened himself against a portrait of Nedir's uncle. He tugged her in beside him as footsteps became an armed guard rounding the next corner.

For a beat, they froze, pinned like bugs under the guard's amber eyes.

The guard moved first. Rigil barely slung his sword out in time to meet a Hamonayan blade flying for his neck. The blow put him off-balance, sending him crashing against the wall with a grunt. One of Nedir's ancestors fell from the wall, the painting's frame cracking under Rigil's boot as Sethe pulled the dagger from her belt. The flash drew the Hamonayan's gaze like a moth to silver flame.

Shoving off the wall, Rigil attacked again, reclaiming the guard's attention. Rigil was the better swordsman, but that hardly counted in Hamonayan fighting. He managed to land a glancing blow on the guard's shoulder, then feinted left and tried another, sparks flying when he swung too wide and nicked the stone wall.

The guard didn't fall for it. Catching Rigil's wrist, he threw his head at Rigil's face.

Rigil's head snapped back, spraying blood in an arc from his nose. Too far away to lunge between them, Sethe could only watch as he careened backward, as the guard drew back and then the cutlass sprang forward, diving for the soft place under Rigil's ribs.

"No!"

Sethe's hands and mind flew out as one, shooting toward the Hamonayan.

She stormed him. Pushed one of her fragments into the Veil to sever his mind from his body, watched through that fragment as the man's soul shot up and away like a gauzy afterimage. The empty body toppled, landing in a heap.

"Oh, tides." Sethe's voice sounded distant, like something flung out over the sea.

Rigil was breathing fast. "Is he . . . ?"

"Stormed."

Miracle of miracles, she managed *not* to sound like she was choking up a fishbone. As Rigil crouched to drag the body toward the nearest door without a word, Sethe couldn't stop staring at those hollow golden eyes. Blank and empty as the eyes of the men she'd left on the road to Zerah Rock so long ago.

"Tie him up." The words were hers, but they surprised her as much as they seemed to surprise Rigil. He nearly dropped the body.

"Why?" he asked. "He's dead."

"Not yet he isn't. I can still bring him back. Please, K'sil."

He hesitated, but obeyed, ripping the guard's belt off his waist and binding his hands and feet together with it. Once he'd finished gagging the man with a handkerchief from his tunic, he tugged the guard into the side room while Sethe slipped into the Veil.

Find that man's soul, she commanded one of her fragments. *Bring it back to his body.* She might be back where it all began, but one thing had changed. This time, Sethe wouldn't see another innocent soul pay the price for her war with Raith Nedir.

"Come on," she said when Rigil had finished hiding the stormed guard. "There are three more guards on this floor."

His steady gaze painted her as she led the way down the hall. Around the bend that had always made her feel like something was waiting to snatch her, past the agate-carved Avenis shrine, where Nedir had made his daily libations, through the first library with its cobalt-and-emerald patterned ceiling, left at the second library, which had always smelled like ashes, even with the windows open to the ocean. The floor tilted down the deeper they went. Like the lines in her palm, every curve and crossing was a part of her, carved into her nightmares as well as her memory from the eight years she'd spent here as a girl. Nedir's pet, prisoner, pupil, test subject. It had depended on the day.

Sometimes, he'd bring her into his study to show her some new plant or hear how her reading lessons were coming along. Sometimes, he'd make Hamonayan curry for dinner, just for her. Sometimes, his fascination with her had almost felt like real affection.

Other times, he'd split her mind open. Which was right about when Sethe had stopped expecting Raith Nedir to be human.

The air still smelled of incense, and the mineral-veined halls still trapped sound like a seashell. By the time the carpet and wainscoting ended at a bare stone staircase, the keep was all but crashing with their footfalls.

"... understandably distressed, but have you considered ..."

At that sound, Sethe caught Rigil's sleeve and yanked him into an alcove where a life-sized statue of Avenis cast a shadow wide enough for the two of them. She bashed her elbow squeezing in, red-hot pain crackling up her arm. Rigil crammed in behind her, his arm around her waist, his breath in her hair. She could only see the bottom half of his face, the smudge of a rusty blond beard coming in, the smear of red where he'd tried to stop his nose from bleeding. It was slightly crooked now, and bruises were swelling around his eyes.

You're still perfect, she wanted to say. Which probably meant she was losing her mind.

"I've done what you asked." Iago's voice this time, accompanied by the soft trip-trip of feet. "I fetched you from Cela and swear to deliver your powder and your *asset.*" His voice warped darkly around that word. "Now, Nedir, I beg you, do not harm my family."

A bead of sweat slid down Sethe's nose and hung there, like a tear. Nedir and Iago reached the top of the steps and passed before the shrine. Behind them, two Hamonayan men labored under the weight of Nedir's luggage.

Nedir looked exactly the same. Bone-white hair tied with a ribbon, a silken robe the color of moonlight, a trailing scent of curry and that briny fungus smell that Sethe associated with powder.

"That, Iago, is entirely up to you."

Iago, by contrast, was a husk of the man Sethe had last seen just hours ago, shoulders curled in, mouth drooping.

So. He was Nedir's ride to Hamonah. Bought with threats, but not loyal.

Nedir and his entourage passed, but Sethe didn't peel herself from behind Avenis's elbow until a faint scent of mold was all that remained. The Avenis statue was grinning at her like a shark circling a wounded whale.

"Iago has been bought." Rigil shuffled out from behind the statue, the violet lantern in Avenis's alabaster hands painting him ghoulish. "Sethe. Do you think . . . Mezaedo . . ."

"He's fine." Her confidence sounded half cooked, even to her. "You heard Iago. He fetched Nedir from Cela. He probably left the tiko ashore with the rest of the crew. Fewer witnesses that way."

Now that there was no danger of crossing paths with Nedir, they took the stairs at a jog. On the lower level, the hall became more tunnel-like. Smooth walls were streaked here and there with rusty ooze, the only light wafting from sconces made of violet glass. Ghost light.

Yes, she'd made this journey before. Young and terrified, sure Nedir would find the broken locks she'd left behind, trying not to imagine what a smuggler might do with a Hamonayan caught sniffing about his cargo.

Little had she known that getting out had been the *easy* part.

If her memory served, they had one last door to break through. Sethe could already feel the tumblers clicking under her hands. This time, she would not stand before that door as a trapped little girl but as a woman seeing a chance at life and taking it. One last bend.

"This is it."

She swung around the corner, expecting an iron door, shaggy with rust—the last barrier between her and the smuggler's cave that had once been her escape.

Instead, she found a blackwood cabinet filling the wall where the door should be. No easy lock to pick. Why would it be that simple?

"Here. Help me." Sethe took up a position on one side of the cabinet. Rigil grabbed the other. Together, they heaved, pulled, twisted, shoved, but the monstrosity may as well have been a wall of solid stone. One with no door, no lock.

No way through.

CHAPTER TWENTY-SIX
RIGIL

A GOOD KNIGHT PREPARED FOR THE possibility of failure. Sethe could be attacked again. Nedir's guards could find them. The world could end.

Somehow, Rigil had never considered that the furniture might conspire against them.

"Could we be in the wrong place?" He faced Sethe in the stone alcove, staring down the tall wooden cabinet that, Sethe claimed, now blocked the entrance to the cavern. "We could have missed a turn."

"What turn?" She heaved on the cabinet again, then settled for kicking it instead. "Nedir and Iago could only have come from here. Tides, if he lured us here to play cat and mouse . . ."

"He doesn't know we're here."

Sethe gripped the dagger in her belt. "This is why I tried to leave you in Hamonah. If he kills you because of me—if he *uses* me to kill you . . ." Visibly bridling herself, she gave the cabinet another vehement kick, then spun back to Rigil. "Ashik. He's still waiting. We could turn back now, forget all of this. Getting out is all that matters now."

Rigil blinked, taking in every shaking, invincible inch of her. It always came back to that. From the streets of Hamonah to the Talons to her days in Melas and beyond, she had never learned what it meant to stop dodging traps for half a moment and just *live*.

And she never would. Not with Nedir hunting her across Er'Rets, lurking on the other side of every bit of karpos she swallowed. She would never be free of his cage, not truly.

Rigil marched for the cabinet.

Stretching from floor to ceiling, it was made of dark glossy wood inset with glass panels, and an eclectic collection of gem-carved objects was arranged on tiers inside. Rigil yanked, rattled, pushed, hoping to reveal a door on the other side. The monstrosity never budged.

But why did none of the figurines inside so much as wobble?

Something about the little idols, the odd shapes arranged in a half circle, jogged his memory, stirring up old lessons from the days of dusty books in Zerah Rock.

Rigil went to his knees and tried to shift the figurines, one at a time. None moved, but the tickle in his memory was fast becoming an itch. Each idol bore a symbol: an hourglass, a stylized moon, a spoked wheel, a bird, a tree. Surrounding each idol was a circular disc that spun on its own, numbered from one to five.

"I'll be ransomed." Rigil surged up onto his heels. "It's a puzzle."

Five idols, five digits. Fandel Barak had once commissioned locks like this in the early days of Zerah Rock. If only Viola were here. Her puzzler's mind would know where to start.

"Where would she begin?" Rigil muttered to himself.

The pattern. Viola would find the pattern.

An hourglass, a stylized moon, a spoked wheel, a bird, a tree. The moon was a symbol of Avenis, so the others might be pagan gods as well. A tree for Dendron, god of nature. A wheel for Nivanreh, god of travel. An hourglass for Isemios, god of knowledge.

"Symbols for the gods." Rigil rested his forearms on his knees. "But why five?"

Teetering visibly between interest and annoyance, Sethe leaned over to study the idols. After running her fingers over each, she pointed to something Rigil had missed—a hand etched into the back of the cabinet, almost invisible.

"The Mythos of the Hand." She flexed her fingers. "Ancient Kinsman religion that some Hamonayans still practice. Five fingers for each god they worship, from most important to least."

Rigil studied the idols. Five gods, in descending order. Avenis had to be first, so he spun the dial around the moon, setting it to number one. Something clicked.

Oh, Viola would be proud.

Sethe, dagger drawn, wrenched a sconce off the wall and held it up for Rigil to work by, all the while watching the hall behind them. *And after Avenis . . .*

He adjusted the dial for Isemios next, and then Nivanreh. Isemios clicked—the god of knowledge was Nedir's second choice, then—but nothing happened when he set the god of travel's dial to three. Some testing confirmed that he had to reset the dials and begin again. This time, he chose Dendron, god of nature, as his third, then Nivanreh. *Click, click, click, click.* He reached for the final idol, an unfamiliar bird, and spun the dial around it to five.

Nothing.

"What?" He reset each figure, tried again. Again, a series of clicks resounded for the first four idols, but setting the last idol to five still gave him nothing. No satisfying click, not so much as a whisper from inside the mechanism. "The bird is the only one left. It has to be the fifth."

"What kind of bird?" Sethe leaned in to peer over his shoulder. "Oh. That's a sunbird. Ancient symbol of Arman."

Rigil frowned over his shoulder at her. "I've never heard that. A two-headed hawk, aye, but not a sunbird. Are you certain?"

She tilted her head so that her hair slanted over her good side. "Remind me, K'sil. Between the two of us, who was raised by the fanatical historian?"

"Nothing happens when I turn the dial," he said, "and Nedir doesn't follow Arman. Everything he does makes a mockery of the Way and the . . ."

Oh. Could it be that simple?

Rigil began again, setting the dials one by one. Avenis, Isemios, Dendron, Nivanreh. When he reached the last carving, he pushed *down* on the sunbird as if to make the symbol of the Father God bow down before the others.

A mockery of the Way, indeed. Arman's emblem genuflected readily, sinking into the wood as a fifth *click* sounded in the alcove.

The cabinet pivoted forward with a creak, bringing a slab of wall with it. Only then did Rigil feel the ribbon of humid air pouring in from behind.

Standing, Rigil dug his hands into the new gap behind the cabinet and heaved until the shelf and false wall were jutting straight out, splitting a dark doorway down the middle.

"Impressive." Sethe exhaled shakily, slid him a weak smile. "Ever think of challenging your father to another game of citadel? I like your chances this time."

Rigil, leaning in to study the doorway, heard his own amused snort vanish into the dark.

Another warm draft blew in from the passage, heavy with moisture and something else as well. Something he didn't need Sethe's urgent arm-whack to identify. The same sharp blend of brine and mildew he had smelled on Raith Nedir in the library at Land's End.

"Is that . . . ?" he began.

She nodded. "Nedir's bloodvoicing powder."

CHAPTER TWENTY-SEVEN
SETHE

CLAUSTROPHOBIC. DARK. REEKING OF Raith Nedir. Now *this* part, Sethe remembered.

Rigil stepped through the opening first, holding the torch for Sethe. As she followed him into the dark, the draft from the tunnel rippled through her clothes and tore past her into the alcove they'd left behind. The last thing she heard was a violet sconce sputtering farewell. Then she pushed the cabinet back into place, cutting the tunnel off from the keep and throwing them into darkness.

The passage smelled of Nedir's powder, an odd blend of salt and decay, plus the odor of wet stone and the things that lurked between walls. Wind tore up the tunnel in warm, wet gusts from the squall outside, almost louder than the crash of waves ahead. It would be a gale before long.

"Will Ashik wait, do you think?" Rigil asked, but he let the question hang when Sethe searched for a reply and found nothing worth saying. Ashik would wait, or he wouldn't. It was out of their hands.

The only way out was forward.

The fungus scent and faint silvery light grew stronger ahead until the cavern was steps away, the entrance undulating with the glow of light off water and crashing with the sound of waves. They hesitated there, listening to the chop and the howl of trapped wind before they swung out into the cavern side by side.

Stepping through that archway put Sethe and Rigil at the back of a cave so vast, it could have been a temple for all the gods combined. The jagged ceiling towered overhead, veined with minerals and pale streaks of mold. Across from them, the ocean crashed into the cavern through an entrance that spanned nearly two hundred paces, like a gigantic mouth open to the tossing sea. That placed Sethe and Rigil in something like the back of the cavern's throat, standing with the tunnel at their backs and the vast sea cave before them.

While some part of Sethe's mind registered the stone ledge she was standing on, the ocean sloshing into the cavern, the ship moored on the water below, it was the light that caught her attention and held it. A faint, silvery glow that seemed to pour from everywhere at once.

"I'll be ransomed." Rigil's voice dipped into soft fascination as he gazed up at the walls. They were covered in a plantlike fur, like moss. It drifted in the wind, bleeding grey light over the water. "It's like moon mushrooms."

Sethe glanced at him. "What?"

"They grow in the Cela Mountains. Ebens believe they feed off moonlight to glow in the dark, but I've never seen moss behave the same way . . ." Catching her flat stare, he trailed off, the pale light coloring him sheepish. "Not relevant?"

"I didn't say that." Sethe shoved a handful of hair from her face. "It's just that *tediously thorough education* coming through."

Outside, the black night was roaring thunder and belching lightning, brightening the massive entrance in bursts of white and blue. Chop sloshed against the walls until the whole cave seemed to be rocking, waves splashing up against the hewn stone path that Sethe and Rigil stood on. The path encircled the whole cavern, following the wall and gleaming with saltwater where the waves had splashed up over the edge. The water itself rippled black and thick as the cloud-covered night outside, shimmering wherever it caught the moss light.

Another path was carved into the cave wall below theirs, accessible by a narrow stone staircase so ships could still dock in the cavern even at low tide. Most of that second path was underwater now, the stairs leading straight down into black waves.

Of course, only one ship bobbed in the cavern, about a hundred paces away. The *Solstice* had been moored along the left side of the cavern, illuminated by the moss, the odd flash of lightning, and a lantern burning low on the ship's stem. Nedir's crew had battened the sails to weather the storm, but the hull showed scrapes where she must have grazed rocks on the way through the Talons. Docked just inside the cavern, rocking with the wild swells the storm was washing in, the vessel was a silhouette against the flashing cavern mouth. A silhouette crawling with the heads of two Hamonayans climbing up from the hold by lamplight.

"Get down," Sethe hissed as thunder cracked outside, the echoes almost deafening. Grabbing Rigil's arm, she yanked him back into the tunnel and sought the Veil for an insect. She nearly jolted when she found dozens waiting—unusually sharp outlines in her mind, crisp as a mast against the sun. The moldy powder scent was worse here. Sharply organic and almost painful, like a wad of rotting leaves crammed into her head.

"The rest of the crew, I take it?" Rigil whispered. "What are they doing?"

Bracing her fingers on the wall, Sethe slipped into the senses of the first beetle she found near the *Solstice*, but gave up when she found the creature's vision too murky to be of much use. Instead, gritting her teeth against her rules about leaving human heads alone, Sethe slid into one of the sailors' minds as they descended into the hold again. She had already stormed a man tonight. What was one more rule broken?

Through the sailor's ever-shifting vision, she saw a dark ship's hold, a burly Hamonayan clambering down the ship's stairs with a crate in his arms. The steps were so sharply inclined, they were nearly a ladder proper, but the Hamonayan never missed a rung, even with his hands full. Sethe's spy was dragging barrels from stem to stern, the ship rocking drunkenly around him.

She had never felt so unnervingly comfortable in another person's skin. It would be so *easy* to reach out and take control.

"That's the last of them," one Hamonayan said from under the hatch, hanging off the angled ladder by one hand and foot.

Sethe's spy shoved a crate against the bulkhead. *"And the* special cargo?"

"It'll keep till morning."

Snapping back into her own senses, Sethe found Rigil watching her in the silvery darkness. "They're loading the shipment now."

He leaned over her to peer into the cavern. She watched the watery light ripple over his face before he jerked back.

"Blight it all. They've finished. Is this the only way out of the cavern?"

If so, the Hamonayans were about to run right into Rigil and Sethe.

She grabbed his arm as her guard began climbing out of the hold. That gave them moments, maybe less. "Come on. Stay with me."

They hurried back into the cavern as lightning cracked again outside, illuminating every tendril of moss and wisp of seafoam for a single, crystallized heartbeat.

"Come on, Misha. I said they'll keep till morning."

Out on the deck, the guards began hoisting themselves up onto the pier. Any second, they could look over and see Sethe and Rigil standing on the edge of the stone walkway.

Into the water, Sethe bloodvoiced.

They hurried down the narrow stairs to the mostly submerged path below, then into the water, as more thunder cracked. When Sethe broke the surface, Rigil was already clinging to the side of the stone path. He pulled her in beside him as footsteps crossed overhead.

"... work to be done, Raji nowhere to be found. Typical."

"Drown and drag 'im. It's done, with hours to spare. Only a madman would attempt the Talons in weather like this."

Bobbing beside her, Rigil met Sethe's eye. Here was hoping Ashik ran on the mad side.

Once the guards had passed out of the cavern, taking their lamp with them, Sethe wasted no time scrambling back up the slick stairs to the upper path. Now that the lamplight was gone, the moss seemed to glow brighter, a pale froth spilling from floor to ceiling and blowing gently in the wind. The mildewy smell was so strong now, Sethe's head felt full to bursting with it.

The upper stone path that encircled the cavern was slick and narrow, growing narrower toward the mouth of the cave, where the *Solstice* was moored for a quick retreat. Tied to an iron spike on the wall, it bobbed below the path, waiting for the tide to bring the deck flush with the walkway. The guards must have used the lower path to load the shipment. The *Solstice* was already flush with that one, and the tide hadn't quite finished washing it out yet.

As they walked along the narrow upper track, she and Rigil both slipped more than once before they passed the *Solstice*'s stern, then its quarterdeck. A gangplank lay on their walkway, sticking out over the ship, useless until the tide brought the ship's main deck a little higher. With the vessel bobbing beneath them and thunder rattling off the cavern walls, Rigil kicked the plank out of the way and dropped onto the deck himself.

"Four-man crew." His face level with her knees, he held a hand up to her, knowing she didn't need it. His lips lifted a little when she took it anyway and jumped down. "Secrecy, I understand, but only four crewmen on a ship this size?"

Once on the deck, Sethe sought the hatch, overlooking the bloodstains Iago hadn't bothered scraping off. "Keeps things simple," she said. "Fewer minds to control, fewer witnesses to dispose of."

When she pulled up the hatch, a wave of urine and that rotten moss scent wafted out, the latter so strong it seemed to shoot straight to her skull. It wasn't pain, exactly. More like restriction. As if her mind, for that instant, had swelled too large for her skull.

She let Rigil descend first, then followed him down the steep steps and into the waiting shadows.

The only light below came from the glow of the moss bleeding through the gaps in the deck, but that pale grid was enough to illuminate mountains of crates cramming the space from stem to stern. Some rose barely to Sethe's knees; others could have housed her comfortably. They smelled of new wood, with a hint of char from the Avenis mark branded into each lid. Recent.

Rigil pried open one of the larger crates and began sifting through the grey dust inside. The *Solstice* shuddered around them, dipping and rising with the chop. "So much."

"We could take it all." Even Sethe heard the hunger in her own voice. The need to ride this gust of luck for every league it was worth. They had the shipment. They had a *ship*. "Rigil, we could sail out tonight, before he even knows we're here. Just cut the moorings and go. Without another brig, Nedir couldn't chase us if he wanted to."

The surf rocked the *Solstice* against the cavern wall, and Rigil caught one of the rafters to brace himself. "In this storm? With a crew of two? We would be broken to bits."

Sir Rigil Barak, right as usual. Sethe swung her arms at the hold. "What do you suggest?"

He scanned the hold, his gaze settling on two unlit oil lamps sitting atop one of the larger crates, probably left there by the guards. He hefted one in each hand, oil sloshing inside.

"Oh." Sethe blinked. "That'll work."

He set to work sprinkling the crates with oil while Sethe opened one after another. Out of curiosity at first, then real intrigue as each box spilled more mysteries than the next. Little carved idols, jars and jars of Poroo ash paint, bone talismans, maps of Cherem, Jaelportian powders.

"More papers," Rigil called from one of the smaller boxes. "Magosian writing. And these barrels along the port side are filled with some kind of elixir."

He was emptying the last of his oil over a keg of what smelled like bad wine. If not for the lamp running out then, they might not have heard the sound trickling from one of the larger crates.

A tiny, tiny whimper.

Sethe was there in a blink, setting her knife to the cords, praying that they'd misheard. Praying to find nothing but Poroo idols when she flipped the lid open and let the light in.

Oh no.

A little girl, face dark with grime, peered out at them through a nest of matted hair.

"Please," she whispered, "Don't kill us. Please."

Something shifted beside her. A boy, raising his head from a bed of straw, eyes darting and swooping as he rasped, "Help me catch them, Kiah. Quick, they're flying away!"

A garbled sound eked up Sethe's throat.

Rigil was already kneeling at the crate, speaking in soothing tones. "My name is Rigil. This is Sethe. Kiah, is it? I believe I know someone who misses you very much."

Sethe stopped listening. The crates had seemed countless when she'd first started investigating, but she burned through the last ones now, slicing and prying, slicing and prying.

Two more children blinked up at her from the next crate in this cluster. The next made five in total. Then six. Nine. All Hamonayan, all bone thin and filthy and begging for food, water, a loved one they expected Sethe to know. Many, like the babbling boy, looked like something had broken inside that would never be put right.

Tremors rattled her fists, something scalding rising in the back of her throat. The girl called Kiah was crying, the sides of her head scored with fresh scars to match the blood under her nails. Another burst of thunder cracked outside, vibrating through the hold. The girl whimpered as if struck.

They're like me. Sethe lurched, breathing hard. "He's made more like me."

And she would take them all. She would see Nedir rot on Ice Island for what he'd put them through, if she had to swim them off this rock one by one. If she had to—

A board creaked overhead, shocking every child to choked silence.

For a long time, no one moved. Even the wind outside seemed to hush.

Then a new sound trickled down through the hatch. A voice. Reedy but confident. Softly singing a hymn to Avenis. A shadow moving between the slats of the deck.

One of the children sobbed, clapped a hand over her lips, and something within Sethe clicked into place.

She looked at Rigil. Rigil, who had been hers for an entire day. Rigil, who had a life waiting for him on the other side of this disaster.

I'll hold him, she bloodvoiced. *You get them out.*

By his face, he might have swallowed a mouthful of Hamonayan rum. Nedir's voice, meanwhile, grew closer, clearer. Wherever he moved, orange light followed through the cracks. He'd brought a torch. Well, all the better to aim a knife with.

Rigil gathered the tikos off to one side of the ladder, in the shadows, taking his place in front of them like a marble guardian. From there, he could watch Nedir descend the stairs but wouldn't be the first thing Nedir saw. That was Sethe's job. And if she did it well enough, he'd whisk the children up that ladder over Raith Nedir's broken body.

Swells slapped the hull. The *Solstice* moaned and pulled at its line. Sethe positioned herself at the base of the steep stairway, Ashik's dagger bleeding cold into her palm as warm lanternlight spilled down the open hatch. A slippered foot fell on the first rung. Then the second. The fourth . . .

Gripping the dagger like her only tether to this world, Sethe lunged for Nedir.

Her legs betrayed her first, buckling on her first step. She fell with a cry, still clutching the dagger but unable to move her arms as Nedir took another languid step down, appraising her over the slope of his nose, a lantern drooping in his left hand. He looked as balanced on the sharply inclined rungs as he did anywhere, robes spilling down to pool at his feet like bilge. He hadn't glanced behind him to see Rigil and the tikos waiting there, poised to move the instant Sethe knocked Nedir off the ladder. Not yet.

"Disappointing, Sedhani." Underlit orange, he smoothed a hand over his hair as if her nonattack had ruffled it. "Force, I would expect from Sir Rigil, but I expected more from you."

One of the children started wailing, and Rigil screened them with his body, sword drawn. Sethe tried to lift the dagger again. Again, she couldn't.

"How are you doing this?" she gasped. "How are you so strong?"

"Incredible, isn't it?" Nedir inhaled deeply. "What my moss can do? When I shattered your mind all those years ago, I knew only a fraction of its potential. It is effective, digestible, highly transportable, but nearly impossible to grow." He tilted his moss-stained fingers to the light. "I had only to introduce it to the caves, and the specimen did the rest. When airborne, the spores are nearly three times more potent than its powdered form. Can you imagine?"

She wanted to ignore him, to defy him, but curiosity was too strong. Reaching out with her mind, she found a thousand fragments waiting to be broken off. And not just hers. Peering into the Veil through a fragment, Sethe could see pieces of the jittery little boy's mind darting about the hold. They had never looked so crisp before, so defined.

Was this what Nedir had felt when he'd swallowed the powder for the first time? This lucidity, this *strength*?

"And this after mere moments," Nedir said, a self-satisfied ooze in his voice. "Imagine what *years* of exposure will do."

He'd read her mind. Sethe tried to break off a fragment only to find it already taken. Already claimed. Surf exploded against the cavern walls outside, shaking the ship and drowning out the dying scream of all Sethe's hopes.

Nedir tucked his hands in his sleeves, warmth seeping into his smile. "So. You see."

No. So busy with the tikos, she hadn't sensed him or thought to check her defenses. Maybe if she had, her newfound strength would have been enough to ward him off before he seized her for himself.

"Unlikely," he said, reading her mind again. "The disparity between our abilities allowed you to hold well enough against the weaker, powdered stimulant, but the spores take time to come to full effect in a new subject like you. Conditioned as I am, I outmatch you after just a few breaths." He smoothed his hand down the front of his robe. "Congratulate me, Sedhani. I found a way to surpass my greatest success. All it took was time."

Sethe stood and stepped back, the dagger rising with her. Her body, that movement—it didn't feel like hers. Because Nedir was already here. Already in her head. All her moss-fed power now belonged to him.

And yet, here she was, tracing the spot on Nedir's robed chest where she wanted this dagger to land. Wanted it *so scuddy badly*.

Seeing the blade, the old scholar inclined his head. "Hmm," he said. Just that.

Sethe's knife moved first. She watched rather than felt it, like she watched her feet pivoting to face Rigil while every muscle contracted against her will. Against her will, Nedir held her tongue, sewed her lips shut against the cries in her head.

Angled in front of the little ones, Rigil took one look at the knife trembling in her hands and shook his head. "Sethe. Don't."

Nedir sat down on the bottom step of the ship's stairs and arranged his pale robe beneath him. "Better, Sedhani."

A scream flayed Sethe's throat as she threw herself at Rigil.

Chapter Twenty-Eight
Rigil

Between Sethe's scream and the flash of metal diving toward him, Rigil became pure instinct. He jerked back. Sethe's dagger grazed his hip, and if pain shot through his skin, it was lost beneath the tidal wave of shock, betrayal, horror.

Sethe. His Sethe. Trying to kill him.

He stumbled back between the crates, trying to draw Sethe away from the children. She plunged after him, tears in her golden eye, a tiny rebellion against Nedir's claws around her mind. With an effort that twisted her face almost beyond recognition, she forced two words through gritted teeth.

"*Fight back.*"

Sword against knife. In another world, the advantage would have been his, a world where he didn't love this woman, where she was more than a feral animal fighting for her life. The *Solstice* spasmed around them, tilting with the waves and banging against the cavern walls like a dog pulling at its leash. Sethe moved with the vessel, in tune with its dips and shudders as Rigil found his stance upon a pitching deck. He might have been a stranger for all the recognition in her face as she dove at him, knocking him off his feet. He hit the floor with her on top of him.

No time to reason with her. No time to plead. Hooking a foot around Sethe's and grabbing her knife hand, Rigil flipped her off.

She crashed into a box of vials, taking the knife with her. Glass shattered beneath her as she fell hard onto the contents. A few of the children screamed, tried to burrow deeper into the cargo.

Good. Until Nedir was out of the way, he wanted them out of mind.

Rigil wouldn't harm Sethe. That vow was his shield as he grabbed his fallen sword and Sethe found her feet, teeth flashing, bits of glass raining from her clothes. The movements were all hers—Nedir was no soldier and couldn't hope to win by controlling her like a puppet. He was likely manipulating her some other way, feeding her false emotions to turn her against Rigil.

But Sethe was still in there. He could not afford to forget that, not when the real enemy sat ten paces away, observing as coolly as a tournament judge.

Sethe darted in again, a shark in dark water. The crowded hold rendered it almost impossible to maintain distance, and so she brought the fight closer, dodging his next disarming move with the reckless grace of a drunken dancer. Her words aboard the *Solstice* resounded in the clash as she ducked inside his next swing: *You've forgotten how to fight like a survivor.*

Rigil grabbed her hand, twisted. The dagger popped free and clattered to the floor. He clamped his boot over the blade, then brought up his free hand to stop Sethe from barreling into him.

Swift and unpredictable as light on water, Sethe grabbed the hand he'd used to catch her and spun toward him, keeping his outstretched arm like a bar between them. Then she looped her elbow over his arm.

And yanked.

Rigil tasted the crack of bone, a sickening sensation with its own flavor and texture. His sword hit the floor. Vomit flooded his tongue. His arm fell to his side, limp. Likely broken.

What had she told him? *Fight with instinct, not style.*

He was too slow to dive for his sword when Sethe kicked it away. The sword skidded into the stern, vanishing behind a box. Almost in tandem, Rigil and Sethe dropped to the deck, grasping for the knife she had dropped. Sethe's hand closed around it first, but Rigil planted his knee onto her knuckles and wrenched the knife from her grip. He found his feet, struggling against the roll and pitch of the deck, grabbing hold of a nearby crate to pull himself upright. An elbow wrapped his throat. Rigil threw Sethe off before she could lock her choke hold, and her roar of frustration shook the ship.

Whirling, he found her climbing to her feet, leaning on one hand for balance like some kind of prowling wildcat.

"Sethe." He tucked the knife back against his wrist as he raised his good hand to her. "It's me. Please. It's Rigil."

There was no point in trying to hide it. Nedir already knew Rigil's weakness, that he couldn't raise a hand against this woman even if she drove a knife through his heart.

When she lunged at him, weaponless and wild with Nedir's influence, Rigil let her momentum carry him back a few steps. Staggering, he pinned her against his chest with his one good arm. She thrashed, kicked at his knees, fought to free her arms.

"I'm sorry, Sethe," he wheezed. "But it's me. You know it's me. Whatever he's telling you, fight this!"

Her head snapped back, narrowly missing his chin. He kicked the back of her knees, sending her to the deck just long enough for him to step back and cock the dagger beside his ear, gripping the handle like a hammer. Not a throwing knife, but maybe . . .

Before Sethe could find her feet again, Rigil pivoted and hurled the knife at Nedir.

A dozen children threw themselves in front of the ladder. The little boy from Kiah's crate took the knife to the thigh and fell without a cry.

All feeling fled Rigil's body, allowing Sethe to slip from his arms. "Madman!"

Nedir descended to the lowermost step and crouched beside the child's fallen body. "My mother was mad, Sir Rigil. I assure you, I am something else entirely."

Instead of turning on Rigil the instant she was free, Sethe staggered toward Nedir, moving like a puppet on fraying strings. Fighting back? Trying to attack him, or help the boy?

She stopped beside Nedir and held out her hand, shuddering to the tips of her fingers.

Resting one manicured hand on the boy's head, Nedir used the other to wrench the knife out of his leg. He handed it to Sethe, who accepted the weapon with wooden resolution, holding it by the blade as if she no longer felt pain. At his feet, little Kiah cried silently over the wounded boy, tears streaming from her eyes even as Nedir held her body still.

Being a knight had taught Rigil patience, control, and knowing when to admit defeat when the odds were simply too steep. Melas had taught him different lessons. Like when to throw caution to the wind.

Sethe began moving toward him again, her face dead except where desperation glowed gold in her eye.

It wasn't a plan so much as a gamble, a last chance to prove that he hadn't failed. He could still save Sethe, still fix this. It was all just another test.

When Sethe darted in for another attack, Rigil threw himself at her but turned and caught her wrist at the last moment, pressing his thumb into the base of her hand until her fingers sprang open. The knife dropped, and Rigil snatched it out of the air, the pommel burning in his hand by the time he reached Nedir.

Nedir, the madman, was ready with his shield of children, a

dozen blank faces gazing blearily at Rigil. Curling his knife hand inward at the last moment, Rigil charged into the children, *through* them, tackling Nedir into the ladder.

The arm Sethe had broken screamed as Rigil struck the wood, but Nedir landed on his lantern, and his scream was louder. The smell of burning cloth filled the air as Nedir shoved Rigil off the ladder.

Even in his frenzy to shed the garment, Nedir didn't release the children. The dead-faced puppets tackled Rigil into a pile of crates before he could regain his balance. One girl grabbed his throat, and he barely managed to keep his hold on the knife with so many tiny hands scrabbling at it.

That bitter smell of burning fabric hit his nostrils as he thrashed against the children, toppling one, tripping another, refusing to use the knife or strike any blows against these tiny bodies. Flames spilled across the trail of oil he had dumped over the cargo, ripping screams from the children as more crates ignited, the heat in the hold ratcheting upward.

"Out!" he roared, willing them to hear him through Nedir's influence. "Listen to me, all of you! Get out while you can! The ship is going to burn!"

Outside, lightning cracked so loudly, it seemed the *Solstice* might break apart around them. Nedir stood over the blaze, teetering on the ship's stairs as the *Solstice* knocked hard against the cavern wall. He tossed his robe, and the charred heap cascaded down the steps. His hair had come undone and fell in white waves around his face, but his tunic showed no char and his face lacked none of its usual serenity. In that moment, the face of a demon from the Lowerlands would have shaken Rigil less.

The children hadn't moved, utterly unswayed by Rigil's speech. Lips pressed, Nedir blinked long at Rigil.

"Fool."

The children resurged. Grabbing, tearing, biting. A small threat, but to a one-armed knight unwilling to kill, a force. One child ripped Rigil's arm behind his back until the world exploded into flecks all shaped like birds in flight. Owls, with golden eyes . . .

No! He could not fail. Not his second chance, his last test.

Sethe appeared before him. A lone figure slashed with scars, a river of tears pouring from the eye she still had, the eye he loved. The children parted for her. Rigil threw one boy off of him, but another took his place, plucking the knife from Rigil's hand like a grape from a Carmine vine. The boy handed the knife to Sethe, who took the handle with trembling fingers. Hard, calloused sailor's fingers he had kissed not an hour before.

It couldn't end like this. He couldn't *let* it end like this.

Then he felt it. A pressure on his mind as, through one of Sethe's fragments, Nedir grabbed Rigil's will. The fight drained from him. Every muscle in his body forgot who it served to bow before Nedir.

And bow he did, dropping to his knees at the foot of the ladder as Sethe came to a stop on silent feet. Her sweat-soaked face flickered burning red. Beautiful as ever—a thought that took Rigil by surprise. So Nedir was controlling his body but *not* his mind. Why?

Foolish question. The old man wanted Rigil to see this disaster coming, to feel the squeeze of torment while watching Sethe suffer.

Nedir regarded him with feline detachment. "I had hoped to avoid this, Sir Rigil. It feels rather like cheating. But if I recall from our citadel game, you are not above that."

Sethe towered over Rigil, hunched around her knife. Begging him with her tears if not with her voice, *begging* him to run, to escape, to survive.

He could do none of them. Couldn't flee, couldn't fight. *There are two kinds of men in this world, boy . . .*

Another crate ignited, spilling fire into the next. Billowing smoke seared his lungs and made a hazy jumble of the cargo. A wave slammed the side of the ship, rocking the *Solstice* again.

But Rigil was at sea, finding Tazeem's waterlogged body. He was at the Battle of Armonguard, watching as Shung carried Bran Rennan's broken corpse out of the watchtower. He was on the road to Zerah Rock, too late to turn back for Sethe.

He was standing before his father, Burr Barak's greatest disappointment.

Arman. The prayer fizzled. Pointless. Pain was a vise on his skull.

Heaving with sobs, Sethe raised the knife.

I love you, Rigil tried to say, but Nedir held his tongue. *Sethe, I love you. Forgive me. Please, forgive me.*

He held Sethe's gaze as his life shrank around him, reduced to the heat of the inferno and the throb in his arm and the smell of burning crates and . . . something else. A prickle in the back of his mind. A brother's voice from another world, telling him that their father was right about life.

It is *a test. His only mistake was convincing us we could pass it on our own merit.*

As if sensing his thoughts—blight it all, he was *reading* them—Nedir forced Rigil to bend his head down until it touched the floor. He felt like a submissive puppy, cowering on his knees and forced into deference. But the prayer blooming in his chest was his alone. Perhaps the only thing that belonged to him now.

Lightness. Years of chasing perfection, waiting to be knocked off Arman's citadel board for an ill step. Sure that Arman's favor was a prize reserved for victors.

And here he'd thought his father was the one who'd never understood grace.

Eagan's voice resurged, warm and knowing. *Do any of us?*

Even in memory, Eagan sounded so sure. Eagan, a man with failures of his own who always found strength in the bleakest, coldest, most impossible places. Two kinds of men. Perhaps Lord Barak had been right. There *were* two kinds of men, yet Arman's grace was reserved not for those who sought to win it but for those who knew they never could. The failures and the runaways. The thieves with nowhere left to look but up. *Arman, what little I have is not enough. It is nothing. I have nothing. Please, Arman, I need You.*

The warmth that poured through Rigil then had nothing to do with another row of crates going up in smoke, thickening the hold with fumes. Nedir still held him on his knees, but something was changing. When he realized what it was, he did the impossible.

He looked up.

"It's all right, Sethe." Hoarse from smoke as he was, Rigil sounded absurdly calm as the point of her knife settled, shaking, against his chest. He shouldn't have been able to speak at all with Nedir's grip on his body, but Arman's heat pulsed through him, freeing, of all things, his tongue.

His silver tongue.

Sethe was fading, exhaustion painting every line of her body. Still fighting that knife.

Fighting, trembling. Losing.

"Sethe, look at me." There she was. Fearless, guileless, selfless, raw as uncut diamond and just as beautiful. Everything he'd ever wanted, Arman had already given him, and there was still one thing he could show her before the end. "I love you. I have loved you since you first called me K'sil and drove me mad with wondering what it meant. I would do anything, would give my *life* to free you from this, Sethe, but I can't. I'm not strong enough.

"I know how hard it is to believe Arman desires your freedom after the traps, the crates, the betrayals, but freedom is not escape, Sethe. It is trusting Arman, trusting that He does love you. All the times you felt trapped, all the times you prayed without knowing why or how, all the times you wondered where He was, He was beside you. *With* you, Sethe."

Sethe's throat tightened, and she must have found a burst of strength somewhere, because she pushed words through Nedir's hold on her tongue. "Are you *insane?*"

Ah, Sethe. Always more fire than fear.

Rigil held her gaze, his body still firmly Nedir's but his words flowing freely from somewhere beyond him. Somewhere warmed by the light of Shamayim. "You have never been abandoned, Sethe, and your bloodvoicing ability is proof of that. Bloodvoicing is Arman's gift. *He* is its source. It doesn't belong to Nedir, not even to you." Lightness, why had it taken him so long to find these words? "Arman wants to set you free, Sethe. Let Him prove it to you."

This had never been about righting a past mistake or saving Sethe's life or even freeing her from Nedir. Arman had given Rigil a chance to finish what he'd started in the alleys of Melas, what Arman had begun in Sethe's battered heart and nurtured all this time. What mattered now wasn't the dream of a shared future or the hope of a restored past. It was the true way, the *only* Way.

This was about freeing her soul.

Breathing deeper than he had in years, Rigil looked at Nedir, then back at Sethe. His Sethe. "Arman doesn't need your help." Then he smiled. "So stop fighting."

CHAPTER TWENTY-NINE
SETHE

IT WASN'T ENOUGH. SETHE KNEW THAT now. What she felt for Rigil was the strongest thing she had. And it still wouldn't save him.

Smoke billowed around her, heat searing her skin and pressing on her lungs as her treacherous hand made the knife bite harder. It was over. They'd been living on stolen wishes. Horror expanded in her like the heat blooming in the hold or the warm blood dribbling through her fingers. Tides, how could he face her like that, practically glowing? Didn't he *know* this would kill both of them?

Freedom is not escape, Sethe. It is trusting Arman.

She could have screamed. Where had Arman been when Sethe's mother had sold her? When Nedir had broken her mind into a thousand pieces? In Melas, Carmine, Land's End. Where in the *tides* was He right now?

Arman wants to free you, Sethe. Let Him prove it to you.

Something wilder than rage warped Nedir's porcelain face now, veins bulging in his temples and down his neck as he clawed the air in front of him, grabbing at smoke. "Now, Sedhani. End it now!"

It was like he couldn't see his life's work burning up around him, like all that mattered was knowing she still belonged to him.

"Do it! Kill him!"

He spoke not to a person but to a pet, something trained to follow orders and to stay chained at his side. Sethe had been fighting that chain all her life. And Arman . . .

If she believed Rigil, Arman had been in the cage with her. In the crate that had borne her far from Nedir when she had needed it most. In the surgeon's apprentice, whose care for the ship's cat had kept her alive on the way. In the boy with too much polish, who had taught her to pray without knowing it.

In the man whose smile now showed her what the love of a Father God looked like.

"Forget the Father God! *Finish* him!"

The old man sounded strained, like the powder was stretching him thin. He couldn't go on like this. Neither could Sethe, but at least she knew they were equally matched.

Or were they?

"Bloodvoicing is Arman's gift, Sethe. He is its source. It doesn't belong to Nedir, not even to you."

Sethe couldn't fight the knife much longer, couldn't fight the alien will pushing her shaking hand closer to Rigil's exposed throat.

Rigil didn't move, didn't flinch. He was on his knees, but his spine was straight as ever, and his bruised, smoke-blackened face had never seemed more serene.

"Arman doesn't need your help," he rasped, lips quirking. "So stop fighting."

Insanity. The second she stopped resisting, Nedir's will would slice through Rigil's throat like an oar through water. She'd tried Arman already. On the road to Meneton, even on the *Solstice*. She'd given Him every chance to prove that those words Rigil had taught her were more than useless hope, so why should this be any different?

It was Mezaedo Chevyah's voice that bubbled to the surface of her mind, sure as sunrise, a potato in one scar-dotted hand as he faced Sethe's challenges across the deck of Myvick's rikoh. Didn't he fear that Arman might fail him, might abandon him like all the others?

Like wind, the squire's answer tore through her: *If Câan could go to the grave believing His Father was still good, that Arman's love could bring Him back again, I figure I can trust that too.*

Sethe's breath snatched. She forgot to pull in another, and Rigil seemed to notice, his gaze hanging on her with that burning way he had of seeing beauty in the most ruined things. His faith was so much more complicated than she had always thought, pocked full of holes and held together by threads, but here he was, asking her to stop surviving long enough to let Arman save them. To lay everything down and trust the Father God's love to be stronger, exactly as Câan had once done.

Arman, freer of captives. Those words were buried in her somewhere, running through her like ore. But words weren't enough. They never would be. Until she actually decided to believe them.

Arman, Father God, father of Câan, freer of captives, Sethe thought the words for Nedir to hear, gasping when she felt them ripple through her like a current of sudden heat. *No trap can hold Him, not even the grave. Whoever He sets free is free forever.*

"Finish him, Sedhani!" Nedir roared from another world.

All right, Arman, Sethe thought. *I'm Yours.*

Dropping her shields, she let Nedir pour in.

It should have been over then. A quick dart of a hand, a flash of a knife, a gurgle of blood running down her fingers like molten metal.

But Sethe's hand, folded around that knife, didn't move a whit.

She glanced at Nedir, found his face waxed over, as if sensing a change Sethe couldn't. Wreathed in smoke, he was more phantom than man. Half the crates were burning now, the smoke so thick

Sethe could hardly breathe. The children had started to wail, some of them struggling through Nedir's hold to crawl toward the ladder, proof that the old man's grip was slipping.

And then his hold on her mind winked out. Sethe's mind cleared. She turned to find him retreating, backpedaling up the ladder.

She darted after him like a shark after blood.

Nedir scrambled up the ladder, tripping on his robes, Sethe close behind. The first two steps had caught fire, but she lunged toward the hatch with only one thought: justice.

"Sethe!"

She spun back in time to watch Rigil yank one of the children away from a burning crate. Smoke was swarming in the hold.

Right. First things first: get the tikos to safety.

Sethe freed the children's minds and Rigil's, all the fragments Nedir had used to possess them fizzing readily back into her. Coming to themselves, most of the little ones flocked toward the ladder but recoiled when they found the rungs burning.

"It's all right!" Sethe hopped over the lower rungs and reached back for the girl in Rigil's good arm, the *Solstice* rocking and writhing on its line. "One at a time! Come on! It's all right!"

They came up one after another. Nine children in all stages of panic, one of them clinging so tightly to Rigil's arm that Sethe had to *pry* him off to lift him through the hatch. After hoisting the first few to safety, she poked her head through the opening to find them swarming around the port rail, little Kiah sheltering three girls in her arms as if she alone could fend off all the pirates in Hamonah. Though Nedir was nowhere in sight, Sethe severed off a fragment and sent it into the Veil to find him. They didn't need any more surprises.

Speaking of surprises. What in the *tides* had Arman just done? Why did Sethe suddenly feel like she was drinking strength from a well with no bottom?

Dripping sweat and coughing smoke, Rigil lopsidedly passed Sethe the last child, a young boy with fingernails like claws, who seemed vaguely catatonic. Sethe heaved him up through the hatch just as something collapsed in the bow, sending a shudder through the whole ship. Flames had nearly encircled the hold now. Only a few kegs along the port side remained. Between the inferno and the thunder in the cavern, Sethe couldn't hear herself breathe.

Rigil began following her up the steps. "What did you say was in those barrels?"

Sethe grabbed the deck. "I didn't."

Wind was howling in the cavern when she emerged on the deck. She gulped sea air, throat peeling from the smoke. When one of the boys gave an ear-splitting shriek, she nearly dissolved. Arman help them, what next?

"Ho, up there!"

Behind her, Rigil's voice stretched tight around a smile. "I'll be ransomed."

Sethe rushed to the rail.

And there he was. Ashik's rikoh was listing hard, water rolling on the deck, the sail ripped down one side. When he saw her on the *Solstice*, he stopped dropping the anchor and waved with all the terrified rigor of a man who had just braved the Talons in a squall.

"Oy!" He squinted up at her, soaked to the skin. White light flashed behind him. "What happened to 'back in an hour'?"

Sethe grinned. "Room for nine more?"

"Keep 'em little. I'll come alongside."

"No!" Rigil limped to the rail, favoring his damaged arm. "Keep your distance, Ashik." He turned to Sethe, panting. "Those barrels. I think it may be Shelosh ink. If the fire—"

"Jump!" Ashik shouted. "I'll fish them out!"

Most of the children went mad at that suggestion, one scar-faced girl wrapping herself around the rail like a monkey. The wounded boy was wailing, Kiah trying desperately to comfort him while glaring at Ashik with naked hostility.

"You need to trust us," Rigil said, trying to calm them enough to make himself heard. The bruises around his eyes made him look like a bandit. "Ashik is a friend. He will take you to safety."

"Kiah." Sethe caught the older girl's shoulders and bent low to meet her. "I need you to be brave now, all right? Please. We both know you've survived worse than this."

It was strange, gazing into that sun-dark face marred with gouges that would definitely scar. It was a strange reflection, the hopeless girl face-to-face with the woman who had found freedom in a storm of smoke and steel. No, in Arman.

When Kiah jumped, hand in hand with two younger girls, the others were quick to follow. Nine splashes in inky water, nine dark heads breaking the surface. Something groaned and crashed in the prow—the deck, collapsing. Flames poured from the gap, reaching for the ceiling.

Sethe's turn. She grabbed Rigil's good arm, ready to jump and never look back.

"What about Nedir?" Rigil shouted.

"Forget him! We have to go!"

"He won't stop hunting you, Sethe." She turned and found his eyes burning lightning blue, bold against his bruising face. "As long as he's free, you never will be."

Another groan as the *Solstice*'s innards combusted. Had the flames reached the barrels?

"Rigil." Sethe seized his face, burying her gaze in his. "It's done. I'm already free."

Letting go and turning to the water, she stepped up to the rail. At the last moment, something moved in the corner of her vision.

Nedir emerged from the captain's cabin, his face sheened with frantic focus as he scrabbled at the hatch like an animal. He was shouting about something he'd left behind.

Pathetic. Mad. In a prison of his own.

Sethe turned her back on Raith Nedir and jumped over the rail.

Only when she hit the water, in that drumming silence underneath, did she realize Rigil hadn't come with her.

She broke the surface in time to see Rigil still on deck, his good hand closing on Raith Nedir's collar just instants before the *Solstice* exploded.

CHAPTER THIRTY
RIGIL

RIGIL WAS AIRBORNE BEFORE HE FELT the *Solstice* heave, and then he was nothing at all.

When he finally peeled his eyes open, his head was still ringing. Two thoughts struck him at once: Those barrels had *definitely* been full of Shelosh ink, and he was not in the water.

Lightness, but the world was loud. The sky spitting and wailing outside, the *Solstice* a groaning mess of fire, the water in the cavern still rocking from the force of the blast. Rigil's arm was bellowing with a voice of its own, only slightly more insistent than the rest of him. He had landed on the upper stone path, moss dripping from the wall to his right. A hard fall that would have killed him had he not fallen face down on Raith Nedir's chest.

Flat on his back, the old man stared at the ceiling, his eyes wide but unfocused, his chest pumping slow, deep-drawn breaths as if breathing were one experiment he had not yet mastered. Sharp pieces of debris from the *Solstice* littered the stone path around them and tossed in the water to Rigil's left, clicking and crashing over the washed-out lower path.

Robeless and dazed, Nedir had never appeared so feeble. A

bird's pulse fluttered in his throat when Rigil shoved to his knees and pressed his arm against the man's neck.

"It's over, Nedir. Now tell me: Where was this shipment going? Who are your allies?"

In and out. Rasping, jagged breaths. This man, so willing to wield lives like rogues in a game of citadel, and here he was, as mortal as the rest of them.

Rigil tried a different tack. "Where is Iago?"

Nedir's mouth curved up in a red-stained smile. "Hamonah is full of captains who ask fewer questions, Sir Rigil. But you still have not asked . . . how I did it. How I reached her through . . . the karpos. In Meneton. On the *Solstice.* You must be . . . a little . . . curious."

"Then tell me something new." Rigil would have to wash a dozen times to forget the buffet of this man's breath on his face, but he didn't know if his body would let him move. "Tell me what you and Coble were planning."

"I've realized," Nedir said dreamily, fingering a cord around his neck, "that boy had no inkling of what his spice was made of, its enmity with karpos. I doubt even his mistress fully understood its potential." He choked on a laugh. "That fool Isbelda. That stupid, wonderful boy. Every bite, defeating the karpos in his blood . . . opening a door . . . for . . . me."

Rigil's entire body went cold at the sight of that worn blue cord. He snapped it from around the man's neck, pulled out a pouch on a string.

Blue velvet, stained orange where a squire's fingers had worried it again and again.

Nedir's eyes were reptilian slits. "If it comforts you, Sir Rigil . . . he was very useful."

"Where did you get this?" Gripping the pouch, Rigil could feel every grain and kernel of spice sliding between his fingers. "Where is he? *What have you done with him?*"

Nedir lifted his head, the halo of hair slowly turning red. His gaze lolled over Rigil's shoulder toward the *Solstice*.

"Oh, no, Sir Rigil," he wheezed. "What have *you* done?"

Rigil shoved Nedir away, forced himself to his knees. He twisted to watch as the *Solstice* keened, the entire upper deck ablaze even as it began to sink against the flashing sky and angry chop that filled the cavern. Behind it, Ashik was pulling a young boy into his rikoh. Sethe treaded water, halfway between the rikoh and Rigil, as if unsure who needed her most. If his squire, if *Mez* was on that boat . . .

It had to be a lie. They had checked all the crates, gotten everyone out. "Lies." Lightness, Rigil sounded as winded as Nedir. "Mezaedo is in Jaelport with the rest of Iago's crew." *It has to be a lie.*

But he knew somehow, even before Nedir's lips peeled from his teeth in a sickly smile. Even before the *Solstice* groaned and lurched in the water behind him. Even before the old man's hand closed on his tunic, his reedy voice wisping through the howling wind outside as he pulled himself closer.

"He was so sure you would find him. So . . . sure you would come. And now . . . drowning in a slaver's hold . . ." He coughed, blood staining the corners of his smile, gaze drifting to the ship even as his breaths grew harsher. "Once a stray, always a stray."

There were no words for the iron gauntlet that grabbed Rigil's windpipe and squeezed at that moment. *Mezaedo. No!*

As he fought to push himself up from his knees—perhaps there was still time, perhaps he could still do something—he all but ignored Nedir's voice trickling from another world.

"I would have liked . . . to play another game of citadel, Sir Rigil. But as that seems unlikely . . ."

It was over before Rigil felt it begin. Nedir's arm jerking, a flash of motion in Rigil's peripheral vision. Impact, then a strange intrusion, something jabbing into Rigil's side that didn't belong there.

Pain.

Then someone screamed. Not him. Sethe. Still on his knees and one good hand, the stone beneath him blurring and undulating in his vision, Rigil turned his head to find Sethe in the water with one hand outstretched toward him. When he looked back at Nedir, prone beside him, the man had gone limp. There was something long and sharp in his hand, a thick wooden splinter from the deck of the *Solstice*, shaped like a spike and drenched in dark red blood.

Stormed, Rigil realized, staring at the man's blank face, panting through the sudden, searing pain between his ribs. Sethe had stormed him. Nedir was gone, soon to be dead of his wounds if he wasn't already. But the blood. Why so much blood?

His side burned. Damp warmth was seeping across his tunic, and he struggled to follow a chain of thought through the fuzz gathering on his vision, the searing inferno in his side. Breathing hard, he curled in on himself. Think, he had . . . to . . . *think*.

Mezaedo. He was here somewhere. On the ship. *Trapped on the ship*.

Arman, I am not strong enough for this.

This time, the admission came easily. And the words of Arman's Book of Life were ready and waiting, surging to Rigil's thoughts now like the voice of the Father God Himself.

YOUR WEAKNESS IS MY STRENGTH.

Scrabbling back to his knees, Rigil wrapped his good arm around his ribs and forced himself to stand through a wash of vertigo. He put his back to the dead Nedir, stumbled up the path toward the wounded *Solstice*, tripping over shards tossed from the deck in the explosion. He was still hearing the Father God's echoes when he jumped off the ledge and onto what remained of the *Solstice*'s burning deck.

He landed awkwardly, the impact juddering up his legs and into his torso, nearly blinding him with a fresh blast of pain as smoke and heat pressed in from the lingering flames. A few steps away, toward the bow, the deck was completely gone, water sloshing in the hold below as the ship keened to port, burning as it sank. A skeleton remained of the ship's ladder, but that part of the deck hadn't yet caught fire. Rigil hurried down the few intact steps to the flooded hold. If Sethe was calling, he couldn't hear her. Or perhaps he was deciding not to.

When he stepped off the ladder, water was swarming into the hold from a crate-sized hole in the *Solstice*'s port hull. The fire had consumed most of the remaining ceiling and burned in oily patches on the water. Rigil's side of the hold was still above water, the deck pitching steeply downward in front of him. A few minutes more and the ship would roll.

"Mezaedo!" Rigil clung to a rafter to keep his feet on the tilted deck, scanning for an unopened crate, some sign of one last prisoner. Heat pressed in on all sides from the burning patches on the water and the tendrils of flame consuming the ship above him. "Mez!"

Rigil! Sethe's bloodvoice was spiky with panic. *What are you doing?*

Could Nedir have been lying? One last attempt at sabotage, as if the stabbing hadn't been enough. A sudden pitch of the deck nearly sent Rigil plunging headfirst into the water. It did succeed in sending him to one knee, and it took a monumental effort to regain the starboard side of the hold and grab one of the nonburning rafters to pull himself upright. The *Solstice* sobbed around him, and thunder rumbled outside, more muted now than before. Ten feet to his right, a burning chunk of the main deck fell from the ceiling like a falling star, hissing as it hit the water that was fast swallowing the hull.

"Mezaedo!"

If there was any answer, it was impossible to hear over the odd pounding in Rigil's ears. Gripping the beam, Rigil blinked against a wave of darkness, unaware that he'd sunk to the deck until he felt the starboard hull at his back. Below him, water was lapping up the floor as the ship listed harder and harder to port. Flames from the nearest oil patch edged closer to the bit of deck he stood on.

Lightness, he was tired. Tired and so weak. *Arman . . .*

That was when he felt it. A hard slap, as if someone was pounding on the deck beneath him. Rigil went to his knees to feel along the floorboards, running his hand in frantic circles.

There. A hatch. Square and almost imperceptible except for the frantic *slap-slap* of some desperate hammering below. Rigil dug his fingers into the groove, clenched his molars against the screaming in his side, and heaved with his good arm.

The hatch swung up on rusted hinges, made of solid iron but covered with wood to help it vanish into the deck. Only by Arman's power did Rigil manage to heave it all the way open, revealing the ship's dark underbelly and a mop-headed boy, shackled and gagged and chin-deep in seawater. For a moment, it was a face from long ago. Young Jaelportian eyes and a flailing hand, sinking while Rigil watched, helpless.

Then reality crashed in, and there he was. Not Tazeem.

"Mezaedo!"

The *Solstice*'s false bottom glowed like the belly of a furnace from the firelight spilling through the hatch. Mezaedo had to tip his head back to keep his chin above the water, and the moment Rigil splashed down into the smuggler's compartment and removed the gag, Mezaedo gulped air in mouthfuls.

"Sirrig." He swallowed water, choked it up again, his dark eyes reflecting the firelight like coals. "Sirrig, it was me. You were right, he was watching through me all along, and now you've got to get out. She's going to roll and you need to go, Sirrig!"

"Are you shackled?" Rigil barked. Lightness, it was hot.

"Sirrig—"

"The lock, Mez! Show me the lock!"

Mez raised his hands above the water, exposing the thick manacles on his wrists. Fighting off another wave of fatigue, Rigil delved into his pocket for the lockpicks and came up with just one.

The ship pitched suddenly, water pouring into the underbelly until Mezaedo was spluttering and Rigil gripping the ceiling to keep his balance. Any moment now, the ship would roll and take them with it. With a bone-splitting crack, another chunk of the deck fell burning into the hold, landing near the secret hatch and raining sparks down on their heads.

Recoiling from the debris, Rigil reached into his pocket again, and this time, something pricked his finger. Not a lockpick but a smooth ring with a crude spike on one side.

Sethe's earring.

"Hold the lock steady, Mez." Again, he sounded shockingly, almost absurdly calm in the lapping dark. He needed both hands, and thank Arman, the water carried most of the weight as he lifted his bad arm and set the pick to the lock, maintaining tension while he applied the long steel pin of the earring. He heard himself saying something reassuring, felt his hand slide the earring into the mechanism, felt the ship heave one last groan around them.

Click.

How he heard that tiny, tiny sound over the moan of the ship and the slosh of the water and the thunder of his own heart, Rigil would never know. The shackles fell from Mezaedo's wrists and sank. The ship cracked again, another chunk of deck falling from the ceiling in a crash of flames. This time, the burning debris fell over the opening, sealing Rigil and Mez below a wall of murderous heat.

Rigil reached up to push the burning wood away but hissed when his hands recoiled from the fire against his will. Pain drove through his palm, the blistering heat shooting straight to every nerve. There was hardly enough room to keep his head above water, and even that air bubble would be gone before long.

Rigil! Someone—who?—was screaming in his head. *Rigil, get out of there!*

Gritting his teeth against the heat, he reached for the blocked hatch again.

Mezaedo reached it first. Mezaedo, who was barely keeping his nose above the surface, whose left cheek was nearly swollen double with bruises, who was pushing the flaming bit of deck aside with his *bare hands*.

The boy cringed, but only slightly, as his fingers met the skin-peeling heat and pushed. And then the hatch was gone, the opening free.

Rigil! That strange voice screamed again, ripping through him like a knife through cloth.

Sethe. It was the last clear thought he had before his world became a blur, tugging Mezaedo through one opening, then another. A moment underwater, a burst of sea air. Thunder and flashing light. A reek of smoke. Hands again, and a hazy impression that Rigil was trying and failing to swim. Pain.

And voices. A young boy's, vaguely Jaelportian. Begging him not to let go.

There was no fear. Only warmth, a dim fatigue, and the shimmering sense that Arman had just rewritten a part of his story. When more hands closed on his arms, pulling him out of the water, that feeling was all he knew for certain, all that made sense in the world.

"Gently! For tides' sake, tiko, he's been stabbed!"

"Oy! Give a man some room to work, will you? Someone take the helm! Come on, stay with me, Kingsguard . . ."

"Sirrig." Something touched his face. Like rain but gentler. "Oh, moldy onions, Sirrig."

It's all right, Rigil wanted to say. *You're safe, Tazeem. It's all right.*

His last thought was of a lemon-gold eye, a face that fit in his hand, a kiss stolen in a Hamonayan alley . . .

CHAPTER THIRTY-ONE
SETHE

WHEN THE SUN FINALLY ROSE OVER the Eversea, it was bleeding red.

Sethe stood at the helm of Ashik's rikoh, her bandaged right hand fused to the spokes, the smell of salt her only reminder that she was still alive and not wandering the Veil like a phantom. The spray tasted metallic, like blood. Everywhere, blood. Her hands felt sticky with it, and every time the rikoh lurched on a swell, she felt her heart sinking and bobbing, untethered in her chest.

The only sounds came from the wind, the rigging, and the children huddled under the mast. Mezaedo had entertained them for a while, making jokes thin enough to tear, telling alternate origin stories for the scars on his knuckles. Some time ago, he'd gone below, maybe to change the bandages on his burned hands. Or to watch Rigil die.

When Ashik's head rose through the hatch, Sethe refused to acknowledge his crimson hands or the morbid news that had to be etched into his face. No, let him tell her. Let *him* speak the words.

It was over. He'd done all he could. There was nothing left to do but grieve.

As he joined her at the helm, leaning backward on the rail, it suddenly seemed impossible. Letting him say it. Letting herself hear it.

So Sethe grabbed at the first thought within reach.

"You were the boy from the ship." The realization struck so suddenly, so quietly, it was like she had always known. "The surgeon's apprentice. You left food by my crate. For the 'cat.'"

No answer. Glancing at him, she found his amber irises turned down, hands buried in his pockets. "I hated that cat."

She tried to laugh. "You saved my life."

An unconvinced shrug. "I gave up on digging myself out of Hamonah years ago, but knowing I'd helped someone off that bilge bucket of an island? It's enough to see a man through." He looked up then, and she saw the smudges under his eyes, the stripe of crusted blood on his cheek. "You should go to him," he said, stepping up to take the helm from her. "It's up to the gods now, but maybe if you talk to him?"

Sethe nearly lost her balance in the undertow of those words.

Rigil. It wasn't over, then. Rigil was *still alive*.

It was up to Arman now.

The cramped space below was surprisingly tidy, an odd blend of surgeon and smuggler. Sethe took her time on details. A low hold, lantern lit and smelling of rum, a tray of needles and thread on the floor, an old white shirt hanging from a beam, missing bandage-sized stripes.

Rigil in a hammock, drawing sandpaper breaths, with Mezaedo Chevyah on the deck beside him, only slightly less deathly.

Rigil looked better than he had during the night, when Sethe had hovered at his side until Ashik sent her away for blocking his light. Even now, though, his lips were blue-tinged, and he didn't stir when Sethe crouched to cross the low hold and run her bandaged hand over his matted hair.

"Rigil?"

Nothing. The barest twitch of the hand lying on his wrapped chest, but that was all.

She wanted to kiss him. She wanted to *shake* him. Instead, she collapsed onto a crate next to Mezaedo, her nostrils full of blood and brine and a flimsy hint of cypress.

"It was me," Mezaedo said softly, his face so bleak she might not have known him if not for his eyes, still too big for his face and glistening in all the wrong ways, one of them bruise-rimmed. Strips of cloth around his hands hid the burns he'd taken pushing that hatch aside before the *Solstice* went under. "Something in my spice, some ingredient my mistress never told me about, must have worked against the karpos. Nedir slipped into my head, heard all our plans, followed us. Even controlled me sometimes, to get to Fateema, Iago. And if you ate something I gave you . . ."

Of course. Escaping Meneton, when the karpos had suddenly given out and Nedir had been there, waiting to slip in—she had eaten one of Mezaedo's blacknuts just before. And on the *Solstice* . . .

Sethe exhaled. "The apricots."

Mezaedo clenched his hands between his knees. He could have been an old, old man, his arms and knuckles sprinkled with those tiny white scars. Sethe caught herself trying to peer into his head, trying to read the thoughts tightening his fingers into knots.

But all she found was a wall. Not like a shield but like an absence, as if his mind had just winked out. She frowned. "Where did you find karpos? Why can't I—" At his blank look, she bit her lip. "Never mind. Where was he sending you?"

"Barth," he said. "I heard him tell Iago."

"So Iago was Nedir's man from the beginning? The one hired to run the powder around Er'Rets?"

"No." Mezaedo rubbed his nose. "I think it was supposed to be that crew from Meneton, Laban and the others. Only, we stole their ship, threw off the whole plan. So Nedir improvised, threatened Iago through me to make sure he had someone to take the shipment. By then, he was already in Jaelport, so he had Iago collect him there on the way to the Talons." A bitter snort. "I guess he was always close behind us, thanks to me. Watching through me, he would have known all along that we were headed to Hamonah."

Sethe frowned, toying with the last few pieces of the puzzle. "He's secretive about his fortress, and no sane captain would agree to sail a passenger into the Talons. That must be why he chose to sail in with Iago instead of using whatever ship he'd taken from Land's End." That had the ring of Nedir's logic to it. "What about the rest of Iago's crew?"

"Iago didn't want them involved. He gave them shore leave when he collected Nedir and his Hamonayans from Jaelport. Tried to let me go then too, but Nedir had other plans." Suddenly, he laughed a hollow-chested laugh. "*That*, I should be used to by now, after eleven masters, but you know, Missethe? Not a moldy *one* of my old masters would have done for me what Sirrig . . ."

When Mezaedo's face twisted, Sethe felt it like a blade in her own ribs.

"He's all I've got, Missethe." Hunched over his knees, the tiko looked lost. And young. Actually, he probably looked a lot like she had once, left alone and afraid on the road to Zerah Rock. "He's all I've got in the moldy world."

Strange, the way Arman worked. Threading people together across time and borders, pulling those threads tight until they met somewhere unexpected. Maybe that was the point of all this. Arman had used this squire to save Sethe's heart. Who better to become to him what Rigil had been to her?

He's not all you've got, Sethe wanted to say. *Should* have said.

But then Rigil coughed to life.

She was at his side in an instant, bent over his face, cupping it in fingers that were probably cold as the grave, but she didn't care, tides take her, she *didn't*. His breaths were coming hard and ragged, every cough ripping the hole in his chest wider.

"Rigil? It's Sethe. Listen to me, you're all right." He coughed again, his entire body spasming. "Rigil! Rigil, come on, breathe. The plan worked, like your plans always do. You didn't even need a scuddy *h-hat*."

Her voice shattered as he went still, coughs fading to silence. Sethe squeezed her fingers shut and felt her soul die.

All her fears that he would hurt her if she let him too close, and this was how it ended. Rigil, gone. She sobbed, brushing her thumbs across his bruise-darkened cheeks, rough with the blond beginnings of the full beard he'd never shown her. "Rigil. Please. Stay with me. *Stay with me.*"

It was a command, not a request. Nowhere *close* to a request.

And hearing it, maybe from the gates of Shamayim, Rigil Barak opened his eyes with a sawdust whisper: "Where . . . would I go?"

His gaze hung on her, smiling and blue as the day they'd met, Sethe and the runaway heir who had bound her heart to his. With a whoop, Mezaedo jumped to his feet and darted toward the ladder, shouting for Ashik.

Thank You, Arman, thank You, thank You.

Sethe touched his cheek. "How about Zerah Rock?"

"Truly, Sethe?" He caught her fingers and squeezed. "I know it isn't . . . the life you want."

"You sandwit. *You* are what I want."

The effort in his laugh was a dart through Sethe's chest, especially when he tried to reach for her with his battered arm and gave up with a groan. Her fault. All of it.

"I do have some conditions." Sethe swept filthy hair off his face. "Shoes, for one. I want them outlawed."

"Done."

It was a joke. Probably. Except he could do that. He was an heir, a future lord, made for a world that soared high above hers.

But Rigil Barak, heir of Zerah Rock, either hadn't thought of that or didn't care.

"You know," he said, still smiling, "this really is like that clerk in Melas."

Sethe snorted. "All you're missing is the split lip he gave you."

"That, and I believe your face was a tad closer."

She leaned toward him. "Like this?"

"I was thinking more like this." He lifted his head until his nose brushed her cheek, and Sethe prepared to stop breathing for a good long while. But then he stiffened and fell back, eyes squeezing shut. "Oh, Isemios's *wit*."

"What?" She jerked back, holding her hands up like they were knives. "Did I do something? Was it me?"

He sighed. "I just realized. I lost your earring."

Oh, for tides' sake. "Are you serious?"

"It was symbolic."

"You want symbolic?" Sethe bent close to whisper, "I'll *show* you symbolic."

Sethe didn't know who kissed who, exactly. What had sparked on a rooftop in Melas and ignited in an alley in Hamonah was reborn when their lips met over his bandaged body. Sethe's hand twisted in his hair, the moment sweeter for the realization that they didn't exist only in the past. Not anymore. Propped on his good arm, he had no hands to hold her face or catch the tears falling from her jaw, but his lips were strong and soft and steadying enough without them.

Nonsensically, through the eyes of some fragment she'd forgotten, Sethe caught herself watching them from outside her own skin. Tear-soaked and radiant, lost in each other, the thieves who had stolen the hearts right out of one another's locked chests.

Sethe, for one, had no intention of giving his back. And a part of her still couldn't *believe* she was going to get away with it.

Chapter Thirty-Two
RIGIL

IF ANYONE ASKED, RIGIL'S JUMPY FINGERS were entirely the carriage's fault. They certainly had nothing to do with Carm Duchy flying past the window or the smell of the Mizrâch Ocean or the sight of that oak he had nearly killed himself climbing once with Viola. Beside him, Sethe slept with her head on his shoulder. She would have blamed his fidgeting on nerves.

Much easier to blame the carriage.

The empty seat across from Rigil and Sethe made Mezaedo's absence throbbingly obvious. Weeks of convalescing in Armonguard had done him good, and by the time Rigil and Sethe had said their farewells, he'd no longer been mumbling Nedir's name in his sleep. He'd chosen to stay in Armonguard, helping to acclimatize the Hamonayan children who, unlike Kiah, had no parents to return to. He hadn't *seemed* out of sorts, but he also hadn't bloodvoiced since the Talons. That worried Sethe. Could a bloodvoicer's mind *be* permanently damaged?

As if Rigil didn't feel horrid enough.

Pressing his head to the back of the carriage, Rigil severed that stream of thought.

Oren Hadar.

The unexpected knock came as the carriage took a turn down another horribly familiar lane.

Rigil perked in his seat. *Your Highness, this is a surprise.*

Sir Rigil, it is good to hear your voice, especially after the reports I received from Sir Eagan. How are your wounds?

Despite the relentless pain in his ribs, Rigil smiled. *Ever-constant companions, I'm afraid, and yet another sign that I've made the right decision.*

The Mârad respects your choice to step back, Sir Rigil. But I'm sorry to lose you. Which reminds me. About your proposal, I concede that it may be valuable to have a spy on Hamonah, but only if you're sure this smuggler is Mârad material.

Rigil leaned forward until his knees brushed the far seat. *I would stake my name on it, Your Highness.* Wind gusted through the carriage as he added, *How fares the investigation?*

Nedir's fortress told us little, Oren answered. *There seems to be no pattern to his interests. It's clear that he was developing the children into weapons, likely for some kind of coup with ties across former Darkness. Coble's son, Erro, denies any knowledge of it, claims Nedir was merely a friend his father funded out of generosity. Land's End maintains that Lord Coble is alive. I suspect otherwise.*

Rigil frowned. *And the others? Rheala and the Eben?*

The former is still under investigation. The latter was last seen traveling north, toward Har Sha'ar. But that is not your concern today.

The carriage took another hard turn, and Rigil winced, only partly from pain. He had forgotten how steely the sky could be here, the heavens themselves a warning to keep away.

Some of the business slid from Prince Oren's tone until he sounded like the prince who had once found Rigil, lost and desperate, on the road to Zerah Rock. *I don't suppose I can persuade you to reconsider your* other *decision?*

Grimly, Rigil smiled for his own benefit alone. *Not this time, Your Highness.*

In that case, lad, may Arman be with you.

Oren's farewell was still resounding when the carriage rolled into Zerah Rock.

As always, the streets were fuzzed with that layer of salt that coated everything near the sea. The smell, that familiar musk— Lightness, even the *air* was conspiring against Rigil, choking him with memories of that cobbler's shop, that granary, that corner where the town cats still congregated in droves. Lamplights flickered, gulls screeched, laughter spilled out of the local inn with its green-painted sign and wilted window flowers.

And the waves. Always the distant, crashing waves. The kind that could break a man to pieces if he didn't keep his feet.

Rigil leaned back from the window as the carriage tilted up Fandel Hill. Only moments away now. Barely moments. Breaths.

Too soon, the carriage rattled to a stop in front of Barak Manor, a blockish monolith with all the personality of a rock and exuding about as much welcome.

Beside him, Sethe stirred as the coachman hopped down to open the door. Her hand rested on his good wrist, right over his pulse.

"Tides, K'sil, *breathe*." She slid their fingers together. "You've done worse than this."

"This is different. It isn't a performance."

Laughing, Sethe adjusted her golden shikana and alighted from the carriage on sandaled feet. She didn't even flinch at the sharp hilltop wind. "Speak for yourself, Kingsguard knight."

Before he followed her out, Rigil smoothed his hands down the front of the fine tunic Mandzee had commissioned for him in Jaelport. When his hand slid over something small and round in his right pocket, he paused. Had he left something there?

Rigil stuck a hand into his pocket and pulled out a blacknut. Unseasoned.

His quiet laugh seemed to echo in the carriage, bouncing off the empty seat where Mezaedo should have sat. "Let me guess," he said softly. "Last one, lucky one."

Rigil was still smiling when he ducked through the carriage doorway and found his soon-to-be bride waiting before the doors of Barak Manor.

Sethe couldn't know how resplendent she was in that shikana. The color seemed made to accent her rich skin. She sprang forward to help him descend from the threshold, and Rigil waved her off, teeth locked. Lightness, had they left the knife *in* his ribs? "Have I told you how beautiful you are?"

"I'm *not* giving you more praise for finding a shikana in Carmine." Sethe's garment billowed in the breeze, looking somehow intentional on her. Wildness and elegance in perfect balance. Frowning at herself, she added, "I still think it's too much."

"It's exquisite. *You* are exquisite. And I do appreciate your consenting to wear shoes for this, Lady Sethe."

"Oh, you know, Sir Rigil. Anything to avoid giving your mother apoplexy."

With a laugh that felt like a breath after drowning, Rigil crooked his good arm. "How do you do that?"

"Easy." She took his arm. "I know you, Rigil Barak. Or Rigil the Nameless, depending on the next hour or so."

Hinges creaked as the doors at the top of the steps began to open for one of Lord Barak's old servants. Rigil grimaced. "You're certain about this? A life with a disgraced exile? We could be left with nothing."

"Nothing, hmm?" She sent him a slitted glance. "How will I manage?"

His fingers ached to run over the feathers tied into her hair, near her temples. Owl feathers, for the name she had accepted from him and kept for him all these years. "I want you to be happy."

She took his arm, fingers curling over his blue satin sleeve. "If you think I couldn't love a Rigil with no title, that ship left the harbor sixteen years ago."

The doors finished opening with the bony creak of too many years gone by, perhaps an unforgivable number. The next few moments would tell.

Rigil forced himself forward, up the first step. The second. One foot in front of the other.

"Also," Sethe said somewhere between step six and the most terrifying moment of his life, "I did break your arm. To abandon you now would be . . . well, scuddy bad form."

Rigil didn't recognize the young manservant who met them at the entrance. As the door clicked shut behind them, Rigil steered Sethe toward the middle of the grand foyer, where the facets of the vaulted ceiling met in a blue-painted star overhead. Veins of gold, hand-painted in the days of Rigil's forefathers, shot through the navy paint.

"I'll fetch the mistress, sir." The servant bowed, exposing the proud yellow lightning bolts sewn into his collar. "Excuse me."

The young man left through an arch to Rigil's left. A Zerah Rock breeze pounded at the tall windows that framed the front door behind them, the wind itself crowding the glass to watch the final disgrace of the heir of Zerah Rock.

Sethe had her head tilted all the way back to study the ceiling. She flicked a glance toward him. "Are you breathing?"

Skirts swished through the library doorway. Rigil swallowed. "No."

Lady Zora Barak did not glide into the grand foyer; she *marched* with all the militant force of an army on campaign, her dark hair severely braided, every footstep cracking on the polished marble floors.

"Rigil! Nearly two hours late."

Beside Rigil, Sethe stopped gawping at the book-lined walls to straighten in her shikana. Rigil bowed as deeply as the wound would allow. Something else for his mother to criticize.

"Forgive me, Mother. I asked the coachman to slow down for the sake of my injury."

His mother slowed when he mentioned the wound. Lightness, that face. It wasn't quite like seeing himself in a mirror: He had her high cheekbones and perhaps her nose, but the darting eyes and dagger chin were all her own. She wore a sleek grey gown with tight sleeves that came to a delicate point over her knuckles, the skirt embroidered near the floor with the pattern of a tossing sea. As a boy, he'd feared the stormy swish of those skirts bearing down on him, always half afraid that those hand-stitched waves might drown him as easily as the real thing.

Rigil took the hand his mother lifted to him, surprised to find it cold as frost. The crease between her brow was sharply defined, like someone had taken a knife to it.

"Oh, Rigil." Her lower lip trembled. "Why do you neglect me?"

Oh, he'd *missed* this. "I was here for the festival, Mother. Not two years ago."

"Please. You left before sunset and never even spoke to your father."

"Well, I'm here now." He managed not to sound like a scolded little boy, mostly on the strength of the woman beside him. "And there is someone I need you to meet. Allow me to introduce Sethe of Hamonah."

"Hamonah?" His mother's thin lips flattened nearly to nonexistence. "Rigil, I am surprised at you. You know I can only tolerate maids from Jaelport. The others simply have no inkling of proper dress. Tempest's mercy, look at what she's *wearing*."

Odd, how hard it was to speak when one's molars were locked together. "Mother, she is not a *gift*. Sethe has agreed to marry me."

His mother's face went blank, her gaze snagging nakedly on Sethe's scars. Apparently, she had developed a twitch in his time away. Perfect.

Just then, Sethe swept into a curtsey so flawless that Rigil nearly joined his mother in gawking.

"My lady, it is an honor to make your acquaintance. I see why Rigil has been so desperate to return to his lovely home."

Sethe kept her lashes lowered—demure, graceful, the perfect noblewoman. As if sensing his stare, she bloodvoiced, *What, you think I never took notes?*

His mother's hands fluttered, lost, until she found a use for them in smoothing her already-pristine gown. "Rigil, I taught you better than to be bewitched by a . . . *woman* like this. No, don't argue. I'll have an antidote made, and we will put this messy business behind us before you meet your father. What of Queen Mandzee?"

"Mother." Rigil had to ease his grip on Sethe's hand before he crushed it to dust. "Allow me to be blunt. I am not bewitched, and quite frankly, I'm not interested in justifying this choice to either you or Father. I came to make peace and face my mistakes, but I ask that you leave Sethe out of it unless you are willing to treat her with civility. Now, is Father here?"

He expected a biting retaliation, some reminder of how much more she deserved.

Instead, his mother blinked, her forehead webbed with fine blue veins. She looked at Sethe, back at him. Reached out, unexpectedly, to brush his cheek with icy fingers.

"In the study," she said finally, hesitating a moment more before turning and drifting out of the foyer as if she had come untethered from the world.

Rigil grimaced at Sethe. "Lightness, I'm sorry."

"Right." Sethe threaded her arm through his. "Because *my* mother was a string of pearls."

Leading Sethe out of the foyer and up to the gallery felt like sailing into a cold, hard wind. Everything in him itched for the warmth of Hamonah, but here he was, climbing the ornate stairs. Gliding past the Barak portraits, past the space where Eagan's likeness had once hung.

Even after all this time, the smell of leather spiced Burr Barak's wing. Rigil found the door to the study ajar, a blast of stale air pouring out like a physical thing. A servant had just pulled a cart out of the room and was carefully rearranging bottles on a tray, pretending not to see as Rigil grabbed Sethe's hand. "Pray for me?"

She mimed tossing him a coin, the Hamonayan equivalent of wishing him well, and he found himself willing the servant to spontaneously dissolve as she seized his lapels.

"Whatever happens in there, K'sil, you're mine and I want you. Understood?"

He looped a lock of her feather-tied hair around one finger. "Lightness, I love you."

Just then, someone inside the room coughed viciously. Sethe stepped back, her touch sliding away.

And then there was only Rigil and his father's half-closed door.

Sick. Not a word Rigil had ever associated with his father. Domineering? Aye. Unappeasable? Certainly. Pushing the door open, Rigil eased over the threshold to land right on a creaky board. The low whine nearly sent him running.

He could have been a boy again, called inside to face judgment.

The room hadn't changed. Wall-to-wall shelves, spilling with books Rigil had never read quickly or thoroughly enough. His distant ancestor Fandel Barak's severe profile was immortalized in paint on one wall, slightly crooked, as if the maid had bumped it while dusting. No rugs, no curtains, nothing of softness. Only the bay window with its view of the crashing sea, the old citadel table before it, and sitting beside it—his father.

Propped in a chair with a blanket over his legs, Lord Barak himself watched Rigil's entrance through Eagan's lazy eyes, an iron grid of wrinkles, and a fast-thinning fringe of dark-grey hair. Rigil found his hand tingling for the steady pressure of Sethe's. Lightness, let her have meant what she'd said. The part about marrying a man with nothing to his name.

"Father?"

His eyes were duller than Rigil had remembered, and when his lips parted, gummed white at the corners, Rigil braced for the worst. But his father just waved a hand at the citadel board before him.

"About time, boy. It's my move."

Citadel. They hadn't traded more than a handful of words in years, and he wanted to play *citadel*?

Well, he certainly wasn't about to argue with the man. Innards twisting, Rigil took his familiar seat across from his father. The room still smelled of seagrass and leather, but now a sour current ran underneath, near the old man's chair.

"Father," Rigil began, "if I may—"

His father raised a hand, absorbed in the half-finished game. "*My* move."

Rigil sat back, jaw working. Whoever had been playing, the wooden pieces were in a sorry state. Defeat was only three moves away, four at most. Poor fellow.

His father settled a hand on his paladin, but eased it off with an unconvinced grunt. "Your grandfather gave me this board," he said suddenly, as if continuing a conversation they'd left off years ago. "The first time I bested him. Did you know this?"

"The swiftest would be to move your rogue to the fourth rank, sir." Under the table, Rigil's fingers tapped out his speech. *Father, I renounce my claim to Zerah Rock. I renounce my right to the Barak name. I understand that I have never been worthy of either, and I accept it. I can live with it.*

The words were poised on his tongue when he studied the board again.

"Wait." *Lightness.* "This . . . this is *our* game. Our last before I left."

His father's gaze slid up to him. "I still don't know what possessed you to pit your serf against my villager. Light knows I taught you better."

Rigil gaped. *What in all Er'Rets?*

"Rogue to fourth rank," his father repeated, as if weighing Rigil's suggestion on some internal scale. "It has merit, but as usual, you play a short game. Ah, yes." Placing a finger not on a piece but on the *board*, he rotated it fully, then leaned back with a satisfied grunt. "Your move."

Rigil laughed, a breathless, disbelieving sound that didn't fit in this room. In front of him, the silver army gleamed in the light, resplendent next to the wooden pieces that had been his only allotment as a boy. Silver was for lords. For leaders. For *heirs*. "I don't understand."

His father's wrinkled face flexed. "I told you. It is a Barak tradition. From one heir to the next."

"But I *lost*." Rigil gestured to the board, the pathetic wooden pieces. Perhaps the man had gone senile? "It's me, Father. It's Rigil. I've failed every test you've ever given me. I came to renounce my claim, to recommend Viola in my place."

"I know why you came." His father leaned back in his chair, looking older than seemed possible considering that Rigil hadn't felt a day over sixteen since taking this seat. Years of bags had piled up under his father's eyes, eyes that darted away now to land on gnarled fingers. "I have become an old man studying this board, boy. I think I know when *I* have lost."

When he slid the signet ring from his finger and pushed it across the board with one vein-swirled hand, Rigil felt his mind leave his body.

This could not be happening.

"Your mother has prepared a banquet," his father rumbled,

sitting back. "Jaelportians, you know. A babe cannot sneeze but someone is throwing a banquet. I had hoped to announce it there." A brusque gesture took in the ring, the board, Rigil's shaking hands. "If it fits, of course."

Rigil was still trying to coax life back into his tongue when a new voice chimed in. "You heard the man, Rigil. Try it."

Swiveling, Rigil found Eagan leaning in the doorway, ready and waiting with a wink. Beside him stood Sethe. His beautiful, beautiful Sethe.

Rigil rose too quickly, shooting a dagger of pain through his ribs. A blessing, that. Proof he wasn't dreaming. "Father, there's someone you must meet."

"Your Hamonayan." The lord of Zerah Rock squeaked back in his chair to scan Sethe up and down. He veiled his thoughts better than Rigil's mother had, but that same stare had found Rigil wanting more times than he cared to count. He found himself bracing for a blunt awakening from this strange hallucination until his father said, "You play, Lady Sethe?"

Rising from a curtsey, Sethe smiled. "Rigil is teaching me, my lord, but he's too cautious. Plays too short a game, I say."

"A short game!" Rigil's father slapped his armrest. "Precisely what I've always said. No foresight beyond the fourth rank. Haven't I said it, Rigil?"

Rigil met her gaze, one brow quirked. *Nicely done.*

She flicked her hair.

"Shall we, then?" Rigil's father made to push his chair out from the table, knocking over the cane propped against the tabletop. The cane fell and bounced off the polished floor. When Rigil bent for it, the old man swiped him away. "Leave it, Son. Rayado?"

There was a stirring at the door, someone slipping in, and then a familiar voice. "Allow me, sir."

On one knee with his hand outstretched, Rigil could only stare at the gnarled little figure that came forward to collect the cane.

Olive skin fractured with creases, eyes as dark as the sea at night. Round cheeks, sallower now with age, but still. A spitting image of Tazeem.

Catching Rigil's stare, the old man smiled. "Hello, Sir Rigil."

"Rayado?" Lightness, the man was still here. Still serving the very family that had cost him his son. "I didn't expect . . . I mean, I never properly—Tazeem . . ."

Guilt clamped its fingers around Rigil's throat as the old man, once like a second father to Rigil and certainly his sister, bent his old spine into acknowledging bows for each of them, Rigil last.

"My lord," he rasped, "I hope I may serve you as I have served your father—loyally and proudly—for years to come. Tazeem would have it no other way."

Rigil couldn't return the man's smile. *Arman, what have I done to deserve this?*

Like light through stained glass, the answer came.

Absolutely nothing.

Still, he had to ask. "Rayado, I know this is impossible, but if there is any way I can make it up to you, any way I could atone . . ."

"I have a thought, my lord." This time, the old steward directed his bow at Rigil alone. Well, Rigil and Sethe, who had stolen to his side and was sliding the Barak ring onto his hand with fingers as warm as the Eversea.

"Yes?" Rigil managed.

A draft blew through the room, scented by the ocean, well-worn books, and somewhere in the keep, a banquet fit for a king.

Watching the ring, the old man smiled through Tazeem's bright midnight eyes.

"You can begin, Sir Rigil, by letting Zerah Rock welcome its lost heir home."

Bonus Epilogue

Thank you for reading *Heir of Light*. We hope you loved the story. Find out what happens next with our Bonus Epilogue, a special gift, available only to our newsletter subscribers.

This Bonus Epilogue will not be released on any retailer platform, so scan our QR code to get your free gift. You acknowledge you are becoming a Sunrise Publishing, Niki Florica, and Jill Williamson subscriber. Unsubscribe from any of the newsletters at any time.

THANK YOU

Thank you again for reading *Heir of Light*. We hope you enjoyed the story. If you did, would you be willing to do us a favor and leave a review? It doesn't have to be long—just a few words to help other readers know what they're getting. (But no spoilers! We don't want to wreck the fun!) Thank you again for reading!

We'd love to hear from you—not only about this story, but about any characters or stories you'd like to read in the future. Contact us at www.sunrisepublishing.com/contact.

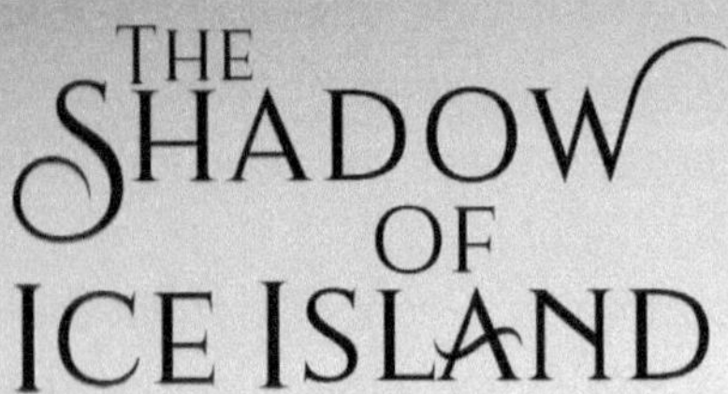
THE
SHADOW
OF
ICE ISLAND

←THE KING'S SPIES→

JILL WILLIAMSON

What happens when a reluctant spy discovers his greatest mission is protecting the woman who stole his heart?

Cole Tanniyn thought his days of danger were over when he traded his sword for a lute. But when the king sends him north as an undercover minstrel to investigate mysterious disappearances from the infamous Ice Island prison, Cole's carefully ordered world changes—especially when Mistel Wepp, the fiery-haired songstress he's falling for, secretly follows him into mortal peril.

She was supposed to stay safe. He was supposed to stay focused. Neither of them expected to fall this hard.

Posing as traveling performers with Kurtz, a gruff former prisoner seeking justice, Cole and Mistel must navigate dangerous taverns thick with secrets while their fake "cousin" relationship becomes increasingly difficult—especially when every shared glance and gentle touch threatens to reveal their true feelings. But when Cole's personal quest to visit his imprisoned uncle becomes entangled with a deadly conspiracy, and Mistel's bold curiosity lands her in the hands of human traffickers, everything changes.

Now Cole must choose: the mission that could free an innocent man... or the woman he loves.

As a web of corruption reaches the highest levels of power, and villains from Cole's traumatic past close in, he faces an impossible choice. With Mistel's life in danger and dark family secrets threatening to surface, Cole must find the courage to fight for love—even if it means defying orders and confronting the demons of his past.

Perfect for fans of sweet romance and swashbuckling adventure, this story weaves together tender love, heart-pounding action, and the kind of connection that transforms two hearts.

Because sometimes the greatest adventure is finding someone worth everything...

CHAPTER ONE
COLE

A SILENCED VOICE CARRIED NO TUNE. That's the thought that ran through Cole Tanniyn's mind as one of the raiders thrust a rusty sword at his chest. He leaped back out of the way and smashed against a set of shelves holding sacks of flour. One tipped off the ledge and thumped on the floor by his feet.

Blazes! Cole had better pull it together, or he wasn't going to find out what it was like to be a Mârad spy, infiltrate the Ice Island prison, and question his uncle.

Because he'd be dead.

While the Tsaftown army had been camped to the east of Mahanaim, Lord Livna had sent out several dozen patrols to check the area. Cole had been paired off with Thakkar Oruk, a living storm; and Alden Wroxton, the silent blade—two of the Fighting Fifteen—and of course, Kurtz Chazir, Cole's friend, traveling companion, and fellow Mârad spy.

Their foursome had happened upon an outpost where two wagons sat empty, each hitched to a pair of rangy mules.

"Let's look inside," Thakkar had said, dismounting his black stallion.

"Grab your shield," Kurtz told Cole. "Sword drawn too."

Cole slid off Cherix's back, drew his sword, and grabbed his shield off the saddlebag, trying not to let his annoyance at Kurtz's continued mothering to show on his face.

He followed the others into a tiny outpost reeking of salted fish and onions. Shelves lined the walls and center of a cramped space no bigger than four peddler's carts hitched in a square. Two men's heads bobbed above the back shelves, while a burly third stood in the front corner, stuffing candles into a sack.

Raiders.

"Ho there. It's me, Thakkar." The Berlander stood with his hands empty, palms raised. "Give me your names so I might know if you are friend or foe."

At that, seven more heads appeared as men, who had been crouched or bent over, straightened to their full height.

Not good. Cole tightened his grip on his sword and moved his shield in front of him.

"We're none of your business," said the burly man stealing candles.

Thakkar quickly drew a pair of hand axes that gleamed in the dim light. "You've had your fill. Take what you've stolen and leave. Now."

The raiders exchanged glances, their expressions defiant.

"There's plenty to share, soldier," the burly man said. "Feel free to help yourself, but you've no right to stop us."

Thakkar sighed, almost pitying. "Have it your way."

That's when the fight had begun.

The raiders surged forward, fierce but uncoordinated in the cramped space. Thakkar met the burly man head-on, his hand axes moving in quick, precise arcs, disarming his foe in moments. Wroxton slipped through the maze of shelves and came up behind the raiders in back, while Kurtz intercepted a bearded man on their right.

Cole found himself face-to-face with a wiry man wielding a rusted sword. The raider lunged, which was how Cole had knocked into the shelves of flour. He barely deflected the next blow with his shield, stirring memories of the Battle of Armonguard and the Eben he'd accidentally killed. He couldn't rely on dumb luck today. If he wanted to live—to reach Ice Island and see his uncle again—he had to fight. So he thrust out his sword.

The raider edged closer, grinning. "Don't know how to use that very well, do you?"

Behind Cole's wiry opponent, Thakkar whirled, hand axes flashing as he felled another raider, who crashed into a shelf, toppling sacks of beans and jars of honey. A barrel of apples rolled past Cole's feet, scattering its contents.

The wiry man feinted left, then swung right, knocking Cole's shield across the room. It hit a barrel and clattered to the floor.

Cole's breath hitched as he tightened his grip on his short sword. The raider pressed forward, and Cole parried every strike. Without the shield, keeping up felt easier than before.

Maybe he really could do this.

The raider struck again. Cole raised his sword, but the man twisted mid-swing and executed a vicious underhand swipe. Cole blocked the blow, but it sent his sword spinning across the floor.

Blazes!

Weaponless, Cole's chest tightened as the raider raised his rusty sword high.

And suddenly Cole was back at the Battle of Armonguard, facing the Eben giant with nothing but the Armonguard flag.

"Lee-lee-lee-lee-lee!" the Eben sang.

Cole's stomach slid into his boots. Without a sword, he did the only thing he could think of. He turned the flagstaff and pointed the sharp end at the giant.

The Eben tossed his spear in the air and caught it with his grip reversed. Ready to throw.

Cole was going to die.

This isn't real. This isn't real!

"Cole!"

Back in the outpost, Kurtz lunged in front of Cole, intercepting the raider's attack with his longsword.

The blades clanged, and the raider stumbled back. Kurtz pressed in, but this time, the end of the raider's sword caught his shoulder. Kurtz didn't slow, but his hiss made it clear he'd been hit.

A chill flared in Cole's chest. He scanned the chaos—barrels, broken shelves, spilled food, scattered tools. Where was his sword?

He crouched, fingers searching debris, and found something heavy and rough—a fallen sack of flour. He ripped open the bag, and when he stood, he hurled it over Kurtz's shoulder.

Flour struck the raider's face, staggering him. Kurtz seized the moment and slammed his pommel against the wiry man's temple. The raider dropped to his knees, his rusted sword skittering away.

At the back of the outpost, Wroxton felled the last raider. Silence followed, broken only by labored breathing.

Thakkar glanced at Cole, hand axes wet with blood. "Nice throw," he said dryly.

Was he being serious? Or sarcastic? Cole didn't know, but his face burned as he picked up his sword from beneath a pile of apples and threaded it into the ring on his belt.

Kurtz clapped him on the back, wincing slightly as he favored his injured shoulder. "Good thinking with the flour, eh?" he said. "You saved my neck there."

Cole's gaze fell on the battered raider, who glared at him through a mask of white powder. Just behind him, Cole's shield lay on the floor. He retrieved it, dusted off the flour, and threaded it over his arm.

Wroxton and Kurtz set about binding the prisoner's hands with strips of rope pulled from the wreckage.

"Now..." Thakkar crouched before the scarred raider. "Let's talk about who you work for."

"We work for ourselves," the man said. "No inbreeding lordling will tell us how to live our lives."

"Do you even know of whom you speak?" Thakkar asked.

"Donediff Hadar is no child," Wroxton added. "He ruled over Er'Rets Point these past five years. His mother is Lady Ginger of Allowntown, and he's married to Yulessa of Xulon."

"He wed a giant?" another of the raiders asked.

"To make sure his heirs don't end up as lowborn as you lot, eh?" Kurtz said.

"Let's get them into the wagon," Thakkar said. "We'll drop them off at the Mahanaim constabulary on our way back."

Cole eyed the growing brown stain on Kurtz's shoulder. "You're hurt."

"Bah!" Kurtz said. "Don't worry about it, eh?"

But that would be impossible. Traveling with Lord Livna and the Fighting Five Hundred was supposed to keep them safe on the journey to Tsaftown, but Cole was starting to wonder if surviving the journey would be harder than whatever waited for them in the frozen North.

The next morning, the Tsaftown army was on the move again. As they headed north over the snow-dusted Allown plains, Cole rode behind Kurtz, concerned by how the brawny man favored his good arm.

Last night, once they'd returned to camp, Cole put up the horses. When he made it back to their tent, Kurtz had already patched up the cut on his shoulder—swore it was just a scratch.

Cole didn't believe him for a second.

Kurtz could have died, and it was Cole's fault. Sure, Cole played the lute well, was unmatched with horses, and had a knack for observation. But if he couldn't fight, how in all Er'Rets could he be a worthy spy and sneak into Ice Island? He simply wasn't strong enough to protect anyone.

Runt of the litter—that's what Nonda Fawst had always called him. He wanted to be strong and worthy, like the Tsaftown soldiers. Like Kurtz.

But he wasn't.

To make matters worse, Kurtz had placed them in the procession six horses behind Jeffrey Korngold, a bard also bound for Tsaftown. The golden-haired man was more talented than Minstrel Harp and bolder even than Kurtz. He was currently playing "The Ballad of the Tanniyn"—the song Cole had sung to Mistel when she'd been stormed to the Veil, the mystical barrier separating the realm of the living from that of the supernatural. Jeffrey's fingers flowed over the lute strings like river water over stone, his smooth, robust tenor twisting Cole's insides into a knot.

> *"Where water meets sky, on vast ocean waves,*
> *A lost man adrift, above a watery grave.*
> *To the skies he prays, 'I have a son, a wife!'*
> *'Oh Arman, how I'll serve you if you only save my life.'"*

Cole hugged his lute, inferiority mounting.

Was it wrong to hate the man?

Ahead, Kurtz guided his horse, Smoke, off the path, waited for Cole to catch up, then fell in beside him on the road.

"What kind of soldier wears his sword on his back and carries a lute in his arms?" Kurtz asked. "If you're attacked, what are you going to do, bash them over the head with the instrument?"

"I would never break my lute."

Kurtz chuckled. "I've no doubt of that. What's with you, eh? Why so melancholy?"

Cole forced himself not to look at Jeffrey. "I'm fine."

"A lie as tall as a redpine," Kurtz said. "Out with it."

Cole sighed and lowered his voice. "Who will hire us with that bard in town?"

"Korngold? Bah! Don't worry about him, eh?"

"How can I not? He does everything far better than me." To further prove Cole's point, Jeffrey ended "The Ballad of the Tanniyn" with a fingerpicked run that resulted in applause and a few whistles from the surrounding soldiers. Part of their mission was to get hired at the Black Boar, a tavern in Tsaftown, but with someone like Jeffrey competing for work, Cole wasn't at all confident in their prospects. "Mistel said she and I performed better together than alone. I wish she could have come."

"Ah. So it's the ginger songbird you're sore about. Why are you still wearing that bracelet of hers, anyway?"

Cole eyed the string of beads around his left wrist. "What else is it good for?"

"Wearing it says 'Don't talk to me, ladies. I'm taken.'"

Cole wrinkled his nose. "It does not."

Kurtz gestured at the bracelet. "It's made of *beads*. It's clearly a woman's trinket. No man would wear something like that unless he's being sentimental."

"Maybe I want to be sentimental."

Kurtz groaned, the expression on his face so exaggerated that Cole couldn't help but laugh.

"What do you care, anyway?" Cole asked.

"Because you keep moping around, and it's my job to guide you through life."

"No one assigned you that task."

"I assigned it to myself," Kurtz said. "A young poet like you should have women tripping over themselves to speak with you. But that frown on your face scares them away."

"There are no women in the army, Kurtz. And even if there were, I have more important things on my mind." Like how they were going to get hired anywhere in Tsaftown with Jeffrey Korngold for competition.

"Bah," Kurtz said. "Talent is wasted on fools, it is. If I could spin words like you, I'd have more women than a king."

"You have had more women than the king," Cole said.

"Stop being so literal. I thought you were a poet, I did. Don't you know about metaphors and hyperbole and all that nonsense?"

Cole raised an eyebrow, impressed that Kurtz knew such terms. "I do, but you've missed the biggest point, my friend."

"What's that?"

"I don't want more women than a king. I'm content with my memories of Mistel."

Except for the part when she hadn't come to see him off. That still smarted, though he supposed he deserved it.

"Enough talk of women, then, if all you can do is mope," Kurtz said. "Talked to Quimby today. He wants to know our plans once we arrive in Tsaftown."

"Get hired at some alehouses and taverns," Cole said. "Unless Jeffrey gets hired everywhere first."

"He can't play every establishment in the north by himself," Kurtz said. "How do you want to handle Ice Island?"

"Don't know." Cole was still shocked that his uncle was alive when he thought the man had died years ago. Prince Oren wanted Cole to question him, see if he'd admit who framed him. "Stop by for a visit, I suppose."

"Jol seems to think we won't be able to just show up. Says the place has been locked down pretty tight lately. We'll have to get invited."

"By who?" Cole asked.

"Verdot Amal." Kurtz said the name as if it tasted bad. "He's the warden."

"And that's a problem why?" Cole asked.

"Because I spent thirteen years on Ice Island for a crime I didn't do," Kurtz said, "and Verdot Amal is the man who made it happen."

Cole's stomach dropped. He'd known getting into Ice Island would be hard. Now it felt impossible. "Well, that's just grand. I need help from the one man who'll probably throw me in a cell just for knowing you."

"Bah!" Kurtz said. "What's thirteen years' worth of hatred when it comes to uncovering the truth, eh? I'm sure you'll think of something."

And suddenly, talking to his long-lost uncle didn't feel like a reunion to Cole—it felt like a trap.

Acknowledgements

First things first, I thank my Author and Finisher for closing doors and opening windows in His perfect timing. To Kate Angelo, who encouraged me to audition for this project; Susie May Warren, for sharing her wisdom and working so hard to learn our characters' names; Jill Williamson, the world's greatest writing mentor; Kelly Fernlake and Andrew Swearingen, who made me feel like family; my actual family for believing in my words even when I didn't; and my brother, Brent, for the sweet map of Hamonah, thank you all a thousand times. This project felt surreal from the beginning, and all these words later, it still does.

A lover of epic stories that glorify an epic God, **Niki Florica** believes Latin is immortal, dreams of being in a musical number (like, a lot) and lives in Canada with her Underwood typewriter and faithful doodle, Reggie. Catch her between writing sessions and she's probably in the clouds: the glassy stare will give her away.

Follow Niki's writing adventures at www.nikiflorica.com.

Jill Williamson is a multi-passionate creative who loves the arts. She's written over two dozen books for readers of all ages and is best known for her Blood of Kings fantasy series, two of which won Christy Awards and made VOYA magazine's Best Science Fiction, Fantasy, and Horror list. She produces films with her husband and teaches about writing at conferences.

Visit her at www.jillwilliamson.com.

BLOOD OF KINGS: LEGENDS

  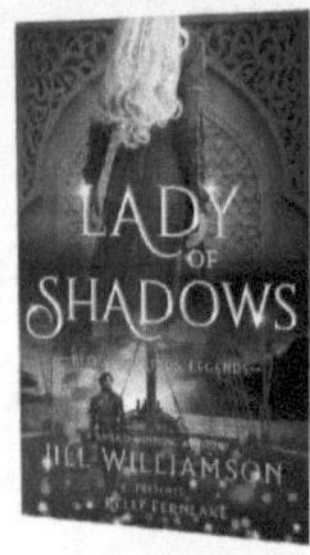 

Award-winning author

JILL WILLIAMSON

with Andrew Swearingen,
Kelly Fernlake, & Niki Florica

Return to the world of Er'Rets in an epic
fantasy series brimming with richly woven
tales of loyalty, love, and sacrifice…

We solve the problem of what to read next.   Available on Amazon

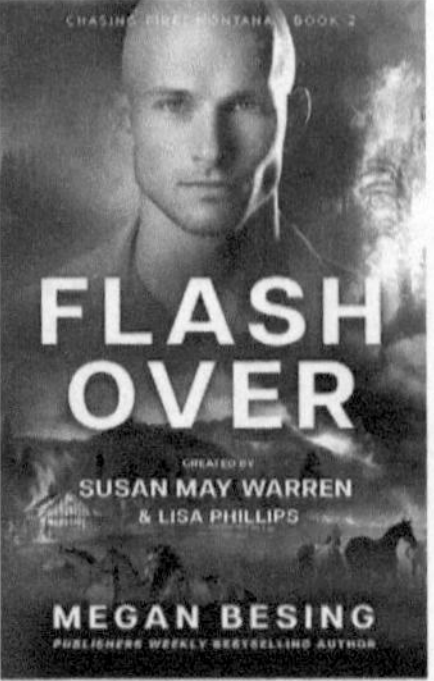

CHASING FIRE:
MONTANA

Dive into an epic series created by

SUSAN MAY WARREN
and LISA PHILLIPS

We solve the problem of what to read next.

Available on Amazon

YOU MAY ALSO LIKE...

When a blizzard strikes Deep Haven and Megan is overrun with catastrophes, it takes a former Ranger to step in and help. But the more he comes to her rescue, the sooner she'll move out... Come home to Deep Haven in this magical tale about the one who got away... and came back.

Still the One **by Susan May Warren and Rachel D. Russell**

Grace Howell leaves her life as a ballerina and returns to Heritage, Michigan, to heal. Teaching dance is just a temporary gig, until she finds herself unexpectedly charmed by small-town life and her growing attachment to Seth Warner, a man from her past with a troubled history of his own.

You're the Reason **by Tari Faris**

Dani Sullivan is determined to revive Jonathon Island's fading charm and reunite her fractured family. Her plan? Reopen the Grand Sullivan Hotel. But without the funds to restore the hotel, Dani's forced to accept help from Liam Stone—a big-city hotel developer whose sleek, modern vision is everything she's trying to avoid.

Meet Me at the Grand **by Lindsay Harrel**

We solve the problem of what to read next.   Available on Amazon

WHERE EVERY STORY IS A FRIEND,
AND EVERY CHAPTER IS A NEW JOURNEY...

Subscribe to our newsletter for a free book, the latest news, weekly giveaways, exclusive author interviews, and more!

follow us on social media!

Shop paperbacks, ebooks, audiobooks, and more at
SUNRISEPUBLISHING.MYSHOPIFY.COM

www.ingramcontent.com/pod-product-compliance
Lightning Source LLC
Chambersburg PA
CBHW030733310726

48969CB00005B/1208